HEROES
OF THE
WATER MONSTER

◆ BRIAN YOUNG ◆

Heartdrum
An Imprint of HarperCollinsPublishers

Heartdrum is an imprint of HarperCollins Publishers.

Typography by David Curtis and Erin Fitzsimmons

23 24 25 26 27 LBC 5 4 3 2 1
First Edition

For all our ancestors who sang songs of hope for us in their moments of melancholy as well as our descendants for whom we sing during our moments of great discord.

PROLOGUE

"SHIYE', MY SON, EDWARD, THERE'S never going to be a perfect time to share this story with you. Come, sit down next to me. This is going to be emotional.

"I was eleven, same as you are now, when your nálí 'adzą́ą́, my mom, told me. I think you are old enough to understand and handle your great-great-great-grandpa's story.

"'Ałk'idą́ą́', in the 1860s, our ancestor lived with his family— his mom, his dad, and his younger brother. Our ancestor was a little older than Nathan while the younger brother was a little younger than you. And they used to live near what is called today Many Farms, Arizona. Like most Diné families of that era, they had many heads of sheep and a wide fertile cornfield.

"One fall, there were rumors going around that white soldiers were burning cornfields and slaughtering cattle. The mom and dad didn't believe that anyone could waste precious food and livestock. So, they continued with their normal routines. There was much to do to prepare for the upcoming winter, such as hauling firewood to keep them warm, hunting deer to make jerky, making winter clothes for their growing boys, and grinding dried corn for their winter meals.

"One day that fall, the brothers were weeding the cornfield while the mom was spinning wool. Their father had taken the sheep out to graze on the last autumn grass to fatten them up. The younger brother saw the dad rushing back with the sheep, sweating and fearful, yelling at the boys to hide in the cornfield and to not make a sound no matter what happened. The mom herded the scared sheep and yelping lambs into the corral. The dad, meanwhile, ran into the hogan and came out with his hunting rifle.

"The brothers hid, pressing their bellies against the dark soil that had produced years of food for them. Then several soldiers riding muscled horses approached the parents. Only the dad spoke a handful of phrases and words in English. From the cornfield, the boys saw their dad arguing with a soldier. The other soldiers pointed their rifles at the mom and dad. Both brothers covered their eyes but still heard the loud shots. The soldiers jumped into the corral and with their knives approached the sheep.

"The older brother did his best to calm down his younger brother. But grief had overpowered their senses and they cried. After the herd quieted, the soldiers heard their crying and then tied their hands. The younger brother looked back and saw that their cornfield had been set ablaze. Then he was forced to walk sixty-five miles to Fort Defiance, Arizona.

"These days, there's no fort in Fort Defiance, but back then there was. And it was built for the sole purpose of relocating the Diné. Under the supervision of General Kit Carson, the US Army was gathering as many Diné as they could so that they could force them to a new place to live, a reservation. But the US Army wasn't prepared for how many Diné would surrender after their livestock were slaughtered, their cornfields charred, and the peach orchards decimated. Food and resources were thin, even in that grim beginning. Nurses stationed at Fort Defiance distributed thin blankets to the prisoners as winter descended.

"For many weeks, the captured families waited and the number of surrendering Diné grew. Finally, it was time to begin the Long Walk to Hwééldi, what we call Fort Sumner, in Bosque Redondo, New Mexico. To give the Diné captives some energy, the soldiers distributed rations of beans, flour, and coffee.

"The boys were about to make dough with the flour when a mean-looking nurse slapped their hands and kicked the flour to the ground. The white flour mixed with the dark red dirt, becoming inedible. She yelled at them. She and other nurses went around wasting flour and beans by tossing them to the ground and walking on them to make sure they were spoiled. Many went hungry that night.

"The next morning, it became clear that the nurses had saved their lives. Because those who had eaten the rations were deathly ill. The soldiers had laced the flour and beans with poison. The sick were left to die, clutching their stomachs as the poison worked its harmful medicine. The rest were forced to march in many long lines eastward, away from Diné Bikéyah.

"Edward, I know you're not the biggest fan of visiting family on Diné Bikéyah. But think about how badly all our ancestors wanted to return. When you listen to what happens next, remember they survived thinking of you. They survived so that you could return to the Four Sacred Mountains.

"On the trail, there was more hardship and death. Those that fell behind were killed. Elderly, young kids, even pregnant women. The soldiers wore thick jackets and leggings, while all our ancestors held on to the thin blankets that the nurses gave them in Fort Defiance. Their own clothes were falling apart. Some suffered frostbite on their hands and their noses, as well as their feet.

"Then came the river named Rio Grande, just outside the young city of Albuquerque, New Mexico.

"The younger brother noticed footprints in the banks heading into the roaring, icy river. Then he saw a soldier ride a horse into the frigid waters, which rose to his knees even with the added height of the horse underneath him. The soldier waved to the western bank and spoke in English. The brothers couldn't understand. One by one, the Diné in front of them walked down the hill and into the river. Our two ancestors didn't know how to swim.

"The Diné shivered as the icy river splashed on their exposed skin. They held their thin blankets above their heads so that they wouldn't get wet in the wintry water. The older brother tried to carry his younger brother across, but they were both exhausted after walking two hundred miles from Fort Defiance. Their frail, starved bodies entered the polar waters, the younger brother crying the entire time. They hugged for warmth, but soon, they had to try to swim.

"Our ancestor held his younger brother's waist, and the boy wrapped his small arms around our ancestor's neck. Their soaked clothes weighed them down. The elderly and the young people around them struggled against the strong current. Blankets of water smothered everyone. Eventually, a sound more disturbing than the screaming of the drowning grew. It was silence. Many bodies sank beneath, did not rise again, and drifted downriver. Those that no longer breathed increased in number. Halfway across, the river took our ancestor's younger brother, carrying him away.

"The older brother couldn't grieve once he made it to the other side because the soldiers kept them moving, threatening them with guns and swords. Many became sick as the frigid air froze their wet clothing. But the soldiers kept them marching. In total, our ancestor walked over three hundred miles in eighteen days.

"Soon, those who survived made it to Hwééldi. In English, it translates to 'Where They Suffered.' The older brother didn't have anyone at Hwééldi. His whole family had been massacred by the US Army. For months after the initial groups were herded there, more and more Diné arrived at Hwééldi. More and more families were broken and destroyed.

"Part of the US government's design and what they did with other tribal Nations was to separate family members from each other. If they noticed a group that was a family, they would force individual family members to walk in different lines. This was to break our hearts and our spirits. But we Diné have our clans. This is why it is so very important that you know your clans, my son. You are Bilagáana, Anglo, through your mom, but from me, you are born for Tábąąhá—that means 'Water's Edge Clan.' Because with the clan system, you can find clan-mothers, clan-fathers, clan-siblings, and so on. And that's what all our ancestors did at Hwééldi. With the clan system, they formed new families if they couldn't find their original family.

"Our ancestor was adopted by a young couple who had come from the Ganado area. They had lost a daughter who became sick after crossing the Rio Grande. The wife was Tábąąhá, like our ancestor. She accepted him as her son and loved him as such. And together, they survived. Through the clan system, more and more families were forged, and in that way, our spirits were saved.

"For four horrid years, all our ancestors toiled the barren, unfamiliar lands. All they planted shriveled and died. The US government had to feed us and gave us minimal provisions. There was rampant starvation. Talking God had instructed our earliest ancestors how to build hogans, with logs and earth. But there were no trees that were suitable for hogan construction.

So, they put blankets on clusters of thin branches to shield them from the freezing winters and blistering summers. But, with each passing year, it became more and more expensive for the US government to keep us prisoners. Hastiin Ch'il Haajiní, in English known as Chief Manuelito, stood with other naat'áanii-s, including Barboncito, Ganado Mucho, Herera, and Delgadito, to negotiate with the US government and sign Naaltsoos Sání, the Treaty of 1868, which allowed our ancestors to finally go home after those four devastating years.

"When our ancestor returned to Diné Bikéyah, he lived with the young couple until he was old enough to reclaim his old home and cornfield near Many Farms, Arizona. It is said that the first night back in his childhood hogan, the older brother had a dream of his deceased family. They were happy he had returned and were able to finally rest knowing he had come home safely. In his dream, he told his family that his descendants would always have a home within the Four Sacred Mountains, and that he had endured Hwééldi so that his grandchildren's grandchildren would be able to live.

"It's important, shiye', that you understand that, yes, we Diné, like all Indigenous Nations, have a past filled with heartbreak and devastation. But we also have a brilliant, shining future."

T'ááłá'í

ONE

FOR EDWARD, MOVING DAY HAD to be the worst in history, second only to the day when an asteroid slammed into the earth, causing the mass extinction of the dinosaurs. His dad, Ted, drove them across the valley of Phoenix, Arizona, in a large white moving truck to their new ritzy rented house in the suburb of Chandler. All the houses looked like clones of each other. The only differences were their front yards. A few had agave plants whose sword-like leaves stuck out of the red volcanic rocks, while most others had grassy lawns that sparkled with moisture.

Edward and his dad had woken up at three in the morning, on a Friday no less, to haul their moving boxes to their new rented house. All to avoid the daytime heat of the Phoenix valley. It was barely eight in the morning, and the temperature was already 91 degrees! This afternoon was supposed to hit 117. In addition to the heat, the air was humid because of the start of monsoon season. The last week of July was the worst time to live in the Phoenix valley. During the day, it would become infernally hot and disgustingly moist like a steam sauna. Only when monsoon rains fell did the heat and humidity break. Edward couldn't wait for October because it would be cooler and, of course, wrestling season would start.

Edward fell in love with the sport when he was five years old. His dad, a former college wrestler, introduced Edward to the wrestling mat, to grappling, and to the four-point stance. Everything just made sense on the mat. When he was old enough to wrestle in tournaments, he enjoyed the adrenaline rush of subduing his opponent. He loved that when he won a match, the victory was his and his alone. And when he and Ted watched the wrestling portion of the Olympic Games, Edward knew that one day he would wrestle for the United States Olympic Team. Edward often envisioned himself on top of the podium wearing a large golden medal around his neck.

The garage door churned opened. Ted parked the boxy white moving truck in the driveway of their freshly leased five-bedroom house. The garage itself was filled floor to ceiling with large moving boxes from their three previous back-and-forth trips. Thankfully, this was the last one. Edward groggily stepped out and went to get his bags from the back of the truck. Small waves of heat wiggled above the smooth black pavement.

Janet, his dad's serious girlfriend as well as Nathan's mom, entered the garage from the kitchen door, holding a bundle of white sage whose tips were ember. She waved threads of smoke to all corners of the garage. Her long black hair was pulled back into a traditional tsiiyééł. Her black graphic T-shirt had an old photo of four Native chiefs holding rifles in between the words "Homeland Security" and "Fighting Terrorism Since 1492."

"I just finished smudging the house," Janet said to Ted.

"'Aoo' 'ahéhee'," Ted said, extending his arm to her.

Janet extinguished the sage, then walked into his arms. They kissed. Edward noticed that she shifted her weight to her left foot with each step.

Edward calculated a way to take her down. Not that he wanted to. He had trained himself to look for takedown opportunities in everyone so that he could automatically spot those openings when he was on the mat.

"Hi, Edward," Janet said, making her way to him. She crouched down to his eye level and squeezed his shoulder. She smiled. Janet had strong mom vibes, which Edward tried to ignore because he wasn't ready to think of Janet as anything more than his dad's girlfriend. Edward had been careful not to get too close to any of his dad's exes. It made it easier to say goodbye. But he and his dad hadn't moved in with any of them before. So, would it be safe to let his guard down?

Janet said, "To celebrate our big move, I was thinking about ordering pizza for dinner."

The moment she said "pizza," visions of delicious dripping cheese, salty pepperoni, herby tomato sauce, and sweet sausage filled every fold of his brain. Edward instantly woke up. "Yes, please!"

"Great." She smiled. Behind her, Ted walked into the house carrying a large box on his shoulder.

Before she stood back up, her expression hardened. She said, "We should tell your dad at dinner about your involvement with the water monster."

Edward nodded. He had been dreading telling his dad more than the gross hot summer afternoons. He tried not thinking about it because it would mean that he had hidden something from his dad. And they never hid anything from each other. It really wasn't all his fault that he kept a secret from his dad because Nathan pretty much prohibited Edward from speaking about Dew, or other Holy Beings, to anyone.

Edward had first seen Dew nine months ago, when his dad invited Janet and Nathan to watch the latest kaiju movie. Edward thought it strange that Nathan brought this tiny hamster-sized lizard with him. Especially since she sat on his head. But no one else noticed, not even his own dad, who would have certainly made a stale dad joke about it. But that wasn't the strangest thing! Oh, no! On the drive to the theater, the lizard actually sang along with the pop songs on the radio! Learning that Dew was a real living water monster from Hajíínéí Bahaane' completely overshadowed when their parents proposed that they should all move in together.

Through the past nine months, Edward learned that Nathan was losing his ability to interact with the Holy Beings because his voice was deepening. Not to mention the occasional trail of acne on his cheeks. Nathan needed to pass on his duties to someone who could see and hear the Holy Beings. Big surprise that Edward turned out to be that someone.

But if Edward was to be responsible for Dew, he needed to tell his dad. Janet said she would help tell Ted when they moved into their new rented house. And that time was going to be during dinner. Tonight!

In his room, Edward unpacked a box labeled "Misc." It was full of things that he didn't have a clear category for, like the few books he had, pencils, and a photo of his late mother. In the photo, she was caught in an eternal laugh. Her fair skin glowed in the setting sun. The sun could have been rising, too. The horizon behind her reddened the edges of her blond hair.

His mom had died when Edward was sixteen months old, before he could form clear memories of her. Edward didn't know how he should feel about his mother. His dad always spoke of her as intelligent and kind. Her absence conquered Ted every year in September, on the anniversary of her passing. Edward placed the photo on his writing desk where his dad, and Janet as well, could clearly see it. He hoped Janet would see it.

He sprawled onto his back on his bed. The ceiling fan silently spun directly above the bed, battling the gross hot summer temperatures. He was too tired to get up and turn on his room's AC. All he wanted to do was nap. But he still had clothes to fold, wrestling takedown posters to put up, his writing desk to organize, and many other things to do. His door creaked open, and the room temperature dropped. Goose bumps popped up over his exposed forearms. It was Dew, the young water monster.

"Hi, Dew," Edward said, forcing himself to sit upright.

"Hi, Edward!" Dew said. Her claws made tearing sounds as she scurried across his light gray carpet to his bed. She looked like a tiny Komodo dragon. Her head was rectangular and narrowed at her snout. Her tail was almost as long as her midsection, where her stubby legs stuck out.

Dew's tiny kitten-sized body had the same diamond designs as a Diné rug along her spine and on her stomach. Today, she was the size of a kitten. Tomorrow she would be the size of a scorpion. The next, maybe a pony. Apparently, all water monsters could change their size by absorbing or expelling water.

Dew said, "I like your room. Oh, yeah! Nathan wants to talk with you!" She darted out of Edward's room.

Dew and Nathan were very close. Almost always, Dew preferred to be with Nathan. That wasn't going to last much longer. Soon, it would be just Edward and Dew. He heaved himself up and ambled his way to Nathan's room.

He stepped into the second-floor hallway, which had four doors. One door led to Nathan's and Edward's bathroom, and the other three were bedrooms. He knocked as he entered the door to Nathan's room.

Nathan's twin bed crouched in a corner. Next to the neatly made bed, a reptile tank sat on a writing desk by the window. The top of the tank was left wide open so that Dew could enter and exit as she pleased. A bookcase opposite the bed displayed pictures of Nathan's nálí 'adzą́ą́ and his uncle, Jet, who was the coolest person on the earth according to both Edward and facts.

Nathan sat on his expensive gaming chair in front of his

computer desk. Dew jumped onto his lap. Leaning back, Nathan turned around to face Edward. The yellow lamp of the reptile tank elongated the shadows on his face. Nathan looked like he was going to deliver a James Bond villain dialogue, especially when he slowly petted Dew's head.

"You wanted me?" Edward asked as he closed the door behind him.

"I have a favor to ask," Nathan said. "Can you watch Dew for the next two days?"

"Sure, no problem," Edward said. He sat down on Nathan's bed. Soreness flared up in his muscles. He had been packing, unpacking, and organizing his new room nonstop for hours. There was a very real possibility of Edward passing out on Nathan's bed. "Where are you going?"

"The Third World. I'm going to see if Mother Water Monster is going to allow Yitoo to mentor Dew."

"Oh, yes, her." Edward stretched and yawned. Ever since Edward had agreed to being Dew's next guardian, Nathan had been stressing out about securing a mentor for Dew. Apparently, Dew had been born in this world, the Fourth World, and needed to learn water monster songs. Yitoo Bi'aanii was the most powerful water monster, second only to Mother Water Monster herself, and both Nathan's and Dew's first choice for mentor. Nathan had said that Yitoo was healing in the Third World, and Edward didn't ask for more information. "Why do you need Mother Water Monster's permission?"

Nathan answered, "Largely because of water monster etiquette.

But I think Mother Water Monster is protective of all her kids. This will be Yitoo's first time being back in the Fourth World since she left so long ago. I hope Mother Water Monster says yes. If not, then we are going to have to find another mentor for Dew."

Edward's eyelids were getting heavy. He remembered what Janet had said earlier. "By the way, your mom wants to tell my dad about Dew during dinner tonight."

"Tonight?" Nathan almost shouted. He started to run his hand through his hair. Was he hyperventilating?

To prevent Nathan from whatever meltdown he was about to go through, Edward asked, "What was it like when you told your mom about the Holy Beings?"

"My mom already kind of knew because she notices every-thing. After Dew hatched in my nálí's cornfield, I had to bring her with me to Phoenix because she didn't like being alone. When I started teaching Dew the three water monster songs I know, I sort of had to tell my mom because of all the things that the songs do to water."

"Oh, because the songs control water around you guys." Edward knew that both Nathan and Dew could influence water with those songs. Maybe he could learn a water monster song, too!

"My dad helped me to buy her noise-canceling headphones for Christmas. And yeah, those headphones protected her from the effects of the songs, but they didn't explain how the steam-ing cup of coffee she was drinking turned into solid ice."

Edward asked, "Think you can freeze the backyard pool to

convince my dad, if we need it?"

Nathan responded, "Do you think it'll come to that?"

Edward never had any issue going to his dad for help or telling him anything. Then again, Edward never had to tell his dad that Holy Beings from the traditional Diné stories were real and that one, possibly two, was going to be living with them in their new rented house! His dad had never let him down before. And he wouldn't now. "He'll believe me."

At dinner, a steamy, dreamy, cheesy pizza lay on the kitchen table in front of Edward. The garlic-infused crust glistened with a buttery sheen. The luscious smell of salty pepperoni begged him to take one tasty bite, which Edward was more than happy to do.

Nathan, sitting to his right, was equally happy to answer the siren song of pizza.

Edward wished he had more time to fully enjoy his pizza before they talked with his dad about water monsters. But Janet and Ted walked into the kitchen, both exhausted from all the moving and unpacking. Janet sat on the other side of the kitchen table while Ted went to the fridge. He knocked on the door, waited a few seconds, then opened it. Edward knew this setup for a dad joke.

Nathan said, "Hey, Ted?"

Edward quickly said, "No, Nathan, stop!" But it was too late.

Nathan asked, "Why did you knock on the fridge?"

Ted slowly turned around, holding in laughter. "Because there could be a salad dressing." Ted busted out laughing. Janet coughed, trying not to laugh with pizza in her mouth.

Edward smacked his forehead. Nathan looked confused and then, after a few seconds of thinking, rolled his eyes. Edward said, "You walked right into it."

Ted pulled out the pitcher of filtered water and sat at the kitchen table. Edward would have given anything to have another dad joke distract from the inevitable conversation.

"Dad?" Edward began. His voice shook.

Almost as if he could sense the seriousness in Edward's tone and voice, Ted focused all his attention on Edward. "Yes, son?"

Edward said, "We have something to tell you."

Janet and Nathan stopped eating and listened.

"We, huh?" Ted said, noticing Janet's and Nathan's quiet demeanor.

Janet encouraged him, "You can do this, Edward."

Beads of sweat collected on his forehead and hands. Edward pushed the words out of his mouth. "So, you know about the Holy Beings from the traditional Diné stories? Turns out they are real. And I can see them."

Ted sat back and crossed his arms, absorbing the revelation. He asked, "Like the Hero Twins and Changing Woman?"

"I can, too, Ted," Nathan said. "But not for much longer, because of puberty."

Ted asked, "How about you, Janet? Can you see them?"

Janet said, "No. You and I can't see them because we're adults."

"That's a bummer," Ted said. He leaned forward, placed

his elbows on the table, and rubbed his face with both hands. Edward could tell that he was confused. "I can't tell if you guys are messing with me."

"I'm telling you the truth, Dad," Edward said.

Ted forced a smile and said, "I'm guessing there's a big reason you all are telling me this now."

Nathan inhaled deeply. "Yeah. For the past two years, I've been taking care of a young water monster who is named Dew. Since I'm becoming an adult, I need to pass on my responsibilities."

"To Edward," Ted said.

"I wanted to ask for your permission first," Edward said. "Because it's a big responsibility and I may need help."

"I'll support you, shiye'," Ted said automatically.

"There's more," Nathan said. "We may need to host a water monster known as Yitoo Bi'aanii, the most powerful water monster here in the Fourth World. I'm going to the Third World tomorrow."

"Third World? Wow!" Ted said. He leaned back and ran both hands through his hair. His short black hair spiked up, giving him a wild rock-star hairstyle.

"I have to talk with Mother Water Monster," Nathan continued. Ted's face contorted with astonishment, and he blinked fast. "If she is okay with it, Yitoo will be staying with us."

Ted asked, "And where is Yitoo supposed to sleep? On my leather couch?"

"In the pool in back," Nathan said.

"Of course! In the pool in back. That makes sense!" Ted said, his voice rising and filled with incredulity. "Guys, I'm going to need the two of you to head to your rooms for a bit. Janet and I need to talk. Get more food."

Edward knew his dad was overwhelmed. He quickly stood up and tugged at Nathan's shirt. They grabbed some slices of pizza and went up the stairs.

Edward heard his dad say to Janet, "I don't like being kept out of my son's life and what he does. If it were me, I would have told you the moment I found out."

"You're right," Janet said, her voice firm and calm. "For what it's worth, I wanted to tell you immediately. The boys didn't want to tell you until now."

"They are boys, Janet. Children. We are the adults," Ted said. "And Edward is *my* son. You don't get to make decisions about what he gets involved in without me."

This was the first time Edward had heard his dad refer to him as his son in front of Janet. Before, Ted was very careful not to emphasize that Janet wasn't Edward's mom. And that included not claiming Edward as solely his. Edward realized that he and Nathan had stopped in the stairway and were eavesdropping.

"Come on," Edward said.

"Okay," Nathan said.

The two of them went into Nathan's room to check on Dew, who was napping in her little lizard tank. This was a rough start to all of them living together.

Naaki

TWO

NATHAN WAS EXHAUSTED THE NEXT morning. After fully unpacking and arranging all his stuff in his new bedroom until midnight last night, he had to pack for his trip to the Third World. Yawning, he slid on the sterling silver ring that cradled his communication stone. He checked the time, ignoring the pop-up news articles predicting climate change doomsday. It was 6:39. Since Uncle Jet was picking Nathan up at seven, he forced himself out of his comfy bed.

Nathan walked to the lizard tank and gently tapped on the glass. "Dew. Time to wake up."

He couldn't see her. Worry swelled his chest, but he calmed himself. She could be sleeping out of view. He tapped a little louder this time.

"I'm up!" Dew said. She crawled out of a dark corner, the

size of a hamster, yawning widely and struggling to keep her tiny eyes open.

Nathan reached in and scooped her up with his palm and placed her on his head. She crawled in circles like a kitten and made herself comfortable. Nathan didn't need to guess that she was asleep after hearing her squeaky snoring. Her gentle weight erased his previous worry. Even when he couldn't see her, he could always feel her. Holding his neck as stiff as he could, he walked over to Edward's bedroom.

Nathan knocked on Edward's door.

"Come in," Edward said.

To Nathan's surprise, Edward was already awake, dressed in athletic clothing, and stretching.

"You're up early," Nathan said.

"My dad and I are going for a run," Edward said. "What's up?"

"Double-checking to make sure you're up for watching Dew for the next two days."

"Yup," Edward said. He lay on the floor and pulled one knee across his body.

The casualness of Edward's tone annoyed Nathan. This was an important job. Dew wasn't just some puppy that he could play with whenever Edward was bored. "Can you be a little more serious about this?"

"I am," Edward said. He sat up and folded in half to touch his toes. "I'm as serious about Dew as I am about wrestling."

Edward's passion for wrestling was borderline obsessive. If

Edward could eat and drink wrestling, Edward would certainly do that. "My nálí's place doesn't have cell phone service, so text me and when I'm in reception I'll respond."

"Got it," Edward said. He stood up and did some forward arm circles. "Hey, Dew."

"Huh, what?" Dew sleepily asked. Nathan felt her limbs stretch and her claws spread out on his skull.

Nathan gently pulled Dew off his head and handed her to Edward. "Go with Edward."

Edward asked, "Wanna join my dad and me on our run?" Edward held her with two hands and placed her on his shoulder.

After another yawn, Dew looked like she was waking up. Her eyes, while not darting around scanning everything, were fully open and alert.

Nathan admitted, "This is the first time that we'll be away from each other." She met his gaze but didn't seem to have the same anxiety that was gripping his throat.

"I'll take care of her," Edward said. He rubbed her forehead with his pointer finger.

"Okay," Nathan said. A million scenarios of Edward messing up rushed through his mind. He felt his phone vibrate, already knowing that that was Uncle Jet texting to say he was here. "Listen to Edward while I'm gone, Dew."

She nodded.

Nathan closed the door as he returned to his bedroom to get his bag. Even though she was next door, he already missed the weight of her body on his head and her annoying pop song that she loved to sing. If he was an emotional mess now, only let-ting Dew go for two days, he dreaded the day when he would no longer see and hear her. But that could still be days, weeks, or hopefully months away. He let himself miss Dew while he rushed to meet Uncle Jet outside.

Thirty minutes later, Ted walked into Edward's room and asked, "Eddie, you ready?"

Edward still had zero ideas on how to navigate his dad know-ing about Dew. He reached to his neck and petted Dew's tiny hamster-sized spine. Toward the end of the pet, Dew lifted her rear end like a puppy. She then leaned her rib cage against his neck. "Dad. Dew is going to join us."

"Um, hi, Dew," Ted said, his head looking at all the corners of the room. This was super awkward!

"Good morning!" Dew chirped.

"Trust me, Dad," Edward said. He grabbed Ted's hand and pulled it to Dew's snout by his ear. Ted looked like ten types of confused.

Dew sniffed and then stood on her hind legs to press her forehead against the tips of Ted's fingers.

"Do you feel that, Dad?" Edward asked, hoping that he would say yes.

Ted's eyes shifted back and forth. With an uneasy smile, he said, "Can't say I do."

Edward's heart deflated. He so wanted his dad to be a part of taking care of Dew with him. They did everything together. To be doing something that excluded his dad was unfamiliar and unnerving.

"If you say she's there, I believe you," Ted said. He straightened up, pressing his knuckles into his back. "How about the trail by Desert Botanical Garden?"

"Eh," Edward responded. It was an all right trail. But it was narrow and, if a biker rode by, which always happened, then they would have to get out of their way.

"How about Tempe Town Lake?" Ted said, balancing on one foot and holding his other ankle in his hand to stretch his quadriceps.

"Yes!" Edward said. Tempe Town Lake was where they went to celebrate, to despair, and to prevail! It was *their* running path. Tempe Town Lake was a man-made river just north of Arizona State University. And alongside it was a smooth concrete running path that stretched for miles. A person could swim in its dirty waters if that person wanted a third arm or some other mutation.

Dew asked, "What's a Tempe Town Lake? Do you think there'll be a water monster there?"

"I don't think so," Edward said to Dew.

"Huh?" Ted replied.

"Talking to Dew," Edward explained.

Ted said, "All righty! We bounce in ten minutes. It's already ninety degrees outside! Woo, this summer we are breaking some heat records!" Then he left Edward's bedroom.

Later, Ted drove the three of them to Tempe Town Lake in

his dark blue SUV. His dad changed the radio from news to a pop station that blared out Jimmy Eat World. Dew perked up on Edward's lap and sang along with the radio. She even vocalized the guitar riff. Yeah, that wasn't going to get annoying anytime soon, Edward thought.

Back at their old apartment, the drive to Tempe Town Lake would have taken fifteen minutes max. Now it was a full-blown forty-five minutes. His dad veered off Loop 202 and headed south on North Scottsdale Road. Then his dad turned westward on University Drive. If they went eastward instead, they would have driven by their old apartment. Edward wondered if his dad missed it as much as he did.

Just when another mid-2000s rock song ended, Ted parked their car in the Tempe Beach parking lot. After getting out, he took a loud deep breath and reached toward the sky. Ted then roared like a bear and said, "Gorgeous morning!"

An elderly white couple with blond hair walked toward a nearby parked car with a US flag attached to its rear, smiled, and waved at them.

"Can you see me?" Dew yelled at them. She scurried up the side of Edward's head, and her nails dug into his skull. Her stubby lizard toes spread across Edward's forehead. Even if she was barely the size of a hamster, her razor claws dug painfully into Edward's sensitive nape. "Oh, I thought you were waving at me. You probably can't hear me, either, but hi anyway!"

Edward positioned her tiny body so that she curled around the side of his neck and said, "Stay still."

Ted waved back at the elderly couple and said, "Good morning!"

"Good morning!" they cheerfully replied.

Moments later, Edward and Ted stretched in the vibrant green grass of Tempe Beach. It was then that Dew decided to sing her favorite song: "I just can't hide this feeling, baby! I want to be your appealing lady! It is in your energy. My sacred reverie, mm, baby!" It was a new pop song that played everywhere. Edward couldn't get away from that song. Especially since Dew loved to sing it at least ten times a day. His dad was so lucky he couldn't hear Dew.

"All right, Eddie," Ted said. "Gonna say this again. You can tell me anything."

"You say that every week," Edward said. That wasn't true. He said it five times a week minimum.

His dad smirked. "At least you know." Ted's voice shifted from the usual upbeat energy to a more serious slow and low tone. "Which is why I'm surprised you didn't tell me about water monsters sooner."

"I'm sorry, Dad," Edward said. "Nathan doesn't like telling anyone about the Holy Beings. He's very protective of Dew."

"When did you find out about Dew?" Ted asked.

Edward raised his voice to talk over Dew, who kept singing louder and louder. "When all four of us went to watch that kaiju movie. We were driving over in Janet's car, and I kept hearing this young girl's voice singing with the radio. That's when I noticed that the voice came from a little lizard on Nathan's shoulder."

"You don't have to yell. I can hear you," Ted said.

"Sorry, she's singing really loudly," Edward said. "Dew, can you sing quieter?"

"Okay!" she said, and whisper-sang.

"Sounds like Nathan doesn't trust me yet," Ted said. Done stretching, the two of them stood up and walked to the concrete trail. When they were on the manufactured gray stone path, a Hispanic couple, about the age of his dad, rang their bike bells. Ted waved at them. They smiled, too, zooming past on their bikes.

"What do you say we try one of those next time?" Ted said, still grinning. "We'll bike to your school. I'll wear those really high bike shorts."

"No one wants to see your legs, Dad!" Edward contended. It wasn't rude if it was true.

"Hey, I got nice legs, okay?" Ted said, "We'll keep that thought on the back burner."

"Burn up that thought completely," Edward said. "Better idea, I get my own bike."

"There's a thought," Ted said. He seemed to be thinking about it. "What if Nathan also got a bike and all three of us went biking on the weekends? You know, just the guys?"

"Can I come?" Dew asked.

"I want running and biking to be our thing," Edward said. In truth, he didn't like the idea of his dad doing anything with Nathan. Ted was *his* dad. Nathan already had a father.

"I hear you," Ted said. They started jogging. "Why don't you think of something for the three of us to do together, then. You may not fully enjoy Nathan, but I think if you two really put effort into it, you might actually become close."

"Sure, Dad." Edward was thankful that his dad had said "close" instead of "brothers." Though, to be honest, what he really wanted was more time alone with his dad. He hoped that Nathan would stay an extra day or two in New Mexico so that he could have his dad all to himself, like before Ted and Janet started dating.

Ted asked, "How does it feel to be involved with the Holy Beings?"

Edward responded, "I'm still figuring things out. Nathan said he'd tell me how to be this guardian person for Dew. But he's been so busy getting things ready for Yitoo that I think he forgot."

"Okay, explain to me. What's a Yitoo?"

"So, you know water monsters, right? After the First Being came into the Fourth World, our world, water monsters followed them. Yitoo was the first one. She's so powerful that she bit into the ocean of the Third World and brought that water here. She created the biggest river that runs through Diné Bikéyah—the San Juan River."

Ted nodded, absorbing this info dump. "And why does she need to stay in our swimming pool?"

"To teach Dew all the water monster songs that she knows. Before you ask, water monsters use their songs to sing down the rain and they can make water do cool stuff. But you and I can't listen to their songs or else the water inside our bodies will be affected. Once Dew knows enough songs, she'll be strong enough to be on her own, and Dew, what do you plan on doing after that?"

"I don't know!" she said brightly.

Edward relayed the info, "She doesn't know."

Ted asked, "How long will this take? Because you still have to maintain your grades. And then there's the wrestling season to think of. If the Olympics is your goal, then you can't skimp on your training."

"I know!" Edward said. "This is actually the best part. I've been practicing my moves with Dew! She's a really good wrestler!"

Dew said, "Thanks!"

"I'm not sure how I can help with the Holy Beings. But whatever you need, ask," Ted said. "As for Olympic wrestling, remember, if there's ever a point where you feel that you want to pursue other interests, it ain't gonna break my heart," Ted said. Another thing that he said far too often. "But it'll be my greatest honor to help you reach that goal, Eddie."

Dew said, "I like your dad."

A warm feeling glowed in Edward's stomach. He had the best dad in the world.

Nathan and Uncle Jet arrived at Nali's mobile home site a little after noon. The two of them stepped out of Uncle Jet's car. Nathan's vision blurred a little at the edges, and the dry New Mexican sun warmed his chilled forearms; Uncle Jet had the AC blasting for the entire five-hour drive. Nathan wiped his glasses clean before putting them back on. The sun was still above the horizon and wouldn't fully set for another eight hours at least.

The mobile home hadn't changed much since Dew hatched two summers ago. Nathan's dad purchased solar roof panels. Nathan then helped Uncle Jet install them on top of the mobile home. Although there was still no running water, having electricity drastically changed the living experience here. Once Uncle Jet secured a job and was able to move into his own apartment back in Phoenix, he bought Nali an electric stove, an oscillating fan, and even an electric kettle for her tea water. Nathan got her a mini fridge last Christmas. Very thankful for the gifts, Nali still preferred to make fires for cooking dinner. She had said it just made the food taste better, and Nathan agreed.

Nali sat by the firepit, where she pulled a fresh piece of frybread out of her cast-iron pan with a pot fork. Next to the fire, a deep aluminum pot boiled pinto beans, mushrooms, and ham hocks. Nathan walked quickly to Nali, and she smiled widely and wrapped him in a hug. As they embraced, he noticed that he was just as tall as she was. Next year, he would for sure be taller than she.

"Shinálí," Nali sweetly said. She tiptoed to kiss his forehead. "I missed you!"

"Shidóó, Nali," Nathan said.

Uncle Jet took off his black sunglasses and walked to the two of them. When he was in arm's reach of Nali, she pulled him into a hug. He said, "Mama."

"Shiyáázh," she said. "You okay being here?"

"I'm good," Uncle Jet said. The last time that he was here, Uncle Jet had been fighting alcoholism and depression. "Man, this is the land that time forgot."

"Or the land that remembers its charm," Nali said. "Wohsą́ ch'iyaan chaha'ohdi."

"We haven't even unpacked," Uncle Jet said.

"Eat first, then unpack," Nali said, already walking toward the chaha'oh. "No" wasn't an answer.

A few minutes later, Nathan poured honey onto Nali's fluffy frybread. He had missed this so much! Uncle Jet sat across the table from them, his back exposed to the cornfield, which was surrounded by the fence that Nathan had mended. In the cornfield itself, several young cornstalks had sprouted out of the dark brown soil. Nathan guessed they were at least a foot tall. He squinted and realized that the leaves weren't vibrant green, but a baked brown.

"Has it been raining here?" Nathan asked, tearing into the frybread.

"Kwe'é doo nahałtin da. No rain," Nali said.

"Dá'ák'ehshą'?" Nathan had to ask about the cornfield.

Nali placed her cup down. "I let the harvest dry out. 'Éí binii-naa, the water pump in the mountains started bubbling."

Uncle Jet explained, "That means the groundwater is running low."

Nali continued. "As much as I wanted to grow more vegetables for myself, I have to think of others who need the water more than I do. So, while I'm staying here, I go to the grocery store to buy water for myself."

Nathan sighed. He had known that taking Dew away from this area would put it back in a drought. But Dew hated being alone. And he hated seeing her sad. When they sang the water monster lullaby together, a small cloud would appear and gently drop small beads of rain around them. But those precious drops were all that fell. And no matter how many times they sang nor how loud, their efforts weren't enough to bring a full rainstorm to the area. Dew needed to learn more songs if she was to fully end the drought here—and if Nathan was to ever fulfill his promise to Pond.

He also felt that by helping Dew become a fully realized water monster he was reducing the effects of climate change. Every day there was another scientific report about the effects of climate change becoming more dangerous and saying that the deadline to make changes to prevent cataclysmic weather patterns was fast approaching. Most articles he read said that the deadline was 2040, less than twenty years away. When Nathan would be his dad's age, he would have to deal with those dangerous weather patterns. How could people not be terrified of that prediction? He knew that not everyone experienced the tangible effects of climate change as he did. Living out here, even for a few months, made it very apparent how dependent life was on stable climate conditions. "Someday, there will be so much rain that you won't have to haul water," Nathan confidently said.

"One success at a time, shináli. Don't forget all that you

have done so far." Nali smiled, her calloused palm rubbing his shoulder.

Out of the corner of his eyes, Nathan noticed that Uncle Jet was staring at the hogan. Nathan couldn't interpret whether he was upset or downtrodden. The last time Uncle Jet had been in that hogan, the entire space had stunk of alcohol and he was going to do something drastic. A feeling deep inside Nathan, maybe his intuition, had told him that Uncle Jet needed help. So, Nathan, despite all the pushback from him, had stayed with him until he asked for help. Even though it was two years ago, Nathan was still concerned for Uncle Jet's safety.

"Háadishą' Dew?" Nali asked.

"She's with Edward," Nathan answered.

"I know he wasn't your first choice," Nali said. She poured herself some tea. This summer she was drinking hibiscus and sage. "We don't see the full design of the Holy Beings, but things happen for a reason. Be patient, shináli."

"I will," Nathan said. Edward still had a lot of growing up to do, being neither patient nor attentive to Dew's needs. It didn't matter because it was too late to find someone else. Besides, Nathan needed to focus on convincing Mother Water Monster to let Yitoo be Dew's mentor. He, however, couldn't overlook that Uncle Jet remained quiet and continued to stare at the hogan.

Táá'

THREE

A LITTLE AFTER FOUR IN the morning, Nathan quietly stepped out of the mobile home. He adjusted the sterling silver ring that held his turquoise communication stone, which allowed him to understand and speak with all beings. It squeezed his finger tightly. Along with his responsibility for Dew, he would soon have to give the ring and stone to Edward. Maybe, a few years from now, when Dew was strong enough to be alone, he'd get it back. He could worry about that later. He had to go into the desert and call one of the Jet Stone Twins to take him to Hajíínéí, the area that connected the Third World to the Fourth World.

A familiar eagerness fueled his movements as he looked upward at the stars. His heart filled with happiness like he was going to meet Pond, then shrank when he reminded himself Pond was no longer here. Every time he was at Nali's mobile home during the night, he experienced flashbacks of emotions.

The phantom feelings were slowly dulling. Now he could enjoy the serene beauty of the desert night sky, which sparkled like an ocean at sunset. Certain parts of the night sky were purple from clusters of stars. Suddenly, an odd shape appeared in the sky, as individual stars shone brighter than others. It was an arrow that pointed to the hogan.

Then Nathan noticed dim orange light pouring out an open window. Worry clouded his thoughts and concern soaked his heart. Nathan had to know if Uncle Jet was okay. Nathan knocked on the door before entering.

"What's going on?" Uncle Jet smirked, standing near the northern window in front of a LED camping lantern. He wore a sleeveless rock band T-shirt and black basketball shorts and was spinning an unlit cigarette between his fingers. His legs stuck out of his unlaced dark boots. The rest of the hogan was filled with black trash bags that contained blankets, pillows, and some of Nali's own rugs.

"I thought you quit smoking." Nathan stepped into the hogan.

"I have," Uncle Jet said. He turned to fully face Nathan. "This is filled with cotton. When I get strong cravings, I spin this and think of all the bumps I overcame to get to this point." He put the cotton-filled cigarette into his pocket. "I still have a ways to go. But like your nálí said, don't forget all you have accomplished so far."

"Why are you awake?" Nathan asked, hoping to prolong this conversation.

Uncle Jet said, "I wanted to check on you for once. You said you'd be heading out around this time."

Nathan stepped deeper inside to scan Uncle Jet's shadow for a pair of eyes. Two years ago, Nathan discovered that an Ash Being was attached to Uncle Jet's shadow and took the form of a pair of eyes. Thankfully, there weren't any. Still, his worry lingered like smoke.

Uncle Jet said, "Don't know how our ancestors managed. These aren't the most comfortable accommodations."

Nathan asked, "Why did you stay in the hogan?"

Uncle Jet answered, "I'm trying this thing called exposure therapy to help me make peace with my past. My therapist mentioned that when a person returns to an old environment, the shape of the land, the smell, it makes you wanna do the things you used to do. You're primed for old habits. You feel old emotions that you had forgotten."

Nathan understood exactly what Uncle Jet was talking about.

"Standing here in this hogan isn't that hard," Uncle Jet said. "It's easy to be here and not want to drink. Because I have those tool sets my therapist drilled into me. And I have you. What's difficult is seeing the marks I left, seeing the shadows of the man I used to be." Uncle Jet pointed to a small dent in the wood panel underneath the northern window. "I threw a glass bottle at this wall, when your nálí and I got into that fight before I left and was arrested in Gallup. Before you came in here and saved me.

"There were times when I blacked out, and someone told me what I did. And I'm like, that ain't me. I'd never do that.

It's like there is this other person who did those moronic things, and I'd think, 'Wow, that person is such a low-life jerk.' But it was me. I did those things. The toughest part of my sobriety is seeing people I care about deal with what I did when I blacked out, how that person I was haunts you all. Sometimes, your nálí flinches when I raise an arm too fast. That is all on me." Uncle Jet lowered his head.

"You never gave up," Nathan said.

Uncle Jet smiled. "I owe you at least that much."

"You don't owe me anything," Nathan said. He didn't like the concept of owing a person a favor for having been helped. It made the relationship feel like a series of emotionless obligations. And families shouldn't keep tabs on who helps who.

"You're too kind," Uncle Jet said. He approached Nathan and grabbed his shoulders. Then his voice dropped and turned serious. "I mean that. Your amazing kindness sometimes blinds you. Make sure when you do help others, it doesn't come at a cost to yourself."

"Sure, I will," Nathan said, looking Uncle Jet in the eyes. He didn't fully agree with what Uncle Jet was saying. Everyone deserved to be helped because everyone was capable of growth and change. Even if helping others put Nathan into tough situations, it was worth it to see that person or being in a happier place.

"You better be on your way," Uncle Jet said, releasing Nathan from his firm grip. They left the shadowed hogan. The soft sands puffed dust into the air with each step they took.

Nathan said, "I can't wait for Dew to know enough songs to finally end the drought."

"Your nálí would love that. All right"—Uncle Jet yawned—"do what you gotta do, then come back. I'll wait right here for you. Might make some coffee."

"I could be gone a while," Nathan explained.

"I'm up and got some Holy Beings to thank when the sun rises." Uncle Jet nodded eastward. The horizon was still full of stars, a few hours away from sunrise.

"I'll see you soon, Uncle Jet," Nathan said. He made his way to the other side of the cornfield.

Once he approached the edge of the desert, he inhaled the cool dry air. He imagined Jet Stone Boy and called out his name in Diné. A few seconds later, a rainbow with a neon glow arched through the night sky from the other side of the plateaus. The rainbow rushed down and slowed as it landed in front of Nathan.

He regretted not reminding himself to not look directly at it because he was momentarily blinded. After Nathan rubbed his eyes under his glasses, the glowing rainbow dimmed, and he was able to see the shiny crystal-like skin of Jet Stone Boy. Nathan sighed, relieved he could still see him. He couldn't wait to see Jet Stone Girl on the other end of the rainbow path.

"Good morning, Jet Stone Boy!" Nathan said, shaking his hand.

"Nathan." Jet Stone Boy smiled. "Are you ready to go?"

Nathan said, "Yes, please."

Jet Stone Boy hummed and pressed his quartz crystal onto

the soft sands, and a rainbow path materialized in front of them. Nathan took a deep breath, never fully prepared for being shot through the air at who knows how many miles per hour, and stepped onto the glowing rainbow. He allowed himself to enjoy this moment while it lasted. Because he had no idea if Mother Water Monster would allow Yitoo to come back up to the Fourth World. If she didn't, he would have to search the entire Diné Bikéyah, in the boundaries of the Four Sacred Mountains, for another mentor.

The cold rushing air pulled Nathan's lips into a smile. He reached his arms outward once his stomach stopped sinking and he was able to breathe easily. The land blurred below him, and the only thing he could hear was his own heartbeat. He wished he could travel like this all the time. Then his stomach started sinking again, which meant they were descending.

Jet Stone Boy slowed their fall the closer they got to the earth. Nathan stepped off the rainbow, pressing his foot against firm ground. Jet Stone Boy hurried to Jet Stone Girl's side and held her hand. The rainbow dimmed out of existence as they ended their singing. With the last of the colorful lights, Nathan saw the petroglyphs of the four trials and the long, narrow cave that led to the entrance of the Third World. He could no longer fit into the narrow opening. His shoulders were now too broad.

"Good morning, Jet Stone Girl. Thank you both for bringing me here," he said to them.

They both bowed their heads and in unison said, "You're welcome."

Nathan said, "I'll call for you two when I'm back." Nathan spun the communication ring around his finger to make it more comfortable and faced the entrance to the shortcut.

Suddenly, a tentacle of water wrapped around Nathan's leg and pulled him off balance. Immediately, Nathan sang the Move song and tried to command the tentacle. But whoever controlled this water clearly surpassed Nathan's ability. The tentacle pulled, and Nathan fell to the ground. He started singing the Change song and commanded the water to turn into mist. Nathan shouted the song, and soon enough the tentacle burst into steam that clouded his vision.

"Who's there?" Nathan demanded, rushing to stand.

An adult woman laughed. Her chuckles bounced off the smooth sandstone around them and echoed around Nathan and the Jet Stone Twins. Once he heard her, Nathan recognized who it was.

"Nathan!" Yitoo called to him.

"Yitoo! You terrified me!" Nathan said, his heart still pounding against his rib cage.

"I apologize. I couldn't help myself," Yitoo said from the top of the canyon. The bright stars and waning half-moon behind her cast a dark shadow on her features. She was as large as a truck! The mist all around Nathan condensed and formed a pathway that Yitoo walked on toward him. Her scales reflected the moon. Unlike the brown-and-green mountain designs of Pond, Yitoo's colorful scales resembled arrowheads in the four sacred colors—white, blue, yellow, black—pointing toward her snout.

Zigzagging down the line of her spine, yellow scales took the shape of crooked lightning.

"Wait a hot minute! What are you doing here?" Nathan asked. He was supposed to go down to the Third World and meet with Mother Water Monster!

"I'm here to teach my youngest sister, of course!" she said with a chuckle. "There are so many songs, and I can't wait to start. She's going to be a powerful water monster, thanks to me!"

Nathan assumed that meant Mother Water Monster had already given Yitoo permission to be up here. His joy and relief overpowered him. The most important thing, Nathan assured himself, was that Dew could officially start her training!

"And where exactly is my youngest sister?" Yitoo asked. She glanced around and then sniffed Nathan. Was she searching for Dew's scent? Then she lowered her head and pressed her forehead against Nathan's chest. Nathan leaned into the gesture, enjoying this gentle side of Yitoo.

"She's with Edward back in our new rental house," Nathan said.

"You'll have to explain some of those words to me, but that may be for the best." Her expression changed, and her large eyes drooped. "I sense great change, even here at Hajíínéí. There is very little moisture in the atmosphere. I'm scared of what has become of my river. I'm going to her. Would you join me?"

Nathan assumed by "her," Yitoo meant her river. "Of course. Jet Stone Twins, would you mind bringing us to her river?"

"No need," Yitoo butted in. "Thank you both for your aid,

but I would very much like to travel as a water monster in the Fourth World again."

The Jet Stone Twins nodded and bowed to the two of them. "It has been our pleasure to assist you both, Venerated Yitoo Bi'aanii and Nathan Todacheenie. Be well."

Jet Stone Girl hummed and pressed her crystal into the ground. She stepped onto the rainbow and disappeared into the air. A few seconds later, Jet Stone Boy disappeared as well.

"I hope we didn't offend them," Nathan said.

"I'm sure they have other things they want to do," Yitoo said. "Hop onto my back, Nathan."

Nathan climbed onto her spine. Once he mounted her neck, a sharp pin pricked his heart. Old emotions that he thought had dulled flared up. He reminded himself this was Yitoo, not Pond. Even though he so wanted to lean over and wrap Yitoo in a hug.

Yitoo seemed to sense the shift in his emotions. "Are you okay, young one?"

Nathan explained, "I'm sorry. Your brother, the Water Monster of the Agave Pond, used to carry me like this."

Yitoo arched her head upward and caressed Nathan with the back of her neck. She said, "I knew him for a few decades after he hatched in the Third World. He was very kind and highly respectful of every being around him. I miss him, too."

Nathan sniffled. For the longest time, it had felt like he was the only one who knew and loved Pond. No one, not Nali, not Uncle Jet, not his dad, not his mom, not Edward, not even Dew, had ever met Pond. He thought he was the only one who truly grieved for Pond. Just that little connection he had with Yitoo soothed the small jewel of grief that would always be in his heart.

"Are you ready?" Yitoo asked.

"Yes," Nathan responded. Only then did Yitoo lower her head.

Without her humming or singing, water poured out of her body and circled them in snake-thin streams. Her size shrank until she was the size of a horse. Then the water she expelled formed a jet that carried them through the dry channels of the canyon riverbed. After Yitoo saw her river, they would make their way back to Nali's hogan, and then Uncle Jet would take them back to Chandler. And finally, after all the stressful months of finding a mentor, Dew was going to learn more water monster songs. Eventually, Nathan hoped, Dew would live at the Agave Pond and sing down the rains.

Yitoo zoomed so fast through the rock valleys of Hajíínéí that Nathan had trouble holding on. If he remembered correctly, her river flowed through the towns of Farmington and Shiprock, New Mexico. Traveling at these speeds, it wouldn't take them long to visit her river and then meet back up with Uncle Jet. An hour at most. Above them, the moon hung in a clear sky, free of light pollution. Very quickly, the scent of corn husks filled the atmosphere.

To their left, rows upon rows of cornfields stood. The field spread for miles. Yitoo slowed down beneath him. The water that propelled them forward collected around Yitoo's wrists and ankles. It swirled around and around and then finally began to harden into icy bracelets that resembled squash blossom jewelry. Nathan was surprised at just how much water had condensed into the diamond-like jewelry. Easily, a swimming pool amount of water condensed into one bracelet.

"What's this?" Yitoo asked. Her voice was the loudest sound in the quiet night. She approached a chain-link fence that had a sign on it.

Nathan read to her, "Navajo Agricultural Products Industry." Nathan thought of ways to explain to Yitoo what NAPI was. "These are fields that grow food for people to eat."

"Do people no longer grow their own food?" Yitoo asked.

Nathan said, "We mainly go to grocery stores that sell food grown in places like this. Or order from a delivery app." He bit his tongue. Would he have to explain what a smartphone app was?

"This area sits on top of a plateau," Yitoo explained. She tilted her head and sniffed the atmosphere. "There hasn't been rain for weeks. How does water get here?"

"I think they divert water from the San Juan River, which isn't too far from here," Nathan said.

"Do not call my river that name," Yitoo firmly said. Her body heated up, and her heart pounded loudly. "My river and I will not be identified by the Pale People. Our name is Yitoo Bi'aanii. Not San Juan."

Two years ago, he had first met Yitoo in the Third World when he was trying to get medicine for Pond. And she called white people "Pale People" then as well. "I'm sorry, Yitoo."

"Thank you for apologizing," Yitoo said.

"If it makes you feel better," Nathan began, "these fields mainly feed Diné. My grandma actually uses their pinto beans in her stews."

"My river still nourishes life?" Yitoo asked. She seemed to calm. "After one hundred and sixty years that I have been gone, she still cares for those around her."

Nathan rubbed the groove between her skull and neck. "Are you ready to see your river again?"

"I have been. For many decades," Yitoo said.

The squash blossom jewelry exploded into hundreds of gallons of water. In seconds, the water slushed, gurgled, and pushed them forward. Yitoo raced through the NAPI fields of corn, beans, and wheat.

They descended into a vein of the canyon that took them down the face of the plateau. Nathan was also very curious as to how this land had looked before colonization, before the crimes of Manifest Destiny. Nathan said, "Yitoo, tell me about your river."

"My river was wide and deep, clean and clear, gentle and fertile," Yitoo said. Her voice lightened. "Beings of all shapes and sizes drank from her. After I had sung the sixteen rain songs, she would swell, like the womb of women. My river was sweet to the taste. That's why the most respected and beloved of all the Holy Beings preferred to drink my waters. Sometimes, when my brothers and sisters were having troubles with their waters, they would ask for some of mine, and I did not withhold. Especially in a desert landscape, water is life. Without it, there is only death."

Yitoo navigated the winding paths of rock spires and sand mounds. Soon, they slowed again. They entered a low ditch that was a long and wide empty clearing filled with soft sand and smooth egglike stones. The water returned to Yitoo's wrists and ankles as jewelry. Nathan hopped off. Before them was a wall of broad-leaf oak trees. Yitoo sniffed the ground.

She said, "My water was never this low. It used to cover this area and reach the height of those riverbanks."

Nathan turned and saw that the banks behind them were tall hills. Her river used to be three times his height and about a hundred yards wide! Yitoo pushed forward through the curtain of oak leaves and branches. Nathan kept close to her, awkwardly avoiding tree limbs.

Then they saw the remnants of her river. Before them was less a river and more a deep, dark, bleeding scar. The water was low and dirty—a feeble stream that meandered back and forth like a lost snake looking for nourishment.

"What happened to you?" Yitoo bowed her head. "My river. My heart. I never should have left you." Spikes poked out of her spine. Yitoo's tusks emerged from her jaws.

A shiver ran down Nathan's back. He had to do something to help her! So he did the only thing he could think of and wrapped his arms around her wide shoulders.

"It's going to be okay," Nathan said into her ear. "It's going to be okay." He briefly recalled holding on to Uncle Jet in Nali's hogan.

"It's my fault. It's my fault my river is almost dead," Yitoo said. Her tears dripped onto the dry bed below. The ground soaked them up like a sponge.

Nathan felt her head lean onto him. She was heavy, but it was okay. He was strong enough to hold her up. Yitoo's body slumped to the dusty riverbed, and Nathan gently lowered her onto the ground. He continued to comfort her.

"I never should have left." Yitoo sniffled.

"You are here now. You can bring your river back to her former health," Nathan said. He let Yitoo take all the time she needed to process what had become of her river. Nathan hated that soon he wouldn't be able to see her. If he wasn't about to lose his ability to interact with the Holy Beings, he most certainly would help Yitoo in any way he could. But he couldn't make that promise, as much as he wanted to.

Dįí'

FOUR

EVERY SUNDAY MORNING, TED MADE Edward call
both his grandparents to update them on what he was doing.
Last Sunday, all four were excited to hear about the new rented
house and how the move would go. Edward couldn't wait to ask
both his nálís for some tips on how to treat Holy Beings. Dew,
for now, was busy chasing a large fly that buzzed around his
bedroom. When the fly flew low to the ground, Dew jumped up
with all her might and snapped her jaws at the insect.

Edward thought about not calling his Anglo maternal grandparents, especially Grandma Lillian. It always felt like Grandma
Lillian treated him like an "indian." When she used to babysit
him, she would call him a "wild indian" when he wanted to play
or misbehaved. She'd frequently asked him if he was ever going
to grow out his hair, of which Edward had no intention. She

never asked his other male cousins on that side of his family to grow their hair long.

First things first. He grabbed his tablet while Dew was still chasing the fly and started a video chat with his nálís.

His Nálí Lady picked up after a few rings. "Yá'át'ééh, shinálí 'ashkii! Yá'át'ééh, yá'át'ééh!" She held her smartphone vertically and smiled at him. Her brown face filled his screen top to bottom. Nálí Lady held her phone close to her face because she needed new glasses. Her yellowed lenses were from an expired prescription. Edward looked at his camera and grinned, showing his teeth. "So very handsome! So, what is the latest news with you?" she asked.

"Yá'át'ééh, Nálí Lady. Nothing. I have a question for you. What do you know about water monsters? Like, do you know anything about them coming up here? Into the Fourth World?"

She looked puzzled, but in an excited way. She loved any opportunity to talk about the traditional stories. She took off her glasses and rubbed her temples. "Coming into the Fourth World? The stories don't say nothing about water monsters coming here to the Fourth World."

"But you know, they could, right? In theory?" he asked.

"Yes," she said, putting her glasses back on. "What's with the interest in water monsters?"

"I'm just curious," he said. "You know, in case I ever run into one. Like what the proper manners would be. How would I treat them?"

Her smile stretched out of the vertical screen. "That's easy. Treat them like Holy Beings, in other words, just like you treat me!"

"Because grandparents are holy." Edward sighed as he completed her normal saying.

"'Aoo', 'aoo', 'aoo', shinálí 'ashkii," she said, chuckling. "The Holy Beings are your Elders, and as such, treat them as you treat me." She pulled her phone to her face and whispered into the microphone. Her chin filled the screen. "Medicine people say if you help a Holy Being, sometimes they'll give you a blessing in return."

Edward sat up. "What kind of blessing?"

"The Warrior Twins helped many different Holy Beings," Nálí Lady explained. "In return, the Twins received lots of material goods, blessings, and favors, which would help them defeat the Enemies of the Diné. If you help Diyin Diné'e, they will bless you same way as the Warrior Twins. That blessing can be help toward any of your goals."

Edward's mind was busy connecting the dots on two things that seemed so very different. Then it dawned on him. He asked, "Do you think a Holy Being, like a water monster, could bless my wrestling career?"

She said, "If you help one, then ask it to guide you along your path to the Olympics."

"That's it!" Edward said. He could wrangle a favor out of the water monsters! Definitely Yitoo, who was the most powerful water monster in the Fourth World. If Edward could get a blessing from her, then Edward was 110 percent certain that he was going to be the greatest Olympic wrestler in history!

This was the best idea he ever had. Once Yitoo arrived here, he could ask if she needed any favors. Edward could hardly wait for this afternoon when both Nathan and Yitoo were to come back. After he finished talking to his Nálí Lady, and his Nálí Sir, he called his maternal grandparents. All through the conversations, he imagined himself on top of the Olympic podium holding a gold medal in the air at the base of a crowd-filled stadium.

Later that evening, Edward wrestled with Dew as they waited for Nathan and Yitoo to return. Nathan hated when they did, but Dew enjoyed herself. Besides, Dew could grow to his size by absorbing water, which made her perfect for practicing wrestling moves. They shot, took down, escaped, reversed, bridged, even did several near falls in the garage where his dad had laid out some wrestling mats. Dew chilled the air with her water monster abilities since Ted hadn't yet installed an AC in the garage.

Ted had gone to work training clients at the gym that he had opened with three other former ASU wrestlers in Old Town Scottsdale. Ted never confirmed one way or another, but Edward suspected his dad trained celebrities who lived in Scottsdale during the winter. Ted normally didn't work on Sundays, but with the expenses of moving, he would need to for a few weeks. Janet was holed up in their bedroom doing research for an article she was writing. So, for most of the day, it was just

Edward and Dew wrestling in the garage.

Edward held his elbows close to his rib cage and his hands forward, ready to shoot in and wrap his arms around one of her legs. Lucky for Edward, Dew was a pretty good wrestler and learned wrestling moves quickly! But she tended to get excited and lose focus. When she got distracted, her limbs had a mind of their own and she often tripped or fell.

"All right, Dew, if I shoot in like this . . ." Edward said as he lunged to her slowly. He reached forward as if he was going to wrap an arm under her shoulder.

Dew stood up on her hind legs. "I do this!"

"Nope!" Edward said. He saw the opening wide and clear and grabbed her hind leg. He pushed against the back of her knee, and her entire stance crumpled. She plopped onto the floor. Edward immediately seized this opportunity and quickly performed a half-nelson hold. "All right, how do you get out of this?"

Dew giggled, enjoying the roughhousing and losing focus.

Edward felt his clothes moisten and his grip on her loosen. She shrank in size, expelling water, and wiggled out of the half nelson with ease. She then slithered behind him, reabsorbed the water, and pushed against his shoulders with all her weight.

"That's cheating!" Edward said, positioning himself in the four-point stance. He quickly planned his escaped strategy. First thing was to hop onto his feet and use his quads to drive back against Dew's weight. Outside, Edward heard the slamming of car doors. "Nathan's here."

"Yay!" Dew said.

The two of them rushed into the living room. Edward nimbly navigated the narrow hallway and dodged the bulky furniture on his way to the front door. Dew, the size of a Great Dane, bumped against the walls. The pictures shook in response.

"Let's not destroy the place," Edward said.

Edward opened the front door and saw Nathan's uncle's black car parked underneath the streetlight. Nathan dug his duffel out of the trunk. Yitoo walked into the streetlight. Her head hung low. She was sad, that much Edward could see. But her posture still exuded confidence, strength, and authority. All the toughest and most accomplished wrestlers had this posture. She was roughly the size of a fully grown sheep, at least for now. Her pretty scale designs amazed him. Jewelry that sparkled like diamonds dangled around her neck and ankles.

"My sister is here!" Dew shouted. She rushed over to them and began to rub her long body against Yitoo, who finally smiled.

Nathan and his uncle hugged. Edward wished that someday he could be as cool as Jet. Nathan's uncle entered the car and drove down the streetlight-illuminated pavement.

Nathan, Yitoo, and Dew made their way back into the house.

Yitoo examined Edward, making him nervous. She asked him, "Haash wolyé 'ashkii yazhi?"

"My name?" Edward answered, dumbfounded.

Yitoo grimaced at the sound of English.

"'Ałtse," Nathan said to Yitoo. He quickly whispered in

Edward's ear, "Don't speak English around her." He quickly yanked off his turquoise ring and held Edward's hand. The small ring pressed against the middle of their palms.

Nathan rarely let Edward hold or wear the communication stone. This must be an important moment. Why didn't Nathan want him to speak English? "Shí 'éí Edward yinishyé. And I'm sorry about speaking English." Weird, he should have been able to speak Diné fluently.

Nathan seemed to notice that the communication stone wasn't working and hastily dashed to turn off the kitchen and living room lights.

Meanwhile, Yitoo turned her attention to Dew, who was excitedly weaving through her legs. On Yitoo's right front ankle was a story bracelet. From a brief glance, Edward saw a long line of people next to a river. Yitoo's tail wagged and accidentally thumped the walls, causing the newly framed pictures to shake. Then Yitoo and Dew booped their noses together. Edward assumed this was how water monsters said hi. They talked in Diné with each other.

After the last lamp was turned off, Nathan leaned over, hands on his knees, sweat dripping down his round cheeks, panting and out of air. He reached and grabbed Edward's hand that held the communication stone. Nathan's hand was slippery with sweat.

When everything was washed in shadows, Edward understood what Yitoo and Dew were talking about.

Dew said, "I'm not allowed to sing the songs too loudly

because there are people around. Oh, and I once burst some pipes!"

Yitoo chuckled. "I'm not sure what pipes are. But I once sang so loud that I made a hurricane in Mom's realm." Yitoo smiled and leaned toward Dew. "She was not happy at all."

"You can create hurricanes?" Edward said. How much power did water monsters have exactly?

Yitoo continued. "Ah, I see you aren't able to speak Diné without the aid of a communication stone. Yet, you also don't scare easily. You may not be much of a guardian now, but that only means you have plenty of room for growth." The corner of her lips curled. She smiled at him!

"I work out almost every day, and I run in the morning," Edward said, feeling a need to impress her.

"You run in the morning?" Yitoo asked. Her eyes sparkled with interest.

"Yes!" Edward said. "Mostly when my dad has time. He told me that Diné used to run in the morning in the old times to remember and honor the Warrior Twins."

"That they did," Yitoo said. "Though I prefer to call them the Hero Twins because they did more than simply fight the Enemies. Did you know their favorite running path was alongside my river?"

"They ran by your river! Did you meet them?" Edward asked. Like fireworks, excitement burst in his chest. The Warrior, oops, Hero Twins were by far his favorite of the Holy Beings! Both

Enemy Slayer and Born for Water combated gigantic Enemies after the First Beings emerged into the Fourth World. When Edward was little, he sometimes pretended that he was Enemy Slayer, who would go and fight the enormous Enemies, while Born for Water would stay in their hogan sending prayers and smoke. They were the reason why he and his dad loved kaiju movies so much!

"Of course! They would drink from my river after especially long runs." Yitoo smiled and stared off into the distance, like she was cherishing a fond memory. "That was a different era. Young guardians," Yitoo said, "I want to say hello to the Holy Beings of this large valley."

"Huh?" Edward said.

"The Holy Beings of the original inhabitants of this area, before the Pale People," Yitoo said, her face scrunched in dismay. "I want to ask their permission to be on their lands."

If Edward understood correctly, she wanted to visit the local deities. He had no idea which Nations were here originally. There was the Pima casino just off the highway. So maybe the Pima? It wasn't like Indigenous history was taught in public school. Even so, that was no excuse to not know whose ancestral homelands they were on.

"I'm sorry," Nathan said. "I haven't even given thought to whose ancestral land Phoenix is."

"My, my," Yitoo said, exasperated. She held her head high. "Whenever Diné leave the boundaries of the Four Sacred Mountains, they pray to the local Holy Beings and ask permission to set foot on their lands. It's a gesture of respect. I certainly was grateful for prayers from any human, Diné or otherwise, when I maintained my rivers."

Nathan said, "I'll do some research and figure out where to meet them if we can."

Yitoo smiled. Her voiced smoothed and her eyes twinkled. "Truth be told, Nathan, I am glad that individuals like you still exist. Not since the Era of the Hero Twins have I seen such a person as yourself."

Jealously, Edward said, "I can research, too." He bet that he could figure out the answer before Nathan could!

Nathan appeared to have finally caught his breath. Beads of sweat no longer popped up on his skin or his hands, which Edward was thankful for. He said, "Edward, Dew. Yitoo and I have something important to share with you."

The atmosphere chilled in the living room. All the energy and joy of meeting Yitoo dispersed. Edward sensed that this was something dire. He asked, "What?"

"Yitoo and I went to see her river," Nathan began.

"My river is sickly and about to dry out," Yitoo said. "At first, we thought the low levels were from my river being diverted to the cornfields on top of the nearby plateau. But I sense foul play, as the dryness of my river, of all of Diné Bikéyah, is unnatural. Something big, something heartless, is stealing massive quantities of my water."

"What do you mean?" Dew asked. Her tail stopped wagging and curled between her hind legs.

"I think there is an Enemy roaming around, today, in the Fourth World," Yitoo said. "A Modern Enemy."

Edward's spine quivered. It was as if all the oxygen had been evacuated from the living room. An Enemy—like Thunderbird, who could summon dangerous lightning storms; like Human-Eater, who could consume entire towns; and Wild Boar, who could run at unheard-of speeds to hunt humans for hundreds of miles—was here in the modern era.

Yitoo finished, "And if we don't confront whatever it is, it could cause horrendous damage to the Fourth World and its inhabitants."

'Ashdla'

FIVE

NATHAN WAITED FOR EDWARD TO absorb the Modern Enemy hypothesis. This had huge implications. If there truly was a Modern Enemy stealing Yitoo's river, was it stealing other sources of water?

"Okay," Edward said, making his way to the sofa and pulling Nathan along with him. His eyes were wide and scared. He plopped onto the dark leather couch, still holding Nathan's hand. "What do we need to do? Where? How do we find the Modern Enemy?"

"First," Yitoo said, "you need to know what one is. We Holy Beings have our own tasks and duties. Sometimes, our tasks and duties complement those of the many beings in the Fourth World. Sometimes, they conflict. As such, we are neither completely evil nor good. An Enemy, however, is a heartless, chaotic being that doesn't care about the suffering it creates. The Enemy known as Human-Eater would devour entire villages as well as slurp entire lakes dry. He didn't care how his hunger and thirst disrupted the harmony of the natural resources. The ability to love and care for many different beings, that's what differentiates Holy Beings from Enemies."

"Okay," Edward said. "Keep going."

"Enemies, like Holy Beings, have many forms," Yitoo continued to explain. "They can be as small as a mouse or as large as a mountain. That being said, whatever is stealing my waters is taking such great amounts that I believe this Modern Enemy is enormous. It could be as large as this house to as large as the Shiprock mountain."

Nathan gasped. Yitoo hadn't mentioned that before. Shiprock mountain was over 1,500 feet tall! That didn't make sense to him, though. If the Modern Enemy was indeed that big, he or others would have seen it by now.

Nathan sat down next to Edward. His heart grew heavy as he said, "I don't know how much time I have left with the Holy Beings. But we need to find this thing quick before I lose my connection with you."

"Otherwise, it's going to be just me," Edward said.

Nathan nodded and squeezed Edward's hand.

Dew, who had been quiet this entire time, said, "Let's find this Modern Enemy and punch its face! Let's go right now!"

"Youngest sister," Yitoo said. "It would be unwise for you to go searching for the Modern Enemy this moment, as you are uneducated. Which is why I believe our best course of action is this: we begin your tutelage this instant. Where again?" Yitoo asked Nathan.

Nathan spoke, "In the backyard pool. If you sing in the bottom of the pool, the songs shouldn't mess with the nearby neighbors or our parents."

Yitoo finished her speech. "Give me four days and Dew will know enough songs to be a powerful ally. After which, we will search for what is stealing my water, find it, and confront it."

Nathan couldn't wait that long. What if he lost his connection by then? He needed to do something now. "Yitoo, do you think Edward and I could do something in the meantime?"

Edward snapped to; he had been lost in thought. He said, "What? Us? Something?"

Yitoo said, "The best both of you can do is prepare. I do not know what the future brings. But there is a very real possibility we may need to combat it."

The last thing Nathan wanted to do was fight. If there was a Modern Enemy out there, they should try and reason with it first. Nothing was truly evil or careless. Nathan had to at least try to communicate, to connect with it. He disliked meeting a being with the intention of combating it. "Can we try talking to whatever this is? Maybe it doesn't understand what it's doing."

"What if," Edward said, "we find the Warrior—sorry, the Hero Twins?"

"What's that?" Yitoo asked.

"We can ask them to confront this Modern Enemy," Edward said.

Nathan couldn't deny that he wanted to meet the Hero Twins. What Diné kid didn't want to meet them? But Nathan held firm. "There's always a chance the Modern Enemy will stop what it's doing after we talk to it."

Yitoo said to him, "How does this sound? After I train Dew, we will seek out the Hero Twins to ask for their assistance in addition to evidence of the Modern Enemy. Now that I say it out loud, the Hero Twins would know best how to deal with an Enemy, with reason or weapon."

Nathan said, "We can do that."

Yitoo said, "Wonderful! Now, Dew, let's begin. With my help, you will be the second-strongest water monster in the Fourth World." She winked at her.

Nathan led all of them to the back door, wanting to do more. He wanted to be the one to talk to this Modern Enemy.

Nathan took a deep breath of air-conditioned coolness before stepping out in the backyard, where the temperature was still in the low hundreds. It was a little after eight p.m. and the summer sun was barely setting. The turquoise water in the pool sloshed about. Edward slid the back door closed behind them.

Yitoo said to Dew, "There is much to learn, and I'm so very eager to teach you!"

Dew hopped up and down. She said, "Yes, please!" Then, in English, she sang, "I just can't hide this feeling, baby!"

Yitoo snarled as spikes shot from her spine. She arched her back like a hissing cat, then spoke in a deep angry tone, the air around them heated even more: "Don't you dare speak the language of the Pale People in front of me."

Dew scurried over to Nathan and curled around his foot, sniveling in fear. Edward released Nathan's hand and bent his knees in some wrestling stance.

Yitoo must have realized that she had terrified them. Her spikes retracted back into her body. She lowered her head, per haps ashamed.

Before Yitoo spoke, Nathan shared the communication stone with Edward. She said, "Forgive me. The last time I heard the language of the Pale People was when soldiers were pointing guns at your ancestors."

A stabbing pain shot through Nathan's spine. He felt Edward's palm go cold.

Dew slowly crawled toward her sister, tail between her stubby back legs. "I'm sorry, Yitoo. I won't sing that song."

Yitoo smiled at Dew and rubbed the bottom of her chin on the top of Dew's forehead. "Thank you."

"That's her favorite song, though," Edward said. Nathan felt Edward's grip on the communication ring tighten.

"It is," Nathan said, backing Edward. If Dew enjoyed singing a pop song in English, she should be allowed to.

"You'll have more favorites," Yitoo said to Dew. Then, to Nathan and Edward, "That's because water monsters at her age learn new songs as soon as they hear them. Infant water monsters hear a melody once, and it never leaves their head."

"I'm not a baby!" Dew protested.

Yitoo said, "Here's a compromise. You can sing that song,

but only in Diné. Never in the language of the horrible Pale People!"

Nathan nodded. That seemed like a great compromise. Yitoo was both compassionate and intelligent. The perfect mentor. And Nathan was even impressed with Edward, who had been ready to defend Dew. Edward might be a good guardian for her. Things were falling into place.

Dew jumped up and down. "Oh, yes, please! Though, some of the words don't translate into the Diné language easily."

"Speaking of the Diné language," Yitoo said. "We'll begin your mentorship by reviewing your pronunciation. The true power of water monster songs lies in the exact melody as well as the strict pronunciation. To fully control water, you, Dew, must speak with the original tone and diction. Not with this dirty accent, tainted by the language of the Pale People." Yitoo looked at Nathan. "Diné clearly isn't your primary language." She shook her head, disappointed.

Nathan had been proud that he had been able to learn as much of the language as he had. Even with the help of Nali and the few available Diné language books, it was difficult! There were several different verbs of "to hold" that depended on the actual shape of the object being held! Yitoo made all his efforts to learn Diné seem small and not enough.

"It's not ideal that you don't speak the Diné language correctly," Yitoo said. "Your ancestors didn't survive the violence of the Pale People so that your language could disappear."

"The Pale People aren't all bad," Edward whispered.

Nathan was certain that he was the only one who heard that. Edward looked mad and unnerved. Nathan rubbed Edward's shoulder. But Edward pushed Nathan's hand off and then stormed into the house and slammed the sliding door closed.

"Is he upset?" Yitoo asked.

Nathan slid the communication ring back onto his finger. "Don't worry," Nathan replied, extremely self-conscious of his pronunciation. "I'll check on him later. Are you going to begin now? Outside of the pool? Because there are people around who might be affected by the song."

"You need not worry," Yitoo responded. "The words themselves are harmless, if spoken without the melody. Here, watch the water." She indicated the pool. She spoke the water monster lullaby. Nathan expected to see something happen or the air to chill. But it didn't. The water remained calm. And the air remained jungly.

"Do you know why our songs control the waters?" Yitoo asked Dew.

"No," Dew said.

"What is melody? What is language?" Yitoo asked.

"Sound," Nathan said.

"Yes. And what is sound?"

"Waves," Nathan said.

"Yes!" Yitoo said excitedly. "Like water, sound is energy that rises and falls. The words create intention, what we want the water to do. Sound waves create tones as well as chords, and in turn power and effect. Voice and volume create the size of the intention. And lastly, we have melody, which is the product of emotion. The more intensely you feel, the more powerful the melody, the greater the effect of the song."

Nathan recalled a time two years ago, when his dad was going to take both him and Uncle Jet back to Phoenix. It was after Uncle Jet finally asked for help and Nathan was preparing for his journey to the Third World. He needed to convince his dad to let him stay with Nali. He was desperate. He only thought of the Change song and was able to fully freeze a bottle of water.

Yitoo continued. "As I have been alive for countless eras, I have experienced many emotions. And you, too, my wonderful sister, so full of potential, will live through many eras. With those experiences, you will become a powerful water monster."

Yitoo led Dew through some pronunciation of the Diné alphabet. She emphasized the unique Diné consonants: the tł', the ł, and the hard-sounding ts' sounds. Dew's lessons were finally starting! Nathan sighed. For the past few months, he had been so stressed out. He hadn't had someone to guard Dew in his stead. He hadn't had an older water monster to teach Dew songs. There were so many ways he could have failed. Not to mention, he had to deal with moving to a whole new place! But somehow, everything had come together. It might take a few more years, but the rain was finally going to return at Nali's mobile home. And if the Modern Enemy was the reason for some of the effects of climate change, then convincing it to stop what it was doing would theoretically stop some of that climate change. That was a very comforting thought. Because dealing with a Modern Enemy was much easier than trying to convince an entire nation that they must change their ways to postpone that 2040 deadline.

Both water monsters' scales and colors slowly became transparent. Like someone turning down the volume, their voices muted. But Nathan wasn't scared of losing his connection to them this time. Yitoo was here. Dew was learning. And Edward was a promising guardian. Nathan snuck away to check on Edward and let Yitoo teach Dew uninterrupted.

Edward went right to his bedroom and sprawled out on his bed. Even with the air conditioner on full blast, hot humid air had fought its way inside his room. The raging heat outside mirrored Edward's frustration with Yitoo. He wanted to FaceTime Andrew, his best friend, and was ready to call him. Then he realized that Andrew wouldn't understand what was happening. How could he? Andrew wasn't Diné. So instead, he pulled up a video of an Olympic championship wrestling match. A wrestler in a yellow singlet swooped in on the other one in a red singlet. Yellow caught Red's knee and drove his shoulder into Red's hip. Edward counted two points for Yellow when he slammed Red onto the mat. Counting the points, however, didn't distract him from his anger with Yitoo.

She kept finding ways to say how terrible "Pale People" were. Did that mean Edward was horrible, too? What was her deal, anyway?

Edward couldn't ignore that everyone in this house was

full-blooded Diné except himself. He was Diné but also Anglo. Neither half of himself made him weaker. He wished he knew someone who was half Diné and half Anglo like himself that he could talk to. His Diné cousins on the reservation teased him for being a city kid. And he didn't get along with the three other Diné kids in his grade at his school. They often hung out after school together when Edward was training for wrestling season. He had never felt so alone, and wanted to go visit Andrew, who never judged him for whatever half he was.

Someone knocked on his door, pulling him out of longing for his old apartment. Edward hoisted himself out of his bed. And as he expected, Nathan stood on the other side when he opened his door.

"Hey," Edward said, going back to his bed and watching the wrestlers on his phone.

Nathan stepped cautiously into Edward's inner sanctum. Nathan looked uneasy about the dirty clothes strewn everywhere, his unmade bed, and the leftover lunch on his desk.

"Are you okay?" Nathan asked, closing the door.

"Sure," Edward said, still moody. Nathan couldn't understand what he was feeling. Nathan's Certificate of Indian Blood said "4/4 Degree Navajo Indian Blood," while Edward's said "2/4." Not like Yitoo having an attitude with "Pale People" would disturb him. "Where's Dew?"

"With Yitoo. They've started the lessons," Nathan said.

"So is she going to sing something other than 'My sacred reverie, mm, baby!'?"

Nathan chuckled. "I hate that song."

Edward suppressed a grin, still not wanting to let go of his anger at Yitoo.

Nathan said, "About what Yitoo said about your white half."

"What about my Anglo half?" Edward snapped.

"I'm sorry that I hurt you," Nathan said as calmly as he could. "I was so focused on accommodating Yitoo that I didn't think about how she speaks about white people would affect you. I didn't say or do anything."

Edward appreciated that Nathan took responsibility for hurting him, even though it was Yitoo's attitude toward Anglos that bothered him. His anger dulled, though was still present.

"There's more," Nathan said. "It's about why we shouldn't speak English around her."

"Ain't that great," Edward said, making no effort to hide his irritation.

Nathan explained, "Yitoo has been healing in the Third World for a very long time. One hundred and sixty years, to be exact. From what I've heard and what she's told me, she became sick from a battle she lost."

"Who did she lose to? Was it an Enemy?" Edward asked. Seriously, what was Nathan trying to say exactly? Whatever he wanted to say he should just be direct. Instead of all this tiptoeing around the subject. Edward wasn't going to put any effort into guessing. Nathan would just have to come out with whatever it was.

Nathan said, "I don't know the complete details. But she was around when the US Army relocated our ancestors to Hwéél-di. Something happened to her during that time. Whatever she experienced was so traumatic that she had to go back to the Third World to heal. I know she has post-traumatic stress disorder. And I think the English language is one of her triggers."

Edward gasped. It felt like he had been slapped. If Yitoo had been here since the Era of Emergence, she would have been here during the Era of Relocation. Ever since his dad told him the story of his ancestor who survived Hwééldi, there was a small wound in his emotional being that didn't stop bleeding. Couldn't stop bleeding. No, that wound had already been there and was always bleeding. It was more like he was finally able to notice that there was a wound that had always been there, that had been passed down to him from the previous generations on his dad's side. There was something more to the shape and texture of this pain that he couldn't identify, at least not yet. Edward's ears rang, and he was dizzy. Nathan looked like he was expecting him to react in this way because he just sat down and waited.

Now Edward was terrified. How would Yitoo react to his Anglo half? Some of his racing thoughts finally condensed into words. "Does Yitoo hate Anglo people?"

"From I've seen so far, yes," Nathan said.

"What about half Diné, half Anglo?" Edward asked.

Nathan said, "We shouldn't tell her about your mom's side just yet. I don't know how she'll react."

Frustrated, Edward said, "Or we just don't tell her at all,

if she's going to be so offended by my mom's side." Edward hoped his annoyed toned communicated exactly how ridiculous this was. It sounded to him like Edward should be embarrassed by his mom.

Nathan shook his head. "I think being honest with her at the *right time* is our best option. I've read a few articles on depression and PTSD. There's a thing called exposure therapy. My uncle Jet said it's helping him make peace with his past. I think it's the best way for Yitoo to process what has happened since Hwééldi. So, I think we should gradually expose her to the current world. Once she understands or at least becomes aware of what has happened in the world since then, we can tell her about your white half."

"Whatever," Edward responded. He went back to watching wrestling videos on his phone. Nathan sighed, seeming to get the hint that Edward was done talking, and left.

It was hard for Edward to see his future self, holding the gold medal. Perhaps Dew could bless him. Then again, did she know how to perform a blessing? Edward tried to think of other options, but he kept arriving at the fact that Yitoo was the most powerful water monster in the Fourth World. And if he wanted to have a powerful blessing, he would have to swallow his frustration and help Yitoo. Regardless of her feelings toward "Pale People."

Hastą́ą́

SIX

THE VERY NEXT MORNING, EDWARD sprinkled some raisins into the oatmeal that his dad made for the two of them in the kitchen. He wasn't in the mood to think about Yitoo's disfavor of Anglos because another thing weighed on his mind. How were he and Nathan going to tell their parents about the possible Modern Enemy?

Nathan, meanwhile, sleepily swayed his way down the stairs. He looked like he had just rolled out of bed, cowlick at the back of his head, his glasses uneven, still wearing his basketball shorts pajamas. Edward watched as Nathan prepared himself a bowl of cereal and then sat at the table across from him. Nathan slumped on his elbows, yawned, then adjusted his glasses.

Nathan asked, "How are they doing outside?"

Edward answered, "I guess all right. They were at the bottom of the pool when I checked on them earlier. Yitoo must be teaching Dew." Right before Nathan could ingest a spoonful of cereal, Edward blurted out, "What should we tell our parents? You know, about the Hero Twins and the Modern Enemy?"

Nathan dropped his spoon in his bowl with a loud metallic clank. He was fully awake now. "I haven't thought of that."

Edward said, "We should tell them everything."

Nathan massaged his eyeballs. "If we tell them, they're going to worry."

Edward added, "They trust us, and we need to be truthful with them."

Nathan looked grumpy, and not from just waking up. He obviously didn't like what Edward had just said. He replied, "I don't think we should tell them everything. My mom is super stressed about the article that she has to write, and your dad already has enough on his plate. If all we are doing is finding the Hero Twins to ask them to deal with a Modern Enemy, our parents don't need to know. Think about it. All we're doing is just relaying a message. We aren't going to be confronting any-thing. That's the Hero Twins' duty. We can say that we have some water monster stuff to do on Diné Bikéyah. Which is true. If we let them know about the Modern Enemy, we're getting them riled up for nothing."

Edward thought about Nathan's points. He had to trust that Nathan recognized when Janet was stressed, because Edward didn't know her like that. But Edward did know his own dad. And that with the move, the financial strain, the extra hours, his dad was doing his best to keep cool. But Edward had to say,

"They're adults. They can handle it."

"If you say so." Nathan eased off. "I'm not telling them, though."

"Fine," Edward said, a little annoyed with Nathan's secretiveness.

Just then, Ted walked downstairs. Edward wondered if his dad had heard any of the conversation. Ted was already dressed to go to work, though to be honest it was no different than if he was going to work out or run. He wore a black compression shirt with gray running shorts.

"Good morning, gents," he said. "For a moment there, I forgot which direction the sun rose. But it soon dawned on me."

Edward said, "Dad, seriously? It's not even eight yet!"

Ted suppressed a chuckle. Then he tousled Edward's hair. "Hey, I got a long string of clients back-to-back for the next few days. With school starting soon, you're going to go with Janet and Nathan here to the store to get school supplies today. Capisce?"

"I capisce," Edward said. He saw the tiredness in his dad's eyes. Edward really wanted to tell his dad about the possibility of finding a Modern Enemy. Then his dad grabbed an energy drink from the refrigerator. His dad only drank those when he was absolutely exhausted.

"Don't you threaten me with a good time," Ted said to the energy drink, and slurped it in several loud gulps before rushing out the front door. "Listen to Janet, both of you!"

His oatmeal finished, Edward took his bowl to the kitchen sink and went upstairs to finish getting ready for the day. Telling their parents what was happening was the right thing. But realizing something is right and doing it were very different things.

Two hours later, Janet took both of them to Target to get backpacks for the upcoming school year. Edward looked at the rows of flimsy neon nylon backpacks displayed in front of him. There were some decent ones, but Edward needed something more durable than what was on display. His new backpack would need to withstand a packed schedule of practices, meets, and long school days.

Just then, an Anglo store employee in a red polo approached them and said in an incorrect and very English-accented Spanish, "Hola, ¿necesitan ayuda?"

"Um, what?" Edward asked.

"¿Necesitan ayuda? Do you speak Spanish?" the store employee asked.

Nathan shook his head while Edward responded, "No."

"Oh, well, if you need any help, just ask," the store employee said, and walked to the end of the wall of backpacks to make everything uniform and ordered. Even though the wall looked organized enough. Edward couldn't shake the feeling that the store employee was watching them.

Janet walked up from behind and said, "Lots to choose from, huh?"

"Yeah," Edward said. "My dad usually gets my backpack

from Dick's Sporting Goods by I-10 and Warner." He also got his workout and school clothes from there. The durable material just lasted longer.

"You can still get your regular school supplies from here," she said. "We'll go to the one in SanTan Village later. Maybe just you and me, huh?"

Edward was caught off guard by the thought of spending time alone with Janet. Was she trying to be motherly? Edward didn't need a mom. He already had one, even if she was just a memory.

Suddenly, her phone played a goofy ringtone. Janet's expression changed, and she reached into her purse. After reading a text she said, "I got to respond to this." Her head arched downward, and her thumbs typed furiously on the screen.

Edward went back to the backpacks. Nathan snuck up by his side, leaned in, and whispered, "Still want to tell my mom?"

Edward faced Nathan. Beyond him, Edward could have sworn that the store employee, who rearranged the display of backpacks in front of him, was watching them. Edward tried to ignore the awkward store employee and whispered back, "Soon."

Edward thought telling was going to be easier, but in fact it was way more difficult. Nathan firmly believed that it was better to not tell their parents everything. Perhaps that was the better option.

"Maybe we don't need to tell them," Nathan whispered, holding a backpack and inspecting its pouches.

The store employee approached them and aggressively yanked

the backpack out of Nathan's hands. "All right, what are you stealing?"

"Huh?" Edward asked, his defenses up. What was happening? His eyes shot around to look for Janet, but she wasn't in sight.

"Stealing?" Nathan asked, sounding just as surprised as Edward.

"Empty your pockets," the store employee demanded. "Right now."

"I don't have anything in my pockets," Edward said, his voice shakier than he expected. Fear bubbled in his abdomen.

Nathan stammered, "M-me either." He sounded more confused than scared.

"Do you want me to get security involved? He's going to ask for your green card; you want that?" the store employee asked, sounding increasingly angry.

"We don't have a green card," Nathan retorted. He sounded just as heated as the store employee.

Edward froze. Nathan was making things worse! Edward quickly reached into his pocket and pulled them inside out to show the store employee.

Nathan stared at the store employee's name tag. "Chad, is it? Did you know my dad is a constitutional lawyer? I bet he would love to chat with your manager, Chad, about this company's policy of racial profiling." The words flowed out of Nathan's mouth without trouble. Every syllable was distinct, and every consonant articulated.

"No need," Chad said, looking unhappy with how things had gone. He skulked away from Nathan and Edward.

Edward's adrenaline still pumped through his veins. Only now did Edward realize he had been ready to perform some wrestling moves on Chad if he needed to. He couldn't imagine the trouble he would have gotten in if he had suplexed Chad.

Nathan dispelled the heavy silence. "I get asked for my green card when I come back from my nálí's mobile home. When I'm darker. Just do what I do, and they'll leave you alone. Never have your hands in your pockets, or they'll think you stole something. If you take something off a shelf, make it very obvious that you put it back. Always smile, even if you don't want to. It makes them feel at ease. Sometimes I'll ask them for help, and that gets rid of their suspicion. Not all employees and security guards are like this. Some are just doing their job. But occasionally, there is one who will follow you while you're in the store."

Edward asked, "Is this happening because I'm getting older?"

"No. It's *been* happening. You're just now realizing because you're older," Nathan said. He grabbed a backpack and guided Edward to the school supplies.

Edward followed in Nathan's steps. Memories of hanging out with his own friends rushed into his mind. Every time a security guard singled him out. Every time a gas station attendant solely watched Edward. And all his friends, Andrew included, who were mostly fair-skinned, telling him that he was overreacting. All those times he brushed off being singled out because his friends told him he was overthinking were transmuted by

Nathan's words. It *had* been happening.

After they got their school supplies, Janet took them to the food court at the Chandler Fashion Center. Edward and Nathan both had burgers and fries. Even with the amazingness of lunch, Edward still stewed over being profiled and for Yitoo's comments against his Anglo half. It was just so overwhelming! With Yitoo, he wouldn't be fully Diné; he would be Anglo. However, to certain people, he was brown. Everyone seemed to have their opinions about and behaviors toward different skin colors and fractions of blood. And since Edward was only eleven, he couldn't do anything about it but endure it. This wasn't fair.

An older security guard walked through the food court, scanning in their direction. Edward's edginess ramped up. He immediately made sure that his hands were in view of the security guard, just in case.

"What are you two going to do when we get back?" Janet asked, pulling Edward's attention away from the security guard.

"Video games," Nathan said.

"Stare at a wall," Edward said.

Janet chuckled. "Your sense of humor is just like your dad's, Edward."

Janet's expression became serious. She said, "Boys, I'm going to go to the Tohono O'odham Nation this evening to cover a developing situation."

"Developing situation," Edward repeated.

"And you're going to report," Nathan stated, bits of burger falling out of his mouth.

"Yes. Seems like this happens once every decade. The border wall between the US and Mexico is going through the Tohono O'odham Nation, which has traditional land in both territories. The wall would divide their Nation into two. If that happens, several families would be separated. The Tohono O'odham are again protesting against the construction of the latest border wall."

"Got it, Mom," Nathan said.

"Sure thing, Janet," Edward said, still watching the security guard, who was finally leaving the food court. Edward's tensed body eased up a little.

"'Bout as much of a response as I was expecting," she said. "I'm going to have to pack as soon as we get back."

"Okay," Nathan said. He pulled some fries out of the carton and chewed on them.

"You two will have to be alone until Ted finishes with his last client," Janet said.

"Yup," Nathan said.

"Make sure to do your chores: clean your rooms, vacuum the living room carpet, and wash the dishes."

"Hey, Janet?" Edward started, nearly dropping his burger. This was his chance to tell Janet about the Modern Enemy.

"Yeah?" Janet said.

Edward froze. The sounds around him became muffled. The lights brightened and obscured everything.

Nathan said, "Edward and I need to take care of some water monster business."

Edward took a huge bite of his burger and chewed slowly, his senses relaxing.

"Oh?" Janet said.

Edward swallowed the lump of beef and bread, then said, "Yitoo wants to show Dew around Diné Bikéyah as part of her training."

Janet asked, "What does that mean, 'show Dew around Diné Bikéyah'?"

Nathan said, "Oh, we'll be traveling to sacred sites, maybe for a few days. I was thinking of maybe setting up base at Nali's hogan."

"Yeah. Nothing crazy at all," Edward contributed. He crossed his toes because his hands were busy holding his burger.

"How many days, because you're supposed to spend the weekend with your dad and Leandra," Janet said.

"I think we should be back before I go to Dad's place," Nathan quickly replied. Edward sensed that Nathan was stretching the truth.

"Will your nálí be there?" Janet asked.

"It's summer. She's there," Nathan said.

"How are you getting there?"

"Uncle Jet," Nathan said.

Did Nathan just lie? Right to his mom's face?

"Fine with me," Janet said. "Edward, be sure to tell your dad. I'm sure he'll want to know what you two are doing. And, Nathan, call me the moment you get to Gallup."

"Can do," Nathan said.

Edward tried his best not to look at Nathan. He was right. Telling their parents about the potential Modern Enemy was more trouble than it was worth. He shoved some fries into his mouth to settle his conscience. Because there was a small voice inside his mind asking, "What if it does become dangerous?"

Tsosts'id

SEVEN

THREE DAYS LATER, NATHAN BROUGHT Edward
out to the backyard pool to talk with Yitoo and Dew. Tonight,
Nathan wanted to take Yitoo to a small park in Scottsdale called
Arizona Falls, the first hydroelectricity station in the valley.
Since they were leaving in the morning to Diné Bikéyah, this
would be the only chance he got to introduce her a little more to
the advances of technology.

Nathan worried he couldn't see the water monsters. He
wished he could have been a year younger so that he could have
more time with the Holy Beings. Nathan slid the back door quietly closed, so as not to wake Ted, who had gone to sleep a few
hours ago. Apparently, Ted had a training session with a client at
six a.m. Nathan and Edward left the dry, air-conditioned indoors
and entered the monsoon atmosphere of outdoors.

The surface of the water sloshed and lapped against the concrete edge of their backyard pool. Nathan peered into the deep end and saw the faint outlines of Yitoo and Dew. Nathan knelt and stuck the tips of his fingers into the pool.

As soon as Nathan did that, Dew launched herself directly upward like a little torpedo! Edward skidded backward, caught off guard by her speed. Dew fell back down. Without singing, she commanded a spire of water to cushion her landing. Nathan smiled, remembering when Pond did that. He estimated that he could see roughly 65 percent of the water monsters. He could see where they were, but the exact details were blurry, like he was looking at them without his glasses. Still, two-thirds was better than no-thirds.

"Hi, guys!" Dew chimed, not caring how loud her voice was. Nathan was relieved he could hear her just fine. She tilted her body against his leg, like always. Even if he couldn't see her completely, he still felt her weight.

"I'm awake now," Edward snarked.

Yitoo's snout emerged from the water. She then hoisted herself out of the pool with her powerful front legs.

"Edward," Nathan said, reaching out to share his communication ring. After a frustrated sigh, Edward's sandpaper hands held his. Nathan hoped that Edward could keep calm if Yitoo spoke negatively about white people.

Yitoo said, "Hello, young guardians. Is holding hands a new custom in this era?"

"Oh, I only have one communication stone in this ring," Nathan explained.

"Would you each like your own?" Yitoo asked, tilting her head.

"Yes, please!" Edward said, very quickly.

Yitoo commanded, "Nathan, if you would, dislodge the communication stone and divide it in half."

"What? Will it still work?" Nathan asked, shocked that he never tried it himself. Then again, he never had a reason to beforehand.

"There are many tricks and secrets that I can share with you." Yitoo smiled. Without her singing, about two gallons' worth of water emerged from the pool behind her and turned into two chunks of ice that hardened and condensed.

At the same time, Nathan took the turquoise communication stone out of the ring and rubbed his pointer finger and thumb together until it became malleable. He rolled it out in a thin line and split it in half. After that, he created two small mounds.

"Place them in the ice, please," Yitoo said. "And hold out your hands."

Nathan approached the chunks that were slowly taking the form of rings. He pushed the two stones into each. He motioned for Edward to hold out his hands. Both reached with their left hands, and the ice chunks hardened around their thumbs.

"Watch, youngest sister; this is something Mom doesn't know how to do," Yitoo said. "Ice, like crystals, can reflect light. We can change the direction of the ice crystals to reflect light at different angles and then create colors." Nathan's ring became half black and half blue, while Edward's became half white and half yellow.

"Are you both ready for our search today?" Yitoo asked.

Edward, still gawking at his new ring, answered, "I am."

"I am, too," Nathan said, surprised that the communication stone still worked even though it was divided in two. "How's Dew coming along with her training?"

"I've learned so many songs!" Dew chirped.

"She learns songs much quicker than I anticipated," Yitoo said. "We've actually gone beyond what I planned on teaching her."

Dew excitedly explained, "She sang the songs at a fast pace, and I was able to learn way more songs! Look at what I can do now!"

Dew lifted the water in the entire pool without uttering a single word and then immediately froze it into a giant ice cube. Still hovering in the air, the frozen water divided into four different-sized chunks. Those four chunks warped as if they weren't frozen at all, then reshaped into four ice sculptures of Yitoo, Dew, Edward, and Nathan, twice the size of their non-ice counterparts.

"Whoa! I can't move and change water at the same time," Nathan said. He was impressed, even a little jealous. He'd never be able to do that.

Yitoo explained, "That's because most water monster songs

are more effective with different physical states of water. For instance, rain songs control water much easier than ice. And snow songs control ice much easier than water."

"That's not all!" Dew said. Then the ice sculptures condensed into smaller versions, making loud cracking sounds.

Yitoo sat down next to Nathan and said, "What she's doing is advanced stuff. She's condensing the ice, pushing all the air out of the water, into something much harder than any metal. It's how I create jewelry and how water monsters can create armor," she said. Her bracelet and necklace jingled like tiny bells. "With enough water, we can make armor that can repel lightning. It took me a week to be able to do what she's doing. And I was very sloppy."

When the ice sculptures were the same size as they were, Dew lowered them into the dry pool. Then they began to move and dance.

"That's amazing," Nathan said.

"I can't be outshone now, can I?" Yitoo chuckled.

Nathan didn't recognize what was happening with the ice sculptures, but something was changing. It wasn't the texture. Then Nathan realized there was color inside the ice! The color was changing to match the clothes that Nathan and Edward were currently wearing as well as the intricate diamond designs on Yitoo's scales.

"Whoa" was all Edward could say.

They were looking at four clones of themselves inside the pool. Not exact clones—more like androids because they lacked small details like wafting hair or the stretching of fabric. It was like watching some stone sculptures move around.

"Okay, I'm bored," Dew said. Then, in an instant, the four ice clones exploded into water that filled up the pool with a loud splash! The colors of the ice mixed and dissipated as the waters calmed into a still mirror that reflected the moon.

Yitoo said, "With the two of you, young guardians, and the current abilities of Dew, I am fully confident we'll find the Hero Twins and, if need be, vanquish the Modern Enemy." Her voice deepened. She squinted. "And once we see to the Modern Enemy, we can plan on what we are going to do with the Pale People."

Nathan's heart dropped, and his mouth went dry.

"They aren't all bad," Edward said. Nathan could see the telltale signs that Edward was getting riled up.

"Don't be fooled by them," Yitoo said. "I've experienced their cruelty firsthand."

If Nathan didn't do something now, this whole situation could turn out very bad. Soon, they would have to tell Yitoo that Edward was half white. But now was way too early. Yitoo first needed to grasp how much the world had changed. That Diné people, like all the other Indigenous peoples of the United States, were considered minorities. That ethnicities other than Indigenous, other than white, now called North America home. Nathan rubbed Edward's back, hoping that he didn't have to tell him aloud to calm down.

At that moment while comforting Edward, he realized he

was again neglecting how Edward felt. He couldn't afford to sit down. He had to intervene. So, he said, "Yitoo, so much has changed since you were last here. Not just the landscape. Not just the cities, the buildings. A lot of people, Pale People and Diné, have changed. Actually, Edward and I were hoping to bring you to a place called Arizona Falls to introduce you to some of those changes."

Yitoo smiled. Her jewelry jiggled and jingled like tiny bells as she stood on all fours. She arched into a downward-dog position and said, "Wonderful! This 'pool,' as you call it, is becoming cramped."

Nathan realized that Edward was tapping his arm. He felt the warm of Edward's breath on his ear.

"Thanks," Edward whispered.

Nathan nodded. He reached back and squeezed Edward's hand. He felt oddly protective of Edward and his feelings.

Before they left for Arizona Falls, Nathan asked Yitoo for some of her energizing sweetgrass. She happily provided some from her medicine bag. And she also pulled out a nearly invisible dark piece of fabric.

Nathan explained to Edward, "Don't inhale a lot; otherwise you'll be up all night."

"Don't you threaten me with a good time," Edward said.

Nathan lit the tips of the sweetgrass and then immediately blew them out. A thin trail of smoke wafted in the air. Both Nathan and Edward inhaled. The delicious smoke flowed into their nostrils.

Nathan saw the dark shadows underneath Edward's eyelids disappear and his posture straighten. Yup, Edward was awake.

"Okay!" Edward yelled.

"Not too loud. You'll wake up your dad," Nathan reminded Edward. "Thank you, Yitoo." He handed her back the braid and took the dark fabric she held in her mouth.

"Yes, thank you," Edward said. "What's that?"

"This," Nathan answered, "is a piece of shadow from the Holy Being known as Darkness. We're going to wear it so that it doesn't look like we are floating in midair." Nathan chuckled at the thought. The shadow fabric was large! He unfurled it and tossed it over all four of them, and there was still enough to easily hide another water monster of Yitoo's size!

"Let's be off," Yitoo said. She commanded her ice jewelry to melt. Like the ice sculptures in the pool, there was more water than the size of the jewelry displayed. Yitoo absorbed all the water, growing.

After Dew jumped into Edward's backpack, the two of them mounted Yitoo's strong shoulders. Nathan made Edward hold the shadow fabric so that he could use the Maps app on his phone. He searched for the nearest path to the Salt River Project canal, a large, interconnected web of concrete waterways that distributed water across the Phoenix valley. Thankfully they weren't too far from a canal. Nathan directed Yitoo to hop over the backyard fence.

After sneaking through several backyards, they came across a waterway. From there, they would head north alongside the

202 highway. These waterways made for perfect transportation trails in the middle of the night, when no one was around.

Nathan said, "Okay, follow the curve, and then we're going to go north."

Yitoo curved the corner and headed north through more dry waterways. They followed the turns and straightaways of the Salt River Project canals, rushing over the Tempe Town Lake and the recreational trails that ran on both banks. Yitoo angled her head slightly to the right. She asked, "What are those large patches of grass there?"

Both Nathan and Edward glanced at what she was staring at. Edward answered, "That's a golf course."

Yitoo scoffed, "You'll have to explain what a golf course is. But that amount of grass needs considerable water." She shook her head.

A few minutes later, the four of them arrived at Arizona Falls. While climbing off Yitoo's spine, Nathan scanned the small park to make sure there was no one else around. This late into the night, Nathan didn't expect anyone to be. They stood on a wide-open expanse of concrete surrounded by a gray fence. Below them was stagnant, polluted water that stank like rotten eggs. To his right was the E Indian Road and four large tennis courts. Nathan walked over phrases and words forever inscribed in smooth concrete below him. One quote caught his attention: "Raindrops on hard dirt make the ghosts rise."

Yitoo appeared shocked to Nathan. Yitoo asked, "What is this place?"

Edward unzipped his new backpack, and Dew crawled out. He said, "You should see this place when there is water, Yitoo. It can be very pretty. My dad and I sometimes run on the trail right there." He pointed toward the other side of the tennis court.

Yitoo sniffed the dirty water. "What happens here?"

Nathan said, "Places like this use water to generate electricity."

"Electricity is like lightning except it can be used to energize those light bulbs you told me about, Nathan." Yitoo spoke in even tones like she was trying her best to understand this new concept.

"Yes, and there are other ways to generate electricity," Nathan said. "But I thought I'd show you this first to introduce you to the modern times. We use electricity for pretty much everything."

"Okay," Yitoo said. She sighed deeply and sat down on her hind legs. "Did the Diné create this?"

"No," Nathan said.

"The Pale People," Yitoo said.

"Yes," Nathan said. "All that you have seen—the rented house, the highways, the cars—have come from the minds of white people as well as African American, Latinx, Asian people, and many other groups. I think Lewis Latimer, an African American inventor, made light bulbs affordable for everyone. And Latimer also invented the first evaporative air conditioner.

There's more to the United States than Diné and Pale People interactions."

Thankfully, Edward was smart enough to let Yitoo absorb this information and not say anything—yet. Yitoo then said, "You've avoided my questions long enough, Nathan. Tell me what happened after the kidnapping of the Diné people."

"The Diné lived in a place called Fort Sumner for four years," Nathan said. "There was much hardship and then the US government . . ."

"Pale People," Yitoo said.

Nathan continued. "Their government released our ancestors and permitted them to return to Diné Bikéyah but reduced our lands to the current reservation. Most Diné still live in the boundaries of the Four Sacred Mountains on the reservation. But that was one hundred and sixty years ago. Since then, big cities emerged, such as Phoenix. There are many others Las Vegas. Albuquerque. Los Angeles. Even some bigger ones like New York City on the other side of this continent."

"These cities, they are full of Pale People?" Yitoo asked. She lay down, as if she was absorbing all the information.

"Many other peoples as well. Some from across the oceans live here. Some were brought here against their will," Nathan said, thinking of all the different races, nationalities, and ethnicities. He sat down next to her and wrapped an arm around her neck. "And we all coexist together."

"I have a question, and I expect a truthful answer," Yitoo

said. She stood up, brushing off Nathan's arm. She sniffed the dirty waters. "Where does the water come from? This valley does not naturally provide the amount of water that this monstrous thing called a city needs."

"I don't know," Nathan said.

"Lake Roosevelt provides most of our water," Edward said. Yitoo grimaced at the English name. "There are other lakes close to Utah and Nevada. I don't remember their names."

"What are their Diné names?" Yitoo asked.

"They aren't Diné. Or they aren't within the Four Sacred Mountains," Edward said.

"I would like to see them," Yitoo said.

Edward jumped in. "I can take you. If it's a favor you're asking."

Nathan noticed that Edward was a little too eager to be doing anything for Yitoo. He wondered what Edward was up to. "I think we should first find the Hero Twins and resolve the issue of the Modern Enemy."

"Yes," Yitoo said. "The Modern Enemy is our priority."

"Are you okay?" Nathan asked Yitoo.

Yitoo said, "Bring me back to the pool."

Nathan nodded. He had expected her to respond in this way.

Dew jumped into the backpack, and then both Nathan and Edward mounted Yitoo. Together, they made their way back to the house. Nathan needed to help Yitoo understand that Diné were able to survive the relocation and adapt to the modern era. These next few moments, when she was absorbing and understanding the new Fourth World, were vitally important.

It was near 1 in the morning when Nathan and Edward dismounted in the back of the house, Yitoo slumped near the pool and watched ripples spread across it. Nathan approached her cautiously and petted her head. Then she started weeping.

"I failed," Yitoo said.

"What makes you think that?" Nathan asked her.

Yitoo said, "The Pale People were free to do what they wanted. The first time I saw one of them, I was confused because they looked so much like the Diné, who respect and honor the harmony that we have built with each other. The only difference is that their skin is pale like bone. I assumed their physical similarities meant the Pale People, too, would respect the natural world. I let them roam and trusted in their goodness.

"Instead, the Pale People forced their names upon the mountains, valleys, canyons, and even the rivers. They forced the name San Juan River onto my waters. They never offered any form of thanks for the water they greedily drank. They kidnapped the original caretakers of the land and implemented their will over the land. They suffered no consequence for their damnable behavior."

Nathan wished Edward didn't have to hear that. He said to Edward and Dew, "Do you think Yitoo and I can have some space?"

"No problem," Edward huffed, and scooped Dew up in his arms. She didn't squirm and sat quietly, staring at Yitoo. He opened the sliding doors and stepped in.

After the two of them entered the house, Nathan said to Yitoo, "You did not fail. You fought hard for the Diné people, Yitoo. We're still here. Edward and I are living proof that you did not fail. Diné have adapted and became a part of the larger global society." He became conscious of his smartphone pressing against his thigh in his pocket.

Yitoo said, "If I hadn't left, if I was stronger, Pond might not have died."

It felt like a strong hand squeezed at both Nathan's heart and throat. Sadness flooded his veins and the back of his eyes.

Yitoo continued. "And not just him. My sisters and brothers, who still live here in the Fourth World, they suffer and die because I was too weak to resist the Pale People."

After the shock of hearing his late friend's name softened, Nathan focused on Yitoo. He said, "You had to do what was best for you."

"If only things had gone differently," Yitoo said. "If I recognized earlier the danger they would bring, I would have ended the Pale People's scurrying about in the Fourth World."

Nathan recognized her thought patterns. He searched her shadow to make sure that there were no Ash Beings in her shadow. Seeing none, he sighed in relief.

"The past happened," Nathan said. Remembering Pond, and Uncle Jet, he said, "It can make us stronger. It has made us stronger."

Yitoo gently leaned onto Nathan. "If only there were more like you, Nathan."

Nathan smiled. Then she ruined his good mood by saying, "It puzzles me why you don't call Edward your younger brother."

His ears buzzed, and the skin on his face prickled. "He's not my younger brother. My mom and his dad are living together."

Yitoo chuckled. "Much has indeed changed. Back then, when two families combined as yours has, it was understood that the children called each other siblings."

Nathan said, "I'm not calling him my younger brother."

Yitoo said, "Father Sun's wife had trouble accepting the Hero Twins as her sons. Someday you might. Keep your heart open to the possibility of being his older brother. There is great pride in helping raise a younger sibling. Dew reminds me that there is promise of a peaceful future filled with justice and joy."

Nathan had seen the love, the bond, and the connection Dew had with Yitoo. He wondered if Yitoo had had the same relationship with Pond. Then memories of the summer two years ago flashed in his mind. Pond in the shadow of a dune, whimpering. Pond in the diagnosis meeting, scared of the words "radiation poisoning." Pond, laughing and smiling, as Nathan rode on his back across the New Mexican desert in the silver light of stars and moon. Pond, exhausted, his rib cage bones showing through his descaled skin. Pond, breathing his last. He started to cry. "I miss Pond."

Yitoo said, "And I miss your ancestors who visited my river before the Pale People kidnapped them."

Nathan, too, began to understand her anger toward white people. If they hadn't mined in the Church Rock Mines, then

Pond would never have been poisoned by radiation. For all the good and convenience that modern technologies had allowed, the original inhabitants were made to suffer for that progress. But Nathan was a descendant of those original inhabitants. Was he no better than the people, white or otherwise, who ignorantly indulged themselves while people who lived on Diné Bikéyah, like Nali, were made to suffer? If he participated in modern conveniences, was he a part of the problem? How could he be a part of the solution?

Tseebíí

EIGHT

LATER THAT MORNING, EDWARD TOOK a big breath to calm his nerves. He stood in the backyard adjusting the new backpack Janet had recently bought him. It was filled with snacks and gear for the upcoming journey across Diné Bikéyah. Nathan, Dew, and Yitoo were in front of him, also making last-minute preparations. Dew, like Yitoo, was making condensed ice jewelry from the pool waters. Nathan was busy on his smart-phone, probably looking at maps. Edward told himself that by the end of the day, he had to ask Yitoo for a blessing.

He had reasoned that if he were to help Yitoo with the Modern Enemy issue, then he would earn her respect and could tell her of his half heritage. And if he became a United States Olympic wrestler, people like Chad from Target would have more respect for his skin color. No, becoming an Olympic wrestler wasn't going to cure the world of prejudice, but he could provide prejudiced people a positive example of someone like him. It made sense to him but didn't feel right yet. Edward tapped Nathan's shoulder and leaned close to whisper, "How are we going to talk with her during the day?"

Nathan looked surprised, like he hadn't thought of that. "I, uh, lemme ask her." Nathan spoke in broken Diné to her. She looked confused. Nathan pointed to his ring and then the rising sun.

"'Ałtse'," Yitoo responded. She stuck her nostrils into the space between her neck and armpits and then pulled out two small strips of shadow fabric. "Yoostsah shaníaah."

Suddenly, the ring around his thumb was pulled toward her by an invisible force. Edward felt it slide off his hand and then saw it floating in the air before Yitoo's snout. The strips of darkness wrapped around the rings, and the bright colors dimmed like they were caught in a deep dark shadow. Both he and Nathan held out their hands again, and the darkened rings slid right on.

"Can you understand me?" Yitoo asked.

"Yes," Nathan said. "What did you do?"

"You may have noticed that the communication stone works when there is more darkness than light," Yitoo said. "You can trick it by wrapping a shadow around it, and it will forever be covered in darkness. It will work in the middle of a bright sunny day now. As long as you don't completely cover it in shadow, it'll still be visible."

"Thank you, Yitoo," Edward said. This was so cool. He liked

the ring very much, now even more with its darker yellow and subdued white colors.

"Yes, thank you very much," Nathan said. "I think we should head north first. That should get us to Diné Bikéyah. After that, I don't even know where to begin looking for either the Hero Twins or the Modern Enemy."

Yitoo said, "Once we get to Diné Bikéyah, we will visit my brothers and sisters and ask them if they know of the where-abouts of the Hero Twins. As we go to my, excuse me"—Yitoo smiled at Dew—"our siblings, we will keep an eye out for any signs of the Modern Enemy. Perhaps the reason it hasn't been discovered is because it has kept itself hidden and no one has suspected its presence. Well, without further delay, let's begin our search for the Hero Twins!"

Dew jumped for joy; her jewelry twinkled with every bounce. "I'm so excited."

"I'm not sure 'excited' is the best word," Nathan said.

"Anxious," Edward pitched in.

Yitoo gravely said, "Be on guard. We may very well uncover the identity of the Modern Enemy. Once we do, it may be inspired to retaliate against our efforts. But fear not. Dew and I should be more than capable of protecting you both."

Edward hated to think of being on Yitoo's bad side. After all, she was the most powerful water monster in the Fourth World. And from what he had seen of what Dew could do with Yitoo's lessons, water monsters were capable of phenomenal feats.

"Let's get this party started," Edward said, another saying he copied from his dad. He hated that he didn't tell his dad the full truth of this journey. He swallowed his guilt and tried to ignore the knot in his stomach.

"Agreed," Dew said. She scurried up to Yitoo, who was absorbing the rest of the pool water and growing to the size of a moose.

"Are you fully prepared? We may not be returning to this valley for some time," Yitoo said.

"Yes," Nathan said. "I've already called my paternal grandma. She'll be cooking dinner for us."

Edward took one last look at the rented house. For the first time, it felt like home. Even if they were only gone for a short time, he was going to miss it. "Ready as I'll ever be."

"Climb onto my shoulders. We leave now," Yitoo said, her voice strong and commanding. She sounded like fear did not exist in her. Like she was dealing with a bothersome pest instead of a Modern Enemy that could cause doomsday damage upon the Fourth World.

Nathan climbed on her upper back first. After he looked secure, Edward jumped on Yitoo behind Nathan. Yitoo pulled the large shadow fabric out of her medicine bag with her jaw and gave it to Nathan, who then wrapped it around all of them.

Yitoo explained, "It would be wise to conduct our search in stealth. Nathan, if you hold on to this shadow, I shall secure you with a harness of water."

Without warning, a thin ropelike stream of water wrapped

around their waists and held them in place firmly. Dew sat on Yitoo's forehead. She sniffed the air, like a puppy sticking its nose out of a moving car. Then water frothed around Yitoo's legs and lifted them over the brick fence and rushed them toward the Salt River Project canal. Once in the canal systems, water propelled them forward just as fast—no, even faster—than a car on the highway! Scared, Edward wrapped his arms around Nathan and dug his face into his shoulder blades. Nathan patted Edward's forearms and leaned forward.

It only took them a few minutes until they were out of the valley and zooming up the Goldfield Mountains. Yitoo jumped onto a ridge and hurried across the spine of the mountain. Using a powerful explosion of water, she launched them from peak to peak until they were nearly at the crest.

Edward glanced back and saw the sprawling metropolis of the Phoenix valley, trying his best to ignore how high they were. The city covered the entire desert landscape. Chandler in the south. Mesa and Gilbert in the east. Central Phoenix. And far off in the northwestern tip was Surprise. Edward couldn't help but love his home city. It was full of wonderful people, amazing opportunities, and the best chimichangas. Yitoo began their descent, and Phoenix valley disappeared out of view. He would gladly fight a Modern Enemy to protect his home city.

Even though the water harness held him tightly, Edward was terrified at how fast they were traveling. The landscape around him was just a fuzzy blur. Edward noticed, however, that he wasn't having a hard time breathing. Unlike when he was on the waterfall slide in Hurricane Harbor for Andrew's birthday party, he was able to breathe normally. Then he noticed that he wasn't hearing any sounds at all. No whooshing air past his ears or the splashing of water, but there was weight around his ear. With one hand, he carefully reached to his ear and felt the cold, smooth surface of ice. Before Edward pulled the ice muff off, Nathan tapped Edward's thigh and shook his head. Edward understood immediately. The water monsters were singing, and the ice muff was protecting him from the effects of the songs.

What felt like forty minutes had passed, and suddenly there was an incredible boost of speed that terrified Edward. The speeding land beside them looked like watercolor streaks. Nausea bubbled in his sternum and dizziness spun his head. Edward felt his upper body leaning to the side. Thankfully, Yitoo slowed to a stop before Edward could fall to the ground.

Edward hopped off as soon as he could. He pointed to the ice muffs, looking at the three of them. Then Nathan commanded the water to melt off his ears. Edward knelt on the ground, focusing on his breath and not on the nausea slowly creeping up the back of his throat. His hands dug into the deep purple sands to the cooler grains beneath to soothe his senses.

"Where are we?" Nathan asked.

Edward heard Yitoo answer, "We must have crossed the boundaries of the Four Sacred Mountains. We are here, at the very edge of Diné Bikéyah."

No longer sick to his stomach, Edward cautiously stood and looked around. Nathan was walking next to Yitoo, searching the wide colorful desert in front of them. Beyond them, Edward had his breath taken away yet again.

"We're in the Petrified Forest and Painted Desert," Edward said. "My dad took me here two years ago."

They stood in the middle of the Petrified Forest National Park. If Edward remembered correctly, the park was twenty miles east of Holbrook. All around them were colorful sand dunes. Flat-top plateaus, with patches of blue grama grass reaching toward the cloudless sky above, stretched to every horizon. Erosion had cut into those flat tops to reveal layers of red, white, orange, and pink sandstone underneath. Stumps of petrified wood lay in rows across the earth to their right. The outside of the rock wood was deep red and resembled cracked canyon walls. But the interior of the wood looked like opal and the inside of abalone shell.

"Whatever name you humans give it, this is the start of the sacred boundaries of Diné Bikéyah," Yitoo said. "And when water monsters enter those boundaries, our abilities are more powerful. Edward, have you collected your bearings?"

"Yeah. Just don't go as quickly or else I'll throw up," Edward said.

"Please," Nathan added quickly.

Yitoo didn't respond and only lowered her body to the ground to let the boys climb onto her shoulders. "For your sake, I will. Hold on for a few moments, as we are very near one of my siblings."

Edward cherished the little seconds he had left standing on the ground.

"It gets easier the more you do it," Nathan said.

"I hope so," Edward said.

Ice covered his ear as he mounted Yitoo. And they were off again. This time, Edward squeezed his eyes shut and fought his motion sickness by imagining the weight of the Olympic medal around his neck.

Just as she said, it took a few minutes for them to reach wherever Yitoo wanted to go.

Edward opened his eyes when he was fully certain they were no longer traveling. The wide-open desert landscape looked almost like his own paternal grandparents' place just north of Chinle. Dry gray bulbs of shriveled grass dotted the entire ground. Pointy slender green leaves of yucca plants poked out of the earth. Edward turned around, and far behind him he could see the faint pink-and-orange outlines of the Painted Desert.

A breeze gently flowed past them, carrying a disgusting smell that made Nathan cough. Edward covered his nose. He felt the ice over his ears melt.

"Follow me," Yitoo said, undaunted by the horrid stench.

They walked toward the dried waterbed with cracked soil outlined by the gray stalks of dead grass. Another breeze wafted past them. Even with Edward covering his nose and mouth, he could taste that smell on the tip of his tongue. It had similar qualities to rotten fruit, but it was much worse. There was also a used-diaper odor to it.

The four of them bravely walked forward and soon discovered the source of the smell: the rotting corpses of twenty horses.

The skin on the horses' cheeks was pulled back, revealing their teeth, white and reflecting the sunlight. Patches of skin dangled on their sun-bleached bones. They looked like they were frozen in a scream. The lower half of their dead bodies had sunk into the ground. Parts of the remaining skin were covered in dried mud.

Yitoo approached the horse bodies almost as if the awful reek didn't affect her nostrils. With her nose, she tapped a few of their foreheads.

"I'm so sorry," she said. "Please know that your death, painful and slow as it was, will not be in vain. I will unveil the Modern Enemy that is stealing water from Diné Bikéyah."

Dew apprehensively approached the horses. Edward realized that this might be the first time Dew had seen death. Her wide eyes sparkled with tears.

Yitoo explained, "They died of dehydration. When ponds or lakes reach a tipping point of drying, the last bits of water flow to the deepest part. These poor beings must have all approached those last drops of moisture as one unit. This ground is lined with clay. And with the weight of all the horses, the ground became a pit of mud that swallowed them all. This happened a few weeks ago, as the last bits of moisture have dried up."

Those poor horses, Edward thought. He'd hate to have been in their position, literally.

"If the Modern Enemy takes more water, this could very well be the fate of all living beings in Diné Bikéyah," Yitoo solemnly said. Then she lifted her chin to the sky and growled. She tilted her head slightly as if listening for a reply.

To Edward's surprise, there was a deeper, grumblier roar.

Yitoo said, "My younger brother will be here shortly. He will tell us what happened to his lake."

Facing away from the bodies of the horses to avoid their smell, Edward scanned the area for Yitoo and Dew's brother, but saw nothing. He turned around—still nothing.

An unknown adult male voice spoke right from Edward's side. "So it is true. You have returned."

"Who said that?" Edward shouted, turning to the direction from where the voice came.

There was movement in a small shadow that looked like the shimmering heat waves on black pavement. The movement in the shadow moved straight upward like a curtain, and a water monster emerged out of thin air! After his body was in full sunlight, the shimmering settled as if it never happened.

"He has a piece of shadow, too," Nathan whispered into Edward's ear.

"Gracious Yitoo Bi'aanii," the male water monster said, bowing. He approached Yitoo, and they butted each other's heads. Yitoo was easily twice his size.

"Clay Lake, my brother, I have missed you," Yitoo said.

"Hi!" Dew chirped and jumped from Yitoo's shoulder blades onto Clay Lake's. She hastily crawled all over him. Clay Lake smiled the entire time.

"I have a new sister!" Clay Lake said. "Such happiness!"

"What happened to your waters, my brother?" Yitoo started. "Those poor horses."

"Their death is my fault," he said, coughing. "I sang and sang and sang with no success of rain. I sang until my throat burned, and then I sang some more. When my voice was the squeak of a mouse, I stopped because the rains were not coming."

Yitoo said, "Brother, what is happening? This severe dryness is not natural!"

Clay Lake responded, "It's been like this for years. Decades after you returned to the Third World was when the changes began. Our songs became less and less potent. There are plenty of us who try to sing back the rains. We have little successes, here and there. But more often, the moisture we summon isn't enough. Some of our siblings, Canyon Mist being the first, elect to live in silence. They don't sing because they feel their efforts are futile."

"This is bad," Yitoo said. "This is very bad."

"It's been like this for a long time," Clay Lake repeated. "What brings you back to Diné Bikéyah?"

Yitoo said, "I'm teaching our youngest sister all my songs. That's my primary reason for my returning. But I suspect that there is a Modern Enemy, here, today, in the Fourth World. And it's stealing the waters of Diné Bikéyah from my river."

"Oh, I am certain your suspicions are accurate," Clay Lake said. He slumped down. "A cruel and heartless entity *is* stealing the waters. As a result, Diné Bikéyah becomes drier and drier with each passing year. Its inhabitants are made to suffer a vast and unending drought."

Edward's heart dropped. There was a Modern Enemy! And it

made these horses suffer. What else was happening because this Modern Enemy was taking waters?

Yitoo said, "The four of us want to find the Hero Twins and ask for their help. The last time I saw them was when they were preparing to confront the Enemy known as Old Age."

Clay Lake responded, "The Hero Twins? Enemy Slayer and Born for Water? I do not know where they are. Their mother, Changing Woman, left westward until she came upon the ocean. Maybe they followed her? I apologize for not knowing more."

"Do you know what the Modern Enemy looks like or where it is?" Yitoo demanded.

"That is the tricky thing—identifying it. Long ago, it was easy to identify an Enemy. But in this era, it's possible for an Enemy to hide in plain sight," Clay Lake surmised. "You know who might? Canyon Mist. She was the first to believe that a Modern Enemy is afoot. She might know how to identify it, or at least the telltale signs of its interference."

Yitoo said, "Thank you very much, younger brother. I know this isn't much. But please take some of my water."

One of the bracelets on her back legs unlinked and floated to Clay, who excitedly opened his mouth to swallow it. After he gulped it down, his faded color momentarily turned vibrant. His dry scales glistened and gleamed. "Bless you, sister."

Yitoo said, "Know that the four of us are working to restore balance to Diné Bikéyah."

Clay Lake nodded. "When you discover the Modern Enemy, vaporize it."

Yitoo said to Edward and Nathan, "Come, we are off to the canyons of Nazlini."

After the three of them mounted Yitoo, she sped off northeastward. Edward was too furious to be nauseous. The image of those dried horse carcasses haunted him. No one else had said it, but there was a great deal of suffering in the boundaries of the Four Sacred Mountains because water was being taken from across Diné Bikéyah.

Náhást'éí

NINE

NATHAN HATED THAT THOSE HORSES had suffered so much. He wanted to find the Modern Enemy as quickly as possible. He had to talk to it, whatever it was, to explain that because of its actions, others were suffering. Nothing was fully heartless. Nothing was beyond helping. Edward's arms squeezed Nathan's abdomen a little too tightly as Yitoo launched them down a tall hill. He squeezed the shadow firmly. And from her growls and the speed at which she was traveling, Yitoo was likely very angry.

Nathan considered that it might be more advantageous for him to talk with the Modern Enemy without Yitoo around. It wasn't ideal, but he might have to separate from Yitoo and find the Modern Enemy himself, after learning how to identify its signs from Canyon Mist. Then would that mean Edward would have to be alone with Yitoo? If she was with Edward, would

Edward be able to handle himself if Yitoo spoke negatively of white people?

Around noon, they whizzed by the Nazlini Chapter House to enter the mouth of the canyon. Yitoo slowed their propulsion to navigate the tight maze of rocky walls. Then Yitoo stopped and roared like she did earlier to summon Clay Lake. Her mighty voice echoed off the pink-orange rock faces. Nathan and Edward crawled off quickly. The soft sands beneath them sank like the beaches of the Third World. A lot of water used to rush through here, Nathan gathered. A river did carve this canyon after all.

While they waited for a water monster to reply, Nathan looked at his phone and realized it was time for lunch. With all this excitement and traveling, he hadn't realized he was growing hungry. "We should eat now," Nathan said to Edward.

Both Nathan and Edward reached into their backpacks to pull out peanut butter and jam sandwiches, small bags of chips, and bottles of water. Nathan grabbed Edward's water and chilled it for him. In the middle of their quick meal, a water monster emerged from around the corner of the canyon wall. She limped forward, holding her elbow against her chest.

"Canyon Mist!" Yitoo said. She hurried to her side. "What happened to you?"

"Imperious Yitoo Bi'aanii," Canyon Mist said, bowing. Her voice sounded like it once had been sweet, but now carried bitterness, like moldy honey. She didn't look at all happy to see her older sister. "I wasn't expecting to see you. Oh, my elbow? You needn't bother."

"Here, allow me to help," Yitoo said. Water erupted from her necklace and wrapped around Canyon Mist's injured elbow. A cool cloud flowed away from the water, like dry ice.

"I said not to bother," Canyon Mist said with disdain. "What returns you to the Fourth World?"

"Oh," Yitoo said, saddened by the rejection. The water returned to her necklace. "Clay Lake directed us to you. He said you think there is a Modern Enemy creating chaos in the Fourth World right now."

"Very likely," Canyon Mist said.

"Can you tell us what we should be looking for?" Edward asked. Like Nathan, he was finishing his lunch and putting the trash into his backpack.

"Now, why would I do that?" Canyon Mist said. She sat on her hind legs and licked at her hurt elbow.

"What's with this attitude, younger sister?" Yitoo asked. "Siblings should help each other."

Canyon Mist stopped licking and said, "I find the idea that simply being family implies an automatic allegiance annoying. Besides, searching for the supposed Modern Enemy is a fool's errand."

Nathan stepped forward. "What do you mean?"

Yitoo asked, "What happened to you, dear sister? You used to be so sweet."

"After you returned to the Third World, Humbled Yitoo"— her voice dripped with sarcasm—"we remaining water monsters had to fend for ourselves. I'm not blaming you for what happened after you left. I would have done the same thing had I suffered what you had. But we had to adapt to the changes brought on by Pale People."

"Horrid beings," Yitoo said.

"As you see, everything changed. All for the comfort of humanity. For many decades after the arrival of the Pale People, we water monsters sang our songs, returned the rains, nurtured our waters. But for what? We received nothing in return. Does being Holy Beings mean we have to automatically be selfless? I used to say yes and continue to smile and sing. But my river in my canyon became polluted and eventually dried up.

"About a hundred years after you returned to the Third World, a number of us remaining water monsters noticed that the rains we were singing down weren't as plentiful. We looked into many possibilities. Were the songs losing their influence? Was it our singing? Was it us? But it became clear that it was nothing on our end. We sang perfectly, beautifully. All the other songs that helped us command water were still powerful. Then I realized what was causing the dwindling rains. Something was taking the water away from Diné Bikéyah. It's the only way.

"When you brought the river from Mom's realm up here, that moisture became the foundation of the water cycle in Diné Bikéyah. Our sixteen rain songs supplement that holy cycle. Your river takes the moisture to the ocean. We sing the songs, and the ocean turns into clouds that travel back to Diné Bikéyah. It rains, and eventually the water returns to your river. It's a beautiful system. But when something takes water away out of that cycle and doesn't give it back, that's when the rains weaken and the land dries.

"So, I abandoned my duties to singing the rain songs and protecting the moisture in this canyon. Oh, don't look so distraught, Inflated Yitoo, you are hardly one to judge another for abandoned duties. In fact, by abandoning my river, I was able to search for the abomination that steals our waters. I traveled across and even beyond the sacred boundaries, knowing that outside of them I am susceptible to death. Just like you did, when the Pale People kidnapped all the Diné."

Nathan asked, "What did you find?"

"The state of the Fourth World. And the influence humanity has had. The cities they created. The roads they use to navigate great distances. The disconnect humans now have with the natural resources they rely upon. It offended me. When I returned, I decided to sing only for myself and nothing else."

"Our duty as water monsters is to protect the water," Yitoo growled.

"I am protecting the water," Canyon Mist said. She stood up and squared herself against Yitoo.

"By letting the land dry and the beings that rely upon it die?" Yitoo said.

"You've not seen the sludge of fracking turn a clear river into dark brown muck. You've not seen the wastewater of a uranium mine spill into a nearby lake. Oh, yes, I am aware of you and your efforts, Nathan, Healer of the Water Monster. You've not seen lakes polluted by trash. By withholding the remaining water, they can't be perverted nor be taken away. So, forgive me, older sister, for thinking your quest is nothing more than a childish attempt to soothe your ego."

Canyon Mist spoke so coldly that Nathan was surprised to feel the air around them grow humid and hot. In an instant, a spray of water slammed against Canyon Mist and pushed her a few yards until her spine smacked against the canyon wall behind her.

Nathan immediately grabbed Edward and pulled him behind his body. Dew jumped from Yitoo's forehead and landed by Nathan's feet. Fear rushed through his body. Nathan commanded water to cover Edward's ears in case the water monsters sang. Then he began to hum the Move song, ready to defend himself and Edward.

Yitoo spoke. "You are a disgrace to all water monsters, unfit to care for the waters in this region."

Canyon Mist roared, and the stream that was pushing against her exploded into plump water heads that pelted everywhere. Canyon Mist dug her paws into the riverbed to stand firm.

"Get yourselves to safety," Yitoo said. The droplets slid down the rock walls and trailed back to her body.

Nathan didn't argue and picked up Dew. The two boys proceeded to run as quickly as they could away from the two water monsters. Once they got a safe enough distance from them, Nathan turned around, ready to aid Yitoo. Though at the display of her power, he would only get in her way.

Canyon Mist walked toward Yitoo, saying, "Disgrace. Unfit. Call me whatever you like. I didn't leave my river when she needed me most." Water flowed out of Canyon Mist's mouth and encased her injured elbow like a support brace, then hardened into ice. Water pooled out of the riverbed, collected at her tail, arched forward. The water tail sharpened to a tip and finally froze solid. She looked like a mixture of a water monster with the tail of a scorpion. Canyon Mist pushed toward Yitoo.

"You will sing your songs and give your river back to the lands and their inhabitants," Yitoo said. Her jewelry melted and spread across her body as her spikes poked out of her back. In a few seconds, her entire body was covered in ice armor.

Canyon Mist said, "Have we not overexerted ourselves? Have we not taken on more than necessary? Let all beings suffer the consequences, and we Holy Beings can start anew." Canyon Mist walked, using the ice brace. "Imagine that, dear oldest sister. Owing nothing to any being. Living for ourselves, instead of indulging the ungrateful greedy humans of the Fourth World who would defile our precious waters?"

Nathan wondered if that last sentence was directed toward him and Edward. He felt guilty because he had never thanked the Holy Being that brought water to the Phoenix valley.

"If you will neither sing nor share your waters, then I will strip them away from you," Yitoo said. She ran toward Canyon Mist.

Canyon Mist raised her ice tail as high as she could, then

swung it down toward Yitoo. "Not without resistance you won't!"

Yitoo dodged to her right, and the ice tail slammed the ground. Yitoo then rammed into Canyon Mist with her entire body, pushing her back again against the wall.

Canyon Mist's ice tail raised again and rushed at Yitoo's chest. This time, the ice tail hit Yitoo with a loud cracking sound. Yitoo's ice armor held strong, no fractures anywhere. The ice tail repeatedly hit Yitoo over and over again. Yitoo endured the assault, then knocked her head against the side of Canyon Mist's right temple. As she did, Canyon Mist's ice tail began to slightly melt. It looked like Canyon Mist wasn't going to last much longer.

"No!" Canyon Mist screamed. The ice tail hardened. She slammed the ice tail to the ground and used it as leverage to hoist her body into the air to get her away from the canyon wall. Her body landed, and she immediately swung at Yitoo's hind legs. The ice tail knocked the bend of her knees, causing Yitoo to slump into the ground. "I did not ask you to come back. I did not ask you to solve the problems that arose in your absence! Just leave me alone!"

The ice tail turned into water that wrapped around Yitoo's body. Using the water rope, Canyon Mist lifted Yitoo and threw her against the opposite canyon wall twenty feet high. Yitoo's body fell. Before her body hit the ground, some of Yitoo's ice armor melted and cushioned her landing.

Yitoo said, "We are Holy Beings of this land. We don't have

the luxury of solitude. We need the many beings who walk, fly, and swim in this world as they need us. Have you forgotten plant life?"

"You're wrong!" Canyon Mist shouted, slowly walking toward Yitoo. "Look at this area! Look at how all the beings manage to exist without my songs and without my water. Look at the happiness I had before you interrupted it."

Nathan did look around. There was plant life. But everything was so dry and just barely alive. The life here, both plant and animal, was submissive to the whims of nature. This wasn't living; it was survival. It was borderline torture.

The water monsters were now within reach of each other. Canyon Mist swung her mighty ice tail at Yitoo with increasingly wild abandon, hitting both the ground and the canyon wall. Then Yitoo caught the ice tail in her powerful jaws. With a mighty yank, she ripped the ice tail off Canyon Mist. Yitoo proceeded to shatter it, and the ice particles fell to the ground, sparkling and chiming like silver bells. Canyon Mist lay still, unable to do anything other than breathe.

Yitoo shouted, "Dew!"

Dew hopped onto Nathan's head and said, "Yes?"

"I have another song for you to learn," Yitoo said. "With this song, you will be able to forcibly take water away from an opponent."

"Don't you dare!" Canyon Mist shouted.

The pieces and shards of ice around Yitoo melted and collected into a large tentacle that began to wrap around Canyon

Mist. When Yitoo sang, the tentacles seemingly stabbed into Canyon Mist and began to draw out her water, causing her to shrink. Yitoo created another bracelet from the moisture that she took.

"You stole the remnants of my river!" Canyon Mist yelled in between deep, hoarse gasps. She was no more than the size of a medium dog. "My heart!"

"Younger sister, I forgive your resisting me." Yitoo spoke calmly to Canyon Mist. "If you change your mind and want to continue singing the rain songs, come find me and I will give you back your river. If not, you have until the next full moon to return to Mom's realm."

Canyon Mist glared at Yitoo. "I will not return to the Third World. Come find me here next full moon. I still will not sing."

"By then, I will have solved the issue of the Modern Enemy," Yitoo said with confidence. "And the four of us will restore the water to all of Diné Bikéyah. It'd be wonderful if you could be a part of that."

Canyon Mist said, "I'll be a part of it! I'll even tell you how to find it! This Modern Enemy you speak of, you've probably already encountered it and didn't realize it. It exists only to consume for its benefit. Go to your river. Follow its flow. Discover where your water goes and certainly you will discover the evidence of the Modern Enemy. Perhaps the next time you see me, it is you who will be asking for my forgiveness. Now leave me alone."

Canyon Mist pushed herself off the ground and limped away.

Feeling that it was finally safe to approach Yitoo, Nathan guided Edward and Dew toward her.

Yitoo breathed heavily. Her exhales released as hot steam. Nathan didn't recognize her eyes. They were fully dilated and a dark green color. He could see his own reflection in them.

"Yitoo," Nathan cautiously asked.

"Let's go, everyone," she said.

"Where are we going to?" Edward asked.

"I don't care," Yitoo responded.

The boys climbed onto her shoulder and Dew rested on her forehead. Nathan agreed that getting Yitoo away from her sister was best. Later, they could form a better plan. He wrapped the shadow around them. In moments, they were exiting the canyon, away from Yitoo and Dew's sister who refused to sing down the rains. Nathan thought he heard Yitoo sniffling. He thought he saw tears flowing into the jet stream below them.

Edward shifted his weight as they exited the canyon, heading westward and away from the Chapter House of Nazlini. They crossed the lone paved road and continued forward into a vast and semi hilly sandy desert. It wasn't as vibrant as the Painted Desert, but there was color and undulating hills, crevices, and plateaus.

Edward detested, yet at the same time was awed by, how Yitoo took away her sister's water. On the one hand, Yitoo was an amazing fighter! She was powerful and tactical, and the stuff she did with water was exhilarating. But on the other hand, she did subdue her younger sister with aggression.

Yitoo stopped in a dry wash with yellow-brown horsetail grass lining the edges of the water bank. The water that propelled them continued its momentum and splashed Edward's legs as they rushed by. The water sank into the ground, staining it dark brown. And in minutes, the wet darkness faded back to its pale color as it quickly dried.

Nathan jumped off immediately and went to hug Yitoo, dropping the shadow fabric, while Edward took his time to dismount. Yitoo didn't resist Nathan, and she wept. Edward wasn't sure he wanted to comfort her. She had said mean things about Anglos, and she did attack Canyon Mist first.

Yitoo was able to say through her sobs, "Canyon Mist used to be so full of love."

"It's not your fault," Nathan told her.

Yitoo said, "My absence has turned her bitter. What renders my heart into pieces is that many more of my sisters and my brothers might have endured similar trials. I wasn't here to protect them."

Edward didn't agree with that. He said to her, "You had to heal. Canyon Mist is just as capable of making decisions as you. She chose to abandon her duties as a water monster. What sucks about that is that other beings suffered for that choice. If she wasn't going to sing down the rains, then by taking her water you can share it. You did the right thing."

Nathan looked surprised. "I couldn't have said it better myself."

Yitoo nodded. "Both of you have tremendous capacities to surprise and amaze me. I am at ease. I only hope that I didn't harm her too much."

Edward could relate to that, like no other. He said, "I once fireman-carried a wrestling opponent and ended up injuring him. After the match, I asked if he was okay. He said he was and that it was his fault because he stuck his arm out when he knew he shouldn't. Maybe you can check in on her, like I did with my opponent, in a few days."

"That I will," Yitoo said. Her sniffling stopped. "That action is both firm and loving, an attitude I hope you cultivate, Dew."

Nathan asked, "Does that mean you'll give the Modern Enemy a chance to talk with and listen to us?"

Yitoo responded, "Nathan, with all your kindness, you must also prepare for the possibility that the Modern Enemy cannot be reasoned with."

"All I ask is that I just talk with it," Nathan said.

Yitoo said, "For you, I will. Now, where to next?"

Nathan said, "I told my grandmother this morning that we would be spending the night with her at her mobile home. It's a bit early, but if you are exhausted, we can head over there."

Yitoo said, "Every minute we don't search is a minute that the Modern Enemy could be growing stronger or causing more suffering. We should listen to my sister and go to my river."

Edward tried to think of places to inspect for signs of the Modern Enemy. Everything they had learned was just too vague. If they went to another water monster, he or she would probably say the same thing about the Modern Enemy; it existed but hadn't been identified. He'd rather search for the Hero Twins instead. But the information they had received about the Twins' whereabouts was just as cryptic. He recalled the stories that his dad told him when he was younger. Perhaps in those stories there was a clue about where the Hero Twins had gone. The Hero Twins, sons of Father Sun and Changing Woman. They traveled to the realm of the Holy Beings to go to the hogan of Father Sun for the sacred Obsidian Armor and the Four Sacred Arrows—Dawn, Rainbow, Folding Darkness, and Lightning. Na'ashjé'ii 'Adzą́ą́, or Spider Woman, told them the weaknesses of the old Enemies. Then it dawned on him where they could go! "We should go to Spider Woman!"

"Who's that?" Dew asked. She quickly crawled up Edward's leg, his lower back, then his shoulder. She leaned up against his neck as he spoke.

Edward excitedly shouted, "Spider Woman! The Hero Twins would always report back to her. She would know where they went!"

"Edward, that's a grand idea," Yitoo said, walking up to him. She lowered her great head so that their eyes met. Then her thin reptilian tongue caressed his short black hair. "I may have to call you both Heroes very soon."

Happiness flowed from his chest to his limbs. Yitoo wasn't that bad. He knew that given time, he could convince her that not all Anglos were like the ones she encountered 160 years ago. There was goodness in her heart.

Dew jumped from his shoulder to Yitoo's forehead, her claws no doubt leaving fresh red scratch marks on his shoulder. Yitoo said, "Spider Woman lives just north of here in the Chinle canyon system. Let's be on our way."

While climbing to his spot behind Nathan, Edward felt as close to Yitoo as he had ever been. After they talked with Spider Woman would be the perfect time to ask her to bless his wrestling career.

Neeznáá

TEN

AS YITOO RAN NORTHWARD THROUGH the lonely desert of Nazlini, the sun was halfway through its downward descent. It still amazed Edward every now and then that the Holy Beings were real. Feeling the dry heat toasting his exposed forearms, he wondered if Father Sun was watching the four of them. He estimated it was at least four in the afternoon.

Yitoo ran up a steep hill that transformed from smooth orange sandstone with a dark purple line running through it to a sparse forest of stumpy trees. With every great heave of her legs, the junipers became taller, wider, denser. Eventually, Yitoo had to slow her speed so that she could navigate the tight clusters of juniper and oak.

Eventually, they came to the edge of Canyon de Chelly, and Edward immediately lost his breath. Directly in front of them, two tall orange rock steeples known collectively as Spider Rock spire rose from the bottom of the canyon and reached toward the cloudless sky. Light reflected off the smooth rock bellies of the canyon wall that surrounded the spire. The afternoon shadows cascaded down the sides of the canyon walls like black paint. This was where Spider Woman lived and where the Hero Twins would reconvene with her.

Edward asked Nathan in a quiet, meek voice, "Are we going to have to go up there?"

Nathan whispered back, "Are you afraid of heights?"

Edward squeaked, "So what if I am? Not like anything interesting happens near cliffs, except death."

"It's just eight hundred feet high," Nathan said nonchalantly.

"Eight hundred feet of annihilation," Edward said, taking large gulps of oxygen to subdue the growing woozy feeling in his head.

"Just close your eyes and hold on to me."

Dew asked, "How do we get there?"

Yitoo said, "Youngest sister, change the air into an ice bridge. You must rehearse the songs while we are not in danger."

Before water could cover his ears, Edward plugged them up with his fingers. He wasn't a fan of ice muffs. Their talking became muffled. Edward pushed a little harder until his breathing was all that he could hear. He thought of his future wrestling career. He saw himself winning state wrestling championships in high school. Being drafted for a college wrestling team. He hoped for Ohio State because a lot of Olympic wrestlers went there. Finally being discovered by an Olympic scout. He felt air rushing against his skin. His stomach rose and fell. Then Nathan tapped his shoulder.

Edward opened his eyes slowly and noticed that they were on the Spider Rock spire. He forced his chin upward and inhaled large gulps of air so that he didn't see how far up they were. He trusted Dew and Yitoo to keep them safe, but his heart kept telling him that they were going to fall off at any moment. Olympic medal, he thought, ignoring the steep cliff at his side that led to certain calamity!

There was just enough space for Yitoo to stand on and to be able to do a 360-degree turn. Then again, Yitoo was about six feet tall, four feet wide, and twelve feet long. Edward whimpered, searching the small area of rock around them. He couldn't handle how close they were to the edge. He pressed his face into Nathan's backpack and squeezed his hands tighter. Edward felt Nathan pat his knuckles.

"Spider Woman, are you here?" Nathan asked. "We are your grandchildren and would like your help, please."

An older feminine voice responded, "Yes, I am home, grandchildren. Please, come inside."

Edward peeked from behind Nathan's backpack and saw a small black hole in the center of the spire. It grew, and as it did, sand trickled inside the dark throat.

"May my youngest sister and I enter, too, venerated Spider Woman?" Yitoo asked. "We are water monsters."

"I would be honored," said the elderly voice. The hole widened even further.

Yitoo lowered a foot and seemed to find a solid surface. Soon, the hole was round enough for Yitoo's large body. She stood on a platform that descended like an elevator. Thankful to be going down, Edward slowly loosened his grip and leaned away from Nathan's back. He descended into the dark shadow, and the heat of the afternoon sun was no more.

Once his eyes adjusted, Edward noticed they were on a platform of clay mud plastered on a weave of pine tree branches. Hoisting them down, four ropes held the surface on which Yitoo stood. All around them was darkness. Above them, the blue afternoon sky remained. Then the aroma of mineral-rich sands flowed into his nostrils, summoning memories of his paternal grandparents' hogan. When they sprinkled water on the floor, it made the ground smell so delicious he was tempted to eat the dirt.

An old woman was huffing below them in the shadows. With each gasp, the platform lowered a few inches. What would Spider Woman look like? In the picture books that his dad had bought him, Spider Woman had the upper body of a human, and her lower body had the round furry abdomen of a spider with all eight legs. But when his paternal grandfather described her, she had six arms and no furry spider parts.

The platform finally stopped. A cloud of dust expanded in all directions around them.

"My grandsons, water monster sisters, come," the elderly voice said. Her voice had the steadiness of mountain streams and the lyrical nature of trees bending in the wind. Edward couldn't see into the thick shadows.

Yitoo stepped off the clay tree branch platform and walked toward the voice. She lowered her body to let the boys off. After stepping on safe ground, Edward searched the darkness. The light from the opening above barely lit anything. Edward took out his phone and turned on the flashlight and shone it around them.

They stood in a round structure, shaped like a hogan, that was far wider and more circular than the thin Spider Rock above. The ceiling was round and smooth. The ground below them was full of soft orange sands with swirls of red and yellow, like the cliffs outside. Edward gazed at the top of the ceiling and was surprised to see the night sky, but the constellations were placed in unfamiliar locations. His eyes adjusted to the darkness, and then he noticed that he wasn't staring at the night sky but a rug of stars, which Edward estimated to be about fifty feet tall and three times as wide. Once he tore his attention away from the beautiful star rug, he noticed hundreds, maybe even thousands, of spiderwebs zigzagging, crossing, and dangling from the ceiling. There were countless looms with rugs in progress. The rugs were so intricate and detailed that they resembled oil paintings in museums. A collection in one quadrant was dedicated to the Hero Twins, depicting them fighting the many Enemies that plagued the surface of the Fourth World so many eras ago.

But easily the grandest rug of all hung behind him, covering half the space. This rug displayed Diné Bikéyah like a map. Edward could see clusters of houses that made up the Arizona towns of Window Rock, Fort Defiance, Chinle, Nazlini, Kayenta, Tuba City, Ganado, and Red Mesa, as well as the New Mexican towns of Gallup, Shiprock, Farmington, Crownpoint, and Grants. There were many more towns that Edward couldn't identify. There were also many mountains, including the four sacred ones in the cardinal directions, as well as meandering rivers, colorful mesas, tree-topped plateaus, wide-open expanses, rocky cliffs of canyons, and mountains covered with evergreen trees.

Among the rugs hung trinkets, kitchen utensils, and various bundles of flowers, plants, and roots with deep vibrant colors. Pushed up against the walls were clay pots filled with water, some with plants, and spools of thread made from her webs. Edward realized that Spider Woman used the plants to dye the spider webbing thread, to create the rich colors depicted on the rugs.

"It warms my heart to see grandchildren after so many years." Spider Woman smiled at the boys, stepping into the cone of light. Her stringy hair, the color of sparkling night stars, was pulled into a tight tsiiyééł behind her head. She wasn't enormous, but she was definitely taller than a normal human and didn't appear to have any spiderlike features. She had a large blanket over her shoulders, though she still shivered. Her blanket glistened in the afternoon light. As she squinted to see them, her plentiful wrinkles collected between her brows and around the sides of her mouth. She must have smiled a lot in her life to have gotten those specific wrinkles.

"Hi, Grandma," Nathan said, bowing his head. Edward quickly followed Nathan's lead and did the same.

Spider Woman spoke to Nathan: "You are very old to be able to see me, grandson. You are already leaving childhood."

"I'm not sure how much longer I have with the Holy Beings," Nathan said.

"Help me sit down, grandson," she said, holding her hand out to Edward.

Nathan took out his phone and turned on the flashlight feature.

Edward held her hand, though he wondered how much help he'd be able to give, considering her height. Her grip pressed against his yellow-and-white thumb ring. She wobbled over to a large rock covered with a large fluffy sheep hide. That must be her bed, Edward thought. Spider Woman turned to sit down. Edward widened his stance to use his legs and leaned back to provide counter-support.

"Oof!" Spider Woman said as she sat down. Her blanket fell to the ground.

She wore a gorgeous rug dress that was woven predominantly with the four sacred colors: white, blue, yellow, and black. Edward would have stared at the dress rug a little longer if he hadn't noticed the four other arms that stuck out of the sides. One pair was rubbing itself for warmth, while another pair was reaching for the blanket. Edward quickly grabbed the blanket and wrapped it around her.

"Thank you," Spider Woman said. She held his arm gently

as he moved to stand up. She stared into his eyes and patted his head. "I see you, my grandson. Don't divide yourself into fractions. You are whole. You are already complete."

Edward wasn't sure what she was talking about. But her voice was so soothing and so loving that he hugged her and said, "Thank you, Grandma."

She smiled and beckoned Yitoo over as Edward went to stand by Nathan. "Benevolent Yitoo Bi'aanii! Welcome back, my beautiful niece."

"Auntie Spider Woman, it gives me pleasure to be in your divine presence." Yitoo rubbed the side of her cheek against Spider Woman's knee.

Spider Woman folded in half and wrapped Yitoo in a grand hug. She said, "The land, the animals, the plants, the many Holy Beings, and I, especially, have missed you dearly."

"Hi, Miss Woman!" Dew said from Nathan's shoulder.

"Oh! And who's this baby?" Spider Woman said, her eyes alight.

"I'm not a baby!" Dew said.

Spider Woman said, "Please, come closer so that I can see you clearly!"

Nathan gently grabbed Dew and placed her on the ground. Dew hesitantly went to her.

Spider Woman said, "Oh, you are most certainly not a baby by any means!"

Dew seemed to relax a little and said, "No, I'm not. I already know thirty-seven water monster songs and about three hundred twenty-seven pop songs!"

"Wow, that's so many! Sing one for me, please?" Spider Woman asked.

Anything but that song, Edward pleaded in his mind.

Dew leaped into the air. She sang, "I just can't hide this feeling, baby! I want to be your appealing lady! It is in your energy. My sacred reverie, mm, baby!"

Before she could continue the song, Yitoo stepped in. "Sacred teacher of weaving, we need to find the Hero Twins." Dew stopped singing and then scurried over to Spider Woman, who picked her up and held her against her cheek.

"Hero Twins?" Spider Woman asked. "Enemy Slayer. Born for Water." She placed Dew onto her shoulder, then pulled at a thread dangling from the ceiling. Down came a jug that swished with water. She said to Dew, "Young water monster, can you put water from that large jug into that boiling jar, please?"

"Okay!" Dew commanded a stream of water from the jug to enter the charred jar that sat on top of a pile of ashes.

While Dew was concentrating on the water, Spider Woman whispered to Edward, "My heart, build a fire, will you?" She pointed with her lips to a corner of the room.

Nathan shone the light to the direction she indicated, and Edward saw stacked firewood. Edward quickly gathered the logs and arranged them next to the jug.

Nathan continued. "Grandma, do you know where they went? Or who would know where they went?"

Edward noticed some flint stones and smacked them together,

starting the fire. It occurred to Edward that the water monsters, maybe even Nathan, could heat the water, but he knew better than to defy an Elder. Plus, Spider Woman had such grand grandma vibes he'd do anything for her.

Spider Woman squinted and rubbed her temples. "The last four Enemies they hunted were Poverty, Sickness, Old Age, and Death. They told me they decided to spare them because those four Enemies taught the Diné valuable lessons, such as the value of humility, the value of taking care of your body, the value of raising and guarding the younger generation, and the value of living. They told me they would be leaving and built me all these wonderful looms."

"Do you know where they went?" Nathan asked. "We need to know because a new threat has arisen."

"A new threat?" Spider Woman said.

"Yes," Edward said. "We believe that there is a Modern Enemy that has already done damage to the Fourth World by stealing the water of Diné Bikéyah. It could do much more harm, and that's why we have to find the Hero Twins, so they can help us identify it and deal with it."

The water boiled. Pungent tea leaves seeped their yellow color into the liquid. The heat from the fire circulated around the domed room. Cedar smoke filled the hollow space.

"Can you help us, Grandma?" Edward asked. "Where did the Hero Twins go?"

Spider Woman's milky eyes looked into Edward's. She had the same eyes as all grandmas, reflecting unconditional love and support for all her grandchildren, no matter how distantly related. And behind her eyes was time-tempered strength and wisdom. But she was no longer smiling. She told them all, "They left for the Fifth World. No one knows where it is, but those that leave for the Fifth World don't come back. Perhaps they don't know how to return. I'm sorry. Your journey to find the Hero Twins is pointless."

And just like that, all of Edward's hope was extinguished. They couldn't chance going to the Fifth World to find the Hero Twins without knowing how to return. His mind desperately thought of different options, different Holy Beings who might help them. Maybe the four of them could convince a whole bunch of water monsters to scour Diné Bikéyah and deal with the Modern Enemy.

"You say you must find someone who is powerful enough to resist this Modern Enemy," Spider Woman said. "Why not you four? Two brothers and two sisters."

"He's not my brother," Nathan said quickly.

"We're not brothers," Edward said at the same time.

Yitoo chuckled. "Just call him your younger brother, Nathan."

"I've heard many grand things about you in particular, Grandson Nathan," Spider Woman said. Nathan blushed a little. If Edward had learned a few water monster songs, Spider Woman would have complimented him, too. "You control waters as a water monster does. With Yitoo Bi'aanii, the most powerful water monster in the Fourth World, by your side, you four would easily subdue any Enemy, ancient or modern."

"I'm not sure. Edward can't listen to the water monster songs," Nathan said.

Spider Woman said, "Like the Hero Twins, seek Father Sun and ask to borrow his Obsidian Armor as well as his Four Sacred Arrows of Folding Darkness, Dawn, Rainbow, and Lightning. Raise the Dawn Arrow above your head, and a beam of light will guide you to the Modern Enemy, as it did with the Hero Twins. Use the Folding Darkness Arrow to cover yourselves in shadow and stealth. Attack with the Lightning Arrow. And when the Modern Enemy is defeated, let fly the Rainbow Arrow across the sky to signify the end of the violence." Spider Woman looked at Edward. "The Obsidian Armor will protect you, my grandson, from the effects of the water monster songs. Wear it to harness its blessings of strength, stamina, and resistance to physical damage."

"Us?" Edward looked at Nathan. "But we're just kids."

"I'm a teenager," Nathan said.

"Barely," Edward said. "I don't think we can . . ." As doubt filled his heart, he heard an echo of his dad saying that Edward could accomplish anything. "Do you think we can defeat a Modern Enemy?"

Spider Woman explained, "It stands to reason that a Modern Enemy would surrender to Modern Heroes."

Confidence radiated from Edward's heart. This was all very exciting. He was being told to go to Father Sun's hogan in the realm of the Celestial Holy Beings and wear the Obsidian Armor that Enemy Slayer himself wore!

"Give everyone some tea, my little one." Spider Woman smiled at Edward.

Edward stood up and poured Spider Woman a cup of steaming tea first. He looked at the bright orange liquid that smelled of corn husks. He poured everyone a cup, then himself last.

"How do we get to Father Sun?" Edward asked.

"Father Sun rests on the crown of the Southern Sacred Mountain, Tsoodził, to have his midday meal when all shadows are their smallest. He and the Guardian of the Mountain will not be happy to be disturbed, but you are his descendants, so he will have to listen."

Edward nodded, taking note of the Guardian of the Mountain. He took a sip of the sweet tea. Its warmth dissolved the knot in his stomach. He felt his lungs absorbing more and more oxygen with each breath. His nerves and anxiousness relaxed, like rippling waters coming to a mirror stillness.

"Thank you very much, Spider Woman," Yitoo said. "I have to admit that I am very happy with this suggestion. It would be my duty, my honor, to resolve the problems that have arisen in my absence."

"Dear Yitoo," Spider Woman said. "Much has changed since you were last here."

Yitoo said, "Nathan and Edward have been introducing me to those changes. Not all of them I enjoy."

"I am that way, too," Spider Woman said.

Yitoo asked, "Wouldn't it be wonderful to revert to the time before the Pale People?"

What was Yitoo implying? Edward wondered.

"My sweet child," Spider Woman started. "You are still healing from the horrors of the Era of Relocation. As am I and as all Holy Beings are. There was violence all across Diné Bikéyah. Outside my home, in this canyon, there were massacres. Entire families pushed over the canyon ledges."

Edward felt a lump of pain burn in his chest, like an ember being blown upon. It seemed like everywhere they went, there were scars of Manifest Destiny.

Yitoo said, "The Pale People have gotten away with so much savagery!"

"Forgive them, for yourself," Spider Woman said, waving Yitoo to come over to her. When Yitoo was close enough, she held Yitoo's cheeks and lifted her head.

"Have they asked for forgiveness?" Yitoo angrily responded. "Even if they did, they can't expect us to forgive their history of bloodshed!"

Spider Woman said, "No. There hasn't been a gesture of responsibility or atonement. But letting go of some of that pain, some of that hatred that you have for them, will allow you to build a happiness that isn't dependent on their actions and apologies or lack thereof. Now, that doesn't mean ignoring what happened or forgetting their horrible actions. No. But you deserve to be happy again. You deserve to love yourself again."

"Everything I have done was for love, except when I abandoned my waters," Yitoo said. "Look what that has done to the Fourth World!" She tried to pull away from Spider Woman.

But Spider Woman gently kissed Yitoo's forehead. "When you returned to the Third World, you were doing it for the love of yourself. Don't ever regret valuing yourself. After you subdue the Modern Enemy, I want to see you again."

"That can be arranged," Yitoo said, sliding out of Spider Woman's hold. "It will be my priority."

"How about me?" Dew asked.

"And please bring the not-a-baby water monster with you," Spider Woman said. "I, too, have songs you might want to learn!"

"Please!" Dew said, crawling on top of her head to her other shoulder.

Yitoo said, "Boys, Dew, finish your tea, and we'll be on our way." Dew hopped from Spider Woman and onto Yitoo's forehead after slurping down her tea. Yitoo said, "Thank you for your words. I have a lot to think about."

It was only a few sips, but the tea seemed to both calm Edward's nerves and inspire him. After they finished their tea, the four of them stepped onto the clay branch platform. Spider Woman hoisted them up, back to Diné Bikéyah. They waved goodbye to her.

Spider Woman said, "Come by anytime. Grandparents especially love it when grandchildren visit."

Edward briefly thought of Grandma Lillian. Even though he didn't enjoy talking to her, she was still his grandma and she still loved him. He told himself that he would make more of an effort to interact with her. But he would have to tell her his feelings about how she made him feel like an "indian" and not her grand-kid. There was a chance she didn't know she was doing that. And there was a larger chance that if she knew, she could stop treating him that way.

"It's getting pretty late," Nathan said when they were out-side. The sun was descending, and the sky had turned a dark orange. "I think we should head back to my paternal grandma's hogan and get some rest."

"Very well," Yitoo said. "But we leave when the moon is high. I want to follow up on Canyon Mist's suggestion. I think we should follow my river for evidence."

"Then after that we can get the arrows and armor!" Edward said.

"Why are you excited?" Nathan said. "We better hope it doesn't come to that, because then we'd have to fight the Mod-ern Enemy."

"Oh, yeah, right," Edward said, but it was hard to contain his excitement. He had just been called a Modern Hero by Spider Woman. He would love nothing more than to don the Obsidian Armor and shoot a sacred arrow or two. His stomach grumbled, and he realized he could use some rest. And then after that, he would ask Yitoo to bless his wrestling career.

Ła' Ts'áadah

ELEVEN

NATHAN'S HIPS ACHED AS HE pushed against the wind that rushed against him. After several hours of traveling on the back of a water monster the size of a small car, not to mention Edward against his back, he had been able to sync his balance with Yitoo's running motions. Still, his inner thigh muscles burned from overexertion and his lower back was stiff. Yitoo zoomed through the flat desert east of Tohatchi toward Nali's hogan site. All around them, shadows spread like dark ink across the desert as the sun sank in the west.

Nathan couldn't wait to be at Nali's, where she was preparing a warm dinner. Nali had texted earlier when she went to Gallup to get food that she would build a fire to cook. Nathan's stomach grumbled loudly at the thought of her fresh, handmade tortillas and steaming fried potatoes with chopped-up pieces of

Spam, and sweet kernels of canned corn mixed in. Truly, Nali's cooking was fit for heroes. Then, after they rested, they would continue on their journey to discover the Modern Enemy, talk with it, and hopefully convince it to change its ways.

Nathan recognized the landscape of undulating dunes with patches of sagebrush. He leaned forward and spoke into Yitoo's ear, "Not much farther. Go a little to the right, down the stream, and we'll pass through Pond's pond, and about ten minutes later, we'll be at my paternal grandma's home site."

Yitoo grunted to acknowledge she had heard him, then huffed as she jumped on the top of dunes.

When Nathan saw Nali's mobile home, he noticed thin strings of smoke that disappeared as they rose into the air, like an unraveling silk scarf. Closer, the fragrance of fried potatoes and Spam tickled the insides of his nostrils, triggering his stomach to growl.

Yitoo slowed her speed. The water at their sides didn't splash as wildly or froth as furiously. She brought the three of them into the cornfield. Nathan eagerly dismounted and stepped on crinkling husks of corn that Nali had stopped growing. After he gave Yitoo back her shadow fabric, he swung his elbows from side to side to limber up his spine. Muscles everywhere were not happy. His toes felt tingly and staticky, like noise on an old television set.

"Young Heroes," Yitoo said. "Rest while we can. We shall leave when the moon is high and our influence over water is strongest. I want to end this search for the Modern Enemy as soon as possible."

"Me too!" Edward said, stretching and cracking his back.

Yitoo did a downward-dog stretch. Her spine popped and cracked in several places. She commanded the ice jewelry off her body and sighed in relief. "But we'll need to get the armor and arrows if we are to confront this Modern Enemy."

"After seeing what you are capable of, Yitoo," Edward said, "I'm not even sure we need the armor and arrows. You're pretty powerful."

Yitoo blushed and held her head high. "Thank you for the compliment."

Nathan led Edward out of the cornfield and toward the firepit, where Nali cooked their delicious dinner. Nali must have noticed them because she was opening the fence to the cornfield, a huge smile on her face.

"Shináli!" Nali said.

Nathan hurried over, despite his toes barely feeling back to normal, and gave Nali a big hug. No matter how short their time away from each other, it was always wonderful to hug Nali after being apart.

"My heart," Nali whispered into his ear. "And you must be Edward."

Edward looked like a deer in headlights. He was balancing on one foot and pulling his other foot upward. Must be some stretch or something.

"That's my name. Don't wear it out," Edward replied nervously.

"Txį', you both must be starving," Nali said. She walked toward the campfire.

Nathan couldn't eat enough of Nali's tortillas, potatoes, and Spam. She had even roasted some green chilis on the fire grill as a special surprise. He leaned back and enjoyed the feeling of a full stomach, especially after a long day of traveling and being out in the sun.

"Edward, tell me about yourself," Nali said to him.

"Oh, me? I'm Edward. Eleven. I'm a boy," Edward said. Nathan wondered why he was being awkward and shy. "Not sure what you want to know."

"What are your grades? Favorite subject in school?" Nali asked. She leaned forward, interested in hearing Edward's response.

"Oh, those? I'm all right in school. Mainly Bs. A few Cs here and there. Favorite subject? Don't really have a subject. Love wrestling, though," Edward said. He seemed to relax and took a swig of water from Nali's blue spotted cup.

"When I was in middle school, I only got one A," Nali said.

"You were in middle school?" Nathan asked. This somehow just blew his mind. This new knowledge of Nali being middle school age conflicted with his image of her as grandmotherly.

Nali chuckled. "Ages ago. Back then, I wanted so badly to run for the cross-country team. One day, I went to the cross-country coach and asked him if I could join the team even though I was a girl. He told me I would have a hard time running in a skirt."

"What did you do?" Nathan said, shocked. How could a coach say something so sexist like that! "Did he get fired?"

"No, he didn't. Back then girls weren't allowed to participate in many sports. Title IX hadn't been passed yet. That was the norm."

"What's Title IX?" Edward asked.

Nali said, "K'ad 'éí, Title IX protects the rights and safety of many different people. But when it was passed, goodness, in 1972, it laid the foundation for girls to do sports, among other activities." Nali chuckled. "It may have surprised the cross-country coach, but I ran a mile and a half every day to get to school and back home in fifteen minutes. With my skirt and tsiiyééł, thank you very much." She sipped her tea. "I remember the first time there was a women's basketball team at my college, years later. So much ruckus over women receiving the same respect as men. There were groups saying that women only needed to be cheerleaders—mostly men, but some women, too. They argued that the funds directed toward women's sport teams could be spent on other more important things. It seems whenever progress is achieved, those that benefited from oppression throw a tantrum. They did back then and still do today. But over time, those tantrums quiet and they figure out that their lives haven't been affected much, if at all."

"Then they find something else to complain about," Edward added.

"The work is never done," Nali said. "Which is why it's

important to remember the struggles of those who fought to make your life fair." Nali sipped her tea.

"Thank you for sharing that with us, Nali," Nathan said.

"Yes, thank you, Mrs. Todacheenie," Edward said.

"Please, Edward. You can call me 'Másání,'" Nali said.

Nathan nearly dropped his fork onto the earth. Did Nali give Edward permission to call her "Grandma" in Diné? Was it because, culturally, Diné kids always call an elder "Grandma" or "Grandpa"? Or was this gesture something more? Something that meant Nathan and Edward were more than just two boys living in the same house whose parents were dating?

"Oh, um, okay," Edward stammered out.

"I'll always have room in my heart for more grandchildren," Nali said. "'Ahéhee' Diyin shí 'éí Diné! I get to meet new grandchildren all over the place!"

All of Nathan's being did not want Edward to refer to Nali as grandma. Or for Nali to call him her grandson. At the same time, Nathan forced himself to chill out. He told himself it was okay for Edward to call Nali "Másání" because Nathan called other elder women "Másání," too. It was simply a respectful Diné gesture. He hoped.

Nali reached over and patted Nathan's shoulder. "Shinálí, I've been meaning to tell you. I'm considering going back to school and getting my master's in education."

"Huh? What? Wow!" Nathan said, all his discontent from earlier evaporating. This was big news!

"If I do, I'm planning on taking summer courses so it doesn't interfere with my job," Nali said.

"Summer courses?" Nathan questioned. Then it became clear why she was telling him this. "So, you won't be spending your summers here at the mobile home?"

"I know you have doings with the Holy Beings. But also, your time with them is soon coming to an end. I wanted to give you time to think about what you'll be doing during the summers for the next few years."

"When are you thinking of going to summer school?" Nathan asked. He was quickly adding months and years in his mind. It didn't matter, he knew, because this was probably his last summer that would be able to interact with the Holy Beings. Doing the calculations distracted him.

Nali said, "With your uncle being stable, I've been able to put some money aside. At the rate I'm saving, I can start classes in three years."

"Okay. How long is it going to be?" Nathan asked. He would be a junior in high school by the time she was starting her master's program.

Nali said, "The program I'm interested in normally takes two years. That's full-time. Part-time it would take me at least five years."

So then four years after he finished high school. An image of the future formed in his mind. Both he and Nali standing side by side holding their degrees. Nathan his undergraduate. Nali her master's. "Nali! If you do that, then we could graduate together!" He nearly stood up, his legs wanting to jump.

Nali seemed to like that idea very much. She stood up, went to Nathan, bent over, and hugged him. "I was hoping you would say that! You can wear James's, your nálí hastiin's, bow guard when we both graduate at the same time."

"Pinkie promise!" Nathan said. Nathan had thought about college very rarely. But Arizona State University and University of Arizona were his most likely paths, and since Nali lived in New Mexico, she would go to University of New Mexico or New Mexico State University. "Even if it's different schools!"

Nali lowered her hand with a warm wrinkled pinkie poking out. Nathan wrapped their pinkies together, solidifying that image of the future in his heart. He couldn't wait to stand with Nali in college gowns holding their degrees.

Edward didn't share in their excitement. He slouched over his food, staring at the fire that was growing brighter with the setting sun. Nathan didn't like that they were leaving Edward out of this happy moment. So, he said, "By that time, Edward, you'll have your first Olympic medal."

Edward snapped to. It took a while for him to register what Nathan had said. Then he said, "I mean, I'd be wrestling for Ohio State, hopefully."

"Oh! Olympics?" Nali asked Edward.

"Yeah, it's this dream I have," Edward explained.

Nathan noticed the waxing new moon rising. A familiar fear rose with it. He vaguely felt this need to learn the three water monster songs and help Uncle Jet. These were just remnants of that summer that occasionally revived with familiar sights and smells. The moon was rising! They needed to sleep because Yitoo wanted to leave the mobile home site when it was in the middle of the sky. He said, "Speaking of dreams, Edward, we should try and get some sleep. Yitoo wants to leave in the middle of the night to follow her river."

Nali sighed. Nathan had told her that they were searching for her missing water, not that they were also searching for a Modern Enemy. She didn't need to worry about that. Especially if Nathan could convince it to change. "Tell me if you need any help at all. That's what grandparents are for. Go to bed. I'll wash the dishes."

"Thank you, Nali," Nathan said.

"Yeah, thank you," Edward said.

While Nali began to gather the dishes, Nathan led Edward to the mobile home. Even though it was barely eight o' clock, they would have to try to sleep. They wouldn't get enough rest, certainly. He was planning on asking Yitoo for some energizing sweetgrass to help them. But that was later. Now he just had to show Edward the mattress in his summer bedroom and then go to the couch where he would sleep. Tomorrow, he hoped, he would be able to chat with the Modern Enemy and convince it to change its ways.

Naaki Ts'áadah

TWELVE

EDWARD WAS IN A DEEP sleep when his alarm went off. It started low and quiet but grew louder and shriller with each passing second. What he wouldn't give for another five hours. He willed himself up from the most uncomfortable mattress in the world, then sat upright for a minute, telling himself that he couldn't go back to sleep. His eyes refused to stay open. After a few more seconds of battling his sleepiness, he stood up and put on bright neon blue athletic shorts and an ASU T-shirt with the Sun Devil mascot in a wrestling singlet. He twirled the yellow-and-white ring on his thumb that held half of Nathan's communication stone to remind himself it was still there.

Now was the time to ask Yitoo to bless his wrestling career. He had wanted to after supper, but Yitoo and Dew were rehearsing the words of water monster songs in the cornfield. "Olympic medal," he said to himself to wake up even more.

Using his phone as a flashlight, he walked down the dark hallway of the mobile home. He noticed that it was nearly one in the morning. He could not imagine spending more than a day here. It was so cut off from everything, not to mention it was spooky quiet. The silence felt like there was a predator outside holding its breath to sneak up on its prey. And there was no running water! His own nálí grandparents had running water, electricity, and internet. He most definitely would not last a week out here. A month was 400 percent "nope."

Nathan sat upright on the dusty couch in the living room where he had slept, also trying to stay awake. He wore brown tattered cargo shorts with pockets everywhere as well as a faded black T-shirt with a video game reference. Edward slumped in the chair beside Nathan.

"You ready?" Nathan asked, his voice deep and grumbly.

"Nope," Edward said.

"I'll ask Yitoo for some sweetgrass," Nathan said. He pushed against his own knees to stand up.

"Yes please." Then Edward asked, "Hey, Nathan, is it cool if I ask Yitoo to bless my wrestling career for, you know, helping her find the Modern Enemy?"

"That sounds fine," Nathan said, yawning. "You should ask her later, in my opinion. She's really focused on finding out what's happening to her water."

Then it dawned on Edward that Nathan, too, would have an opportunity to ask for a blessing. He asked, "Did you know we could get a blessing for helping the Holy Beings?"

Nathan tied his shoes with a strong knot. He said, "Yeah."

"So, are you going to ask for a blessing?"

"If she offers one," Nathan said. "I mean, I kind of already asked a favor from the Holy Beings for taking care of Dew. I'm afraid to ask for more."

"What did you ask for?"

Nathan didn't answer for a few seconds. "I asked them to help me find someone to take care of Dew when I can't see her anymore. Then the next day you were able to see and hear Dew." He stood up and navigated the dark shadows to the front door.

Edward absorbed that information. Nathan could be so self-less at times, it was admirable. "You know it's okay to ask for things for yourself sometimes."

Nathan opened the door and, in the moonlight, smiled. "I asked you to take care of Dew, didn't I? Let's go."

Edward stood and considered that he technically had two blessings he could ask for: one for helping Yitoo, one for helping Dew. When the time came, he was going to give one of his blessings to Nathan. All Edward really needed was one. But Nathan was right; perhaps after they found the Modern Enemy would be a better time to ask for it.

The two young Heroes, Edward and Nathan, walked out of the mobile home in the middle of the night and made their way toward the cornfield, where Yitoo and Dew awaited them. Edward noticed that he and Nathan were stepping in sync with each other. Tall and strong, under the light of moon and stars,

Nathan looked brotherly. Even if Nathan was still very much a *Nerdasaurus rex* at times. They entered the cornfield through the gate in the fence and approached Yitoo and Dew.

"Were the two of you able to get some rest?" Yitoo asked.

"Not a whole lot," Edward responded. He rubbed his eyes. Sparkles of fireworks burst inside his eyelids.

Nathan said, "Yitoo, I was wondering if we could use some of your sweetgrass."

Dew asked, "When will I get my own sweetgrass?"

Yitoo gently tapped Dew's spine with her snout. "I'm not sure. Normally, Mom gifts us a medicine pouch when we leave the Third World to the Fourth World."

Dew asked, "So, we should go see Mom and ask for my medicine pouch, right?"

Edward noticed Yitoo shift her weight from the back to the front. She looked uncomfortable. Was this about the question?

"You can see Mom when you learn all my songs," Yitoo said. "And yes, Nathan. Of course. Do you have something to light the tips with?"

Nathan reached into his backpack and procured a small lighter.

Edward hovered closely to watch. Yitoo put her snout into the bend of her right armpit. When she turned to face Nathan, there was a pouch in her mouth. She handed, or really mouthed, it over to Nathan, who then untied the top of it. Edward was struck with amazement when Nathan reached his entire arm into the pouch. It was like his whole arm disappeared! Nathan smirked and then pulled out a bundle of braided sweetgrass that was the size of a yardstick. Nathan also seemed surprised. He then held the kernel-sized flame to the burned end of the bundle.

"Edward, you first," Nathan said, cupping some of the smoke and wafting it toward him.

Edward sniffed, still not used to how the sweet grass awakened him. The smooth smoke slid down the back of his throat. It felt like energy was gliding through his veins to every inch of his body, from his heart to his fingers and toes. His weariness washed away. It wasn't erratic energy like when he tried some of his dad's coffee and wanted to backflip an entire marathon. He just felt focused, alert, and motivated. Edward wondered if he could coax a bundle for himself to have before his wrestling matches.

Nathan wafted smoke into his airways, and the tiredness of his eyes transformed into wakefulness.

"Let us be on our way, young Heroes," Yitoo said.

Edward smiled. He could get used to being called a "young Hero."

"Let's get this party on the road, or the river!" Edward said, just about ready to jump into the air and high-five Nathan.

Yitoo chuckled. "The Hero Twins were always excited at the beginning of their adventures, too. I must admit I am disappointed we are no longer going to find them. I miss them so very much. But time flows forward. And it's my privilege to see the new generation of Heroes ready to battle, ready to fight, ready to succeed on behalf of the Diné. Nathan, Edward, I hope you both know how truly special you are."

"Thanks, Yitoo," Nathan said. His voice sounded so soft that Edward wondered if Nathan was blushing.

"Yes, thank you," Edward followed. There was hope for Yitoo to understand that not all Anglo people were terrible. He would tell her about his mom's side, eventually.

A steady stream of water erupted from her ice jewelry and wrapped around her spine, creating a harness for the two of them. Yitoo gave Nathan the shadow fabric as the two of them sat on her back. Nathan tossed the shimmering cloak over all of them, and the water harness tightened around them. It was odd, because though the harness was made of ice, it wasn't freezing his exposed calves. It was comfortably warm. Water continued streaming from the jewelry, this time floating to her ankles. Yitoo spoke to Dew, who had crawled onto her forehead. "Now, let's follow my river and see if we can find evidence of the Modern Enemy. Youngest sister, if we sing together, we can travel twice as fast. Edward, make sure your ears are closed."

"I'm on it!" Nathan said. "Here, put these in. My uncle left a pair here." In the palm of his hands were high-quality foam earplugs in camouflage colors and connected by a bright green string. "He uses them when he practices his shooting. He says they're some of the best on the market."

"Thanks," Edward said. He rolled them between his fingers until they were thin enough to slide in his ear canal. The plugs expanded until he could barely hear Yitoo and Dew talk in a muffled language. Soon, he only heard the air entering and leaving his throat. He gave Nathan a thumbs-up. Then he leaned into

Nathan's back and wrapped his arms around Nathan's abdomen, ready for the rocketlike propulsion forward.

Edward held his breath. Yitoo shot forward so fast that it felt like he was being torn in half. His lower body was glued to Yitoo while Nathan's and his upper bodies were being pushed back by the air. Both he and Nathan leaned forward to escape the pressure of wind.

Nathan's back was warm and solid. Edward had gotten comfortable and felt safe with Nathan in front of him. He had to remind himself that Nathan was not his older brother.

About an hour later, Edward peeked to his side and saw the dark rocky formation of Shiprock, more shadow than rock. The moon was in the middle of the sky, high and bright, as thin as a smile. Edward was thankful for the warm ice that held him against Yitoo because the air around them was as chilly as the inside of a refrigerator.

They sped past Shiprock and continued until they reached a paltry river that was nearly dry. Edward didn't have to forcibly lean forward as Yitoo slowed down beneath them. Edward heard their mumbles and saw Nathan pointing. He wanted to unplug his ears but decided to wait. He didn't want to chance hearing a water monster song that could turn him into a human Popsicle, or evaporate all the moisture inside him, turning his blood to red sand.

The water returned to the jewelry around Yitoo. Easily hundreds of gallons condensed into her bracelet. Yitoo continued forward, running instead of using the water to jet them forward.

Nathan's arm reached back and tapped Edward's rib cage, then pointed to his ear. Edward got the hint and yanked the earplugs out. He could feel the glorious air in his ears! He could hear something other than his breathing.

Nathan said, "I thought you could use a break, so I asked them to run for a bit."

"Thanks," Edward said. Nathan always thought of others and their comfort—something that only now Edward was beginning to appreciate.

Yitoo navigated the dry, meandering riverbed. They were running away from Shiprock heading west. There was very little water and a feeble stream that zigzagged back and forth on dirt and stones like a lost snake looking for nourishment. But like the water at Arizona Falls, the water was rancid and had turned green. Rusted bikes poked out of the surface. Edward was anxious to solve this riddle of the Modern Enemy's form. He carefully scanned for otherworldly footprints, finding only dryness.

"My heart," Yitoo said to her river. "I must borrow you. I will return you."

The stream snaked its way up her ankles and into her scales. As her size grew, the river lowered even further. Television sets, chairs, and other refuse were revealed when the waters lowered. The green algae that rested on the surface of the water clung to litter like wet T-shirts. Yitoo sprinted as fast as a sports car over the dried riverbed, as massive as a school bus.

"Edward," Yitoo said, "do you mind putting those things

back into your ear? I feel we have a great distance to cover, and when Dew and I sing, we are able to travel much faster."

"No problem," Edward lied. Of course, he wasn't going to say no. His ears no longer ached, so he could withstand the earplugs for the sake of faster travel. He quickly shoved them in and tapped Nathan's shoulder.

Much faster than before, Yitoo launched forward like a rocket ship. With his strong wrestling grip, Edward held on to Nathan. Yitoo navigated them down the riverbed, away from small towns, and into empty desert. Eventually, the riverbed deepened and widened into a canyon. The canyon depth was roughly the height of his rented house and as wide as the 202 highway. Huge amounts of water must have been rushing through here when it was full. But now the droughty riverbed gouged deep into the rock bed like a scab.

Edward couldn't guess how far they had gone because of how fast Yitoo traveled. About an hour later, the tiny stream morphed into a thick vein of water that rose to Yitoo's ankles. Soon, it was an actual river. But it wasn't moving. It was just sitting.

Suddenly, Yitoo reduced her speed to a gentle walk. Edward quickly took out his earplugs, thankful for the break. Each step she took on the calm river created gentle ripples that made the reflection of stars flicker and dance up and down. The smooth white-orange sandstone walls at either side of them curved and blocked their view in front of them.

Yitoo pressed forward with slow caution, almost as if she

didn't want to see what was around the corner. As she forced herself forward, dread grew inside Edward's stomach, though he couldn't figure out why. Were they about to find out what was taking her water on the other side of the canyon? Yitoo rounded the canyon corner, and they all came upon a large lake.

She said, "This lake is not natural. What is this abhorrent creation?"

Nathan said, "We are at Lake Powell, near Page, Arizona."

"That over there is halting my river," Yitoo said. She took them to the nearby dam and examined the concrete wall.

"This is the Glen Canyon Dam," Nathan explained.

Yitoo launched them out of the water and onto the dam itself. Of course, she had to walk to the edge of the tall walls. The water on the other side was many hundreds of feet below. Edward squirmed and whimpered. He pressed his eyes into Nathan's shoulder blades.

"They are collecting *my* waters. There is more to this mystery. Look," Yitoo said. Edward did his best not to think about how high up they were as he peeked down toward the bottom of the dam. "This man-made lake creates a disruption to my river, but it isn't the only thing messing with my waters. We must press forward. Edward, please place your earplugs back in."

"Don't worry, Edward. I'll let you know when you can open your eyes," Nathan said.

"Okay." Edward quickly inserted them into his ear canals and squeezed his eyes shut. He whispered to himself, "Olympic medal."

Suddenly, his stomach upturned, and Edward let out a loud scream. They were falling! He peeped his eyes open and saw that Yitoo had created an ice arch that they were sliding down toward the bottom of the dam. It was still too fast for Edward to feel safe. But at least they weren't falling to their deaths. Edward closed his eyes again, too terrified to watch the ground rise to meet them. He felt fat globs of water splash his entire body. He opened his eyes, and they were already zooming forward at the bottom of the dam in the thin river.

At one point, Edward thought he could hear muffled singing. He quickly pushed the earplugs deeper in just to be safe. All around him, the landscape blurred by them. They were in a canyon, turning and rounding rocky edges with astonishing speed.

Edward noticed that the sky was brightening. The eastern horizon was a deep purple, and the stars were dimming. With this faint light, Edward realized they weren't in just any canyon—they were in the Grand Canyon! Majestic maroon sand-rock plateaus surrounded them. A deep purple color sliced through the rocks, and underneath that was a dazzling white line of rocks. Each color was layered on top of each other on the face of the canyon. As cool as it was, they still sped forward. Edward made a mental note to himself. He would have to ask his dad to take him here. Maybe Nathan could join them.

After they exited the Grand Canyon, the river flowed southward. And eventually they left the boundaries of the Four Sacred Mountains. Edward knew because Yitoo's influence over the water weakened, and their speed slowed. He looked around him and noticed the landscape. They sped through small towns, lakes, mountains, and canyons. Arizona was such a beautiful state. Edward was ashamed that he had seen so little of it. Phoenix valley was cool, but the rest of Arizona was stunning and gorgeous.

The air around them was warming, almost feeling like the humid air of Phoenix. Yitoo was determined and headstrong. They followed the river and came across another area like Lake Powell. But once Edward realized they were going to slide down another very, very tall concrete dam, he closed his eyes.

After his stomach settled from the fall, Edward noticed that the river was widening. Before the river was thinner and flowed fast. Now it was opening, and its flow slowed.

Eventually, they came to a large lake, and the sun was hovering a few feet above the eastern horizon. Edward didn't bother to take out his earplugs because in moments they were following an aqueduct, heading eastward.

There was an uncomfortable familiarity to the landscape, to the atmosphere. He recognized the unique saguaro cacti. Edward thought of the journey they had taken thus far. Directly from Yitoo's river in Shiprock. Her river combined with the Colorado. It turned into a lake in Page, then back to a river that led to another dam, then turned into another river and eventually to the lake they just left. Yitoo's river, her water, was being diverted to here.

The more they traveled eastward, the more a suspicion grew in Edward's mind. He hoped that it didn't lead to Surprise,

Arizona. Edward noticed they were slowing down and that Yitoo was simply walking on the water. Nathan tapped Edward's rib cage and motioned to take out his earplugs. They dismounted and stood facing a terrible sight.

"This can't be," Yitoo said, anger in every syllable.

Edward's fear was confirmed. The aqueduct that took water from the river they were on was being directed through Surprise, Arizona. A shiver ran down Edward's spine. The aqueduct they were in would eventually connect with the Salt River Project, which distributed water through all the Phoenix valley.

Yitoo screamed, staring at the faint outline of the downtown skyscrapers, the patches of green grass of the two hundred golf courses. Spikes shot out of her spine in front of and behind Edward. Both her lower tusks and upper tusks were displayed like sharp white knives. Her scream echoed into the marrow of his bones.

Edward didn't know if his own blood was warming from Yitoo's lamentations or his own fear. His wrestling instincts went on high alert. Because Yitoo now looked like she was ready to attack. She was enraged. She was dangerous. The tips of his fingers and toes went numb as he lost his breath, waiting to see what Yitoo would do next.

She said, her voice deep, "Phoenix is stealing my waters."

Táá' Ts'áadah

THIRTEEN

EDWARD'S HEAD SWAM IN CIRCLES. The air rushed into his lungs suddenly. His temples became fuzzy and tingly. Nathan reached toward Yitoo's neck.

Yitoo glared at the glimmering skyscrapers of downtown Phoenix that stabbed at the air like the spines of cacti. She said, "After all my struggles and sacrifices, the Pale People won."

Nathan rested his palm on the back of her skull. Should Edward do the same? Edward summoned his limbs to bend and move his body toward the other side of Yitoo. Meanwhile, Nathan comforted Yitoo, "It's okay."

Dew leaped onto Nathan's shoulders when Edward finally placed his hand at the base of one of Yitoo's spikes. Did all water monsters have spikes like this? Did Dew?

"Yitoo," Dew said, her voice meek and small, "is Phoenix

really taking your river?"

Yitoo's breathing evened from her deep guttural growl into a calm flow of a desert breeze. Her spikes and fangs receded. Her head drooped, and her shoulders sagged. Even in sadness, she was still powerful and intimidating.

"We have irrefutable evidence that Phoenix is taking my river," Yitoo explained. Every syllable dripped with loathing. She spotted something in the distance. "What is that?"

Edward squinted and saw nothing out of the ordinary. "What are you looking at?"

"Those tall colorful pipes, as you call them," Yitoo said.

Edward recognized what she was referring to and dreaded explaining to her what it was. Because it was one of his favorite places to have birthday parties.

Nathan answered, "That's Hurricane Harbor, a water park."

"They use my water for frivolity," she said. Edward sensed she was doing everything in her power to not scream. "I must return to Diné Bikéyah. We must convene with our brothers and sisters."

The way she said it implied that it wasn't up for discussion. His dad could scare Edward when he was angry. But Yitoo was a whole different level of scary. Edward was terror-stricken.

"Okay," Edward said. He felt that the best idea would be to get her away from Phoenix. Sometimes when one of his team-mates lost an important match, Edward and others would take him away from the wrestling floor to help him cool off. That's what Yitoo needed right now. To cool off. He struggled to think of what to do once they were away from Phoenix.

Nathan said, "Don't be angry, Yitoo."

Yitoo grunted, "That is something I cannot do." She faced north. "Let's be on our way."

Edward wrapped his arms around Nathan, who held on to the shadow fabric that hid them. During their previous trip northward, Yitoo's feet gently brushed the top of the soil. Now her claws dug deep gashes into the ground, leaving behind dark brown scars on the desert floor. Edward held Nathan and dug his face into Nathan's shoulders. Edward couldn't tame this feeling he had that something terrible was going to happen. Like he was standing in front of a tidal wave that was soon going to swallow him.

That feeling did not leave Edward and instead grew bigger and heavier the two hours they traveled back to Diné Bikéyah. Yitoo pushed herself even harder. If anger and despair could be felt, Edward was feeling it emanate from Yitoo's throbbing heart, from the roiling pulse of her veins, from her forceful exhales of overexertion. Edward could only be grateful that the anger wasn't directed at him. Suddenly, Yitoo stopped running and summoned water from her jewelry to jet them forward.

When they returned to the Painted Desert, Yitoo slowed them down, and once she stopped, the water returned to her as jewelry. The mid-morning sun peeked above the horizon, illuminating the colors of the sands and plateaus.

Edward dismounted and stretched his legs. Nathan folded up the shadow fabric and put it into his backpack. Blood reentered his lower extremities, awakening his toes. Yitoo huffed. Edward noticed that her eyes were red, not from anger, but from crying. She kept blinking, but small tears twinkled at the creases of her eyelids.

"Are you okay?" Nathan asked her.

"Yeah," Edward said, following Nathan's lead.

Yitoo said, "There used to be valleys of yucca, hills of sagebrush, and lakes so deep the colossal Enemies of the Diné could swim in them."

Edward examined the flatness of the land. The small juniper trees around them were bare. Edward pulled at a nearby branch, and it snapped off. A cloud of dust bloomed around Edward's body. He coughed as several dragonflies darted away from him.

"Now it's dying," Yitoo said. "The groundwater drained."

Yitoo tilted her head upward. Dew scurried to Yitoo's face and rubbed the side of her long tummy against her cheek. "I'm sorry that Phoenix is taking your river."

"I appreciate that, and I appreciate you, my lovely youngest sister," Yitoo said. "Will you help me summon our siblings?"

"Okay! How do we do that?" Dew asked. She jumped down to the earth and landed with her legs outstretched.

"Nathan, would you mind fishing out my braid of wind?" Yitoo asked.

"Actually, do you mind if I do that?" Edward asked. Ever since he saw Nathan's arm disappear into Yitoo's medicine pouch, he had wanted to do that himself.

"Go for it," Nathan said.

Yitoo pulled her medicine pouch out of her armpits and low-ered her head for Edward to reach in.

Eagerly, Edward thrust his entire arm into the bag. He made sure to use his left hand, which didn't have the communication stone. He wouldn't want to lose it in the medicine pouch. And as expected, his arm did not meet resistance. There was cool moist air. Edward tapped and touched different surfaces. Some felt like crystals, others like pebbles.

"It helps to think of what you are reaching for," Nathan said.

Once Edward had that thought in his head, his hand wrapped around flowing air that pushed back against his grip. It felt like holding your hand open out a car window on the 101 freeway. Edward pulled his hand out of the medicine pouch and held the invisible braid of wind to Yitoo. He could see the path of the winds he was holding. It was like thin strips of plastic wrap were flowing in an endless loop around his hand.

"Edward, hold one end to my snout," Yitoo commanded. "You might want to stand on this." Water rushed from her jew-elry and froze into a solid platform.

Edward stood on it, still mesmerized that he was holding wind in his hands. Actual wind! Once both his feet were on the ice platform, a fountain of water elevated him ten feet into the air to match the height of her head. Dew scurried onto Yitoo's great forehead. Edward reached with his hand that held the wind braid toward her snout.

Yitoo let out a deep roar. A second later, Dew roared. Dew's sound was more like that of a kitten hissing compared to Yitoo's alpha lioness roar. The petrified stumps of wood shook around them. Numerous bugs and birds darted away. Small lizards scrambled out of dark hiding spots. The wind braid pushed Yitoo's and Dew's roars away from them and into the atmosphere.

Edward felt the wind leave his hand like beach sand falling off his palm.

Yitoo stopped roaring and then so did Dew. "We wait," Yitoo said. "They will come to us."

Not more than five minutes later, Edward spotted a water monster rushing toward them. Edward recognized the patterns. It was Clay Lake! He seemed to be in much brighter spirits than yesterday. He stood more confidently.

"Sister, I am here," Clay Lake said.

"Thank you for coming so quickly," Yitoo simply said. It unnerved Edward how calmly Yitoo was acting, compared to earlier, when her tusks and fangs were exposed. It felt like she wasn't just angry, but also thinking and planning. "I will inform you shortly why I have summoned you, once our siblings have arrived."

Nathan said, "Is that Canyon Mist?" He pointed with his lips to the north.

It was. After she stepped off her stream, she limped forward.

"Canyon Mist! What happened to you?" Clay Lake asked. He immediately sniffed some of the bruises on her spine and side.

"I did that," Yitoo admitted.

"What do you want?" Canyon Mist asked. "One doesn't roar like that unless it's an emergency."

"I will explain soon. But first . . ." Yitoo said. She slowly approached Canyon Mist, who cowered yet snarled. "I have to apologize to you. I was wrong, and you were right. I didn't know how bad things had gotten up here in the Fourth World."

Yitoo bit her anklet and handed it to Canyon Mist.

"You're giving her back her river?" Nathan asked.

"I am. And I can only hope for your forgiveness, sister," Yitoo said.

Canyon Mist gripped the anklet in her jaws and bit down, crushing it. Water gushed around her face and sank into her scales. Canyon Mist grew back to her original size. "I don't forgive you."

Yitoo blinked away tears, surprised. She said, "I respect that, but please stay and listen. This affects all in Diné Bikéyah "

Canyon Mist rolled her eyes. "I heard Dew's roar. I'm staying for her. Not for you." She slumped down onto the ground and began to gently lick at the bruise on her rib cage.

Two more water monsters approached from the north. Three came at the same time from the east of them.

"Yitoo!" a water monster with one missing eye said.

"Mountain Fog!" Yitoo said. "Where is Plateau Rain? You two were always together. Tell me!"

Mountain Fog said, "Her groundwater was entirely drained. She gave her own moisture to save the area."

"Oh, Plateau Rain," Yitoo said.

Two more water monsters arrived from the west, each in terrible shape. Edward saw in their bodies, their movements, decades of pain.

A frail water monster whose scales hugged his skeleton, said, "I am all that is left of the Church Rock area. We have lost many brothers and sisters."

Nathan held a hand against his mouth. Edward leaned close to him and asked, "Are you crying?" As they talked, the others described similarly sick or deceased water monsters.

"No," Nathan said. "I'm not."

"It's okay to cry. You always do anyway," Edward said. He patted Nathan's shoulder.

"My groundwaters are all but gone and the hills that once were green and lush have become brown and deathly," said a female water monster who just showed up.

"They are all in pain," Nathan said.

A tenth water monster showed up. He had a scar across his shoulders.

"My lake is a puddle," said a tailless female. "My waterbed has been diverted into a pool that is used for fracking."

"Who are these children?" the water monster with the shoulder scar asked.

Edward shook his head. He had gotten so caught up in what was going to happen that it took him a second to realize they were looking at him. Were they expecting him to introduce himself? If he had to, then he would have to reveal that his mom's side was Anglo through the traditional Diné introduction.

"My dear brother, Shaded Marsh," Yitoo said to the scarred water monster. "They are Nathan, formerly the Healer of the Water Monster of the Agave Pond, and Edward, the caretaker of our youngest sister, Dew," Yitoo said. "But after today, they will be known as Modern Heroes. They are our very own Heroes of the Water Monsters."

Some of the water monsters bowed their heads. While it was exciting to see so many water monsters in one place, there was a sinister mood in the air. Edward noticed that Shaded Marsh simply glared at Edward as if he were examining a poisonous bug. Could Scar sense that Edward was not fully Diné?

"Siblings! Siblings!" Yitoo boomed. "I have made a horrible discovery. My rivers are being drained away from the Four Sacred Mountains and being diverted toward the abomination known as Phoenix, where they treat water as a toy!"

Most water monsters growled and hissed at the word "Phoenix." They said, "Do not mention its name!" "Nor Las Vegas!" "Nor Albuquerque!"

"What are these words you speak?" Yitoo asked.

"There exist more cities like Phoenix that steal our waters," Canyon Mist explained. "Hence why I no longer sing the rain songs. Because no matter how long or loud I sing, it will be diverted to those horrid places."

Yitoo growled in response. Her spikes emerged, and her tusks dripped with drool. The air heated around them as she spoke. "Then it is time that I ask for your blessings. For, in the name of our deceased sisters and brothers, in the name of the mountain rains being drained away from the pine trees, in the name of the rivers that once were clean and wide, in the name of the stolen mists of the canyons that nurtured cornfields . . ." She stopped and took a deep breath.

Edward's heart dropped. What was she going to say?

Yitoo finished, "I declare, here and now, Phoenix as the Modern Enemy of the Water Monsters!"

Díí' Ts'áadah

FOURTEEN

EDWARD'S BLOOD DRAINED FROM HIS limbs. His fingers and toes tingled. He looked to Nathan, who also appeared to be shocked by Yitoo's declaration. His own thoughts were drowned out by the water monsters' cheers. What did declaring Phoenix, his home, as the Modern Enemy mean?

"Lend me your strength!" Yitoo shouted. "I will take our waters and return them back to their home! All Pale People will learn to respect our waters!"

Mountain Fog came to Yitoo and said, "We will join your side."

Yitoo said gently and sweetly, "This is my mistake. As such, I alone should fix it."

"You're wrong," Canyon Mist said, standing up. All the excitement disappeared, and every water monster waited for Canyon Mist to continue.

"Younger Sister," Yitoo said, lowering her head. Edward figured it was because she was ashamed for having just recently attacked her.

Canyon Mist continued. "I'm still a long way from forgiving you. But this mistake is shared by us all. We all allowed the Pale People to fester and multiply. We all should contribute our efforts to resolving this problem."

Edward bit his tongue. They were talking about his maternal grandparents like they were disgusting bugs. His blood bubbled with anger. But he was too scared to do anything, like when Chad had asked him for his green card.

Mountain Fog said, "We want to help."

Edward waited to hear what Yitoo would say. In the Hero Twin stories, when an entity was declared an Enemy, it was up to the Hero Twins to destroy it, both physically and spiritually. But, then again, the Hero Twins did spare the last four Enemies, known as Poverty, Old Age, Sickness, and Death, because they were of value to the Diné for the lessons they taught.

Clay Lake said, "Though you are the only one strong enough to leave the boundaries of the Four Sacred Mountains and complete our goal, I and others want to help."

Yitoo seemed to think.

The anger Edward felt was reaching its limit. This was going to affect his dad, his friends, and everyone in Phoenix, including Grandma Lillian and Grandpa George. He needed to do something, say something, against all this. But he felt completely powerless and outnumbered. Who was he, a small half Diné, half Anglo boy, to oppose the strongest water monster in the Fourth World? If he spoke, no one would listen to him.

Yitoo said, "When I return with our waters, those of you who still wish to help can do so by bringing them back to their original owners."

Edward stared at Nathan, hoping that he would speak up against Yitoo. Nathan, however, averted his gaze from Edward. Was he avoiding him? Was he siding with Yitoo? He couldn't contain the words in his heart. Edward felt the words escape his throat. "You're going to be hurting everyone in Phoenix, and they've done nothing to you! If you take away their water, we all will suffer. Even the Diné who live in the Phoenix valley. Like Nathan, his mom, my dad, and me." Edward stood his ground, not moving an inch, surprised at how brave he was.

Yitoo coldly replied, "Are the Diné who live in Phoenix even real Diné if they no longer live within the Four Sacred Mountains? Tell your parents to return to Diné Bikéyah, where they should have lived in the first place, and they will be safe and have access to my waters."

She didn't care about hurting the entire population of the Phoenix valley! She was being so heartless. Had this indifference always been there?

"We are Diné, no matter where we choose to live," Edward said.

Yitoo continued. "Grandson, understand that Phoenix is an abomination that steals my waters. Yes, the inhabitants are going to suffer when I take back our waters. But Diné Bikéyah suffers.

The animals suffer. The real Diné themselves suffer because of Phoenix. For harmony to be restored, it's high time the Pale People suffered consequences."

"That sounds like revenge, not harmony," Edward said.

"The only way they will take responsibility," Yitoo said, clenching her jaws, "is to force them to."

"I do not condone this," Shaded Marsh said. Silence spread across the group. They all turned to face him. He said, "Water is meant for nurturing and sustaining life."

Some of the other water monsters gasped. Two others walked to his side. Edward glared at Nathan and hoped that he noticed how angry he was with him for being quiet.

To his surprise, Nathan made his way to Edward. All the water monsters, including Yitoo, were looking at Shaded Marsh.

Yitoo said, "Brother, you are courageous to oppose me. Phoenix takes our waters and uses it not to sustain life but for meaningless entertainment! They build amusement parks using our waters, feed water-draining plants that are not native to our land. While the real Diné themselves, the animals, even our siblings, we dry up and die."

Several of the water monsters cheered.

While Yitoo continued talking, Nathan whispered to Edward, "You have to stay away from Yitoo." There was fear and urgency in his voice. "She can't find out you're half white."

Nathan was scared for him, Edward realized. If Yitoo did find out about his Anglo half, how would she react? All he could say was "Okay." Then, after some of his senses came back, he said, "You aren't going to help her take the waters, right?"

Nathan grabbed his shoulders, "Look, Edward. All Yitoo wants to do is return the waters to their original place in Diné Bikéyah. Once we do that, we have solved the issue of the missing water. Phoenix can do without golf courses or water parks."

Edward nearly shouted, "Phoenix will be in a water crisis!"

Nathan retorted, "Diné Bikéyah is in a water crisis right *now.*"

Edward shook his head. He couldn't believe what he was hearing, nor the look that Nathan had. The world spun, and Yitoo's words were being overpowered by increasingly loud buzzing in his ears.

Edward heard Shaded Marsh speak from the side. "I will not be a part of this."

Nathan continued to hold Edward's shoulders. Edward was too shocked to do anything about it. In a tiny squeak, he said to Nathan, "I can't be a part of her plan."

Nathan responded, "Then you should go back to my nálí's mobile home and wait for us there. You'll see. Once balance has been restored, everything will be okay."

"I guess so," Edward said, following Nathan to Yitoo's side. He hated that in this moment, when he needed to act, to resist, all he could do was quietly obey commands.

Shaded Marsh said, "We all endured the horrors of the relocation, oldest sister. True harmony cannot be based on ruthless counterattack."

Yitoo said, "Pretty words are useless when the oppressors

ignore our songs and voices. When you are ready to be on the rightful side, I will welcome you with an open heart. Together, we will heal the land from the blight of Phoenix." She lowered her nose to the earth and said, "Please hang on, Mother Earth. We will no longer sit idly by. We will fight for you."

The ground trembled. Was that the actual Mother Earth responding to Yitoo?

"Know that I love you," Shaded Marsh said, bowing to Yitoo.

Edward wanted to follow him and leave this group. It took all his willpower to not shout out that Phoenix wasn't the Modern Enemy. That no one in Phoenix should suffer for something they probably didn't know they were doing. But Shaded Marsh, and two other water monsters, left the group, leaving Edward feeling even more powerless against the other water monsters, who were growing more energized with every word Yitoo spoke. Even Nathan was joining in. The fire in his heart to speak up had been a momentary sparkle like a smashed light bulb.

The twelve remaining water monsters, Nathan, Yitoo, Dew, and Edward stood in a circle. Edward's head hung heavy on his shoulders from fear.

Dew's little claws scratched his exposed shins as she crawled up to his shoulder. She said, "I don't like what's happening, Edward. I'm scared."

He pressed the side of his head into her warm little rib cage. "Me too."

"There is no time to waste," Yitoo said. "I will return to the human-made lake where our waters are being held captive. Please wait at your home sites, and I will return with your water."

Cheers erupted around Edward and Dew. After a few moments, Nathan spoke. "Actually, Yitoo, I think it might be a better idea if we split up."

Edward couldn't believe how brave Nathan was in this moment. He wasn't sure if he could smoothly suggest anything to Yitoo with his anger.

Nathan continued. "We must check in with our parents. Edward has to go back to my grandma's hogan."

"I'll take him," Dew said.

Yitoo's voice sparkled with vivacity. "Yes, things are falling into place. Dew, Edward, return to Nathan's grandma's home and complete your task. While you're at it, tell them to return to Diné Bikéyah. Await us there, and we shall regroup after I return the waters. I am asking all three of you to grow up so incredibly fast. For that I apologize. But if this world is to have a future, we all need you to be as capable and independent as the rest of us."

"I'll be fine," Dew said. "Edward's a great Hero."

"That he is," Yitoo said. She smiled at Edward.

Edward swallowed the words "don't," "smile," "at," and "me." Each syllable was fiery and spicy. He had an urge to kick the ground to dampen the anger in his chest! But, having seen Mother Earth respond to Yitoo, he decided against kicking a Holy Being. Edward nodded. "Cool."

Nathan continued. "I'll go with you, Yitoo."

Yitoo said, "It would be my honor to have your company, dear Healer and Hero."

Nathan adjusted his glasses and climbed atop Yitoo's broad shoulders.

Yitoo said, "Brothers, sisters, our path to harmony begins with this first step!" Yitoo and Nathan rode a jet stream of frothing water northward, to take water away from Phoenix.

With Dew on his shoulder, Edward turned and left the remaining, celebrating water monsters. He felt that if he stayed, they were sure to offer help to get to Nathan's nálí's hogan. And Edward was in no mood to accept help from anyone that viewed Phoenix as an Enemy.

He walked and walked. His legs picked up a fast pace, and then he started running. Edward needed to get away. He didn't want anyone, or any Holy Being, to see how seething he was. In all his training with his dad, he was taught to not let emotions cloud his ability to strategize. And during the announcement that Phoenix was the Modern Enemy, he let his emotions flare up and override his instincts. He should have come up with a strategy to subdue Yitoo! He was so angry that neon polka dots appeared in his vision.

"Edward, you're crying," Dew said.

That's when he felt the tears at the sides of his eyes, the snot plugging up his nose, and the burn in his lungs and thighs. He came to a stop and knelt on the ground.

"Everyone I know is going to be hurt," Edward said.

"That's why I can't be a part of that," Dew said. Her lilt, the melody hidden in her throat, was gone. Her tone was much more mature.

"Youngest sister and young Hero," said a familiar voice. Shaded Marsh emerged from the nearby sagebrush. "You both oppose her?"

"Yes," Dew said.

Edward said, "How can we stop her?"

"It's impossible to stop her. Even if all water monster siblings teamed up, she would still have a great advantage over us with her knowledge of so many water monster songs. You need a stronger water monster, one that Yitoo will have to listen to."

"Mom," Dew said.

Were the two water monsters talking about seeking help from Mother Water Monster?

"Do you know how to get to Hajíínéí?" Shaded Marsh asked.

"No idea!" Dew said. Some of her youthful energy reemerged.

"I can bring you," Shaded Marsh said.

Edward approached the water monster, ready to mount his neck.

"What are you doing? I am not a horse!" Shaded Marsh said, upset.

Edward explained, feeling foolish, "I'm sorry. I thought all water monsters carried people like this."

Shaded Marsh said, "Water monsters with good knees."

Edward knew about joint injuries: they were a wrestler's worst nightmare.

"Then how are we going to get to Hajíínéí?" Dew asked.

"I travel by other means," Shaded Marsh said. He stuck his nose into his armpit, bit at something, then held it between his teeth. It was a sparkling quartz crystal. Still gripping the crystal with his teeth, Shaded Marsh explained, "Inside this is a rainbow path. Stay close as I sing this rainbow path into being. It will take us to Hajíínéí."

"Okay." Edward reached out and touched Shaded Marsh's shoulder. "Is this okay?"

"I will allow it," Shaded Marsh said.

Edward held his breath as Shaded Marsh hummed, creating a rainbow path that jetted them through the sky. Hopefully they would reach Mother Water Monster and prevent Yitoo from putting the entire Phoenix valley into an unprecedented water crisis.

'Ashdla' Ts'áadah

FIFTEEN

EDWARD SOARED THROUGH THE SKY on the arch of a rainbow. Noon light flooded over the vast flat desert and splashed onto the sandstone plateaus, igniting their peachy colors. Had he known that this was how they were going to be traveling, he would not have joined Shaded Marsh. He would rather walk! It took all his effort to hold his head up and not peer below.

To Edward's surprise, Dew was quiet the entire time. She was transfixed by Shaded Marsh's song, which controlled the rainbow path by connecting the clear crystal with a thin water tentacle downward to sustain the colorful path. Whoa! Edward could see through the rainbow trail. Immediately, dizziness unanchored his sense of balance. He closed his eyes and leaned against Shaded Marsh for the rest of the flight.

Edward figured they were descending when his stomach

dropped. Then the blowing air stopped, and his stomach settled.

"Feel free to let go of my neck," Shaded Marsh grumpily said.

Light squeezed through Edward's tight eyelids. Both his arms were wrapped tightly around Shaded Marsh's neck. He let go, and his knees buckled as he walked a few steps on firm earth.

"Afraid of heights?" Shaded Marsh asked.

"What, afraid? Me! Psh!" Edward said, finally stabilizing his knees. "I punch heights in the face as a warm-up."

"Thank you for bringing us, older brother," Dew said.

They stood in a maze of sandstone walls and spires. Edward's steps in the deep soft yellow sands created tiny puffs of dust in blades of sunlight that cut through the rock formations. In front of him was the opening to a small cave. On top of the opening were petroglyph symbols that Edward couldn't decipher.

"Edward, over here," Dew said from behind him.

Edward turned around expecting to see a grand entrance. But there was just a solid wall of smooth sandstone with striations of white, orange, and purple. If there was one thing that was becoming easier to do, it was to trust in Dew and what she was capable of as well as what she knew. If this slab of rock in front of him was where they were going, then that's where they were going.

Suddenly, his phone vibrated. Edward snuck a peek and saw that his dad had texted. *I'm suspicious of our new stairs. I think*

they're up to something. Checking in on you guys. Love you.
Text me an update.

Shaded Marsh slumped down into the sands with a loud har-rumph. "I must rest; my knee has lost its cartilage and standing for prolonged periods causes me great pain."

Edward put his phone back into his pocket. He needed to focus on the task at hand. "Sounds like an arthritic flare-up. My dad sometimes works with clients who have arthritis," Edward said, remembering when he helped his dad study for a corrective exercise specialization. Ted had Edward perform a plethora of arthritis-specific strengthening exercises and stretches. "Try icing it first to dull the pain for twenty to thirty minutes. Then apply heat for fifteen minutes to stimulate blood flow. Then stretch."

Shaded Marsh nodded. "I'll try your suggestion." He inhaled and was about to sing.

"Actually, older brother!" Dew rushed in. She stood on her hind legs and placed her small front paws on Shaded Marsh's lips. "Can you wait to sing the songs until Edward is out of hearing distance? We don't want to freeze him solid or evaporate him." Dew then scurried to Edward's feet.

Shaded Marsh chuckled. "I forgot. It'd be mighty helpful for you, young Hero, to not be susceptible to our songs."

"I couldn't agree more," Edward said.

"Maybe that's what we can ask my mom for!" Dew said, jumping up into the air. "Nathan drank some of her water! We should ask her if you, too, can drink her water so that you won't be affected by our songs!"

"Yes, please!" Edward said. If he could listen to the songs, then maybe he could learn to sing them as well and one day influence waters like a water monster, and like Nathan.

Dew asked, "In the meantime, Edward, would you close your ears?"

Edward pulled the earplugs from his pocket and inserted them. Soon, he hoped, he wouldn't have to do this when a water monster sang. Dew's mouth was opening and closing.

Then the strangest thing happened, at least since a hole opened to the dwelling of Spider Woman, and his traveling on an actual rainbow. The rocky wall in front of them jiggled like Jell-O. Edward tapped the bottom of the canyon wall with an apprehensive foot. Undulating outward from the point of contact, the entire sandstone face wobbled. This wasn't rock. It was water!

After this realization, an opening, tall and wide enough for them to comfortably walk through, appeared. Dew must have stopped singing because the jiggling stopped and the wall was solid to the touch.

Before taking the earplugs out of his ears, Edward made sure that Dew wasn't singing. She wasn't, but instead was busy crawling up the side of Edward's leg, up his spine, and stopping at his shoulder. She wrapped her body against his neck like a large cat. Edward reached to her forehead to pat her.

Dew said, "Let's go and meet my mom, Edward."

Edward took a deep breath and walked into the dark mouth of the hidden cave. He hoped that in a few hours he would be able to withstand the effects of the water monster songs. More than that, though, he hoped that Mother Water Monster would be able to help them with Yitoo before she caused great harm to his friends, his teammates, Janet, his dad, and all who lived in Phoenix.

Nathan twisted his upper body to loosen the muscles in his lower back as Yitoo finally slowed to a walk. For three hours, they were jetting, and his lower body was feeling it, including the muscles in his hands that held the ice harness. Smooth orange plateaus and sharp canyon edges surrounded them to the front and to their left. To their southeast was the proud figure of Naats'isáán, Navajo Mountain. The sun was already in the middle of the sky.

Nathan's spine shivered, and his neck felt colder than usual. He missed the warmth of Edward holding on to him and Dew wrapped around the back of his neck. He felt like he had let them down somehow. But they didn't know the conflict in his heart. A huge part of him agreed with Yitoo because he had been trying so hard to bring back the rains to not only Church Rock but to all Diné Bikéyah. He couldn't sit around and read more articles about the encroaching deadline of climate change. Something had to be done now.

Yitoo jumped into a canyon where water pooled and continued running. Nathan guessed that she didn't want to sing because her song might echo off the walls of the canyon. And that was a good call because he wouldn't want to destroy this beautiful area. They rounded a corner, and Nathan gasped. They were at the Rainbow Bridge National Monument! Yitoo ran underneath the tall arch of pink-and-orange sandstone rock.

"We are nearing our destination," Yitoo said.

"Okay," Nathan responded.

All throughout his elementary and middle school years, he had heard of the growing concern about climate change. That the increasingly abnormal weather patterns were a result of carbon emissions caused by humans. Phoenix was getting hotter. Diné Bikéyah was getting drier. The tornados in the middle of the United States were more violent. The hurricanes on the East Coast were growing stronger. The weather was only going to get worse. And that scared him. How was the weather going to behave in the future when he was an adult? How would the weather be when he had children and grandchildren? He had to do something to slow down the advance of hostile weather patterns, like a megadrought. If he did, he could feel less responsible for the way the modern world was.

Yitoo navigated the meandering canyon that turned and curved according to the whims of the water below them. They descended lower as the walls of smooth, sun-bleached rock reached higher and higher. The temperature chilled with each foot they went down. Then they reached the end of the canyon. Right before them was a vast body of calm deep blue water that reflected the clear sky above them.

Yitoo said, "My waters. They hold you captive as they did the Diné so many years ago."

Her last sentence hit Nathan hard. He already knew it. The water in his kitchen faucet, the swimming pool in his backyard, the shower water in his bathroom, came from this water before him. Nathan agreed that Yitoo was doing the right thing by taking back her waters. She was the one who had brought them there in the first place.

Yitoo sang a song that was new to Nathan. As she sang, the water flowed toward her ankles like a charmed snake. Suddenly, more and more tentacles appeared. All of them wrapped around Yitoo's legs, neck, and waist. Hundreds, thousands, of gallons of water gushed and splashed Nathan's legs. It took about fifteen minutes for the entire area to be drained completely. All that water had condensed into jewelry of considerable size. She had taken the entire Lake Powell!

"Yitoo," Nathan said. "I thought you were taking back only your water. Your river isn't the only one that flows into here."

"I'm taking back what has been stolen. If you ask me, this is only a fraction of what has been taken throughout the many decades since I have been gone." Then Yitoo said gently, "Returning my waters will correct the imbalance on Diné Bikéyah."

Her words soothed his anxious conscience. While Phoenix valley did receive water from Lake Powell, it wasn't the only source. And if they left the other sources alone, all people in Phoenix wouldn't be without water. They could go without pools, without their concrete lakes like Tempe Town Lake, their numerous golf courses, and their water parks. Nathan felt he was a part of the solution. Nathan could bring moisture back to Diné Bikéyah and finally fulfill his promise to Pond. There was no simple answer to his inner conflict. No matter if he chose to help Yitoo or oppose her, someone was going to suffer. And the question quickly became: Which home of his was going to have to hurt? And hadn't Diné Bikéyah endured enough?

Edward stretched on the icy platform that was zooming downward to the Third World. He lay on his back, pulling one knee to the opposite floor. He had no idea what to expect, but if he needed to do something physical, he was going to be ready. Dew was mimicking his movements as best she could with her stubby lizard limbs.

It felt like they had descended for a least an hour. But finally, the icy platform emerged from the rocky column. He viewed the dark water world as the icy platform continued downward on a spire of water.

"Wow," Edward said.

Unlike the Fourth World, this world had a ceiling. Poking out of its rocky roof were tree-sized crystals that glowed a soft dim blue color. The entire sky looked like an eternal night sky. Down below was an ocean of calm water. Edward expected a fishy odor but was pleased instead to inhale a subtle eucalyptus smell.

Dew crawled up his body and rested around his shoulders. "I wonder if my mom will be mad at us."

"Why would she be mad at us?" Edward asked.

"Because you don't have permission to be here," Dew said.

The closer Edward got to the endless ocean below them, the sweeter the water smelled. Also, more islands popped into his vision like stars blinking alight during dusk. A few seconds later and a hundred feet lower, the icy platform rested on a beach as big as a football field. An enormous water monster, fifty yards long, inspected the two of them.

Edward bowed. Mother Water Monster wasn't as scary as he thought she was going to be. "Hello, Mother Water Monster."

"Me?" The water monster laughed, in a deep, unmistakably male voice. "Not very observant, this one. Flattered you think I'm my mom. Why are you here, youngest sister?"

"Where's Mom?" Dew asked. "We need to talk to her about Yitoo Bi'aanii."

The water monster's expression changed at the mention of Yitoo's name. His tail curled to the side of his abdomen, and his head lowered. He was scared. "I wouldn't if I were you. Their last argument was terrifying."

Edward shook his head in disbelief. "What do you mean 'terrifying'?"

The male water monster responded, "Yitoo and Mom had a big disagreement about her going back to the Fourth World."

Edward said, "I thought Yitoo left with Mother Water Monster's permission?"

"I think it's best you hear it directly from Mom," the scared water monster said, ambling away from them. "Just touch her water and she'll know that you are here." He then hopped into the ocean and swam away quickly.

Dew and Edward walked to the edge of the island. She stepped forward and dipped her toe into the waters. Nothing happened. The dark blue waters before them remained still. The surface reflected the crystals that jutted out of the rocky ceiling. Both sky and water twinkled like stars. A small wave rose and fell. Edward's nerves calmed a little.

After a gentle, quiet minute, Edward had to ask, "Should I just drink the water? I mean, it's here. I'm here. Let's have a party."

Dew shook her head. "Terrible idea. Mother Water Monster is very strict, especially with humans. She'd drown you without hesitation. Or maybe even pull all the moisture out of your body."

Edward understood why the male water monster was terrified of Mother Water Monster. "Got it. Only with her permission. Wait a hot minute. Circle back. You said I don't have permission to be here. Dew! What is she going to do to me?"

Before Dew could answer, the ocean divided in half before them. The ocean floor trailed off miles into the depths of the ocean, and Mother Water Monster was at the end of the hallway of ocean. While most water monsters looked like a Komodo dragon, Mother Water Monster had alligator qualities. Scales aggressively poked out in two rows from her shoulders to the end of her tail. Coal-black claws emerged from her thick muscular limbs. Unlike her children, she had no designs on her scales. Suddenly, Edward wished he had her permission because Mother Water Monster had noticed that he was here and then hissed at him.

"This human does not have my permission to be here!" With every step she took, she absorbed water, increasing her size. When she was the height of a sand plateau, she displayed her pale fangs that were as long as telephone poles to Edward. Her eyes were red with rage.

A tidal wave rose behind her and rushed toward the two of them. Edward held his breath and squeezed his eyes shut as the wall of water slammed down on him.

Hastą́ą́ Ts'áadah
SIXTEEN

THE WAVE KNOCKED EDWARD DOWN, and water invaded his mouth and nostrils. He landed with his face pressed into sand. The weight of the water felt like an elephant stepping on his back. He was going to suffocate if he didn't do something. He slid his hands under his shoulders for maximum leverage. All the muscles in his chest, shoulders, and arms burned as he pushed to save his life. The edges of his vision darkened, and his lungs stopped burning from lack of oxygen. A calm feeling expanded outward from his chest. This was it, his end.

Then, as soon as it began, it stopped. The waters engulfing Edward simply flowed back into the ocean, allowing Edward to gasp for air. The darkness in his vision turned to television static. His lungs stung like they were pierced with needles as fresh oxygen flooded into them.

Edward noticed Dew's lips were moving. But he didn't hear

a thing. That's when he realized that his ears were covered in ice again. He pried the muffs off and was finally able to get his bearings and stand firm.

Dew explained to Mother Water Monster, "I told you about Edward! He's Nathan's replacement."

Mother Water Monster's angry gaze made Edward shiver in fear. He wasn't eager to be crushed by water again.

Mother Water Monster said, "Regardless, this human does not have my permission to be here."

"Mother Water Monster!" Edward said. "I'm sorry for coming here without your permission."

Mother Water Monster's facial expression softened. "At least he has manners. Are you going to sing my songs to me now?"

"What?" Edward asked, dumbfounded. Was he supposed to sing songs? He knew Nathan should have taught him some of the songs!

"The last five-fingered being sang me my songs to prove his intentions," Mother Water Monster explained.

Dew said, "Nathan and I didn't teach Edward any songs. I thought since I was here with him, he wouldn't need to sing any."

Mother Water Monster said, "I suppose the fewer five-fingered beings that can sing my songs, the better."

Edward wasn't a fan of her attitude, even if he was to treat her like a grandmother. He wondered if all water monsters except Dew held a grudge against humans. Edward tried his best to remain calm and bit his tongue.

Dew continued. "We need your help. Yitoo Bi'aanii has decided to take all of the waters from Phoenix, the hometown of both Nathan and Edward."

Mother Water Monster asked, "Why should I care about Yitoo Bi'aanii or this Phoenix?"

"Mom, many humans are going to suffer," Dew explained.

"Let them suffer," Mother Water Monster spat.

"Mom!" Dew said. "That's so cruel."

"Was it cruel of them to kidnap one of my children?" Mother Water Monster asked in response.

Edward couldn't just stand around when Mother Water Monster was so indifferent, so heartless to what was going to happen to his home. He had to say, "You can't blame the rest of humanity for the mistakes of a few."

"Quiet, Edward!" Dew whispered. "You're only making things worse."

Mother Water Monster chuckled over Dew's whispers. Then she said, "That's very easy for you to say when you are not the one to endure the consequences. Tell me, child. What do you know of my realm? Do you know that when any of my children leave, their absence troubles my waters? I am their parent as much as this vast ocean is. Water feels. Water thinks. Water cares. When my children leave, my waters mourn and turn dark blue. Now think about what happens when one of our children is kidnapped. Both the water and I suffer heartbreak and rage."

Edward was about to say something, but Dew shushed him.

"When a child of mine leaves, for whatever reason, my realm

becomes unstable as we become accustomed to their absence. The water, not having eyes in the same way you and I do, still feels that absence. But, as I can't communicate what has happened, the water only knows that my child is gone. Now you speak of your oldest sister. Dew, do you know that she left my realm without my permission?"

Dew shouted, "She wouldn't!"

"I told her that she wasn't allowed to be your mentor. After Nathan and you came here and asked for her, I gave it much thought and decided against it. She still has much healing to do. I feared that should she return to the areas where she was traumatized, she would again fall ill. So, I told her no. She made a big fuss. Still, I wanted her to heal and gave her space. But I soon found that she had run away. As such, she is to never return here." A tear escaped from Mother Water Monster's eye.

Edward couldn't believe that Mother Water Monster had not wanted Yitoo to teach Dew the songs. Furthermore, that Yitoo had disobeyed her own mom and left the Third World. But what did this mean for the fate of Phoenix?

"Mom, please," Dew said. "I don't want innocent people to suffer."

Mother Water Monster said, "My youngest daughter, I will not aid this Phoenix and the five-fingered that live in it. The five-fingered shape the environment that they are in for comfort, taking no account of other beings who lived there prior, nor the expense their comfort accrues. Generation after generation repeats the same idiotic patterns, thinking themselves blameless. Year after year, era after era, they grow in number, and the little costs their ancestors accumulated multiply. The environment they lived in, the original beings that lived there, not just five-fingered—also winged, also finned, also many-legged—suffer for their comfort. When the time comes for consequences, when the environment says, 'No more,' when we say, 'Enough is enough,' they play the victim while still indulging in their conveniences."

"I don't understand," Dew said.

Mother Water Monster said, "In time, you will. When you have your own waters, you, too, will make decisions that will affect more than just the five-fingered. Your sole duty is to your water, as its protector." Mother Water Monster sighed. "I supposed your different perspective is my own fault."

"What do you mean?" Dew asked.

"Youngest daughter, Morning Dew, do you know that you are the first water monster to be born on the surface of the Fourth World? I'm tired of my children returning here weakened, sick, or deathly ill. My heart never numbs from hearing of their demise, such as Agave Pond. I sent you with Nathan in hopes that by being born in the Fourth World you would develop immunity to their pollutions and obscenities. An unintended consequence is that now you belong to two different worlds."

"So, you are saying I shouldn't do anything?" Dew asked. "Just let my oldest sister do as she pleases?"

"No." Edward stepped in. "Violence and intentionally causing others to suffer is not the answer."

Dew nodded. "I can't sit around. I'm going to do something,
with or without your help."

Mother Water Monster turned toward the ocean behind her. A
tentacle of water emerged from the ocean and scooped up Dew
to carry her to Mother Water Monster's head.

"In order to resist your oldest sister, you must have your own
waters," Mother Water Monster said. "Any waters that originate
within the Four Sacred Mountains will respond to her demands
over others. Waters that do not originate from her rivers, however, will not bend so quickly to her will. Drink of my water to
call it your own."

"Thank you, Mom," Dew said.

Mother Water Monster said, "There are still many consequences and effects of your birth in the Fourth World that have
not yet been revealed." Mother Water Monster turned her large,
swiveling eyes on Edward. "I'll overlook your transgression of
entering my realm without permission this once. But you are not
allowed back here until I deem you fit."

"Um," Edward said, digging the tips of his shoes into the
sand. Mother Water Monster seemed to have lost some of her
anger. This was as good a time as any to ask her. "Mother Water
Monster? Do you think I could drink some of your water so that
the songs don't interfere with my soft, moist internal organs?"

"No," Mother Water Monster scoffed. "You have potential,

young five-fingered. Maybe one day you will live up to your responsibility, but not today." Mother Water Monster walked into her ocean.

Dew jumped off her head and dove into the waters. A second later, Dew emerged as large as a horse. Edward rubbed his eyes. Not only was she physically larger, but she also looked older. Her limbs had extended outward and were no longer infantile. Her dark scales were bolder, and her light scales were more vibrant.

Mother Water Monster's gigantic scaly body disappeared under a blanket of water. The waters didn't ripple but remained as smooth as glass.

"She was very helpful," Edward said sarcastically. Shouldn't mothers not want their children to fight?

"Not in the way that we were hoping," Dew said. "Climb onto my back."

Edward had a sneaky idea. Dew had increased her size with Mother Water Monster's water. Perhaps, then, when they got back to the Fourth World, he could drink the water she had received to grow. Bing bang boom, he would drink the waters from the Third World! Eager to go back, Edward immediately straddled Dew. "How was she helpful?"

"She told us how to confront my sister," Dew said. "If we need to."

"I don't want that," Edward said. He had feared the potential Modern Enemy when they were searching for it. But the idea of squaring off with Yitoo was far scarier.

"Me neither," Dew said. Ice formed underneath her feet and pushed the two of them toward the ceiling. "Let's pray it doesn't come to that."

Nathan leaned forward as Yitoo jogged to the area where Clay Lake resided. In the back of his mind, he knew that people in Phoenix were going to be put in a difficult position. He could envision the towns, the cities, the farmlands that grew food, where the water was being diverted to, and how they would react to the sudden loss of water. But if there was going to be a future, with a comfortable climate, this was how it had to be.

Nathan was frustrated with the older generation, who had damaged the climate and put him in this position in the first place. For years, for decades even, the older generation was warned about climate change. They didn't listen then and mostly still didn't. It must have been easy for them to assume that climate change wasn't a big deal. They weren't the ones who were going to be living in the future. It was his generation that would live in that world. It was his generation that would have to navigate those dangers.

Mostly, he was angry with himself because he also enjoyed modern conveniences. He loved burgers and fries. He enjoyed the blast of AC in his dad's SUV when he drove him to Nali's on the I-40. He was just as guilty as the older generation.

Yitoo slowed to a walk as they approached the lake with the

dead horses. Clay Lake was already there, sadly nudging the bones of a pony.

"Younger brother," Yitoo said. "I have returned with water to give to you."

"Sister," Clay Lake said. "You are saving the land and the beings that dwell on it. I only wish I could be of more help."

"The best way to assist me," Yitoo said, "is to be safe."

"That I can do," Clay Lake said.

Yitoo commanded the water to flow from her body to the cracked earth around the horse corpses. Thousands of gallons of water flowed from one of the bracelets Yitoo wore. The air around them became ten degrees cooler. And the ground darkened as it thirstily drank down the life-giving moisture.

Clay Lake eagerly walked into the spray of water. He opened his jaws and gurgled. He then rolled onto his back and let the water stream down his smooth tummy. His scales, once dull and lifeless, sparkled and seemingly sang in the sunlight.

Nathan looked up and saw thousands of rainbows encircling each plump droplet that was launched into the sky and fell back down. There was now an actual pond forming around the bones of the horses, and it was quickly growing wide and deep. The sound of splashing summoned a whole array of beings. Winged bugs flew to the edge of the pond. Birds followed shortly and stood in the shallow end. They ruffled their feathers and washed themselves clean, singing all the while. Small rabbits, prairie dogs, and even lizards crawled out of the earth and ferociously drank. The bones loosened from the center and floated away.

The clinking sounds they made were replaced by the rejoicing animal voices.

Ten minutes later, all the water from the bracelet had finally been released.

"Yitoo," Nathan said.

"Yes, young Hero?" Yitoo responded.

He said, "Thank you for coming back and doing what you are doing."

"You're welcome," Yitoo said. "There is still much more water to return. Then we have to discuss our next plan of action."

Nathan's gut feelings, his intuition, were aligning with Yitoo's actions. There was no denying that taking the water back was the right thing to do. Returning the moisture might even be reversing the effects of climate change in a way that was immediate and meaningful. And he was helping. Nathan was a part of the solution.

Tsosts'id Ts'áadah
SEVENTEEN

BY THE TIME EDWARD AND Dew emerged into the Fourth World out into the canyon of Hajíínéí, it was five thirty. Light shadows were dripping down the rock face. While Edward's energy dampened, Dew seemed to be as energetic as ever. Her head darted left, right, up, and down.

Edward was surprised. "What? We were in the Third World for, like, eight hours!"

Dew answered, "Time flows slower in the Third World."

What luck that time flowed slower in the Third World and they would be gone for only an afternoon! Then Edward said, "We should make our way back to Mrs. Todacheenie's home. "Do you know how to get there?"

Dew nodded. "From here, yeah. It'll take a while. I don't have enough water to jet-stream us there *and* to be large enough for you to hop on my back."

Now seemed as good a time as any to enact his cunning plan. Edward said, "Speaking of water. Now that we are away from Mother Water Monster, do you think you could share the water she gave to you with me?"

"What for?" she asked. Her head tilted to the side.

Edward explained, "So, I was thinking. She gave you the water, the water you now carry inside you. If you were to give me some of what she gave you, then I'd be able to listen to water monster songs! What do you think?"

Dew took a moment to consider. Edward didn't think it would take this long for her to say yes. Then finally, she said, "That's not how it works."

Edward's chest deflated. "How could it not work? That's her water, and if I drink it, it should allow me to listen."

"Technically, it's my water," Dew clarified. "And it's no longer Third World water. It's Fourth World water now. To listen to our songs by drinking her waters, you would have to drink it in the Third World, and you'd definitely have to have her permission."

"Seriously?" Edward asked. He was 100 percent certain that that would have worked! He couldn't think of any other way to be able to listen to water monster songs. If he couldn't hear the songs, then he was just a helpless hindrance.

"Seriously," Dew responded. Dew led Edward away from the shortcut to the Third World. Up ahead, Shaded Marsh was asleep on his side. His stomach inflated and deflated in a calm tempo.

Edward ran his fingers through his hair, frustrated that things were not working out. Yitoo was taking her waters back. The Hero Twins were no longer in the Fourth World. Mother Water Monster didn't let him drink her waters. Should he even bother trying? He was just going to fail again. He felt so angry with his own ineptitude. He huffed loudly.

"You okay, Edward?" Dew asked.

The last time he felt this downtrodden was when he lost a wrestling match that would have qualified him for state championships in his age group. His dad had told them that it was important to keep trying and to learn from setbacks. Edward answered, "Let's just find a way to Nathan's grandma's place."

Shaded Marsh woke and lifted his head off the ground. Perhaps from moving too quickly, he groaned in pain and rested his head onto the soft sands. He said, "Welcome back."

"Thank you, older brother," Dew said. She sniffed his exposed tummy, scrambled to the other side of him, and then sniffed his spine and finally his hind leg. "You're in a lot of pain!"

"Nothing new," Shaded Marsh said. "My knee doesn't like it when I travel on the rainbow path too often. Change in the atmospheric pressure, I assume. I'll just rest here for the night and should feel better tomorrow."

Dew asked, "Is there anything we can do?"

Edward examined how Shaded Marsh was moving and trying not to move. This was beyond manageable knee pain. This was an arthritic flare-up. Every few seconds, Shaded Marsh winced in pain. Edward knew of a possible way to help Shaded Marsh, but he felt his efforts would probably backfire, like everything else. His inner voice told him to keep trying and to learn from his setbacks.

"Edward's advice of alternating hot and cold has already done wonders," Shaded Marsh said. "This is just part of getting old. Every day is a wild guess as to what is going to hurt next."

"I think I can help even more," Edward said. "I mean, stretching is supposed to be one of the best treatments for managing arthritis." Edward approached the knee that was in pain. He hushed the negative voice that told him he was going to fail. "I can help you stretch your knee."

"At this point, I'll give anything a try," Shaded Marsh said. His mask of strength crumbled, and his snout curled in pain.

"First, let's get you fully on your back," Edward said. "Can you roll?"

"I'm afraid to move," Shaded Marsh answered.

"Okay," Edward said, examining Shaded Marsh's body position and searching for any possible way he could roll him onto his spine. Then he saw an opening. Shaded Marsh's upper body was mobile. If he were to start with the upper body, then the lower body would have to roll, too. "I've got a plan. Dew, can you step back?"

Dew listened and watched Edward work. Edward wrapped a wrestler's grip around the shoulder blade on the ground. Gently, slowly, and intentionally, he drove his feet into the ground and turned Shaded Marsh's upper body.

Shaded Marsh breathed heavily and winced. He said, "Keep going."

Finally, both of Shaded Marsh's shoulders were on the ground, and the lower half was moving. Then, finally, all four legs were in the air, like a cat exposing its tummy. Quickly, Edward pushed sand up against Shaded Marsh's sides to prevent him from rolling over. Secured, Shaded Marsh seemed to relax.

Edward said, "Okay, I'm going to bend the knee that hurts and hold for thirty seconds. We'll do that three times, and then I'll help with some other stretches."

Edward placed his forearm at the back bend of the arthritic knee and with his other hand pulled the foot downward. Some of his confidence was returning. And finally, instead of Nathan and Dew with their fancy songs, he was doing something.

Nathan's cell phone vibrated as Yitoo walked underneath him, approaching the canyon entrance east of the Nazlini Chapter House. To their left, down in the lower valley, was the Nazlini Community School. The swings and slides of the playground were covered by a layer of red dust. He quickly looked at his phone and saw a long line of texts from his mom asking him where he was and that Nali hadn't heard from him. His mom's more recent texts asked him if he was involved with the disappearance of Lake Powell. He couldn't deal with his mom just yet, nor Edward for that matter. They wouldn't understand. At least not until harmony was restored to Diné Bikéyah.

Yitoo stepped off the low plateau with five enormous steps and walked over the only paved road that ran southward toward Ganado. Nazlini was such a small town that he didn't expect anyone to be driving around. Regardless, he tightened his grip on the fabric of shadow. His cell phone lost the single bar of reception, so he slipped it back into his pocket.

Five more minutes and they were in the canyon, with its walls of wind-sculpted smooth orange rock, ceiling of empty blue sky, and floor of a dead stream. Nathan wondered how Canyon Mist was going to react to seeing Yitoo again. Every sibling they had run into was gracious for the water they received. And the land, quenched from the drought, released perfumed air as a sign of thanks. Bugs, birds, and animals all emerged from their hideouts and slurped up the water. It wasn't too big a stretch of Nathan's imagination to envision that one day humanity would be just as desperate for water.

"Sister," Yitoo called out. Her voice bounced off the striped rock walls.

They didn't have to wait long for a response. Canyon Mist emerged from beneath the sands. Small specks of dirt rolled off her scales as she shook herself clean. "Yes?"

"I have come to give you more water from my river," Yitoo said.

Canyon Mist scoffed, "Oh, joy, what should I do with the extra water?"

"Whatever you feel is appropriate," Yitoo said.

"I feel it is appropriate to keep it for myself," Canyon Mist said.

Yitoo quietly huffed, "That is your decision," she said. If she had teeth to grind, they would be coarse.

Nathan felt the need to dispel the awkwardness between the two sisters. There had to be a more thoughtful and tactful way to get them to talk to each other. "Canyon Mist," Nathan started. "Why do you feel the need to not share? I'm not judging; I'm just curious."

"Yes, please tell me," Yitoo begged. "I want to know."

"You both should have realized by now, having seen how desert cities interrupt water cycles." Canyon Mist then spoke directly to Yitoo: "It's great that you are giving your waters to us. But it will never be enough. Because you are treating the symptoms and not the problem. When a jar has a hole at the bottom, it will always lose water. Diné Bikéyah has such a hole. Bring as much water as you want, it will always be drained away by the Pale People."

"The Pale People," Yitoo snarled.

"I hate them, too, sister," Canyon Mist said. "I bore witness to their crimes. I saw their murderous inclinations. They claim holiness but commit the evilest acts on others."

Yitoo said, "No matter how much water I return to Diné Bikéyah, the systems in place will always benefit the Pale People and the cities they scurry in."

"Yes!" Canyon Mist exclaimed. For the first time, Nathan heard joy and excitement in her voice. "That's what I've been conveying to you! Your efforts mean nothing. So, why even bother? Let them destroy themselves with their conveniences."

"That's where I disagree," Yitoo said. "Yes, if we sit back, they will inevitably destroy themselves. But they are destroying more than themselves. They are damaging the land now. They are harming the environment now. I sat back and let them infest Diné Bikéyah one hundred and sixty years ago. Recall the horror they enacted on all Indigenous Nations, not just the Diné. I fear, the longer we wait, the more irreversible the damage to the world they will cause. This demands an active approach."

A sinister smile crossed Canyon Mist's snout. "Then it is very clear that we must attack, oldest sister."

"What?" Nathan shouted. He felt like he had heard an avalanche, a landslide, a volcano eruption.

"*I* must attack Phoenix," Yitoo clarified.

"Why stop at Phoenix? It's not the only city that steals our water," Canyon Mist said.

"Then all the desert cities," Yitoo said.

"The most effective strategy for all the desert cities would be with the Maelstrom song," Canyon Mist said. "That will cause great damage to their structures and means of living."

Yitoo said, "For that, I will need more water."

"Summon all of us again," Canyon Mist said. "We will give you all the moisture we have."

"That may not be enough, but let's start with that," Yitoo said.

Nathan couldn't speak. He was too shocked. He wanted to

help restore balance and bring moisture back to Diné Bikéyah. But Yitoo was now talking about attacking Phoenix and the other desert cities! He was going to need Dew's and Edward's help to calm Yitoo down.

"This would be the perfect opportunity to teach Dew the Maelstrom song," Yitoo said. "Canyon Mist, I hope you know that I will never forgive myself for harming you so."

"When you wipe the cities of the desert off the surface of this world, all will be forgiven," Canyon Mist said. "Would you like my help summoning our siblings?"

"Please," Yitoo said.

The two of them lifted their snouts high, like howling coyotes, and let out a terrifying roar. Their summons echoed off the walls of Nazlini Canyon. Nathan could hear small clips of words and phrases. Soon, it sounded like an orchestral choir of roars. A thin tentacle of water from Yitoo's bracelet reached into her medicine pouch. Immediately after the tentacle came out, strong winds scented with juniper expanded outward. It was her braid of wind, and it carried the voices of the water monster sisters out of the canyon.

"Are you ready, Nathan?" Yitoo asked once the echoes quieted.

"Huh?" he responded.

"The three of us are traveling to the location where the star fell just near Dook'o'oosłííd," Yitoo explained in her usual calm and loving voice. "There, my siblings will donate their waters to me."

"What about Dew and Edward?" Nathan said.

"The summons that Canyon Mist and I just gave will travel all across Diné Bikéyah with the help of my wind braid," Yitoo said. "Dew will hear it and know where to meet us. Hopefully their errand will be complete. Let's not delay, Nathan."

Yitoo bowed her head so that Nathan could climb onto her shoulders. After securing himself with the ice harness and covering themselves with the shadow fabric, the three of them headed westward. All Nathan could think about was that his friends and so many people in Phoenix were going to be in danger.

Edward held his breath as Shaded Marsh took a few uncertain, wobbly steps forward. Dew hovered near his pained knee, ready to assist. One. Two. Three. Four steps in, and then Shaded Marsh smiled.

"The pain has halved," Shaded Marsh said, almost joyously. He lifted his leg into the air, bending, stretching, and twisting it at different angles. "The pain is still present; however, it is much more tolerable."

"Glad the stretching helped," Edward said. "But now you're going to have to add stretching to your daily routine as well as balance exercises to strengthen the joint."

"This morning, I would have ignored you," Shaded Marsh began. "But I cannot ignore the results. Thank you."

"No problem," Edward responded. He stretched himself. It took a lot of effort to stretch a water monster the size of a horse!

Just then, a terrifying roar soared through the air around them.

Edward's spine shivered, and his knees buckled. He heard angry voices and recognized Yitoo's. Both Dew and Shaded Marsh tilted their heads to listen to the message. Dew's eyes dilated, and she stood facing westward.

"What was that?" Edward asked.

Shaded Marsh answered, "Another summons. Yitoo beckons us to meet at the place where the star smashed into Mother Earth, near the western sacred mountain Dook'o'oosłííd."

"Meteor Crater," Edward said.

"And she wants us to donate our waters to her," Shaded Marsh said. He looked scared.

"Why would she want to do that?" Edward asked.

They weren't quick to answer. Finally, with a heavy voice, Dew said, "She's planning on attacking the desert cities, including Phoenix."

Edward's heart dropped, and the shock stole the air from his throat. "She can't."

Dew turned to Shaded Marsh and asked, "Brother, can you bring us there? We have to stop her."

Shaded Marsh quickly moved forward a few feet, then screamed and doubled over in pain. "My knee!" he shouted.

"Are you okay?" Edward asked, rushing over to his knee. Could he have made it worse? "Did I do this?"

"No, young Hero," Shaded Marsh said. "I was overconfident in my pain levels. As I was turning, I put my entire weight on my knee as I would before I had the pain, and now it's back. I'm afraid I won't be traveling anywhere for a while. Dew, come here and get my crystal from my medicine pouch."

Dew rushed over and dug her snout into his armpit. After a moment of searching, her jaws emerged from his body holding the quartz crystal like a delicate piece of thin glass.

Shaded Marsh said, "Youngest sister, you must sing the Rainbow Path song. Imagine the place where you want to go, then step on. When you are on the rainbow, keep the location in mind and the rainbow will bend to bring you both closer to your destination. The Jet Stone Twins have mastered this way of travel, using the stars. They can pinpoint exact locations of where they want to travel. We, as water monsters, will never have their finesse. Just like they can sing our songs and never be as powerful. Even without the precision of the Jet Stone Twins, traveling by rainbow is the fastest way to cover great distances."

Dew froze in place, lowering her gaze toward Shaded Marsh. She looked ashamed.

Shaded Marsh said, "What? Don't tell me you don't know the Rainbow Path song. I saw you listening ever so purposefully to my singing. You picked up the song. Without my permission, I should probably add."

"I'm sorry I learned the song without your permission," Dew said.

Edward wondered if it was rude for water monsters to learn songs without the permission of the singer. Like water monster etiquette or something.

"In time, you may have to learn more songs this way,"

Shaded Marsh said. "Now, hurry. You must convince Yitoo that there is a better way. I can already feel moisture and life returning to Diné Bikéyah. She has already taken the waters back, I'm sure, thereby endangering those who had previously relied upon them."

While grateful for this perspective, Edward kept wondering why a water monster would want to help them. After all, it would be in the best interest for all water monsters to have their waters returned, right? "Shaded Marsh, why are you helping us? I mean, isn't what Yitoo is trying to do a good thing for you?"

Shaded Marsh said, "I agree with some of Yitoo's sentiments. That our waters are not to be trifled with. Our waters should be respected. True, our waters that are diverted to the desert cities are sometimes used for frivolity. But that doesn't mean our waters don't sustain life there. My life-giving waters, my life-sustaining waters, are being used by many peoples and beings in places so very far from their origins. And I think that's wonderful. If we were to take all their water away, what are they going to do? Yes, I wish they would not toy with our waters, but they, too, need water. There is a new balance that is needed to be found. Between their need for water, and for our own need. For many years, their needs have outweighed ours. And what we have found ourselves in is a tipping point of the old balance. I hope your generation, Edward, will find a modern balance."

"A modern balance," Edward said. The words weighed heavily on his tongue and lips. That felt like the answer he was looking for. The real way to resolve this crisis.

"Dew," Shaded Marsh said, "sing the Rainbow Path song."

Dew nodded and then sang. After two verses, an arm of water emerged from her shoulder, and it lowered the quartz crystal to the earth. Glowing ribbons of red, orange, yellow, green, blue, indigo, and violet flowed out of the glass prism like scarves submerged in water.

Shaded Marsh said, "Now, align the colors while imagining the location."

The ribbons at once lined up as a rainbow and then shot into the sky.

Shaded Marsh added, "A warning: Do not land in a lake, or any deep waters, lest you sink to the bottom. No issue for water monsters, but for non-aquatic beings, such as the five-fingered, it could be disastrous."

Edward nodded, closed his eyes, and then, with his hand on Dew's forehead, stepped forward. The scary and familiar sudden blast of air pulled his cheeks back. They were on their way to Meteor Crater to defy Yitoo.

Tseebíí Ts'áadah

EIGHTEEN

THEY LANDED A FEW MILES east of Meteor Crater. Dew then sprinted, pushing herself harder than Edward thought possible. They torpedoed westward through the landscape of low brush and sunset-colored sands toward the churning cumulonimbus clouds that looked like a volcanic eruption. The top narrowed to a tip, like a wide pyramid. Several bolts of lightning ran across the underside of the clouds as well as through their interior, lighting them from the inside like an ominous paper lantern. A few seconds later, Edward heard the pandemoniac cracks of thunder.

When they were a few miles south of Winslow, Arizona, Edward felt his phone vibrate and heard the unrelenting emergency alarm go off. With one hand holding on to the ice harness that held him to Dew, he reached in his pocket with the other and saw: *EMERGENCY ALERT: SEVERE. August 2, 6:52 PM. National Weather Service: SEVERE THUNDERSTORM WARNING in effect for this area until 9:00 PM for DESTRUCTIVE winds. Take shelter in a sturdy building, away from windows. Flying debris may be deadly to those caught without shelter.*

In addition to the weather warning, he saw a long string of messages from his dad that grew in concern, urgency, agitation, and frequency.

They entered the shadow of the vast clouds and immediately were slammed by strong gusts of wind, nearly causing Edward to drop his phone. He would have to respond to his dad later. Then he leaned forward and hoped that Dew could go faster. On the earth were large basketball-sized hailstones. In between grunts and deep breaths, Dew said, "Keep close, Edward! We're almost to my siblings!"

Edward worried about Nathan. He convinced himself that it wasn't the word "sibling" that brought Nathan into his thoughts. Nathan had sided with Yitoo earlier. Was Nathan still helping her now that she was going to attack Phoenix?

It was as dark as dusk. The only source of light was at the edges of the clouds. The gray clouds, ominous and spinning slowly in a clockwise circle like swirling ash, extended for miles in every direction, even engulfing the tips of Dook'o'oosłííd, expanding over the flat desert behind them. A clear path of bright blue sky was miles away. Dew approached the bottom of the meteor impact site.

Edward looked up at the mouth. There were several water monsters singing at the crest of the crater. Even with the earplugs muffling their singing, he could hear the militaristic nature of the lyrics, short and quick, like punches. He pushed the foam tips deeper into his ear until he could hear only his pounding heartbeat.

Glancing to his right, Edward saw the visitor center that looked like it had been evacuated. There were no vehicles in the parking lot.

In moments, Edward and Dew approached the edge of the shelf cloud. Dew slowed before walking underneath the ceiling of apocalyptic clouds. Directly in front of them was the anthill-like mound that was the crest of the impact site. Miles around them, the land was still recovering from the meteor's devastation, as the only plant life was weeds and grass. The dark shape of Dook'o'oosłííd interrupted the flatness toward the west, and some very distant smooth rock formations stood out in the north.

When they got to the top of the impact site, Edward wanted to keep staring at the hypnotic sky, as the clouds were in constant motion, like smoke from a forest fire. But what was before them was even more breathtaking and alarming. Twelve different water monsters stood along the rim of the impact crater. They tilted their heads upward, singing in unison.

At their center was an actual waterfall! The clouds rolled, collided, and condensed into the thick river-sized stream of water pouring into the crater. The entire basin, 540 feet deep with a 3,900-foot diameter, was filled with dark sloshing water. Waves slapped against the walls, spraying Edward's exposed skin. Lightning up above discharged, illuminating every terrifying detail before him. Not too far from them, Yitoo and Nathan spotted them and made their way toward them.

Nathan could see that Dew was conflicted. She might be excited to see so many water monsters singing together and, like him, also worried at the damage they could cause. Edward, on the other hand, was staring directly at Nathan with an angry expression. Edward and Dew must know about Yitoo's change of plans, Nathan figured. The sun descended further, and the far-western edges of the cloud formation glowed like polished gold. Minute by minute, the light of the setting sun crept underneath the cumulonimbus ceiling.

The four of them stood next to one another. Yitoo then said with her lips curved into a smile, "Youngest sister, look at how many of our siblings answered my call! They are all eager to enact change in the Fourth World, though this is hardly enough water. What do you think, young Heroes? You know better than I how resilient Phoenix and the other cities of the desert are toward storms."

Edward didn't respond, so Nathan thought carefully about how to phrase his response. "Monsoon storms used to be very powerful when I was younger. Sometimes it'd rain for hours. The streets would flood. But all the rain and water would drain away as quickly as the storm arose."

"I'll need more water, then," Yitoo said.

Dew meekly asked, "Do you think maybe instead of using the water to attack Phoenix, that we could, you know, just give it back to Diné Bikéyah?"

Yitoo said, "Canyon Mist has revealed to me that the water

will only be taken away again. There is a system at play that favors these desert cities, to the detriment of the land. The only way to restore balance to Mother Earth is to rid the earth of them fully and completely."

"Maybe the people who live in desert cities can learn," Nathan said.

Yitoo responded, "They've had years to learn and to adapt. Do you honestly think they'll change now?"

Nathan wanted so very much to say that people living in the Phoenix valley would change, that they would learn. But it wasn't true. They had been told plenty of times that climate change was real and would cause greater and greater weather phenomena. But still, they mistreated the water and didn't give a second thought as to where the water came from and from whom they took it. They went back to their normal routines. Just like he himself did.

"Siblings, please end your singing!" Yitoo shouted above the voices of the twelve water monsters.

The twelve stopped singing at once and stumbled to the ground, exhausted. Immediately, the waterfall at the center disappeared and the clouds seemed to calm. It was still a terrifying sight for Nathan. Up until now, Pond and Dew were his only source of interaction with water monsters. He thought they would love all humans. Then an unsettling thought overtook him. If Pond was still alive, would he also support Yitoo? Would he want to attack the cities? No, Nathan told himself. Pond was kind and respected all life.

Edward, meanwhile, pointed to his ears. He still had his ear-plugs in. Nathan nodded for him to take them out.

"What's happened to them?" Edward asked.

"They overexerted themselves," Yitoo explained. "Brothers and sisters," Yitoo began. "Thank you for the gift of your waters."

"We want to join you!" a male water monster said, still lying on the ground. Other water monsters standing along the rocky circumference of the crater rim roared in agreement.

"Please," Yitoo said. "I must implore you all to respect your limits. Just singing this long has completely depleted you. You could die outside of the boundaries of the Four Sacred Mountains! I can't lose any more of my brothers and sisters."

"Neither can we lose another sister," a water monster shouted.

"I will be safe. I have the Heroes of the Water Monsters with me," Yitoo said. She indicated Nathan and Edward with her snout. She stepped onto the water and walked to the center. "They will protect me as I venture beyond the boundaries of the Four Sacred Mountains yet again. And I will travel to the heart of the ocean. There, I will sing, sing, sing"—each time she said it louder and more lyrical—"into existence a magnificent hurricane!"

The water monsters cheered. West of them, the sun's rays took on a dark purple hue, and the turbulent clouds resembled lilac silk billowing in the wind.

Nathan desperately tried to find a way to insert himself into this conversation but couldn't find one. He couldn't steer their energies any more than he could direct an avalanche.

Yitoo continued. "I will sing for two days. With the unlimited water and the power of the Maelstrom song, I will bring torrential justice upon the Pale People. They will endure the violence their own ancestors enacted on the Diné! And finally, the ghosts of the past will know peace and happiness. Because Mother Earth will be cleansed of the Pale People."

Nathan froze. What could he do? He was just a kid. Yitoo, as tall as an elephant, towered over them. Even though he had met Mother Water Monster when she was as big as a mountain, Yitoo was far more alarming. She had purpose. She had a goal. And nothing could get in her way.

"No!" Edward screamed. His voice cracked.

"Young Hero?" Yitoo said, turning to face him.

"You can't do that!" Edward said. He had waited for Nathan to say something, do something, but he was just standing there! Someone had to stand up to Yitoo and had to do it now.

"I will listen to you with an open heart," Yitoo said.

Edward shouted so all the water monsters could hear, but also so that Nathan understood what was happening. "You are going to destroy my home! Not only that, but you are also going to murder—yes, murder—many people. Some of those people are my friends."

"Are your friends Pale People?" Yitoo asked, walking toward them.

Edward thought of Andrew, then himself, and proudly said, "Yes."

Yitoo said, "They have nothing but bloodlust and domination in their hearts. The evil that resides in their souls is unforgiving, heinous, and everlasting."

"No!" Edward yelled. He walked closer to the edge of rock and water. He had had enough of Yitoo talking about his mom and his maternal grandparents that way.

"Your Pale friends will betray you. The same way they betrayed your ancestors," Yitoo said.

"They *are* my ancestors!" Edward said. He didn't regret saying that as much as he thought he would.

Yitoo stood a hundred feet away from them. Her front half lowered, like a lion ready to pounce. "What?"

"Edward," Nathan said from behind him.

"I'm half Pale People!" Edward said slowly and with clear pronunciation.

All the color drained from Yitoo's face. Her spikes rose from her spine. "You lied to me!"

The sunlight changed from dark purple to an orange red and the bellies of the clouds reflected the color. Instead of smoke, the entire sky of clouds now looked like it was on fire. The clouds rolled and slammed into one another. Lightning bolts raced across the sky.

Dew crawled to Edward's side and faced Yitoo. "He never tricked you."

"Youngest sister!" Yitoo said, pacing back and forth. "Do not give your heart to this impostor. His kind only inflicts agony on others."

"Have you forgotten that he's also Diné?" Dew said.

Edward felt honored that Dew was standing by his side and opposing Yitoo. He shouldn't ever feel ashamed about either half of himself.

Yitoo spat back, "His blood is tainted, filthy. He's not full blooded, and therefore he is not a real Diné."

Her response was as bad as Edward had expected. But he also felt freed: of no longer having to hide, of no longer having to hold his tongue when someone spoke ill of either part of himself. He no longer felt like he had to be ashamed because he was only half Diné. As far as he was concerned, he was Diné because he knew his clans. He was Diné because he participated in ceremonies. He was Diné because he could speak some words of the Diné language. And if he wasn't brown enough for Yitoo, and if he was too brown for people like Chad, then that was their problem.

Edward said, "Yitoo, if you attack the cities, then you are no better than those who attacked the Diné."

She yelled, "I'm far better than those cowards!" In an instant, a sharp-tipped icicle shot out from beneath Yitoo and flew directly at Edward.

It was as if time slowed. Edward clearly saw the sharp spear-like tip of the ice zooming through the air toward him. He was too slow to dodge in time. Dew screamed his name, and a watery tentacle emerged from the water in the crater. It reached for the icicle, but it was too slow. Edward held his breath and stared at Yitoo in the eye. He wanted her to know that even in his last minute, he wasn't going to back down. He prepared for the impact.

Suddenly, another watery tentacle shot up and wrapped around the icicle, halting it mere inches from his chest.

"Dew?" Edward managed to choke out.

But Dew was just as confused. She wasn't controlling the tentacle.

Nathan stepped forward with his arm reaching at the icicle.

"Nathan?" Yitoo said. She sounded as shocked as the lightning that zipped through the clouds. "What are you doing?"

"Protecting my younger brother." Nathan clenched his fist, and the tentacle responded by shattering the icicle spear into tiny harmless shards.

Nathan squared off with Yitoo, who looked enraged with boiling resentment. He consoled the part of himself that had believed in the gentler side of Yitoo. He quietly grieved that the possibility of peace was gone. Nathan was not going to let Yitoo hurt Edward or anyone else!

"Brothers, sisters, leave," Yitoo commanded, a low growl in her throat. "These children must learn a valuable lesson." Yitoo turned and walked to the center of the water-filled crater.

"Edward, get away from here," Nathan said.

"I want to help," Edward said.

"You can't," Dew said. "You can't listen to the songs."

Nathan saw the frustration on Edward's face. He really did want to help the two of them. Nathan advised Edward, "The best way you can help us is to be safe."

The other water monsters were descending away from the crater as quickly as their energy could allow. Edward sprinted to create as much distance from them as he could. Edward fought back the tears that were welling in his eyes. For all his strength and abilities in taking down opponents his size, he was powerless against water monsters. And the fate of Phoenix lay in the hands of Nathan and Dew. He had to trust that they would do their best, and that that would be enough.

Just then, his cell phone vibrated. His dad was calling. He let it ring, deciding to call back when he got to the empty parking lot of the evacuated visitor center.

Nathan, at the same time, watched Yitoo stand at the center of the water-filled crater. The clouds still roiled and rumbled like a never-ending firestorm in the sky. Dew stood by his side.

"We have to stop her," Nathan said.

"Yes," Dew said.

Nathan climbed on top of Dew, and the two of them approached Yitoo.

Náhást'éí Ts'áadah

NINETEEN

AS NATHAN AND DEW GOT close to the center of the crater where she stood, Yitoo spoke. "Youngest sister, you did not
witness when Pale People burned the cornfields and slaughtered
the sheep of the Diné. I did! I watched as Diné surrendered to
the Pale People and were gathered at a place called Fort Defiance, while other Diné resisted and were killed in brutal ways.
I should have drowned every single Pale Person the moment
I saw them. Including half- and quarter-bloods, because rage
flows in their very veins.

"It was the design of the Holy Beings that brought you,
Nathan, to the Third World and inspired my return to the Fourth
World. It's so very brave of you to stand against me. However, I will not repeat this warning. For if you do not stay your
opposition, you will be siding with the Enemies. And I will not
repeat my mistake of letting the Pale People, or their allies, live.

Beloved youngest sister and kindhearted Healer, join me. Let's save the Fourth World."

Yitoo lifted her head high, exposing her neck. Nathan recognized this gesture because Pond, even Dew when she was large, would do this. She wanted them to hug her. Nathan didn't need any time to consider. Even though climate change was fast approaching, and Yitoo was offering a quick solution, this was not the right answer. Nathan didn't once think that Dew would go to Yitoo. She remained by his side.

"Yitoo!" Nathan shouted. There was nothing he could say that would change her mind, but he still cared for her. The only words that surfaced from his heart were "There is still love in you."

"Very well," Yitoo said with a deep and heavy sigh. Before Nathan could react, a rope of water wrapped around his waist and Dew's neck and pulled them into the crater.

The warm water invaded every atom of Nathan's being. He immediately commanded the liquid out of his nasal cavity and throat. But he couldn't stop the invisible force yanking his waist. Nathan closed his eyes and focused on finding the source of the pull. In the darkness of closed eyes, he found it. When he opened his eyes, the fiery light reflecting from the clouds grew dim as he was pulled toward the bottom of the crater. He tried his best to keep the water out of his lungs while also severing the connection. But he couldn't. The pressure around his chest grew with every foot that he sank, restricting his ability to breathe.

Just then, Dew appeared in front of him. With a mighty jaw snap near his belly button, she severed the pull. Nathan wrapped his arms around her neck, and together they ascended to the surface.

As they got closer to the surface, Nathan heard the muffled singing of Yitoo and the outbursts of thunder. A surface of ice expanded outward underneath her feet like thick spiderwebs. Was she trying to freeze them? Dew's momentum launched them a few feet into the air. As they fell, all the water in the entire crater froze. They landed on a smooth mirrorlike surface that reflected the fiery sky above. Dew sang the Change song. In response, the ice underneath her warped and wobbled but refused to melt.

"This is my water," Yitoo explained. "Its allegiance is to me. Let that be another lesson for you."

Nathan quickly dismissed his plan of controlling the water. To wrestle control away from her water would be like having a tug-of-war with a tank. Still, he needed water to be able to resist her and protect himself. "Dew, may I borrow some of your water?"

"Of course," Dew said. Her size shrank from that of a horse to that of a donkey as water streamed out of her toward Nathan. "I think we have a chance of overcoming her. She taught me the song that she used to strip water away from Canyon Mist. Let's try that on her!"

"Okay," Nathan said. Nathan commanded the water to wrap around his arms, then his shoulders. He hardened it into armor. It was nowhere near the density of Yitoo's ice armor, but it was better than nothing.

Four streams of water emerged from the sides of Yitoo's torso and solidified into ice arms. She spoke: "Demonstrate what you have learned from me!" The ice arms rushed toward them. Yitoo adjusted her posture and with each mighty footstep cracked and splintered the ice underneath her. The four ice arms snatched Dew and lifted her high into the air.

"Hold on, Dew!" Nathan shouted. He sang as loud as he could the Move song and commanded the tentacle holding her to stop. But nothing happened. Yitoo was too strong.

Lightning, bloodred from the sunset, exploded across the clouds. Yitoo slammed Dew downward. The ice where Dew was going to hit warped and softened. When she hit it, there was an explosion of slush. Dew had wrested control over some of the water! The ice water mixture submerged Dew's body. Dew then jumped out, and the slush covering her hardened into armor.

Dew yelled, "Please stop, sister! Nathan and I will overcome you!"

Yitoo said, "You really do hold such promise. It's a shame I won't be able to teach you the Maelstrom song. It's one of the most powerful water monster songs. It would have been an amazing sight to see how powerful a hurricane you would have summoned, youngest sister."

Dew growled at Yitoo, "I would never cause such destruction on this world!" Dew charged Yitoo, who directed all four ice limbs at her.

Yitoo must not have considered Nathan a threat because she was outright ignoring him. Not wasting an opportunity, Nathan tried to command the ice limbs to stop again. It took all his concentration to wrestle Yitoo's control over the appendages. Nathan noticed an interruption in Yitoo's control when she was focused on attacking Dew. It was subtle, like feeling the texture of cotton versus wool. The ice limbs were just barely bending to Nathan's command. He forced himself to sing louder, his vocal cords strained, his mouth dried.

"Excellent effort, Healer," Yitoo said, turning to face him. "But you lack the proper pronunciation. The consequence of assimilation!"

Dew nimbly swerved to the side as Yitoo swung an ice limb at her, like a fly dodging a baseball bat. Just then, with all his mental might, Nathan forced the ice limbs to stop, and miraculously they did!

Dew took this opportunity to jump onto Yitoo's spine and bite down on the two front ice tentacles. Under Dew's control, the two tentacles tightly wrapped around Yitoo's legs, causing her to lose balance.

"Bah!" Yitoo screamed as she fell over. The sun had fallen slightly lower, and the color of the clouds was turning from dark red to black. "Allow me to dissipate any hope you may have of stopping me," Yitoo said. The tentacles around her legs burst into mist, and she stood up. She unleashed a terrifying roar, and an ice wave twenty feet high rose behind Yitoo and rushed at Nathan.

"Nathan!" Dew shouted, jumping and landing next to him.

Before the wave could smother them, Nathan sang the Move

song and commanded the water to flow around him. He then reversed its course and made it flow back toward Yitoo. Dew sang the same song, and they harmonized. The wave returned to Yitoo taller and stronger. That was it! Singing together made their efforts twice as strong! They had a chance. They could defeat Yitoo! Dew must have realized this, too, because her lips curled into a smile.

Their wave gained height and speed, then slammed into Yitoo. She chuckled as the wave did nothing to her stance. "It breaks my heart to see such talent go to waste."

In an instant, water suddenly emerged from below them and wrapped around their legs and necks. Then it hardened into ice. Dew threw her head in the air, still singing. But a chain of ice closed her mouth shut. And finally, Nathan's mouth, too, was covered in ice. Nathan tried his best to command the water, any of the water. Nothing.

"Within the boundaries of the Four Sacred Mountains, you will never be able to stop me," Yitoo explained. "I will mourn you for many centuries. And I will chant of your bravery to the next generation."

Nathan looked up and saw the clouds. Years ago, when Nathan visited Meteor Crater with his school, the tour guide had said that there were iron deposits sprinkled about the impact site. And during thunderstorms, the iron would attract the lightning. Nathan hummed what he could remember of the Storm song that he had overheard Yitoo teaching Dew. Thunder began to increase in frequency and intensity. Dew noticed and hummed loudly. A bolt of lightning struck the northern rim of the crater. Then another struck the eastern rim.

"No!" Yitoo said. She expelled as much water as she could.

Nathan was able to melt the ice around his mouth. He then melted the ice around Dew. They continued to sing, and more and more lightning bolts appeared.

Nathan stopped singing to say, "She's too powerful."

Dew nodded. Nathan mounted Dew, and they fled as fast as Dew could, leaving the crater with a jet stream.

In the distance, Nathan could see Edward's neon blue shorts against the brown-and-gray landscape. He was waiting for them in the parking lot of the visitor center. Nathan pointed to him, and Dew streamed over. After scooping up Edward, Dew took them far away from Meteor Crater. Only when they were a mile away from the clouds did Dew finally stop.

"We couldn't stop her," Nathan said, panting heavily from the fight.

Dew huffed and slumped to the ground, exhausted.

"I called our parents," Edward said. "They're on their way. We need their help."

From where they stood, they saw the silhouette of Yitoo standing in the middle of Meteor Crater. Water rose and washed over her in a huge ball. An even larger and more terrifying version of Yitoo emerged from the cocoon of swirling water. She stood sixty feet tall, the height of a four-story building, and was as long as an airplane. She tilted her titanic head upward.

"Rest easy, brothers, sisters, Holy Beings, Mother Earth, for I travel to the ocean!" Strands of wind carried her booming voice across the land. "In two days, I will return with a hurricane that will wash clean the Pale People and their cities off this surface world!"

Nathan wept. Yitoo was free to summon the hurricane, and no one could stop her.

Naadiin
TWENTY

AFTER YITOO WENT BEYOND DOOK'O'OOSŁÍÍD westward, Edward, Nathan, and Dew walked away from the visitor center on Meteor Crater Road to the I-40 highway. Each footstep was filled with silence as they processed their fresh defeat. The clouds above them had dispersed, and the last rays of sun had disappeared beyond the western horizon. Exhausted and downtrodden, Edward slumped in the middle of the road. As night had fallen, there was no chance of a vehicle driving on the road. Nathan and Dew joined him.

Edward scrolled through the news headlines on his phone. The entire Phoenix valley had declared a state of emergency, and the city had implemented strict water regulations. Even Andrew, through a text, said that all the stores had completely sold out of bottled water, sports drinks, and beverages. But, the valley was still drawing water from other sources. Edward could only imagine the many areas that were suffering droughty conditions so that Phoenix could have reliable water.

Nathan said, "I thought she'd listen to me." Each word was saturated with anguish.

Edward's tongue bloated like a balloon. He really wanted to tell Nathan to get over Yitoo. But Nathan really cared for Yitoo and was heartbroken. So, Edward rubbed Nathan's shoulders. Then his hand shot back as if Nathan was a hot ember. There was still awkwardness between them because Nathan had said that Edward was his younger brother.

"How long until your parents arrive?" Dew asked.

"At least another hour," Edward said. When he had called earlier during Nathan, Dew, and Yitoo's fight, Ted and Janet had already packed and were waiting for a word from either Edward or Nathan.

"While we wait, we should figure out what we do next," Dew said.

"I'm not in the right mind space to think right now," Nathan said. "I'm too . . . I'm too everything. Pissed off."

Dew stood up and rubbed her cheeks against Nathan's shoulder. "Take your time to process what you are feeling. Edward, any ideas?"

The pressure on Edward was immense. He felt as though the fate of the entire world had been placed upon him. While he had to respect that Nathan had to sort through his emotions, Edward needed Nathan to figure out what to do next! If Edward decided on doing something that was wrong, he was going to doom everyone.

Edward shouted, "Why me? It's not like I can help you guys fight Yitoo anyway!"

Dew slumped. Her face contorted into an unfamiliar forlorn expression. "I don't know what we should do."

If Edward had been able to fight alongside them, things might have gone differently. Suddenly, he remembered something important. "Spider Woman said the Obsidian Armor would let me hear the water monster songs! That's it, isn't it? We go ask Father Sun for the Obsidian Armor and the Sacred Arrows like we had originally planned. And then we stop Yitoo, together."

"In the middle of the Pacific Ocean," Nathan added. There was a note of hopelessness in his words.

"Outside the Four Sacred Mountains, we will have a chance!" Edward said. "Remember how much weaker her influence over the water was in Phoenix? I think you and Dew could match her abilities, and with the Sacred Arrows, I can subdue her."

Nathan explained, "Outside Diné Bikéyah, she's also susceptible to death. If she doesn't stop, we may have to fully end her."

"You said there was still love in her," Dew said. "We just have to remind her of that."

"I really hope so," Nathan said. "I can't lose another friend." Tears flowed out of Nathan's eyes.

Dew wrapped her front legs around his shoulder, and Nathan leaned into her. Dew shot Edward a look that he understood to mean "get over here." Edward dropped that awkward feeling about being called "younger brother." Nathan needed comfort. Edward leaned against him and let Nathan feel his emotions.

An hour later, Ted drove Janet's SUV up to the chain-link fence where Nathan and Edward were sitting. Edward held his breath, nervous at seeing their parents. They could very well be angry. The SUV parked, and both jumped out of the vehicle and rushed toward them, leaving the vehicle running.

"What is going on?" Janet asked Nathan, her eyes wide with a mixture of fear and anger. She held him at arm's length. "All of Lake Powell has disappeared, and Ted tells me that you were fighting a water monster? You told me that you would talk to us if you needed help!"

Ted wasn't saying a word, which unnerved Edward. It meant that his dad was mad. He said, "Dad."

"You promised to keep us in the loop," Ted said.

"Nathan, Edward," Janet started. "Talk to us."

"We need to get to the Southern Sacred Mountain, Tsoodził," Nathan said. "Edward and I can explain everything on the way there."

While Janet drove eastward on I-40, Edward and Nathan told their parents what had been happening and why they needed to go to Grants, New Mexico, where Tsoodził is located. There was a long silence, and all Edward and Nathan could do was wait for their parents' response as they sat in the back. The only sounds were the hum of the engine and Dew, near their feet, licking a bruise that she had sustained during the fight. Edward stared out the window and looked at all the vehicles on the busy I-40 highway. No one knew of the arriving danger. Edward wanted to shout at the top of his lungs, to have a sign on top of the SUV that said in big bold letters, "There is a massive hurricane coming!"

Finally, Ted broke the silence and asked Janet, "You holding strong with the driving?"

"I can get us to Gallup, and then you'll have to drive from there," Janet answered. She shook her head. "Two days until Yitoo attacks."

"Yeah," Ted said. Edward recognized the frustration in his dad's voice.

"I'm sorry, Dad," Edward said.

"I am, too, Mom," Nathan said.

"We'll talk later about you two keeping this a secret from us," Janet said.

They were taking this much better than he thought they would. Edward unplugged his phone from the center console. He navigated news websites to see if there were any signs of a hurricane developing. By now, Yitoo should have reached the Pacific Ocean. No news yet. Then he began to research facts on hurricanes.

"How's Phoenix doing?" Nathan asked.

Janet said, "We are in a water crisis. Phoenix had contingencies in place. The valley has two primary sources of water. There's the Salt River Project that gets water from the Salt River dams and the Verde River dams northeast of the valley. And the Central Arizona Project, which diverts water from Lake Powell and connects to the Salt River Project. Yitoo's actions have affected that source of water. Phoenix is using water from the SRP as well as artificial groundwaters to mediate the water crisis."

Ted contributed, "There's a citywide ban on watering lawns. We're even being encouraged to limit our showers."

Janet continued. "Outdated state and federal regulations that were made in the first half of the twentieth century are complicating how Arizona, Utah, Nevada, and California can react to the disappearance of Lake Powell. While the government squabbles, communities that got their waters directly from CAP, including the Havasupai Nation, are suffering."

"Dad, how do you feel about Yitoo?" Edward asked him.

His dad looked surprised. "Huh?"

"Yitoo, what she's doing. How do you feel about it?" Edward clarified.

Ted responded, "To be honest, I'm still dealing with the whole 'Holy Beings are real' thing. There's a part of me that says this can't be real and that I should just drive us to your nálí's until the water crisis in Phoenix is over. How do *you* feel about Yitoo?"

His dad sometimes did this. Repeat his own question back at Edward. And that's what Edward was hoping for. He needed to talk this out and have someone help him think it through.

"She's bad but also good," he started.

"Tell me what makes her bad and what makes her good."

Edward said, "Well, she took the water. She's putting a lot of people into a water crisis. Including the Havasupai Nation. That makes her bad. But it *is* her water, so she should get a say in it. And Nathan says that she is bringing the water back to Diné

Bikéyah. So that makes her good because the animals, plants, and people here also need the water. I'm just so confused."

"Eddie, as you get older, the less you start to see the world as only good and evil. There are shades, levels, and different perspectives. You see, son, in Yitoo's perspective, she is doing what she believes is right. You are doing what you believe is right by resisting her," his dad reasoned.

Janet said, "In my opinion, if the Phoenix valley hadn't been so quick and greedy to hoard water for itself, external communities such as the Havasupai wouldn't be in this much of a dire situation."

"That's not all, though," Nathan said. His voice was sounding sleepy. "Yitoo was present when our ancestors were forced on the Long Walk to Hwééldi."

Ted shook his head in disbelief.

Two months ago, Ted had told Edward about his ancestor's survival of Hwééldi. Since then, the relocation story had embedded itself in his memory and his heart. It was as though an invisible weight had been placed on his skull and compressed all his vertebrae. After he heard the last word of the relocation story, something inside him irrevocably changed. He couldn't separate himself from all that pain, misery, and injustice. He couldn't escape all that history of heartless genocide or brutal relocation, nor the destruction caused by Manifest Destiny, because it was everywhere. Yet, Edward was also the product of his Diné ancestor's horror and hope, terror, and triumph. Edward *was* the story.

His great-great-great-great-grandpa had survived. Edward could not imagine the amount of strength his ancestor needed to be able to simply live during the Long Walk. He was glad that his ancestor had been adopted by clan members and that those clan members, despite not being related by blood, had treated his ancestor like a member of their family. He looked at Nathan and Janet. Could he do the same?

Nathan broke the silence. "Mom told me that our ancestor eluded capture by hiding in Canyon de Chelly. But on my nálí's side, my ancestor was a teenager. They held her at Fort Wingate, outside Gallup, before they forced her to walk. She met her husband down at Hwééldi. We don't know much about him because he never talked about it even after they returned to Diné Bikéyah. They only thing we know is that he had had a previous family that didn't make it."

Edward wanted justice, even if it was 160 years after the horrible crime had been committed. For the first time, he was ashamed of his mom's heritage. He had to ask, "Was Mom's ancestor a part of the Long Walk?"

Edward could hear his dad switching on adult mode in his voice. His voice was smooth and low, and he took extra time, each word heavy with thought and care. "No," Ted said calmly. "Your mom's side, well, you should talk with your grandparents about this, but your másání and cheii grew up near Chicago. Their family emigrated from Brussels in the early 1800s. The rest you are going to have to hear from them."

Even if his mom's side didn't directly kill Native people, they did benefit from the deaths of Native people and the relocations of Native Nations. Everyone did, even his best friend, Andrew. This story was going to take some time for Edward to process, to grapple with. For the most part, the image of his ancestor's parents being shot, the US Army slaughtering the sheep corral, and his ancestor's brother drowning in the river, were the only things he could envision. He couldn't stop his brain from imagining the Anglo adults in his life, Andrew's dad even, being the US Army soldiers who committed those atrocities. His love of the Phoenix valley had been shattered.

"I was so angry when my mom told me my ancestor's story," Janet said, interrupting Edward's running imagination. "I was angry with my white friends. Not only because of that history, but also because now I could see and understand that their experience of the United States was better and easier than mine in many ways.

"In your grandparents' age, it was illegal for them to perform ceremonies like the N'dáá. When I was your age, racist mascots and inaccurate stereotypes in movies were far more common. All these things still exist. Today, people still falsely claim to be Indigenous, those descendants of the Cherokee 'princess.' I hear that one reason people claim that is because it distances themselves from the relocations. If they are descendants of Indigenous people, they aren't the bad guys; they're the victims.

"Ted and I, our generation, carried the torch your grandparents did, your ancestors did. We work to make sure the United States government honors its treaties with Native Nations and its promise that all people are equal. And soon, it'll be your turn to continue the work of making this world better for your descendants, no matter what heritage or multi-heritage your children are."

"Yitoo said I wasn't Diné," Edward said. "Because I'm half Anglo."

"No, she didn't!" Ted exclaimed.

"Oh, Eddie, that must have been hurtful," Janet said.

Edward said, "It's true! I'm barely half! If I marry someone who isn't Diné, then my kids will be further diluted. They'll be one-fourth. And if they, too, marry someone who isn't Diné, then my grandkids won't be Diné because they'll be one-eighth. So, I have to marry and have kids with a girl who is Diné or else the blood is going to dry up."

"Eddie," Ted said. "You are not going to have any control over who you love. Your heart will love who it wants. Don't let blood quantum dictate your romantic options. I have no regrets about loving your mom. Don't forget you can see and hear the Holy Beings! No matter who you marry, I'm certain your kids, my grandkids, will also be able to see them because they will be Diné."

His dad's words felt like a soothing balm of mint spreading on a burn scar.

Janet mm-hmm'ed and added, "Blood quantum was *never* how our ancestors decided who was a member of our Nation. We have our own ways to identify members and how to incorporate multiple heritages. With Diné, it's through the mother and the clan system. How do you think our ancestors dealt with marrying people from different Nations? Because Diné were marrying other Nations long before Plymouth Rock. We didn't call each other fractions.

"Blood quantum is an outdated product of the US government. It's how the United States defines us and shouldn't be how we define ourselves. If we were to solely use blood quantum for identifying ourselves, then yes, the blood will dry out. There will be no more full-blooded Diné people. That's what they want. Because when we can no longer fulfill the blood quantum requirement, that means we are no longer Diné, and the treaty contracts, like Naaltsoos Sání, that the United States made with our ancestors will be voided. And our resources, like water, like uranium, like coal, become available for extraction. We as sovereign Nations have the power and ability to identify our own tribal members through means other than blood quantum. And, Eddie, I don't *ever* want to hear you call yourself half this or half that. That's colonization nonsense!"

Nathan said, "Sorry for calling you half Diné."

Edward hadn't realized that by using fractions to identify himself he was making himself smaller. By using the word "half" to quantify his identity, he was accepting that he wasn't whole and that he'd never be as Diné as Nathan or as Anglo as Andrew. He was never going to be a complete person by dividing his identity into fractions. "What should I call myself, then?"

"I feel 'multi-heritage' is far better than fractions," Janet said.

Edward loved the movements of his mouth when he said,

"Multi-heritage." He averted his eyes when he saw Janet smiling at him through the rearview mirror. Then another thought popped up in his mind. "If we get through this, can we go to Hwééldi?"

"*When* we get through this," Ted corrected him. "Yes, we'll go to Hwééldi." Even though his voice was calm and steady, Edward could hear that his dad was just as scared as he was.

A knot formed in the back of his throat, and his stomach gurgled with anxiety. This was the same feeling he felt when he was going to wrestle someone much older and stronger than he, but times a thousand. The knot closed his airways and made his head swim. Even though their parents were helping them, Edward knew that he and Nathan were going to have to face Yitoo by themselves. He hoped that, with the Obsidian Armor and the Sacred Arrows, they would be powerful enough to stop her.

"Try to get some sleep, guys," Janet said. "Including you, Ted."

Edward didn't protest and welcomed the rest. He climbed to the very back of the SUV, shifted and contorted his body, and finally closed his eyes after a long, hard day. He did his best to silence the fear inside him that whispered, "You won't be strong enough," but couldn't mute it.

Naadiin Dóó Bi'ąą T'ááłá'í
TWENTY-ONE

NATHAN WOKE UP WITH A crick in his neck. He had had to adjust his body in a strange configuration to be able to sleep across the seats. He reached up to massage the stiff muscles, but Dew's warm, sleeping body prevented him. He let his hand rest on her tummy and felt it rise and fall as she breathed. She stirred and stretched her limbs outward, spreading apart her toes, causing Nathan to move his neck into another uncomfortable angle.

Cautious to not awaken Dew, he sat up and looked out the window. He vaguely remembered that Ted had pulled the SUV into a wide empty parking lot last night. The area around them reminded Nathan of the Chuska Mountains, where Nali pumped her water. Tall pine trees with dark red bark reached toward the clear baby-blue sky. A rust orange bed of dried pine needles blanketed the ground. Clusters of gray oak trees with bright green leaves swayed in the cool air. Far in the distance, the bare crown of Tsoodził loomed above the forest canopy.

He quickly grabbed his phone and figured out that it was eight thirty in the morning, and they were at Coal Mine Campground a few miles east of Grants, New Mexico. His stomach grumbled for Nali's cooking on the firepit. Fried potatoes. Spam. Corn. And her handmade tortillas.

Nathan reached over the seats to wake Edward. Not wanting to wake their parents, he poked Edward's forehead and whispered, "Edward. Wake up."

"Huh?" Edward blinked himself awake. Instead of grumpily ignoring Nathan, a flash of fear crossed his face momentarily. He exhaled loudly and calmed himself.

Nathan then petted Dew from her snout to the end of her tail. She yawned; her thin tongue extended outward. She then smacked her lips like she was eating lemon sorbet, her favorite. He whispered, "Dew, we gotta get going. We need to get to the top of Tsoodził when the sun is at the highest point in the sky. Otherwise, we'll have to wait a whole other day."

"And that's something that we can't spare," Edward said. He was hunched over his smartphone. "Yitoo's started singing." He handed his phone to Nathan.

On the screen was an article that showed there was an unusual weather phenomenon occurring in the middle of the Pacific Ocean. A large area of low pressure had appeared and was growing strong. The strangeness of this pocket of moisture rising into the air was that it wasn't moving westward. It was stationary despite the rotation of the earth. And even odder, it was two hundred miles above the equator, where hurricanes almost never formed.

Nathan nodded. "Let's go. Be quiet."

Edward noticed their sleeping parents and mouthed an okay, then quietly climbed to the middle row. Nathan's heart beat loudly and sharply, like the ticking of a clock, when Edward reached for his dad's phone to unlock the SUV without setting off the alarm. Nathan whispered under Ted's barely audible snoring, "Careful."

Edward's arm extended to the dashboard where Ted's phone rested. The tips of his fingers tapped the bottom, and the phone tilted and swayed. Suddenly, the phone slipped right off the dashboard. Quickly, Edward snatched the phone before it could fall beyond his reach. Then, after Edward entered his dad's passcode, he disabled the alarm and unlocked the SUV.

Nathan, Dew, and Edward snuck out of the vehicle. The last one out, Nathan closed the door like he was laying a sleeping toddler to rest.

Dew scanned the landscape, while Nathan and Edward adjusted the straps on their backpacks. She said, "I can get us to the top of Tsoodził from here."

"Wait, sprinkle some tádídíín," Nathan said, pulling his own corn-pollen pouch out of his backpack.

Edward pinched some of the fine bright yellow powder in between his thumb and middle finger and then handed the pouch to Nathan. Edward sprinkled the fine golden pollen onto the ground before them. Ted had said that only medicine folk were allowed to set foot on the mountains to gather sacred medicine and sands. The medicine folk had to sing ceremonial songs the entire time they were on the mountain to protect themselves and as a gesture of respect. Nathan and Edward quickly asked permission to ascend Tsoodził's sacred spine.

Dew sniffed the ground. "This area has a lot of water. I think I can sing some up so I can absorb it. Then I'll be able to carry both of you on my back. Close your ears, Edward."

Edward had already plugged his ears before Dew had asked.

She sang another song that Nathan had never heard before. After three seconds, water appeared beneath Dew's feet, like she was standing on a sponge. The pristine water disappeared beneath her scales, and her size increased. When she was large enough to carry both Nathan and Edward, she stopped singing and lowered herself to the ground.

Edward took the earplugs out and climbed onto her shoulders. Nathan sat in front of Edward. A rope of water wrapped around their waists and solidified, securing them onto her spine. Dew then zoomed through the forest of pine and oak toward the top of Tsoodził. The wind rushed past them, stinging his cheeks. Edward leaned into Nathan's back. A brotherly desire to protect Edward stirred within Nathan. He had felt this way earlier when he called Edward his younger brother at Meteor Crater. He shook that fresh memory out of his head. He had to get himself ready to talk with Father Sun.

Dew sprinted the entire way to the top of Tsoodził. Edward dug the side of his face in between Nathan's shoulders the entire time. He hated to admit it, but he felt safer with Nathan in front of him.

"Edward?" Nathan shouted to Edward. "Do you remember what the Guardian of Tsoodził was?"

"Guardian," Dew asked. "What is that?"

"Not long after the First Beings emerged from the Third World," Nathan explained, "First Man placed mounds of sands he had collected from the First Worlds. Those sands rose and rose and became the Four Sacred Mountains. At the top of the mountains is a post that holds the sky in place. First Man then placed Guardians at each mountain to protect them and the posts that prevent the sky from falling."

Edward tried to recall what his nálí 'adzą́ą́ had told him. "The Guardians are Bear, Mountain Lion, and Porcupine, and, depending on who you ask, either Bull Snake or Wolf."

Nathan said, "My nálí told me Bull Snake protects Dook'o'oosłííd."

Edward said, "Porcupine is north, Dibé Nitsaa', because its quills are often black."

Dew slowed her speed when they neared the top of Tsoodził. "So, the Guardian of Tsoodził is either a bear or a mountain lion."

If Edward had to choose between either, he would've asked if there was a third option that involved a ladybug. Edward scanned the forest around them. It blurred and stretched into smears of dark green from Dew's speed. The Guardian, bear or massive murder cat, could be anywhere. Dew ran through a clearing that offered an expansive view.

To their left, there was a well-worn hiking trail that snaked its way up the northern side of Tsoodził. Faded aluminum cans glimmered, and shards of broken glass sparkled in the light of the mid-morning sun. Even this far away from the trail, Dew ran over empty chip bags and other light plastic rubbish that must have floated in the winds. Edward couldn't believe it. Tsoodził was a sacred mountain, and yet it was being treated with disrespect. This was unacceptable.

To their right, Edward spotted the dark red trail of lava rocks that ran for many miles south through El Malpais. The lava rocks formed a narrow trail toward the base of a nearby mountain, which widened the farther south it traveled. His nálí 'adzą́ą́ said that these petrified lava flows were actually the blood from Yé'íítsoh, Human-Eater, that the Hero Twins killed. When Yé'íítsoh was struck in the neck by an arrow, his blood poured out of him and was going to make a path that traveled to all sacred mountains. If the blood had created a circle, connecting the Four Sacred Mountains, then Yé'íítsoh would be reborn. Thankfully, Born for Water confronted Yé'íítsoh's spirit and was able to overcome it. Then the blood flow stopped and hardened into the dark lava rocks he was looking at.

The air grew cooler the higher they ascended. Edward nervously looked to his left, to his right, behind them. No bears. No mountain lions. He reasoned that a bear would be the one he would want to face, if necessary. While a bear would be massively powerful, he, Nathan, and Dew could run away from one. A mountain lion, on the other hand, would be able to chase them at high speed and climb trees much faster than a bear would.

Dew would be able to use water to defend them, but that would mean Edward was once again unable to help. He couldn't wait to wear the Obsidian Armor and finally be a part of the defense. Would the three of them, even with armor and arrows, be able to subdue Yitoo? He repeated in his mind that they could and would. They didn't have the option of losing to Yitoo another time.

Suddenly, a cluster of oak trees violently shook. Green leaves fell to the earth, and several bluebirds flitted away. Dew halted. Edward arched his spine to help pull Nathan back so that they wouldn't be launched forward. After Dew came to a complete stop, the three of them froze with anticipation. This was it. The Guardian of the Mountain was nearby.

"What do we do?" Edward asked.

"We should try talking to the Guardian," Nathan said.

Edward thought that was a terrible idea! A guardian guards. The very word itself suggested attacking and defending. "You always want to talk first! I say, freeze first, talk later."

Nathan said, "This is a Holy Being we are talking about. We still need to respect it." Without waiting for Edward's response, Nathan dismounted. Edward quickly followed his lead. The three of them approached the dense cluster of oak trees. Abundant leaves hid the Guardian from their view. But a lone tree in the middle of the cluster shivered.

Nathan called to it, "Hello, Guardian of Tsoodził, Southern Sacred Mountain."

No response.

Something felt off to Edward. Of all the Holy Beings he had met so far, none of them felt the need to hide themselves in this manner. Edward's mind raced through different scenarios. None of them included the possibility that the Guardian was shy and nervous.

Nathan and Dew carefully approached the stand of oak trees. The lone moving tree stopped.

Nathan pressed forward and said, "We are here to talk with Father Sun and would like your permission very much."

Goose bumps appeared on the back of Edward's neck down to his shoulder blades. They felt like the tip of a knife sliding down his skin. Something with bloodlust was watching them. Edward couldn't stop his knees from shaking. He whispered, "We're being hunted."

"What?" Nathan turned to face him.

Before Nathan could fully turn, Edward said, "Don't! Act normal." Two things Edward knew for certain: the Guardian was hunting them. And if they acted surprised or different from before, it would attack. "Pretend I didn't say anything. Or else it'll pounce on us."

Edward fully meant to say "pounce." Because bears didn't hide from their prey. Felines did. Which also meant that this Holy Being wasn't giving them the option of talking first. He needed to find a way to turn around without arousing suspicion from the Guardian. He whispered, "Nathan, keep asking for permission. Dew, get your water ready to defend or attack."

He hoped the Holy Being didn't smell fear because Edward was nothing but scared for all their lives.

Nathan continued. "Oh, great Guardian of Turquoise Mountain, please allow us to talk with Father Sun."

"Let me call your mom and my dad," Edward said loudly. He pulled his phone out of his pocket. He unlocked it and called his dad. It didn't matter that there were no cell phone bars. He needed a reason to search around them. Holding the phone, he turned around and rapidly tried to pinpoint something out of place. Nothing directly behind them. He turned slightly, facing the lava rocks. There was a clear meadow on the south face of Tsoodził. Nothing. As soon as Edward turned around to face the hiking trail, he gasped and dropped the phone.

"Everything all right, Edward?" Nathan asked.

Edward bent over and let Dew's body block his reaction. He had seen a pair of tractor-yellow eyes reflecting in the sun. It wasn't easy to gauge the size of the Guardian. But Edward guessed the length of a school bus and just as tall as one with its belly on the ground. The moment their eyes made contact; Edward felt its immense desire to eviscerate its prey. And he was on the menu.

"I'm fine," Edward lied loudly. He grabbed the phone and held it to his face. He didn't dare look in that direction again. He stood up and spoke into the phone, facing the meadow.

Edward explained, "It's in the shade of the pine trees toward the trail. It's going to kill us if we don't attack first."

"Close your ears, Edward," Nathan commanded.

"What? I can't hear you?" Edward pretended. Then he pressed the phone fully against his chin, almost to the point of cracking his screen. With his other hand he plugged his ear. "Now!"

In the silence, Edward yelled in horror as in seconds a mountain lion with velvet fur, the color of sunflower petals, had already snuck up on them. It leaped into the air and landed in front of them with an earthquaking thud. Edward lost his footing from the ground shaking beneath him. What great help he was. Its tree-thick tail slammed into Nathan's chest, sending him flying yards away from them.

The Guardian lifted a paw and slapped Dew across her jaw. Dew dizzily walked forward and then was pinned under the Guardian's other paw.

"Leave her alone!" Nathan shouted.

"Dew!" Edward cried, reaching toward her.

Then the most horrifying thing happened. The Guardian bit down into the back of Dew's neck. Dew squealed a blood-curdling wail that made Edward nauseous. Dew's body went completely silent and limp.

Naadiin Dóó Bi'ąą Naaki
TWENTY-TWO

"WHAT DID YOU DO TO her?" Edward screamed, running toward the Guardian.

"Dew!" Nathan shouted through coughing fits, still recovering from the tail slam to his chest.

The Guardian's yellow eyes darkened, and his lips curled backward, revealing fangs that were as long as Edward's forearm. The deadly teeth held Dew's lifeless body in the air, and her face was frozen in an expression of anger. That's when Edward noticed that Dew was blinking. She was alive!

The Guardian spoke with a deep male voice and a hiss that sounded like a gas leak. "This water monster is yet alive. Like my infants, there is a nerve that runs parallel to their spines, and when bitten, they will go completely limp. She will remain in my mouth until Father Sun decides what to do with you both."

"Close your ears, Edward!" Nathan shoved his hand into his

backpack and pulled out a bottle of water.

"Dew's alive!" Edward shouted.

"What?" Nathan asked. A few tears gleamed on his cheeks in the late-morning sun.

The Guardian asked, "Why do you wish to meet with Father Sun?"

Edward stood as tall as he could, but he still had to tilt his head upward to make eye contact with the Guardian. "We are Father Sun's grandchildren. We are Diné. And we have to ask to borrow his Obsidian Armor and Four Sacred Arrows to save the people of Phoenix."

Nathan was holding, actually holding, the water that was in the bottle in his hand. The water warped and formed a glove over his fingers and the thumb that wore his black-and-blue communication ring. The few tears that emerged from the corner of his eyes flowed into his water glove. He must really want to attack the Guardian.

The Guardian said, "You did not sing the required songs nor recite the proper prayers." His brows scrunched angrily.

"Forgive us, we don't know them, great Guardian," Edward explained. "But we did offer corn pollen at the base of your mountain."

"That you did," the Guardian said. "It's a shame how much of the prayers and practices of the Diné are being forgotten. But as you are yet still youths, I will forgive your lack of knowledge and permit your presence on my mountain."

"Thank you," Edward said with a respectful bow. Was

bowing what he needed to do? Better safe than sorry. Especially with a murderous cat as large as a school bus.

The Guardian said, "Father Sun will arrive momentarily. If you wish to speak with him, await at the top of the summit."

"What about our friend, the water monster?" Edward asked.

The Guardian growled, "She stays with me. Father Sun has no patience for beings not related to him. You better hurry. He will be lunching soon."

"Come on, Nathan," Edward said. The water had frozen in his hand and covered his entire right arm. "Dew is safe."

With that, Edward pulled Nathan toward the top of Tsoodził. They hurried the remaining distance to the peak. At the top, Edward could just barely make out the very faint outline of the Sandia mountain range. At whose base lay Albuquerque, New Mexico, another one of the cities that was taking water away from Diné Bikéyah.

Nathan, out of breath, finally made it to his side. Above them, the sun shone in a vast light blue sky, devoid of any moisture and cover. Down below him, Edward's shadow was pointing directly north.

Just then, in front of them, a large pole shimmered into existence. It was decorated with feathers and sacred stones in intricate geometrical designs. The ancient pole extended into the sky and the tip of it was far beyond their vision. This was one of the poles that held up the sky!

Edward was even more breathless than before, when a large fancy moccasin, with deep red buckskin that glowed like red embers and soles as white as rainbow opal, emerged out of thin air several feet above them. The foot stepped onto the mountain. A muscular leg followed the moccasin, and another leg and foot appeared from nothing. An ageless man, four times their height, stood before them. He wore pieces of the sky at different times of the day: a waist cloth made of the starry night sky covered his legs, a blanket of peach sunrise wrapped around his shoulders, a glowing strip of the baby-blue midday sky pulled his thick black hair into a tsiiyééł. Everything about him glowed softly. Around his neck, he wore a necklace of massive turquoise nuggets that were as big as Edward's head. Not that Edward had a big head or anything.

Father Sun sat down and crossed his legs. He looked at Edward, then at Nathan. After a tense few seconds, he sighed and said, "Pity that I won't be having a quiet lunch." His large arm reached into his sunrise blanket and pulled out a corn husk bundle that he placed onto the mountain. He unwrapped it, and inside was a thick grayish-blue goo that smelled like delicious sweet corn. Father Sun brought the bundle to his lips and slurped the contents. Almost as if he was ignoring Edward, he curtly asked Nathan, "What do you want?"

"We seek help! A water monster aims to harm a great many Diné," Nathan said. "May we borrow the Obsidian Armor and the Sacred Arrows your sons, the Hero Twins, once used?"

Father Sun slurped down more of his lunch. He smacked his lips and said, "Why would a water monster combat the Diné? Did you upset her?"

Edward said, "It's complicated. It would take too long to explain."

Father Sun chuckled. "I have all day! I am aware of the water monster you warmly call Yitoo. As I travel across the sky, I watch what happens upon the Fourth World. I've seen everything that has happened. I even saw you and this young one walking up Tsoodził. Very good of you to sprinkle pollen before placing your feet on Tsoodził. The Guardian otherwise would have seen to your deaths in such a way that would have seemed accidental. Back to the topic at hand: I didn't want an explanation of what's going on. I wanted to know if you were truthful. And your non-answer was evasive. Not a good first impression."

"Keep quiet!" Nathan whispered to Edward. Then, to Father Sun, Nathan explained, "We showed Yitoo Bi'aanii where her waters were being diverted to. That has angered her greatly."

Father Sun pulled out from the inside folds of his dawn blanket a clay cup. He tapped the bottom of it on the peak of Tsoodził, and it filled with water. After a sip, he said, "You don't think it's reasonable for her to do what she wants with her waters? She wants to protect her waters from those who would misuse their life-giving moisture."

"It's reasonable, yes," Nathan said slowly, to buy himself some time to think of what to say next.

Father Sun tapped the cup again, and like before it filled with water that he sipped.

Nathan continued. "Yes, taking her waters back forces all desert cities to adjust their water consumption, but she wants to intentionally harm people. She cannot be allowed to destroy the cities!"

"Let her," Father Sun said. He finished the last of his lunch and licked the tips of his fingers.

"What?" both Edward and Nathan shouted.

"Cities are unnatural," Father Sun said. "They also exist outside the boundaries of the Four Sacred Mountains. I couldn't care less what became of them. To be honest, if it were me, I would not stop at destroying just the cities of the desert. Why not wipe the entirety of humanity off Mother Earth? I am weary of the five-fingered beings altogether. Both their selfishness and pride are offensive."

Edward said, "But you are the father of five-fingered beings. You're supposed to take care of us."

Father Sun said, "I am obligated. All five-fingered, Diné and non-Diné, are guilty of the mess they are creating and will soon have to deal with. This Fourth World is beyond saving." Father Sun stood up, patting his knees from the rusty dust of Tsoodził.

"Please, Father Sun," Edward pleaded. "We need help."

Father Sun reached up into the air. His fingertips pulled at a piece of the sky. The sky moved and folded like fabric. Behind the sky was a bright mist, both cloudy and ethereal. His hand disappeared into it. "I do not have to be bothered by modern Diné. Long has the blood thinned by intermixing. Such as this one here."

Father Sun looked at Edward. And the face that he had, it was like he was looking at a disgusting bug. No one, Holy Being or otherwise, had the right to look at Edward like that.

Nathan said, "He's Diné. Whether you like it or not."

Edward could have said that himself. But he was glad Nathan did. Even though it was still odd to think of him as a brother, it was becoming easier every time Nathan protected him.

Father Sun smirked. "I assure you I don't."

Edward hated needing Father Sun's help. But the truth was, they did. He let Father Sun's attitude toward him run off like water on metal. Edward recalled that when the Hero Twins asked for help, they were met with the same resistance from Father Sun and had to pass several trials. But among them, Father Sun favored Tsidił, the Stick Game. Edward spoke up. "We'll play you for them. The Stick Game."

Father Sun seemed interested. "Now, there's a suggestion I like!"

Edward recalled his dad telling him the rules. There were twelve flat sticks. One side was painted white and the other black. The sticks were tossed to the ground. Whoever's color was more numerous won. "Three out of five. We win, then you lend us the Obsidian Armor and your Sacred Arrows."

Father Sun sat down and said, "And if I win, you two will never bother me again."

Edward quickly checked in with Nathan, who nodded at him. "Deal."

Father Sun reached into his sunrise blanket and pulled out twelve sticks the height of Nathan. Though to call them sticks would be inaccurate because the white side was made of milky quartz and the black side sparkled like coal.

Father Sun said, "Since these are my tools, I get to choose the color. White."

"Then we are black," Nathan confirmed.

Edward and Nathan stood side by side facing the towering Father Sun. The fate of the Fourth World rested on the two of them winning this bet. Edward gulped.

Father Sun held the sticks in his palms and rolled them. Their white and black sides spun as he rubbed his hands. "Four, three, two, one." He held out his large arms and opened his hands.

The twelve sticks bounced off Tsoodził. Edward watched closely as they spun and twirled in the air. The sticks clinked like bones as they tapped one another. It took only a few seconds for the sticks to stop moving. Edward counted and felt his heart rise to his throat. They had won the first round: eight black sides up!

"Well, well! Beginner's luck." Father Sun laughed. He gathered the sticks and mixed them up as he did before. Another toss.

Edward counted twice to make sure. But they had lost this round, with only three black sides up.

"Tied," Nathan said.

The third round, Father Sun began to sing a song that made fun of Nathan and Edward's efforts to stop Yitoo. Edward wondered if Father Sun even cared if he won or not. The sticks stopped.

Before Edward finished counting, Nathan said, "Seven black!"

They just needed to win one more round! They could beat Father Sun at his own game! Though Father Sun didn't seem bothered or anxious. Was this indifference or confidence? A seed of distrust sprouted in Edward's heart. There was something off about this game.

Father Sun won the fourth round, with ten white sides, which meant that they were tied again. And this final toss was going to determine everything. Edward watched Father Sun closely. He noticed a subtle smirk at the corner of his mouth. They weren't going to win. Edward knew a cheater when he saw one.

Father Sun continued his song describing how Edward and Nathan were losers and tossed the sticks into the air. They jumbled downward, knocking against one another, clicking all the while. Nathan coughed in surprise when the sticks stopped. Edward stared at Father Sun the entire time and watched the smirk grow into a full-blown mocking smile, like a puncture in an apple will grow mold that spreads.

All the sticks were white. They had lost.

Father Sun gathered his sticks and stood up, dusting himself off. "That was entertaining. Now, leave me alone."

Nathan yelled at Father Sun, who was reaching into the sky, "No, please!"

Father Sun laughed. "Enjoy the mess that you five-fingereds have created." Father Sun's hand pushed against an invisible surface. Ripples extended outward from his palm. His fingers scrunched, and a portion of the sky rolled together like a blanket. Father Sun pulled the sky open and lifted himself off Tsoodził.

In seconds, he disappeared; his mocking laughter hushed.

The two of them stood, dumbfounded at what had just happened. Would any Holy Beings help them at all? Edward wondered. Yitoo was already in the Pacific Ocean, summoning a hurricane. They had absolutely needed this plan to work.

Nathan said, "I don't know what to do." He slumped down and hugged his knees.

Edward rubbed Nathan's neck. "Don't be sad, Nathan. Be angry. Father Sun cheated us."

"What?" Nathan said.

Edward explained, "Do you think it odd that he chose the winning color? Also, I was watching his face. He knew he was going to win."

Nathan stood up. "How sure are you about this?"

Edward answered, "I don't have proof other than my gut feeling. But I'd say ninety-five percent." Edward examined where Father Sun had disappeared. There was still bright yellow ethereal mist pouring out and dissipating, like flower pollen blown into the clear blue sky. "There." Edward pointed. "Let's follow him."

Nathan took notice of the opening left behind by Father Sun. "We'd be going into the Celestial Realm. To steal—"

"Not steal. Borrow," Edward clarified. "We'll return everything after we deal with Yitoo. Serves Father Sun right for cheating."

"Okay," Nathan said apprehensively.

Edward plugged up his ears and asked, "Can you make a

ladder out of ice or something to reach the opening?"

Nathan smiled and his mouth moved. The water from his arm rose upward like a snake. The top of it attached to the hole in the sky. Nathan wrapped his arms around Edward, and both ascended toward the Celestial Realm, home of the sky Holy Beings.

Naadiin Dóó Bi'ąą Táá'
TWENTY-THREE

EDWARD STOOD UP ONCE HIS entire body was inside. He and Nathan were on top of the clouds. He looked down and saw the face of Mother Earth. This far up, everything looked like one big blur of colors and shadows. He was able to see the veins of dry riverbeds spreading like spiderwebs across Diné Bikéyah. All of them connected with Yitoo's river. He looked ahead and saw the curvature of the atmosphere. Up above were the stars. Nathan stared at the stars as well, his eyes locking onto the Milky Way galaxy.

"It's so pretty up here," Nathan breathed.

The constellations hung far above them like magnificent chandeliers. Some sources of light, however, were on the same plane upon which they stood. Edward squinted. He could just make out the blurry details of hogans that shimmered like silver stars. There were thousands of them across the distant horizon.

Edward said, "Those must be the houses of the Celestial Holy Beings. Which house do you think belongs to Father Sun? I guess the biggest one."

"Those glowing things are hogans?" Nathan asked, scanning the distance through his glasses. "Hold on. Is that—"

Edward looked eastward and saw a stunning lady wrapped in a robe of night sky, much like Father Sun had worn the daylight sky. Her skin shone with a silver light and was splotchy like the surface of the moon.

"Moon Lady!" Nathan said. He ran toward her.

"Nathan, wait!" Edward said. He reached for Nathan, unsure if stepping outside their square of cloud would mean that they would fall to the surface of Mother Earth. But Nathan kept running. Underneath his footsteps, an invisible surface rippled like water. Nathan waved his arms and Moon Lady saw him.

Edward inched forward, apprehensive about the invisible surface they were on. He was reminded of the Skywalk attraction in the Grand Canyon, where one could walk over the maw of the canyon and onto a thick sheet of glass. It terrified him then as it did now. He slid his foot forward to make sure he could press down without falling. Slowly he made his way to Nathan and Moon Lady, who were hugging each other.

"My brother will not help you," Edward heard Moon Lady say to Nathan. "He's at the middle of his life and is reevaluating his commitments. He believes that the Diné have thinned their blood by intermarrying with other Nations too much to be his grandchildren. He's eager to abandon his duties so he can spend more time with his own family."

That's right, Edward thought. Father Sun had a family up here. In the story of the Hero Twins, Father Sun had come down to Mother Earth and gifted Changing Woman with a pregnancy. Much time after that, the Hero Twins had come here to talk to Father Sun and encountered Father Sun's actual family, including his wife. Edward wondered how Father Sun's wife would welcome them, if at all. They weren't her descendants. "But we have to get the Sacred Arrows," Edward said, still slowly sliding his way toward the two of them.

"Hello, my grandson." Moon Lady pulled Edward into a warm hug. Edward appreciated that she fully accepted Edward as her grandson in a way that Father Sun didn't. "Do you intend to slay this Yitoo?" She looked at Edward, her eyes cooling his very skin. "Try not to be so rushed. Killing a Holy Being will have major consequences, some of which will not manifest until generations after."

"Thank you, Moon Lady, for your advice," Nathan said. "But we just want to stop Yitoo."

Edward desperately hoped they could accomplish that. "We don't want to kill anything."

She pointed toward one of the glowing hogans with her lips. Edward had no idea what she did, but the hogan she pointed to brightened just enough so that he and Nathan could identify it. Moon Lady said, "Brave youths. You are more powerful and influential than you know. I trust that you both will find a satisfactory conclusion. And, Nathan," she sang sweetly, "you still owe me a favor." She winked at him. The invisible floor below her twilight-blue moccasins rippled. She sang a night chant about how Coyote interrupted Changing Woman when she was placing the stars in the cosmos and walked away from them.

"Thank you so much, Moon Lady!" Nathan called.

"Yes, thank you!" Edward shouted. Finally, a helpful Holy Being!

Nathan took off running toward the glowing hogan. Edward held his breath, didn't dare to look down, and forced himself to move forward. And for the most part, his fear was soothed. If he held his chin high and didn't glance below and absorb the massive distance between himself and the surface of Mother Earth, he could do this.

Nathan suddenly stopped running and pointed downward. "Edward. Look."

"No, I'm good," Edward pushed out of his throat. Looking down was the last thing he wanted to do.

"Oh, yes! You're scared of heights," Nathan said. "I think you really should, though."

"I said I'm good," Edward lied. He looked at the tail end of the Scorpius star formation. His mind, desperate for a distraction, pushed forward a memory of his paternal grandpa telling him the Diné name. "Gah Hahat'ee, Rabbit Tracks."

Nathan said, "It's cool, Edward. We're all scared of something. I used to have this huge fear of spiders."

Edward asked, "What are you wanting me to look at?"

"I can see Yitoo in the Pacific Ocean," Nathan said.

"What?" Edward couldn't understand how Nathan could see from this distance. His eyes looked down toward the surface of the earth. His heart rate shot up, and his ears rang. A circular portion of the floor had become like a large magnifying glass. The range of the Santa Monica Mountains in California became clear. The tall skyscrapers and streets of Los Angeles and San Diego became visible. Still, the floor adjusted and moved westward, where a range of clouds, more massive than the entirety of the mountains in California, was accumulating and churning. In the middle of the clouds was a calm area, the eye of the hurricane. In the middle, Yitoo sat on the calm waters, singing.

Nathan offered, "Do you want to hold my hand? You can close your eyes, and I'll guide us to the hogan."

"Please," Edward feebly said. Watching the floor display of Yitoo conjured every ounce of nausea and dizziness that his body could produce. Even though the invisible surface pushed against the bottom of his feet, he felt like he was falling. He squeezed Nathan's hand and shut his eyes. Not seeing where he was going was so much less scary.

Nathan jogged. He could understand Edward's fear of heights. Nathan pulled Edward toward the hogan that shone in the distance with the same colors of the noon sunlight. As they got closer, Nathan noticed that the walls of the hogan were made from glowing clouds. The top was covered with tiny grains of sand that were as yellow and bright as corn pollen. Surrounding the base of the hogan was a carpet of light gray clouds. A cloth, shining like the cluster of stars above them, covered its entrance.

"Okay, Edward, you can look now," Nathan said when they reached the front of the hogan. It was enormous, easily the size of the Grady Gammage Memorial Auditorium at ASU.

"So, we just go inside?" Edward asked, and reached for the starlight blanket.

Nathan grabbed Edward before his outstretched hand touched the cloth. "Don't. You'll burst into flames if you touch it."

Edward asked, "Do you think if we wait long enough . . . ?"

A loud, unfamiliar voice from behind startled them. "Who are you?"

They both jumped and turned around. Edward immediately plugged his ears, waiting for Nathan to do something with the water on his arm. In front of them was a tall child, probably eight years old, from the roundness of his cheeks and the stubby length of his legs and arms. But he was twice their height!

"I'm," Nathan coughed out, "I'm Nathan, and this is Edward." Nathan wasn't sure if he should call Edward his younger brother in this moment, because earlier when he did at Meteor Crater, Edward acted awkward. Maybe Edward didn't view Nathan like that.

"Are you my dad's other children?" Tall Boy asked.

"Yes, we are his descendants from Changing Woman," Edward explained.

"Oh. Her." Tall Boy sighed. "My mom doesn't like her."

Nathan felt that was reasonable. Tall Boy's mom was Father Sun's wife. He could only imagine the anger she must have felt when she discovered that her husband had had children with another woman. But did that make this tall boy before them their half brother?

"I think that makes us brothers," Nathan said slyly. Perhaps there was a way he could convince this young boy to help them gather the items.

"Yes! It does!" Tall Boy shouted. "I love meeting family members!"

"Quiet out there!" a loud female voice shouted from inside the hogan.

Tall Boy said, "I'm sorry, Mom, I'm just talking with my new brothers!" He pulled the starlight curtains aside and pushed the two of them inside the hogan.

Edward and Nathan stumbled forward. As he stood up, Nathan stared into the angry eyes of Father Sun's wife. Her arms were crossed over her chest. She wore a dazzling rug dress that glittered like precious gems. Her shimmering black hair that looked like corn silk was pulled back into a loose ponytail. She was standing above a large clay pot in which she cooked a stew with enormous vegetables.

"More of Changing Woman's grandchildren." She pouted and stirred the stew.

"We're sorry for intruding," Nathan began.

"You *are* intruding. I don't want anything to do with *her* descendants," Tall Lady said. "So, be on your way and leave my family alone."

"But, Mom, they are my brothers," Tall Boy said.

"You have siblings, my heart," Tall Lady said. "They'll be

back any moment, and you can play with them. Look at these two. If you play with them, you'll smush them into paste."

"Please don't play with us," Edward pleaded.

"But, Mom!" Tall Boy said.

"Young man, if you persist with this attitude, you will not have dinner tonight," she said.

Tall Boy pouted and left the hogan. In the commotion of his exit, Nathan saw the Obsidian Armor and a quiver that held the Four Sacred Arrows resting on a shelf at the very top of the cloud walls behind the angry Tall Lady. They were so close!

Nathan explained, "Ma'am, I hate to bother you further, but we would like to borrow Father Sun's armor and arrows to deal with a new threat in the Fourth World."

"Not my problem. See yourselves out of my home," she said, and pointed with her lips toward the starlight cloth.

"Um, we can't touch the blanket," Nathan sheepishly explained.

"Nothing but a nuisance. Mosquitoes are better company than the two of you!" she said. She stopped stirring and made her way to the front door.

Nathan didn't want to think of the size of the mosquitoes in this realm.

Suddenly, to his side, Edward spoke up. "Ma'am, I know you don't like that we are descendants of Changing Woman, and I apologize for what Father Sun did to you. And it must have hurt you a lot."

She halted. "What's it to you how I feel?"

"Because it was a really crummy thing to do," Edward said.

"Yes, it was," she said. "I have waited eras, countless years, for him to apologize to me. When he did, it was so insincere. Then the Hero Twins showed up and took his tools away from my husband. I'll admit that I experienced a little joy seeing how it angered my husband. I wouldn't mind the opportunity to inconvenience my husband once more."

Nathan worried about what direction Edward would take this conversation. From the looks of it, he could suggest that Tall Lady betray Father Sun to experience that little joy again. So, he said before Edward could seize upon that opportunity, "I don't think you should give us the Obsidian Armor just to anger Father Sun."

Tall Lady said, "You do realize you are arguing against my handing you the items you journeyed here for."

"Yeah, Nathan," Edward snapped, and jabbed his arm.

Nathan said, "I do. But I see that the decisions, choices, and actions we take and do with the Holy Beings have consequences that will last much longer than I will be alive." More than that, he was familiar with two arguing adults. "When my parents first divorced, they did small things to annoy each other. And even though the actions were small, their intention was to harm each other, and that's big. Somewhere along the way, they realized that angering each other wasn't doing either of them any good. The pain of the other didn't make either of them happy. It was just pain. They both had to talk through their feelings and are now able to respect each other. I want that for you and Father Sun."

"Me too, I guess," Edward said. "But he still cheated us!"

"What did you say?" Tall Lady asked.

Edward said, "We played the Stick Game with him, and I'm certain he cheated."

"Did he use his own sticks?" Tall Lady asked.

"Yes," both Nathan and Edward said.

"Did he choose white?"

They nodded.

Tall Lady asked, "Did the final round result in all white?"

Edward shouted, "See! I told you, Nathan! Father Sun cheated us!"

"That man is going to teach our son that cheating is okay," Tall Lady said, shaking her head. "Tell you what. I'll give you permission to use his armor and arrows. Return them when you are both done. Don't worry; my intention isn't solely to anger him. It's to punish him for not playing fair and setting a bad example for our son. And if he doesn't like it, then he can find another place to sleep. You are his descendants, and he needs to uphold his responsibilities toward you."

Nathan felt his heart fill with joy. They had done it!

Tall Lady turned toward the shelf. She reached up and grabbed the armor and quiver. An odd thing happened. Both the Obsidian Armor and quiver holding the Sacred Arrows grew! The Obsidian Armor now looked like it could easily fit Tall

Lady. How was Edward going to wear it?

Tall Lady bent over and extended the items to them. When Edward reached for the Obsidian Armor, it shrank to a size that Edward could wear. Edward gleefully put on the shirt-shaped armor. Once he popped his head out of the opening, the armor spread across his body like iridescent ink. It covered his arms, fingers, legs, knees, shoes, and the base of his skull. Even in between his toes, which felt weird and tickly.

Nathan reached for the quiver, but Tall Lady said, "I don't recommend you touch the quiver." She handed it to Edward and immediately a spark of lightning zapped Edward's hands. The armor dispersed the electrical energy in waves of colors that ran across Edward's body. The quiver shrank to a size that Edward could wrap around his shoulder.

Nathan said, "I hate to be rude, but we must be on our way back to the Fourth World."

She said, "I don't mind the brevity of your visit. Thank you for treating me with respect."

"But the door," Edward said.

"The Obsidian Armor will protect you," she said to Edward. Tall Lady had turned around and was back to stirring her stew.

Edward held his breath and pulled the starlight blanket. He did not burst into a blazing ball of fire. Nathan slipped through, and the two of them waved to Tall Lady as they exited. They sprinted their way back toward the entrance to the Fourth World. Even though they were successful, Edward grew worried. Because now that they had the armor and arrows, this meant they were on a one-way path to Yitoo. The weight of the quiver on his shoulders increased. The straps rubbed against his armpits aggressively. They would have to use these deadly weapons against her. And if she didn't stop, would they have to end Yitoo?

Naadiin Dóó Bi'ąą Dį́į́'

TWENTY-FOUR

NATHAN COMMANDED THE WATER AROUND his hand to slowly lower them to the top of Tsoodził. Edward, of course, had his eyes shut and his arms squeezed Nathan's waist all twenty-four feet down. They placed their feet on the sacred mountain, and then Nathan commanded the water rope to unlatch from the opening in the sky and to wrap around his arm. He was surprised at how easily the water responded to his thoughts. He no longer needed to hum or think of the water monster songs. It simply did what he thought. When he did hum or sing, however, his commands were much more powerful.

"Where's Dew?" Edward asked. He adjusted the shoulder straps of the quiver and positioned its wide mouth so that he could easily reach over his shoulder to grab one of the Sacred Arrows.

Nathan scanned the slopes and quickly spotted a cluster of

shaking pine trees. "There."

The two of them sprinted toward the commotion. Nathan readied the water around his arm to fight the Guardian. Just before his legs were ready to quit, Nathan spotted Dew sprinting through the forest. Not far behind her, the Guardian swiped his mighty paws at her scaly tail, missing by inches. Dew launched herself forward with a jet stream, narrowly avoided the powerful swipe of his paw. Dew hopped from tree to tree, to redirect her momentum and to confuse the Guardian.

"Dew!" Edward shouted.

Nathan stopped to catch his breath.

Dew heard Edward and looked in his direction, coming to a stop. She smiled.

"What are you doing?" Edward screamed. "Keep running!"

The Guardian pounced on her. The two of them disappeared behind a cloud of dust. Above them, trees shook violently as their bodies slammed against the trunks. Birds and squirrels darted away from the combat.

The dust quickly thinned, revealing a startling sight. The Guardian was on his back, belly up to the sun, playfully swatting at a large tentacle of water that was equally lightheartedly jabbing at him.

"Dew?" Edward asked.

Dew chimed in, "We got bored waiting for you, so Mr. Guardian was showing me how to pounce. And we kind of got carried away."

The Guardian rolled onto all fours and crouched low. His ears folded back against his head, and his pupils dilated as he faced Dew, who held the same posture. Dew reabsorbed the large tail of water, increasing her size to that of a horse, though compared to the Guardian, she was still very tiny. For a few tense seconds, they pulled their legs closer to their torsos, waiting for the other to make a move.

A nearby twig snapped as a squirrel jumped to a higher branch. Dew launched forward, and the Guardian sprinted away from her. She chased after him like an energetic puppy that had been stuck inside all day.

"I was not expecting this," Nathan said, his breathing finally back to normal. He wiped beads of sweat off his forehead.

"They're playing," Edward said, gawking.

Dew caught up with the Guardian and jumped onto his back. Dew's water took the shape of a large lizard skull, which chomped onto the back of the Guardian's neck. In response, the Guardian rolled over.

The Guardian said, through heavy huffing, "I've not had this much delight in ages."

Nathan and Edward approached the two Holy Beings, who lay on the ground. The Guardian was licking the webbing in between his toes. Dew was also cleaning her face with her long lashing tongue.

The Guardian said, licking the top of his paw and rubbing his face with it, "I find it odd that a water monster and a five-fingered, both that can sing down the rains, visit my mountain. The last being that could summon rain was the Magnanimous

Yitoo Bi'aanii. On occasion, Yitoo would visit me upon my mountain, and we sat there." The Guardian nodded to a dusty patch near the top of Tsoodził. "One winter, I saw hundreds, thousands, of Diné leaving Diné Bikéyah in multiple long lines. Yitoo took it upon herself to follow the Diné, knowing full well she would be susceptible to death outside the Sacred Boundaries. When she came back, she was ghostly and wouldn't tell me what happened to her. I heard later that she returned to the Third World to recover."

Nathan, Edward, and Dew sat silently. Nathan scanned the land below, the trail of deep red volcanic rock. In the 1860s, his ancestors were forced to walk through here, beyond the protection of Tsoodził.

The Guardian said, "I know that all three of you mean to stop Yitoo and the hurricane she is currently singing into existence. I don't know whom I wish to support. But I will side with whoever benefits my mountain. Now that you have the Sacred Arrows in your possession, do you know how to use them?"

"Kind of?" Edward said. "Spider Woman mentioned briefly how to use them."

"If you can promise me this, I will instruct you on their use," the Guardian said. He stopped grooming and held his head high.

"What's the promise?" Nathan asked.

"Be kind to Yitoo," the Guardian said. "All Holy Beings experienced the kidnapping of the Diné to varying degrees. I bore witness on my mountain to the atrocious acts. My spine is still shaking from what I saw done to the children," the Guardian said. His voice trembled, and his eyes glistened with tears.

"I want to save her," Nathan said, and he meant every word.

"The last thing we want to do is to end her," Edward said. "But yes, we *will* do our best to be kind to her."

"Thank you," the Guardian said. He stood on all freshly cleaned fours. "Let's start with the Dawn Arrow. On its own, it will shine brightly in dark areas. But if the holder thinks of a being, Enemy or otherwise, its shine will collect and point to the current location of that being. As for the Folding Darkness Arrow, a demonstration will be more fruitful. Please grab it."

"Do you mind handing me the arrow?" Nathan asked Edward.

"Won't you get hurt?" Edward asked, remembering Tall Lady's caution.

"The Lightning Arrow zaps anything indiscriminately," the Guardian explained. "If you, wearer of the armor, hand any of the other three arrows to Nathan, he will be safe."

Edward swung the quiver around. This was the first time he had taken a moment to fully investigate the sacred arrows. One fletching end was yellow, red, and orange, the colors shifting like the arrow was on fire. Another was frizzled like arm hairs standing on end, and a brief spark appeared. That was the Lightning Arrow. A third was covered in all the colors of the rainbow. And finally, there was a fletching that looked like the tail feathers of a crow. Edward pulled the Folding Darkness Arrow out of the quiver and handed it to Nathan.

"Grasp the arrowhead," the Guardian said. After Nathan did so, the Guardian continued. "Notice how the shape of the arrow will change into that of a stone knife. All the arrows do this. Once you release it, let it fly, or drop it, it will return to the quiver, and it will resume its shape of an arrow. Now Folding Darkness Knife. Grab the shadow of the nearby tree."

Did he just say to grab a shadow? A familiar voice of doubt told Nathan to ask for clarification. But Nathan trusted that the Guardian knew what he was talking about. So, holding the Folding Darkness Knife, he reached toward the shadow and grabbed it! It had the texture of ooze and mist. He pulled the shadow off the ground, amazed that he could do that now!

"Now cut it," the Guardian said.

Nathan swiped at the base of the shadow with the Folding Darkness Knife. And like a sheet, it was shorn.

"The Holy Being known as Darkness is the only one who can permanently cut off a shadow. Once you let the shadow go, it will return from where you cut it. But before you let the shadow go, Nathan, put it over yourself."

Nathan dropped the shadow over his body like a shawl.

"You disappeared!" Edward said.

Nathan took this moment to sneak around to the other side of Edward. He tapped Edward, who then screamed when Nathan reappeared.

"If you decide to let the arrow fly, it will blot out nearby sources of light, the sun, the moon, the stars, fires, electric bulbs," the Guardian explained. "Now, the Lightning Arrow. Nathan, I recommend you not handle it. Only the brother wearing the Obsidian Armor should handle it, for pressing its arrowhead anywhere will make you experience the shock of ten lightning bolts at once. Should you let it fly, it will conjure a storm of lightning. As for the Rainbow Arrow, use this one at the end of your excursion to signify your victory. Letting it fly will not only signal to the Holy Beings your victory, but also has the power to end any storm. Be sure that Yitoo Bi'aanii is fully defeated before using this arrow or else its effects will be nullified and the storm itself will not respond. Lastly, holding the Rainbow Knife will allow you to confront the spirit of a downed Enemy and exorcise it, letting it rest. I hope that you will not use the last effect of the Rainbow Arrow."

"I agree," Edward said.

Nathan smiled at Edward. He was glad that out of everyone who could be at his side confronting Yitoo in the Pacific Ocean, it would be Edward.

The Guardian said, "Be on your way. You have many miles to travel. And Yitoo Bi'aanii's hurricane grows in strength every minute."

At that, both Nathan and Edward climbed upon Dew.

Before Nathan could thank the Guardian, Edward said, "We appreciate your help, Mr. Guardian!"

Dew sprinted forward and down the mountain to meet up with Ted and Janet at the campsite.

Nathan beamed with pride for Edward. Finally, he was becoming the respectful, kind, and strong guardian that Nathan had wanted all along for Dew. Once this was over, Nathan would be comfortable fully entrusting Edward with Dew. That is, if they defeated Yitoo. A big, massive and terrifying "if."

After a heated conversation with their parents at Coal Mine Campground, Nathan had asked Janet and Ted to drive to Nali's place. To help cook an early dinner, Nali asked Nathan and Edward to chop some wood when they got there. As he swung the ax up and down, Nathan practiced his pronunciation of the more difficult words in the Change and Move songs. Edward, meanwhile, carried the pieces of wood to the fireplace. And Dew was fast asleep in the cornfield. Despite the circumstances, Nathan enjoyed this moment, being with his mom, Nali, and even both Ted and Edward.

Two years ago, Nathan had never imagined encountering a Holy Being. So much had happened since then. Pond. The Third World. Dew. Yitoo. He knew that his time with the Holy Beings would soon end. That was the way it was for Diné people. At birth, the Holy Beings watch the Diné babies. Then, after the Diné babies' first laugh, they take a step away because laughter signifies the happiness of and love for the infant. All through childhood, the Holy Beings take steps further and further away from their grandchildren. A series of long goodbyes. Even when he lost his ability to see and talk with the Holy Beings, they were still a part of his life. But he wasn't the only one they were raising.

"Nathan," Edward said, jolting Nathan out of his thoughts.

"What's up?" Nathan asked, leaning the ax against a large stump.

"Your nálí 'adząą says it's time to eat," he said. "Hey, I was thinking about this. I don't want my dad or your mom anywhere near the ocean. And we can travel quicker without them. Dew is borrowing a quartz crystal from her brother Shaded Marsh. So, we can travel by rainbow path. Did you want to leave after they fall asleep?"

Nathan had shared similar feelings. In all honesty, he wanted everyone in Phoenix to leave. But being deceitful wasn't a great idea. Had he been upfront with his mom a few days ago about their search for the Modern Enemy, she might have been able to help. "We owe it to them to tell them the truth and not sneak away."

"We'll probably be grounded," Edward said.

"I think we already are for not telling them about our search for the Modern Enemy," Nathan said. "Let's eat and then try to explain why we need to go on our own."

Dinner was quiet, tense, and filled with fear. Even Nali's steak, potatoes, and flour tortillas couldn't improve the atmosphere.

"Thank you, Louella," Janet said to Nali.

Nali smiled. "Cooking for guests is a great pleasure."

Edward's knee bounced up and down when he finished his meal. Nathan shared his desire to get moving.

"I was thinking I'd take the first driving shift," Janet said to Ted. "We can switch when we gas up in Flagstaff."

"Should we head toward Los Angeles or San Diego?" Ted asked Nathan.

"About that," Nathan said, swallowing both the juicy steak and the knot in his throat. He thought it best for now not to mention that Edward agreed with him. "You all should stay here."

"No chance," Janet said flatly.

"Ain't gonna happen," Ted responded.

"You promised to let us in on your Holy Being duties, son," Janet said.

"Ge'! 'Ashiiké dá'sinootts'ą́ą́, listen to them," Nali contributed. She folded her arms and sat upright. Her glasses reflected the pile of red embers.

Nathan explained, "We can get to Yitoo faster without you guys. Also, none of you can listen to water monster songs."

Janet said, "Do you expect us to just sit here and wait while you two boys go and fight a powerful Holy Being?"

Ted said, "What she said."

"I was thinking about that," Nathan said. "And remember in the Hero Twin stories, how one of the brothers, Enemy Slayer, would go and confront the Enemy in person while the other brother, Born for Water, prayed in a hogan?"

"That's right!" Edward jumped in. "You all can pray for us."

"Is this the best way we can help?" Nali asked. Her expression was stern and stonelike.

As calmly as he could, Nathan explained, "Unless you guys can listen to water monster songs, handle the Sacred Arrows, and travel over the Pacific Ocean, the best way for you all to support us is to stay here in the hogan." Of course, he wanted his mom by his side. He even wanted to rely upon Ted during the upcoming battle. But for their parents' safety, the adults couldn't be anywhere near Yitoo. "Edward, Dew, and I are the only ones who can stop her."

The three adults sat, soaking in this information. Nathan could tell that not one of them liked hearing they couldn't be involved.

"Doo shił yá'át'ééhda," Nali said. She poured herself another cup of steaming tea.

"Shidóó," Janet said. "But I see their point."

"Oh, no way," Ted said. "You're children! You can't do this on your own!"

"Ted," Janet said.

"No, honey," Ted said. "You don't get to make this decision for Edward. And Nathan for that matter. Neither of you have my permission!"

"Ted." Janet cradled his hand. "I'm just as terrified for Edward as I am for Nathan. And before you say it, hold your tongue. I care just as much for Edward as Nathan. If there were any way we could be the ones going in their place, you know we would do whatever it took. Look at our sons, our brave sons."

Nathan felt awkward when Ted stared at him. Was Ted worried for Nathan, too?

Janet spoke, "They have been dealing with the Holy Beings. They know things we don't. We must trust them. If they think it's better for us to stay here—no, Ted, you're listening now, not just to me, not just to Nathan, but also to Edward."

"Dad," Edward said. "Please stay."

Ted stood up and was ready to leave the firepit, but Janet said, "It has to be both of us in agreement, honey. We're their parents."

"Louella?" Ted asked Nali.

"Ha'át'ííshą'?" Nali responded.

"Is your hogan set up?" he asked.

"'Éí dooda. It's set up for sleeping in, not for praying," Nali said.

"Do you mind if I start on that?" Ted asked.

"'Aoo'," Nali said. She stood up and dusted off her purple skirt. "I'll help, too. Janet, can you go to the cell phone reception area by the highway to call my sons? They both need to get here quickly."

"On it, Louella," Janet said. She jumped up and rushed to Ted. "That was very strong of you."

"I can't get through this without you," Ted said, resting his head on her shoulder. "Please tell me our boys will be safe."

Janet led him to the hogan, rubbing his shoulders.

Nathan and Edward stood up, while Nali approached them. She pulled them into a hug. "You keep asking bigger and bigger things of us."

"We can do it, Nali," Nathan said, leaning into her hug.

Nali said, "Go. Don't you dare think of getting hurt out there, or else you're going to be grounded."

"I told you they'd ground us," Edward said.

Nali released them and wiped some tears off her brown cheeks. "Right, keys to the hogan."

"Come on, Edward," Nathan said. "Let's wake Dew and be on our way."

They woke Dew up in the cornfield when the sun was setting, and the dark orange sky was quickly becoming maroon. Nathan scanned the faraway faces of the sandstone plateaus reflecting the darkening sunlight.

Dew asked, "Are you both rested?"

From the sleep he'd gotten on the drive and the food they had eaten, Nathan felt ready to go. A quick glance at Edward told Nathan that he was also ready to face Yitoo. Together, they nodded.

"Let's go, then," Dew said. With a last yawn and downward-dog stretch, she was fully awake. Nathan and Edward scrambled onto her spine. Her color began to dim, and her features softened. But Nathan could still feel her heartbeat.

Dew explained, "I'll get us to the edge of this land surface with the rainbow path. Then, once we reach the ocean, I'll have to cover the rest of the way on foot."

"We can't use the rainbow path on the ocean?" Nathan asked, positioning himself in front of Edward.

"Not unless you want to fall to the very bottom of the ocean floor," Edward said, grabbing Nathan's shoulders with a firm grip.

Nathan offered, "I can hold on to the Dawn Arrow while we travel to the Pacific Ocean."

Edward seemed to think about what was being proposed. "Oh, because we'll be flying through the air like we don't value our lives? And I'll be too terrified to open my eyes? That's what we are talking about here?"

"In so many words," Nathan said.

"Be my guest," Edward said, reaching into the quiver and pulling out the Dawn Arrow. It shone like a warm candle. With the sun quickly descending beyond the horizon, the radiance of the Dawn Arrow cut through the growing shadows.

Nathan held it. "So what do I do?"

"The Guardian said to think of the being and hold it high," Edward said.

Could it really be that easy? Nathan thought of Yitoo, how she fashioned jewelry out of ice, and held the arrow skyward. He thought of her pretty voice that taught Dew the songs of rain. He thought of her tears, when she saw what became of her river and when she hurt Canyon Mist. He thought of her smile when she returned the water back to Diné Bikéyáh. There was so much good in her. Then the Dawn Arrow shot forth a narrow beam of light that pointed southwest. "That way."

Dew held the crystal with a watery arm and began to sing. Strings of colors emerged from the angular crystal. While she wove the colors into a rainbow, Edward cut a piece of shadow with the Folding Darkness Knife and covered all three of them. Dew then tapped the ground, and a rainbow appeared and shot into the sky. Continuing to sing, she stepped on the rainbow with the boys on her back. Nathan held the Dawn Arrow high above his head, and Dew adjusted the rainbow as close as she could toward its direction.

Nathan took a deep breath as they were whipped backward. Edward dug his face into Nathan's shoulder blades again. Nathan's heart dropped, not because they were quickly ascending, but because the three of them were heading into the heart of a hurricane to fight the most powerful water monster in the Fourth World, in the middle of an endless supply of water.

Naadiin Dóó Bi'ąą 'Ashdla'
TWENTY-FIVE

EDWARD, NATHAN, AND DEW SOARED through the air on the spine of a rainbow toward the Pacific Ocean. Sunlight lessened as night deepened the darkness across the land.

Edward didn't think he would ever become numb to the experience of flying with no seat belts and empty air all around. But roughly one hour of rising and falling later, he was able to open his eyes on their ascent and recognize the landscape below. Behind them the rows of streetlights in Phoenix, where all his friends and his home were, sparkled like strands of gold caught in the last rays of sunlight. When they fell to the earth, he closed his eyes and forced himself to imagine they were on a roller coaster. His grip strength was waning from squeezing the shadow fabric.

Nathan had to switch his arms that held the Dawn Arrow a couple of times through their voyage. Edward wanted to help, but even with the ice harness that held him securely in place on Dew's back, he would most likely drop the Dawn Arrow. "Thank you for holding the arrow," Edward whispered to Nathan. He wasn't sure if Nathan heard with the blasts of wind.

A while later, the sun had fully descended. To his right, Edward saw two bright sources of electricity in the darkness: San Diego and Los Angeles. If they couldn't stop Yitoo, those two cities would be first to be destroyed. At his position in the sky, he could clearly see how vast both cities were. Like Phoenix, the two cities spread out for miles. A terrifying realization dawned on him. He now saw that these cities were unsustainable. They were truly monstrous in their size and their consumption of natural resources. But while Yitoo wasn't fully wrong, she couldn't be allowed to destroy them.

They continued heading farther south of San Diego into Mexico. Edward didn't know any of the cities beyond the Mexican border.

On their final descent, Edward bravely peeked to see where they were landing. Just a bit to their right, Edward spotted the unmistakable markings of a golf course as they approached the earth and a nearby highway. Before they landed, Edward quickly read a large sign by the highway that read Bajamar Ocean Front Golf Resort.

Edward quickly jumped off Dew and let go of the shadow fabric, ready to kiss the earth and almost vowing never to travel by rainbow again. Not something he'd ever recommend. One star out of ten. His cheeks prickled and tingled as blood returned to them. Nathan's hair stood on end like he had been electro-cuted.

The three of them faced the ocean that slammed against the rocky cliffside beneath them. The waxing new moon rose behind them. Swirling apocalyptic clouds spread for thousands of miles across the western horizon. Lightning bolts blazed inside the clouds like the base of a volcano igniting. The clouds made the Sandia Mountains of Albuquerque seem like gentle hills, Camel-back Mountain seem like a pebble, and the three of them like a water droplet compared to Niagara Falls.

"No matter what happens from here," Nathan started. He wrapped an arm around Edward and pulled him close. With his other hand, he petted the top of Dew's skull.

"Save the speech for when we win," Edward said before Nathan could finish that thought.

Dew leaned into Nathan's hip and said, "There is still the possibility of reasoning with her."

Edward didn't know how to respond to that. At least to Edward, it was clear that Yitoo had made up her mind and couldn't be reasoned with. And they had to stop her, no matter what. Losing was not an option. He finally said, "It's up to her how this will end."

"Yes, it is," Dew agreed.

Edward sensed sadness in her voice. In the dim beam of light that pointed toward the hurricane, Edward could see that both Dew and Nathan were hurting. They weren't accustomed to confrontation. He couldn't imagine the conflict Dew must have been enduring. To resist, to possibly end the life of her own sister. Dew truly held massive strength that was surprising for her young age.

As for him, all his years of training to be an Olympic wrestler had taught Edward to handle his fears, his sadness, and his anger when dealing with a tough opponent. It was his turn to lead them toward Yitoo. He put his dream of Olympic gold to the side so he could focus on the immense task in front of him. He wiggled out of Nathan's hug and grabbed the Dawn Arrow. "It's my turn to hold on to this. Nathan, Dew, I know that you're conflicted about Yitoo. But she wants to harm millions of lives. We cannot let that happen. Steven, Weslee. Your cousins. My cousins. Everyone in the valley—they don't know it, but they are counting on us."

Nathan nodded. "She shouldn't hurt others."

Dew contributed, "Our waters are meant for nurturing, not for destroying."

Edward held the Dawn Arrow to his chest and summoned forth thoughts and memories of Yitoo. Of her calling him filthy for having Anglo ancestors. Of her speaking ill of Anglo people in front of him. Of the pain on her face whenever she spoke of Hwééldi and how her anguish was like his when he learned of his ancestor's story. The light of the Dawn Arrow focused forward, pointing to the center of the hurricane.

Edward sat in front of Nathan this time on Dew's back. With a jump, she landed on the surface of the ocean and instead of diving deep, she ran on the surface like it was land. Water gushed out behind them like they were engine-propelled, and their speed increased. This was the first time he could hear the song and the words, thanks to the protection of the Obsidian Armor. Edward savored every syllable. The water splashed onto them, first cold and then warmer the farther they got from land. Edward held the Dawn Arrow higher to guide Dew as she ran right toward the hurricane.

The clouds grew large and the thunder violent. Rolling waves, like living hills, slammed into each other, sending thousands of gallons of salt water to splash everywhere. The smell of brine and fish invaded Edward's nostrils. Then they reached the underside of the clouds of the first hurricane rainband. According to the research he had done earlier, hurricanes looked like one giant vortex of clouds; underneath the spinning dome were several large rings of clouds that resembled a bull's-eye target. The outer rings were the smallest rainband, and the closer to the eye of the hurricane, the more powerful the rainband. In Category 5 hurricanes, winds could exceed 157 miles per hour. Edward prayed that this was only a Category 1 with winds between 74 and 95 miles per hour. But from the size of it, he couldn't lie to himself. It was going to be difficult no matter the categorization.

In front of them, drops of rain as plump as baseballs splatted on the ever-moving water surface. As they entered the first rainband, they were completely submerged in water as if they were standing underneath a shower on full blast. He spat ocean water out of his mouth constantly. The water stung his eyes, and he tried his best but couldn't clear his vision enough to see where they were going. Immediately, strong wind currents almost knocked Edward and Nathan off Dew. Behind him, Nathan dug his face into Edward's back.

Edward leaned forward, raising the Dawn Arrow higher, and yelled, "Push through, Dew! Nathan!"

"Yeah?" Nathan shouted through the roaring thunder above them.

Edward asked, "Sing something to get all this rain off our backs?"

"Okay!" Nathan shouted.

Edward couldn't hear Nathan sing amid the explosions of splashing water around them, the lightning cracking above like the earth was split wide open, and the banshee screams of the wind.

Then, as quickly as they were bombarded by the overwhelming rain above, it stopped. Edward glanced upward and saw an invisible dome upon which the globs of raindrops smacked and rolled away. Nathan sang loud and true, keeping the rain away from them.

Finally, they broke through the first rainband. The rain above calmed some, and the wind wasn't trying to pry them off Dew. Somewhere up ahead, Edward could hear Yitoo singing. This was the Maelstrom song, and it was the prettiest song he had ever heard. There were no words, only a sorrowful melody.

Their respite was short lived as they approached the second

rainband. "Keep singing as long as you can, Nathan," Edward said. "Dew, get ready for a stronger rainband coming up."

"Gotcha!" Dew said.

"Okay!" Nathan shouted.

Dew jetted them forward. Up above, lightning bolted across the sky endlessly. From the brief flashes of light, Edward witnessed Yitoo's rage. Dark waves the size of four-story houses rose and slammed into other waves. The clouds rolled violently, like they were boiling. Everywhere water splashed and steamed. Edward told himself to not be scared. But he had never been so terrified in his entire life.

Dew rushed up a frothing rising wave that quickly doubled in height, towering over them. Her speed slowed as they neared the top. She was just barely able to jump on top of it before it crashed downward. Sliding down its powerful back, Dew said, "I don't think I can push forward! This storm is way too strong!"

They couldn't retreat. But if this was only the second rainband of who knows how many, their task was going to be nearly impossible. Edward's wrestling brain kicked into gear, and he tried to analyze the waves for any clearing. But it was too dark to see anything other than the path that the Dawn Arrow pointed toward. All the while, Nathan's singing protected them from the onslaught of rain above.

Wait a minute, he thought, rain is water. "Nathan, if you continued to sing and went underneath the surface, would we be in a bubble?" Edward asked, turning to view his answer.

Nathan nodded, not once stopping his singing from the torrential amount of rain slamming the invisible dome above them.

"Dew! Change of tactics. Dive underwater like a submarine!" Edward shouted.

"I don't know what a submarine is, but here we go!" Dew said, jumping up and then angling her body downward. With a strong swing of her tail, they launched under the turbulent surface of the ocean. As Edward hoped, Nathan's singing created a pocket of air where they could breathe. He squeezed the Dawn Arrow, and it continued to shine their path toward Yitoo.

"Let's keep going," Edward said, not having to shout above the wind, waves, and thunder.

Dew pressed forward, occasionally being pushed by the invisible jet streams. Above them, the ocean erupted and exploded, like bombs were constantly detonated every few seconds.

"Nathan, Dew, I know this is scary, but together we are just as strong as Yitoo. We can overcome her!" Edward shouted.

After what felt like half an hour, a curious and beautiful thing happened. First, the ocean above them finally calmed. And then the water around them began sparkling a dazzling neon green. Streaks of phosphorescent lime danced on the invisible dome like the northern lights Edward had seen in YouTube videos.

"I think we can surface," Edward said, putting the Dawn Arrow back into the quiver.

Dew responded by ascending and breaking into the crisp, clear air. Water splashed around them, continuing to glow as they fell back to the ocean. The moon shone down brightly above a calm clearing of water and sky. About forty miles in every direction, a wall of inky black clouds rolled from the seafloor toward the upper limits of the sky.

"We're in the eye of the hurricane," Nathan said.

A cool and strong breeze blew around them, rippling the surface of the water, causing it to glow that mesmerizing emerald color.

"What's making the water glow like that?" Dew asked.

"Tiny little organisms. It's bioluminescence," Nathan explained.

Then Edward heard Yitoo singing. "She's there." Edward pointed with his lips.

"Yitoo," Nathan said, his voice heavy with care and concern.

Dew jogged toward the center of the eye, where Yitoo sat singing the Maelstrom song. She was the size of an elephant. Her melody resonated with the surface of the water around her, creating cymatic shapes of intersecting geometry, like a mandala of circles and triangles. In her voice that sang the Maelstrom song, he could hear her pain and underneath that her love for Mother Earth.

As they got closer, Edward could see the intricate details of the dazzling ice armor that Yitoo wore. The ice armor must have been made with this ocean water because it glowed softly like a jade candle. Each of her scales had a piece of ice that sparkled like a kaleidoscope. The armor slid smoothly like skin as she swayed from side to side. Her eyes were closed until the three of them were eight feet away, close enough to see the tears in her eyes.

Yitoo said, in the middle of her verse, "Say what you have to say, then leave."

"We are here to stop you," Edward said.

Yitoo didn't even look at him and acted as if he wasn't there.

"Nathan and I also think you must be stopped," Dew said. She bared her tusks, and spikes grew out of her back.

Nathan shifted his weight and stepped off Dew. To Edward's amazement, Nathan pressed his foot against the surface of the ocean and stood tall. Nathan looked like this was a revelation to him as well because he very carefully stepped away from Dew and reached his arms out to Yitoo, as if inviting her into a hug. "I know you are hurting. I know you are angry. There is a ceremony that my uncle had, that I think you would benefit from. The N'dáá."

She stopped singing altogether. For a moment, storm clouds slowed their roiling and churning. She said, "I know what an N'dáá is. I sang protection songs at the very first N'dáá for the Hero Twins."

Nathan said, "We could have one for you! Of course, you'll still need to talk with someone about your pain."

Yitoo said, "Mother Earth is in pain. Diné Bikéyah is in pain. What you are talking about will take precious time that no longer exists. I need to cleanse the Fourth World of the Pale People as well as their allies here and now."

Yitoo wasn't even acknowledging him! Edward was getting

frustrated. He said, "You are wrong. The world isn't just Diné and Anglos! There are Nahiłii, Latinx, Asian American and Pacific Islanders, Arabs, Muslims, Jews, and more groups! You'll be harming them, too!" Anger built up in his chest. He looked at Yitoo's dark red eyes. Yitoo, who was putting everyone in danger, who wanted to destroy his home. "You can't just destroy homes and kill innocent people."

"Your filthy Pale ancestors did," Yitoo barked back. Her demeanor and tone immediately became soft and sad. "The winter of the kidnapping, I left the boundaries of the Four Sacred Mountains to follow the Diné. I did my best to alleviate their suffering. The children that could see me," she choked out, "received a small amount of comfort from that.

"Soon, we came across the banks of a roaring river. The Pale People rode their horses into the frigid river. Holding guns at their backs, they forced your ancestors to cross those deathly cold waters.

"One by one, the Diné walked down the hill and into the river. The elderly and youth struggled against the strong current. Blankets of water smothered them. I did my best to calm the waters. But I couldn't sing. I was too shocked at everything around me. So, I tried to push as many Diné across as I could. But more and more Diné were forced to cross the river. There was a curtain of bubbles that arose from all the violent thrashing of the drowning. Their screams quieted. Their bodies became cold. When I'm alone, I still hear their screams. When I sleep, I dream of the faces of those who sank beneath the river and did not rise again.

"I stayed in that river. I spent days, weeks, saving as many as I could. Pain stabbed my lungs. My throat flared up in fiery anguish. I grew sickly. I grew weak. Even though I was exhausted. Even though I had no nourishment. Even though I became haunted. I stayed until the very last line of Diné crossed the river. Only then did I permit myself to return to Diné Bikéyah. But the thawing of spring didn't warm my heart. I had to return to the Third World so that I might survive.

"The Pale People destroyed families. They joyfully stole land and resources. Not only from the Diné. From peoples all over this surface. Such violent tendencies do not vanish unless we eradicate them, just like the Hero Twins did with the Enemies of Old. I envy your hearts; they've not hardened. Seeing as I have the necessary heart to do what must be done, it is up to me to save this world."

Edward so wanted to suplex-slam Yitoo, even at her size. There was no reasoning with her. Edward said, "If you're will-ing to destroy countless lives, then *you* are no better than the soldiers were!"

Dew pleaded, "Please, oldest sister, I love you! Stop now."

"I didn't fight during the Era of Relocation, and look what it did to the world. Nothing will stop me this time," Yitoo said. The sea began to flow toward her from all directions. The water slipped in between the armor scales and was absorbed into her body as she grew in size. The bioluminescence in the water caused her to shine in the middle of the dark ocean.

"Nathan!" Dew shouted. Nathan wrapped his arms around her neck as she jumped to turn around. She ran from the waters that were being sucked up by Yitoo. Each step Dew took illuminated underneath her.

Edward glanced backward and saw Yitoo grow beyond any height he had seen before. Soon, all Edward could see were four massive feet, each as big as the 1,500 foot tall Shiprock spire, and she was still growing!

After four terrifying minutes of absorbing the ocean, Yitoo stood one mile tall into the sky and her forehead seemingly touched the bottom of the moon. Her entire body looked like Dook'o'oosłííd itself was walking. Edward estimated she was at least one mile tall and three miles from snout to tail. Her eyes looked like two devastating black holes, devoid of light. She roared and the green bioluminescence of her ice armor changed to a crimson red. Black storm clouds spewed from her mouth, and the winds became even more furious.

Yitoo bellowed, "If saving this world means ending all three of you, I'll suffer that sacrifice."

They were three-quarters of a mile away from her, when Yitoo shifted her weight to her front legs and raised her titanic tail into the air. The ocean bent underneath her front side and rippled outward, destabilizing Nathan's grip around Dew's neck. He fell backward into the water.

"Nathan!" Edward shouted, and reached out for him. A strong wave carried Nathan away from them.

Before Dew could do anything, Yitoo slammed her enormous

tail onto the surface of the ocean. An atomic splash with an equally devastatingly loud boom erupted behind her. The splashing water shone so brightly that Edward had to close his eyes until the bioluminescence dimmed. Then Yitoo roared, and the splash collected and formed a red tidal wave two hundred fifty feet tall. It was heading directly toward the three of them!

Naadiin Dóó Bi'ąą Hastą́ą́

TWENTY-SIX

NATHAN FOUGHT TO KEEP HIS head above the surface. His heart was broken, and he couldn't make a solid surface to stand. He was going to have to become someone he didn't want to be. Someone who would use the water monster songs to harm another. The towering red wave rushed at him. He spun wildly, searching for Dew and Edward. Finding neither, he faced the wave less than a quarter of a mile away, frozen in fear.

Then a blade of light cut through the night and landed on his chest. It was Edward, still sitting on Dew's shoulders, holding the Dawn Arrow above his head! They raced toward him.

"Hurry!" Nathan shouted. The undercurrent pulled him closer to the wave that had doubled in height to five hundred feet. Its frothing crest was breaking, and water crashed down. Nathan calmed himself. He had to sing, but to do that he had to overcome his heartbreak. Meanwhile, Dew zoomed toward him.

"Submarine!" Edward shouted to him.

Nathan got the hint. He sang the Move song and imagined a sphere around him. Dew leaped as the avalanche of water cascaded down. Nathan opened his arms and Dew slammed into Nathan's chest, pulling him deep underneath the surface of the ocean to avoid the massive wave. Nathan watched as the wave pummeled the ocean surface, the crimson bioluminescence highlighting every vehement collision. The undertow tossed them around like rag dolls and pulled them away from Yitoo.

Two minutes later, the energy of the water weakened enough for Dew to ascend. She emerged on the raging ocean surface, about four miles away from Yitoo, who stood in the middle of the wide hurricane eye. Behind them the remnants of the red wave exploded against the hurricane wall.

Still holding on to Dew's neck, Nathan found pressure pushing against his foot. The water under his shoe glimmered green as he put more weight on his foot. He released Dew. Nathan stared at the immensity of Yitoo. Every step she took created forty-foot-high waves.

Edward thought as hard as he could. How could they take down Yitoo? Then a plan formulated. "I have to use the Lightning Arrow on her."

Dew said, "Her armor will protect her from the Lightning Arrow."

Edward replied, "Then we'll have to smash through the armor to create an opening."

Nathan said, "She'll probably repair it once it cracks."

Edward said to Dew, "Grow as large as you can, then wrestle with her, the same way you and I did. Only this time, use anything and everything at your disposal to keep the ice armor from re-forming. I don't have great aim so I'll have to use the Lightning Knife instead of the Lightning Arrow. Nathan, can you get me onto Yitoo's back to use the Lightning Knife?"

Nathan said, "Yeah."

Dew said, "Afterward, I can take her water and lock her in ice chains."

"Then we'll take her back to the Third World," Nathan said, hopping onto Dew behind Edward.

Edward realized that Nathan didn't know that Yitoo wasn't allowed back to the Third World. If she wasn't allowed back in the Third World, and was unhappy in the Fourth World, could she possibly go to the Fifth World? He would have to worry about that later because Yitoo was now gearing up to launch another wave at them. "Let's do this!"

Dew sprinted and then commanded a stream of water to propel them away from the hurricane wall behind them to Yitoo at the center of the eye. The water that Dew commanded changed from moss green to the color of yellow amber.

Yitoo noticed them and lifted her enormous tail. Her front legs pressed the ocean down, creating a deep depression miles across. Yitoo's tail ascended toward the cloudless sky. Scarlet waterfalls dripped off her tail.

Edward said, "Take out her front legs! She'll lose balance."

"On it," Dew said. She started singing, the loudest he had

heard her sing. Nathan joined in and then the ocean underneath Yitoo's front right foot changed from red to yellow, and her entire leg plunged into the briny waters. Her chin smacked against the surface as she struggled to regain her composure.

Edward shouted, "Close the distance!" He estimated they were three miles from Yitoo.

Yitoo dug herself out of the ocean and stood tall. Yitoo said, "Youngest sister, my heart will surely break when you are no more. I will tell future water monsters of your bravery and strength." She began to sing again. Then a terrifying sight materialized. The surface of the sea around Yitoo began to vibrate as if it was boiling. The bioluminescence made the entire ocean glow, increasing in brightness.

"Oh, no! She's creating a megatsunami!" Dew yelled. In between Yitoo's feet, the spine of a bubbling crimson wave rose.

"Submarine?" Edward asked.

"Not this time," Dew said. "The undertow is going to be way too powerful and way too deep. I have no choice but to match her singing." Dew stood strong and copied the words of Yitoo's song. The water around them sparkled like interlacing chains of gold.

Yitoo's crimson wave powered toward the three of them. Meanwhile, an equally large golden wave rushed in front of Dew. In mere seconds, the two waves smacked together and instead of canceling each other out, the waves doubled in height in between the two water monsters. Already it was as tall as the Glen Canyon Dam! More and more waves from both Yitoo and Dew added to this great singular wave, causing it to rise even farther into the sky and grow wider. Dew and Yitoo sang as loudly as they could. It was a battle of wills.

"Dew, we have to stop this wave!" Edward shouted.

"If I stop singing. She'll launch. This wave," Dew said in between verses. During the brief moments she stopped singing, the entire wave lurched in their direction.

"Let me help!" Nathan hopped off Dew.

"Be careful!" Edward said.

Nathan sprinted forward, and his wet clothes weighed him down. Running on the ocean's surface was like sprinting through quicksand with shoes caked with cement. His lungs hated every movement he forced his legs to make. Then he came to the base of the megatsunami that expanded both in height and width like a bell curve on a graph. It had quickly grown to size of Camelback Mountain, 2,100 feet tall.

He had to stop to catch his breath and to stop the fire in his legs and arms. He leaned against the wave's surface. He tossed his chin upward, to breathe easier. The stars twinkled calmly on the black ceiling. The clusters were different than the ones at Nali's mobile home. Then several stars shone brighter than the others. His mind connected the dots between the stars, and he saw Nali's mobile home and, to the side, her hogan.

He didn't understand what was happening. But the stars that formed the exterior of Nali's home site dimmed and a new set of stars brightened. He saw inside the hogan this time. Five adults sat around a fire. In his mind, Nathan said, "Nali, Uncle Jet, Mom, Dad, and Ted." Nathan knew without a doubt that he was seeing what was happening now. The adults were in the hogan, praying for them, as Born for Water had done for his older brother.

Then his nose smelled the undeniable scent of sweetgrass and cedar. The aches in Nathan's body disappeared, and like embers covered with dry kindling, a renewed source of energy sparked in his heart. He sang the Move song and a stream, not as strong as Yitoo's or Dew's, appeared under his shoes and helped him ascend the wave.

As he approached the peak, Nathan remembered Yitoo teaching Dew the basics of the water monster songs. Certain songs have better control over different states of water. A rain song wasn't going to control snow like an ice song, for instance. The song that Yitoo was singing had a lot of water references, and therefore was a water song. If he could freeze this wave, then Yitoo's singing would have almost no effect on it!

Nathan stood at the very top of the wave that was now twice as tall as Yitoo herself. Dew's waters shone a sunny yellow, while Yitoo's glowed a menacing red. In between both colors was a strip of orange that extended for many miles to his right and left. He had to do something now before the wave grew any higher!

Nathan sang the Change song. His right hand chilled. The coldness that started in his right hand spread through his entire body and to his toes. A thick platform of orange ice formed under his shoes. He held his hand high, collecting his intentions, his emotions, and his voice. With all his strength, he slammed his hand down onto the ice at his feet. The ice beneath him spread out for miles in every direction and froze the entire wave.

Down at the base of the yellow side of the two-mile tall iceberg, Dew took no break when the wave instantly froze and launched her upward. Edward leaned forward and closed his eyes as they sped to where Nathan was standing.

At the top of the mountainous iceberg that he created, Nathan struggled to shape a megaphone with the ice underneath him. He would never stop believing in Yitoo's goodness. He would do anything he could to find that kind, caring, and nurturing side of her again. He called to her through the megaphone, "Yitoo, please stop blaming yourself for what happened after Hwééldi. Please stop blaming yourself!"

Yitoo approached. Each giant step sent a wave that slapped and splashed against the bottom of the iceberg. "I will finish the Maelstrom song and destroy all desert cities, even if you are in my path. My resolve is my advantage over all three of you. The only way to stop me is with my death!" She sang the Maelstrom song again, regaining control of the hurricane, and then struck the red side of the iceberg with her massive shoulders.

Nathan quickly thought of angles as he formulated a way to break Yitoo's armor. There was a specific angle that he had to remember to create what he needed. He decided a forty-five-degree angle would work best. Nathan sang the Move song. He knelt to touch the ice beneath him. He felt every neuron in his brain fire as he concentrated on warping the red side of the iceberg to the angle he wanted. Pain stabbed the folds of his brain, and then his nerves were set on fire as he forced the iceberg to bend to his will. But it wasn't happening.

On the yellow side of the iceberg, Dew and Edward were halfway up to him. Meanwhile, Yitoo had just broken off a colossal chunk that crashed into the ocean, spraying green bioluminescent water everywhere.

Nathan had to create the forty-five-degree angle! He closed his eyes and listened to the water. He could feel it. The ocean had feelings! Could that be why it was so resistant to his commands? Had he been forcing the ocean to do something it didn't want to do?

"Please, will you help me?" Nathan whispered to the ice beneath him. He sang again, this time asking the iceberg to change its shape instead of forcing his will upon it. The orange color flickered beneath his hand like a candle resisting the wind. Then the ice underneath him turned a bright blue and easily responded to his request. Streaks of glimmering cobalt blue spread through the entire red side of the iceberg and took on the angle he needed.

Just then, Dew and Edward finally arrived. Nathan crumpled onto his hands and knees, unable to do more. Warping the shape of a two-mile-high iceberg had sapped all his energy.

"Wow, Nathan," Edward said, hopping off Dew. He rubbed Nathan's shoulder.

In between heavy breaths, Nathan said to Dew, "Boulders. Break. Armor."

Dew nodded and sang. Sections of the top of the iceberg cracked into long quarter mile long triangular pieces and changed from red to yellow. As soon as the pieces formed, they began to slide.

At the bottom, Yitoo sang and swiped at the base of the iceberg with her front legs. She looked up, but it was too late for her to move as several triangular pieces slammed into her. Each impact created a thunderous clap. And then a lightning-like crack formed in one of her crimson armor plates. Dew directed all the slivers toward that weak spot. The crack expanded until it finally shattered. With the integrity of her ice armor compromised, more and more scales cracked, then shattered. Her entire front half was now armor-less.

At the top, Nathan had finally regained his strength. With Edward's help, he stood up and said, "Avalanche." He sang the Change song, and Dew joined him. Large sections of iceberg glowed in both blue and yellow and then exploded into colorful snow that cascaded down toward Yitoo.

In mere moments, millions of pounds of snow torpedoed downward. Its force crushed Yitoo, rolling her onto her back and pushing her half a mile away from the base of the iceberg.

Edward said, "Phase two, Dew, you're up." He tightened the quiver and calmed his nerves. He saw Yitoo recovering from the avalanche. He was going to have to stand on her to use the Lightning Knife. "Nathan, can you get me on Yitoo?"

"Yes," Nathan answered. He was no longer leaning on Edward. "Let's go. She's already repairing her armor."

"Good luck!" Dew said, readying herself to jump.

"Dew!" Edward said. "When I use the Lightning Knife, make sure you're not connected to her. And she shifts her weight to her left front leg. Her shoulders are stiff— Oh, and be careful." He hugged her neck.

"Oh, Edward," Dew said. She pressed the bottom of her

chin against his shoulder.

"Go!" Edward said, terrified for Dew and the harm that she was going to face.

Dew leaped off the peak of the iceberg, and a torrential amount of red and blue ice melted and turned into golden water that coiled around her legs, her shoulders, her neck, her abdomen, and her tail. The glow of the water transferred into Dew's body, causing her to shine like dawn sunrays. She doubled in size, tripled, quadrupled for a few seconds until her shoulders were the size of city blocks. Even with all her growth, she was barely two-thirds the size of Yitoo. Dew's front legs slammed into the ocean, and a giant wave sprang forth and washed the snow away from Yitoo, who was standing back up.

Indiscernible amounts of water from the ocean surged around Dew. Amber-colored ice armor quickly coated Dew's legs, then spread across her spine, abdomen, and tail. There was something strange about Dew's armor. It gave her a new shape. She had pointed, triangular ears. Her tail was long and thin. Her legs were taller and no longer stubby. Her ice armor gave her the shape of a mountain lion.

"Sister!" Dew bellowed. "Remember your lessons of compassion!"

"Enough!" Yitoo roared. Her scream spread for miles; the ocean gleamed red in response. "Allow me to remind you of our lessons, and how much you have left to learn!" Seawater snaked up her legs, and then sprouted out like extra limbs from her shoulders and her hips and hardened into ice. A final appendage appeared from her tail, with a sharp, pointed tip that she aimed directly at Dew. She looked like a horrifying combination of spider and scorpion, glowing in the dark of night. Her crimson armor was slowly repairing itself.

Edward was awed at the sight of the two titans preparing to fight in the middle of the Pacific Ocean. Yitoo began to approach Dew, each of her eight legs moving in coordination, creating three-story-high waves with every step. Dew lowered her front half and swatted a paw, ready to engage Yitoo.

Edward immediately pulled out the Folding Darkness Knife and gripped a piece of the earth's shadow. "Nathan, I need you to get me to Yitoo."

Nathan nodded and said, "I have an idea, but you're not going to like it."

"I don't like anything about this," Edward said, silently praying Dew wouldn't get hurt. He began to cut a large section of shadow to hide the two of them.

Nathan, meanwhile, was directing a blob of water around his shoulders. What looked like blue wings began to form and extend out from Nathan's shoulders.

"Oh, great, now we're going to paraglide," Edward said, realizing he would have to cut a much larger piece of shadow to hide them.

In the ocean, Dew rushed forward. Yitoo swung her mighty scorpion tail at Dew's face. Dew pressed her body low, narrowly avoiding contact. She then swerved to Yitoo's left and caught an ice leg with her jaws. Yitoo tugged but couldn't release it. The scorpion tail slammed into Dew's side. Dew groaned but held on to the ice leg.

On the top of the iceberg, Edward stood in front of Nathan, who had made a harness to secure them together after wrapping them and Nathan's ice wings in shadow fabric.

"I'm going to aim for Yitoo's forehead region," Nathan said. "You can keep your eyes closed until then."

"Works for me," Edward said. His heart pounded, and his throat constricted with anxiety. His knees buckled, and his entire spine ached. But his trust of Nathan overpowered his fear. Edward closed his eyes and shouted, "Now!"

Not a second later, Edward felt his body lift into the air, and the two of them drifted toward Yitoo. Edward braved a look and saw that Dew had released the red ice arm and was running in a large arch around Yitoo, dodging the tail. Yitoo's eight arms were busy turning her massive crimson body. Dew saw an opening as Yitoo's arms crossed, almost tying themselves into a knot. Before Yitoo could untangle her arms, Dew zoomed forward and slammed into the back of Yitoo's right front knee with her forehead. Dew's amber tail scrapped off newly formed scales.

Floating above the two titans, Edward and Nathan were a hundred yards away from Yitoo. Nathan guided them, and when they were close enough, water rushed forward and created a blue blob on top of Yitoo's forehead. Edward felt his stomach upturn as they dropped and landed in the blob. It exploded upon impact. The water swirled around Nathan and formed into turquoise armor. Edward quickly grabbed the

Dawn Arrow and swung it in the air to let Dew know they had landed on Yitoo.

In front of Edward and Nathan, Dew spotted the arrow and stopped running. It looked to Edward that she was at a loss on how to fight Yitoo without endangering him and Nathan. Then she sang, and a swirling yellow waterspout rising from the ocean wrapped around Yitoo's pointed tail, three miles away from Edward and Nathan. Yitoo groaned.

This was it! This was Edward's chance! He quickly reached for the quiver. But Yitoo shifted her body, and her red ice limbs became water and swatted at Dew. Edward slid and rolled as Yitoo took a single step. He felt like a fly on a horse. Nathan anchored himself with ice to Yitoo. With a blue tentacle, Nathan grabbed Edward's arm and prevented him from sliding off Yitoo.

Yitoo smacked Dew with bone-shattering strength with her red tentacles. With each impact, parts of Dew's amber armor fell into the ocean.

"I have to help Dew," Nathan said, creating a chain and affixing it to Yitoo's scales.

"Go," Edward said. "If I use the Lightning Arrow while you're on Yitoo, you could get electrocuted too!" Edward wouldn't risk shocking Dew nor Nathan. He grabbed the chain that Nathan created.

The turquoise armor around Nathan melted and pooled around his legs. He then rushed toward the closest tentacle near Yitoo's right shoulder with a jet stream. He jumped onto it and rode it to Dew.

Edward, meanwhile, held on to the chain as Yitoo swayed. Then the quiver's strap snapped. It slid toward Yitoo's eyebrows, getting stuck between two scales forty yards away from him. Edward screamed, "No!"

A minute later, Nathan landed by Dew's right ear. The glow of iceberg on his left helped him to see that Yitoo's four water limbs had attached to Dew's in several spots and were pushing her under the ocean's surface; two tentacles by each shoulder, one on her hips, and the last on her forehead. "Get up, Dew!" Nathan shouted, though she might not hear him.

Yitoo approached Dew with mighty, thundering steps. Her crimson ice armor continued to repair itself. "You will live at the bottom of this ocean, encased in ice for a multitude of eras." Dew struggled to pull her lower half out of the ocean. Yitoo towered over Dew and said, "Once Mother Earth has recovered with the eradication of the Pale People, I will allow you to resurface." Yitoo sang the Maelstrom song again then butted her head against Dew's shoulder. Dew cried out in pain.

Nathan slipped but regained his balance as Dew recoiled from the blow. He stared at the red tentacle that was pushing Dew's forehead. It was as thick as a soccer field. He reached out and pressed his hand onto the surface and closed his eyes. His sense of touch expanded from his hand until, in his mind, he felt the vibrations of the push. He could break it!

Nathan sang, asking the tentacle to change to steam. Deep in the center of the red water, a glimmer of blue appeared. Nathan held strong, and the gleam grew stronger. Immediately, a huge cloud of bubbles appeared in the center of the tentacle and expanded outward until . . . *poof!* A thin, glowing mist covered everything. Nathan wiped his face and spotted the closest tentacle, which was near Dew's right shoulder half a mile away.

Meanwhile on Yitoo's forehead, Edward was slowly crawling on his stomach toward the quiver, which was still stuck between two scales. He was getting closer. He did his best to hurry but could only go so fast without sliding off and falling off Yitoo one mile down into the ocean. Edward's fingers were so close to the quiver! Four, three inches! He didn't dare scooch closer. He was barely able to hold his position. He extended his hand. Two inches. He felt the tendons in his elbows, wrists, and fingers ache as he stretched to get closer. He saw the crimson ice armor re-forming and making its way toward him. *Reach!* Edward shouted in his mind. One inch! Half an inch! Yitoo's armor was one hundred yards away.

Dew was submerged up to her front legs. She struggled to pull herself out of the ocean, but the remaining three red tentacles were too strong. Nathan had gotten to the tentacle by Dew's shoulder and saw the surface of the ocean coming upon him. He tried to sever the connection of Yitoo's water but rushed back to Dew's forehead so that he wouldn't drown. Dew's entire body was almost completely submerged. Just her head poked out of the ocean.

Then, miraculously, there was a spark of light above Yitoo's right eyebrow. It was Edward holding the Dawn Arrow. What was he going to do? Was he going to launch it?

"Dew!" Nathan shouted, hoping she could hear. "Close your eyes!"

Edward hoped he had gotten their attention by waving the Dawn Arrow above his head. Dew's eyes saw the arrow and immediately closed. Edward wound up his arm and threw it. The Dawn Arrow flew high into the sky and shone like a brilliant sun. Before it could get brighter, Edward turned around and saw the deep outline of his shadow against Yitoo's scales. The advance of the ice armor stopped. He ran toward the chain and grabbed it.

"My eyes!" Yitoo shouted, stepping backward.

Edward quickly knotted the strap and placed the quiver on his chest so that the mouth was in front of him instead of on his back. Once the Dawn Arrow had disappeared, it materialized in the quiver. Yitoo's body moved and shifted. The winds screeched by Edward's ears. If he hadn't grabbed the chain, he would surely have fallen off.

He had hoped for a stable surface to do what he had to do—especially when he would be holding a million jolts of lightning energy in the palm of his hand. He prepared the Lightning Knife and waited for the exact moment that Yitoo and Dew were disconnected.

Nathan felt the ocean recede from behind him as Dew pulled herself out and stood proud. Nathan approached the second water limb by her right shoulder and turned it into steam. Dew pressed forward, slamming her front paw into Yitoo's chin. Bits of crimson armor chipped off with loud splashes.

Nathan saw an opportunity and asked the ocean underneath Yitoo's back leg to weaken. Yitoo lost her balance, and her left front leg rose into the air. Dew mightily roared and rushed forth to jam her mountain lion forehead into Yitoo's stomach.

Yitoo stopped singing the Maelstrom song and roared. Suddenly, the last two tentacles detached from Yitoo, wrapped around Dew's ankles, and completely froze. The whole iceberg to their side was obliterated into a snow flurry while the entire ocean surface in the eye of the hurricane froze. Yitoo said, "You have learned much, youngest sister. An apt student. Had I taught you a year more, you would have indeed surpassed my skills. There will be more youngest siblings." She walked across the frozen surface of the ocean and then tapped the ice. Icicles shot upward from the ocean and impaled Dew's armor. "Ones that listen to their Elders." She sang and Dew's amber armor completely melted, flowing back into the ocean.

Edward realized this was his opening! He swung the Lightning Knife downward. But before the tip of the knife could touch Yitoo's scale, a tentacle of red ice as thick as a telephone pole wrapped around his shoulder joint, holding his entire arm inches above the bare scale.

Yitoo said, "I will gladly forget your kind, you horrible Pale Person."

Edward used his free hand to push the knife downward. Mere centimeters away from touching her scale, the knife wouldn't budge further. He put his entire body weight on it, but the ice tentacle held strong. Edward was quickly losing his own stamina.

The Obsidian Armor creaked and groaned. Was it breaking? Yitoo couldn't be allowed to win. She just couldn't! He wished his dad was here, by his side. He wished Janet was here. But he stopped when Yitoo's tail of crimson water attached to Dew's exposed body and began to drain away the ocean that had given Dew her increased size.

Nathan tried desperately to melt the ice around Dew's ankles. But Yitoo's command was too strong. Dew was already half her kaiju size and only shrinking faster. They were running out of options. This wasn't how it was supposed to end.

"Nathan!" Uncle Jet's voice said through the darkness. Nathan looked up and saw Nali's hogan in the stars again. "Nathan, can you hear me?"

"Uncle Jet? Is that you?" Nathan said aloud. He briefly recalled the third trial to the Third World.

"Yes, it's me!" Uncle Jet's voice said. "Nathan, I can see you in the fireplace! Don't give up. We are here for you. You and Edward can do this!"

Suddenly, a cloud of smoke that smelled like cedar appeared in front of Yitoo's face and entered both her mouth and nose. Gently at first, like a clearing of the throat, she coughed. Then, gradually, her cough escalated to that of a hoarse heaving. The crimson water tentacle that was draining Dew warped and wobbled. Nathan immediately sang and evaporated it. Dew yanked her hind ankles out of the blocks of ice. She was no longer connected to Yitoo.

Edward screamed at the top of his lungs, "AHH!" Every

muscle of his arms and upper body flared in response as he again pushed the Lightning Knife closer and closer to Yitoo's body.

The red tentacle of ice wrapped under his armpit and pressed against the back of his neck. His wrestler instincts recognized this as a half-nelson grip. His hand peeled the ice off his neck; then he turned and pivoted his hips away from it. The ice pushed his body backward and slammed his back onto Yitoo's large scale. With the added strength of the Obsidian Armor, Edward wrapped his arms around the ice and quickly bridged his entire spine to redirect the flow of the tentacle away from his body. The momentum made the ice slide off him and hit Yitoo's own scale. He then swung his legs to move his body out from under the water. He was free!

"No!" Yitoo screamed.

Edward jabbed the tip of the knife against Yitoo. Immediately, ribbons of lightning raced across Yitoo's body. They covered her entire body from head to tail, shoulders to toes, and entered her throat as she howled in pain.

Even if she wasn't his favorite Holy Being, he hated hearing how much pain she was in. Still, he held the knife on to her. More and more bolts of lightning raced from the tip of the knife throughout her massive body. But finally, after a few seconds that felt like an hour of seeing Yitoo squirm and spasm, the lightning disappeared and her entire body fell against the ocean, creating one last final wave that began to melt the ice all around them. Yitoo lay limp, and smoke emerged from her mouth.

Naadiin Dóó Bi'ąą Tsosts'id
TWENTY-SEVEN

EXHAUSTED, EDWARD REACHED INTO THE quiver that rested on his stomach and pulled out the Rainbow Arrow.

"To signal the end of the fight," he said aloud. Standing, he wound up his arm and threw the Rainbow Arrow upward. Like the Dawn Arrow, it raced across the sky, this time leaving behind a long rainbow tail that sparkled and glowed in the night sky. As it arched over the clouds in the distance, the stormy winds slowed. The churning oceans calmed. The lightning became less frequent. And the most beautiful sight appeared: the clouds began to disperse, slowly but surely.

Edward slumped down on Yitoo. They had won.

Dew slowly approached Yitoo's limp body. A tentacle appeared from Dew's neck and rushed toward Yitoo. It wrapped around Yitoo's body like a sparkling golden snake. Once it had completed several revolutions around her titan-sized body, Dew tugged at the tentacle, and water began to pour out of Yitoo in multiple massive waterfalls. Her body shrank as the water returned to the ocean. Dew, meanwhile, expelled water until she was the size of a motorcycle, perfect to seat two young Diné.

When Yitoo was her normal sheep-sized self, Dew and Nathan approached her, to find Edward swimming toward them. Nathan requested water to lift and place Edward at his side. Yitoo had a few scars and several bruises on her body. A scale or two was missing. But she was breathing.

"She's still alive," Dew said.

Nathan jumped off Dew and rushed to her. He saw that Yitoo was crying and hugged her. He considered what she must be feeling. She blamed herself for the state of the Fourth World, the death of her siblings, and the relocation of the Diné. It was a lot to carry. Nathan had also blamed himself for Pond's passing. Back then, he felt like all the work, all the effort, even he himself, wasn't enough. That his best meant nothing. So, he said to Yitoo what he had wanted to hear, "You did everything in your power to make things better. Your best made all the difference in the world."

Yitoo said through sobs, "Will your ancestors ever know peace? Will Mother Earth?"

Edward thought about both his Diné and Anglo ancestors. To him, they were equally valuable. Without both, he wouldn't have been here. He then said what he was feeling. "The Diné of the Era of Relocation are at peace."

Yitoo's red eyes glowered at Edward. She pulled away from Nathan.

Edward continued. "My Diné ancestors of the Long Walk suffered so that they could return to Diné Bikéyah. They fought and resisted relocation because they wanted to give their children, their grandchildren, to give *me* the option of living in Diné Bikéyah or elsewhere. They rest easy because the Diné didn't die out. Our language didn't die out. And the ceremonies are still being performed."

"What about your lesser half? They suffer no consequences," Yitoo said.

"He doesn't have a lesser half," Nathan said.

Edward said, "Thanks, Nathan, but if you don't mind, I can speak for myself. Being multi-heritage doesn't make me lesser. My Anglo ancestors have caused many people to suffer and benefited from bloodshed. But Nathan's and my generation, all of us—Diné, Anglo, and other groups—are changing for the better. We are respecting each other and learning to not repeat the mistakes of the past."

"Your answer is unsatisfactory," Yitoo said. "The descendants of the Pale People must atone for their crimes."

"Yitoo, harming the descendants of those that harmed our ancestors isn't going to heal anyone," Nathan said. "That is work that you have to do on your own, for your own happiness."

"Why is it that it's always us that has to do the work?" Yitoo pleaded. "Aren't you exhausted, having to teach them, to remind them of their past sins?"

Nathan said, "You're right. It's not fair."

Edward said, "We still do it, because our own descendants depend on it. The work we do today, our grandkids will benefit from."

Yitoo said, lifting her neck and exposing her throat, "End my suffering so that I will finally know peace. The moment I am strong enough I will fight you. So go on, use the Lightning Knife on my flesh and the Rainbow Knife on my spirit!"

"No," Edward, Nathan, and Dew said in unison.

"You will not be killed," Edward said. "But you are not welcome in the Fourth World."

"I'd rather die here and now than return to the Third World a failure!" Yitoo said.

"Then go to some other world," Edward said. "Somewhere where you can start again without humans. Like the Fifth World."

Yitoo shook her head. Her tears stopped, and her eyes cleared.

"Fifth World?" Nathan asked.

"A new beginning," Yitoo said. Her voice sounded happy. She blinked away some tears. "Free from the five-fingered. Very well, I agree to your banishment." She stood feebly, groaning. "What of my river?"

Dew stepped forward and said, "Those waters are yours, and you are free to do what you want with them. When I am strong enough, I will return to the Third World to bring back the river. That river will be mine, and I will see to its protection."

Yitoo smiled. "Know this, when the day comes that the

Fourth World is uninhabitable, *all* humankind, Diné or otherwise, will not be warmly welcomed to my domain."

Edward said, "When that time comes, all our descendants will have learned their lessons from the mistakes made in this world."

"Doubtful," Yitoo said. "For all the strengths of humans, forgetfulness dooms you all to repeat mistakes over and over again. Go on, young Heroes. Make my banishment official."

Edward said, "We will give you four days to return the waters that aren't yours back to their regular spots and make arrangements. In four days, you will be banished from the Fourth World as my ancestors were from the Third World."

Yitoo limped eastward. Edward hovered his hand above the Lightning Arrow in the quiver.

Nathan sensed Edward's fear and wrapped his arm around his shoulder, pulling Edward into his side. He said, "Everyone is going to be safe."

For the first time in these long terrifying days, Edward exhaled and let go of the fear that had gnawed thousands of holes into his heart. The air felt crisp, and the sky was clear. The sun rose and the last of the hurricane evaporated like smoke in the breeze.

Naadiin Dóó Bi'ąą Tseebíí

TWENTY-EIGHT

FOUR DAYS HAD PASSED SINCE their fight in the middle of the Pacific Ocean. The two Heroes stood in the middle of the river Yitoo Bi'aanii, between the towns of Shiprock and Teec Nos Pos, waiting for Yitoo to show. This was the final day for Yitoo to leave before she was banned from the Fourth World. To their southeast, rays of morning sunrise extended outward on the tip of the volcanic rock formation of the Shiprock peak.

Initially, Nathan wanted to return the borrowed sacred items immediately. But Edward felt it necessary to hold on to the Obsidian Armor and Sacred Arrows until Yitoo left for the Fifth World. A breeze scented with juniper and sage blew across their exposed skin. To their left, Uncle Jet sneezed. Ted, Janet, Nali, and Nathan's dad stood, more apprehensive with every passing minute.

Mainly for himself, Edward said, "Yitoo will show up."

Nathan rubbed his shoulder. "She will."

Edward and Nathan searched the horizon and the riverbanks for any sign of Yitoo. Four days ago, after Dew, Yitoo, Nathan, and Edward entered the boundaries of the Four Sacred Mountains, Yitoo wanted to visit her siblings to say goodbye. Edward did not trust Yitoo and probably never would. But when Dew volunteered to travel with her, Edward's concerns eased. And in those next three days, all Edward and Nathan did was eat and sleep. Bruises and soreness popped up everywhere, in places neither knew they could be bruised or sore. For Nathan, it felt like his bones had bruises and his throat was going to be scratchy and dry for the rest of his days. Though he didn't mind it that much because having a deep, scratchy voice made him sound older.

Nathan squinted, searching for the water monsters. Edward, at his side, also appeared to still be looking. A warm, proud feeling spread through him as he looked at Edward. Dew would be in good hands. Edward was going to be an amazing Hero. Nathan reached out and pulled him into a hug.

Caught off guard, Edward asked, "What's this about?"

Nathan replied, "I'm just glad you're here. And thank you. For being by my side."

Edward smiled and said, "'Ahéhee', shínaaí."

Now it was Nathan who was caught off guard. This was the first time Edward had called him older brother. He responded, "'Aoo', shitsilí."

As they released each other, they heard the pitter-patter of multiple pairs of feet walking in the dry river basin toward them. They looked and saw a herd of water monsters walking their way. Nathan sighed in relief. He could still see them.

Edward controlled his reflexive impulse to grab an arrow from the quiver on his shoulders. Yitoo's face, the mere shape of her, sent all his alarms on high alert. Flashes of her in the ocean, tall enough that her head touched the ceiling of the sky, appeared in his mind. He couldn't inhale but remembered his dad's training on breathing.

Nathan noticed Edward's change in attitude and felt an immediate urge to protect him. So, he stepped forward and in between him and Yitoo. Edward more than likely had developed PTSD, like Uncle Jet. But Nathan wasn't as scared of that as he once was, having helped Uncle Jet through his own diagnosis. And even though Nathan's interaction with the Holy Beings was coming to an end, he vowed to always be there for Edward, in any way he could. Because deep in his heart, Nathan knew that Edward would be there for him, too.

Nathan counted about fourteen different water monsters walking toward them. He saw shades of color, like smeared water paint. Dew was among them. But there was something different this time. A cascade of joy welled up in his chest when he saw Dew leading the water monsters. Memories surfaced of when he first saw her, hiding in Nali's cornfield, scared and cold. He had held out his hand, and she immediately jumped into it, like a puppy, eager for affection and warmth. He closed his hand. And she fit perfectly. He remembered promising to never leave her alone, to protect this tiny being who was the entire world to him. And he remembered telling his mom about Dew so he could get a fish tank for her. Dew didn't sleep in it for months and instead slept in the curvature of his warm neck. Her gentle snores sometimes woke him. She now walked with her head held high, as if wearing a crown. Every step she took was with intention and determination. The herd of water monsters stopped a few feet in front of them. Dew approached Nathan and Edward and nudged Nathan's thigh. Relief ran through him, as he could still feel her physical presence. But barely.

"Nathan, Edward," Yitoo said. "I am ready to begin my journey to the Fifth World."

"Is this your farewell committee?" Edward asked.

Behind them, Ted whispered to Janet, "Are the water monsters there? I can't see a thing."

"Ge'," Nali said. "Let them do their thing."

Yitoo explained, "These are my brothers and sisters who want to join me on my way to the Fifth World. They, too, have had enough of the five-fingered."

Nathan clearly saw Canyon Mist among their number. So many water monsters. With their absence, the will of the weather was going to become more and more erratic and violent. But that was the point, Nathan figured. It wasn't only just up to water monsters, or any other Holy Being, to stave off the effects of climate change. Their generation, Nathan and Edward's, and all future generations were going to be the ones to have to navigate that unknown. Nathan remained hopeful that with the increased severity of weather phenomena, all humans could view each other as family and work together toward the common goal of turning things around.

"It crossed my mind that I owe you a blessing, Edward," Yitoo said. She didn't sound particularly happy.

Edward's thoughts of Olympic gold rushed to his head, but he held his tongue. The last Holy Being he wanted a blessing from was Yitoo.

Yitoo continued. "Dew has informed me that you have ambitions of achieving golden status in Olympic wrestling. Seeing as you provided me with the idea of heading to the Fifth World, an idea I very much love, I will provide you with a final blessing."

"No, thank you, Powerful Yitoo," Edward said. He would rather Dew bless him than any other Holy Being. But he also had a different idea in mind. Throughout these past days, he had noticed that Nathan never asked for anything for himself. "If I am owed a blessing, I want you to bless Nathan so that he can still see the Holy Beings."

"Edward!" Nathan said. He sounded surprised. "You don't have to do this."

"I know," Edward said. "But you deserve to get what you want too sometimes."

Nathan hugged him. "Thank you."

Yitoo explained, "There is no blessing we can perform that will permit Nathan to interact with us beyond puberty. The only way we Holy Beings can allow Nathan to continue to see us is to halt his aging. He would be forever his current age."

"I don't think that's a good idea," Nathan said. "Thanks for thinking of me, Edward. It's okay. Just get the blessing for your wrestling career. You deserve it."

Edward felt strongly that Nathan too deserved something. Suddenly, he remembered one possible thing that would make Nathan happy. "Then can you bless Nathan so that he graduates alongside his paternal grandma?"

"Very well," Yitoo said. Edward sensed that she preferred to bless Nathan. "Since I'm leaving, I'll ask other Holy Beings to guide these two toward their graduation, whatever that means. I misjudged you, Edward," Yitoo said. Her voice and expression were as warm as an ice cube. "Perhaps the Diné side of you is the source of your strength."

"I am strong because I'm me," Edward said to her. He didn't care if she disagreed. And anything she said to disregard his Anglo heritage, he wasn't going to care about. He didn't need her or people like Chad to validate who he was. He was both Diné and Anglo. End of story; get over it.

"I really wish I could hear this whole conversation," Ted said behind them.

"Dew," Yitoo said to her. "Bear my warning. The future for this world is grim. I still recommend you join us and let the five-fingered deal with their own mess."

"I will be powerful, because I had an amazing teacher," Dew said. "And will have amazing teachers among my siblings who remain here. The Diné, like other Nations, have been through many grim chapters of history. Yet, the Diné continue to hope, to live, to thrive. I understand and respect your warning. But I'm not scared. I will do my part and be brave about whatever we will face. Because I am not alone. I have Edward and Nathan with me here."

Dew's voice was becoming muted. And to make matters worse, her color was dimming. Nathan was losing sight of her again. Something about this felt different. Like the hazy heat of Phoenix versus the dry oven heat of Diné Bikéyah. Something deep in him knew that this was going to be the last time he saw the water monsters. Nathan felt like someone had pulled his heart out and threw it into a cluster of cacti. He tried to hold back his feeling of heartbreak for the moment.

"Very well," Yitoo said. "Please, when you learn more songs from our siblings, remind them that my Fifth World will always be available to them. And, Edward and Nathan, know that when the time comes for your descendants to journey to the next world, they will have much to prove if they are to join me. I was going to outright ban five-fingereds from my Fifth World, but knowing you, Nathan, and the endless love and kindness you exhibit, maybe there is a chance humanity will finally remember and take responsibility for their actions. A small chance, but still one, nonetheless. Come, siblings, let's wash ourselves of the scars of this world. Our new world awaits."

"I want to say thank you to all of you." Edward spoke up. "For everything that you have done for us through these many eras. I'm sorry that you have endured so much and hope that the Fifth World will be a happier place for you all."

With that, Yitoo led the herd of twelve water monsters into

the dry river. Yitoo soaked up the last remnants of river and distributed them to her sisters and brothers. Like crumpled-up sponges, the water monsters soaked up the moisture. Their scales refracted in the rising sun. Their joints moved with increased mobility. Their eyes darted back and forth, as if looking for a new adventure. They had been resuscitated. After the last drop of the river was gone, the herd of water monsters walked westward.

"How are they going to get to the Fifth World?" Edward asked.

Dew answered, "Moon Lady is going to meet with them in the Pacific Ocean and guide them to the path that leads to the Fifth World."

Nathan hugged the space where he heard Dew's voice come from. He felt her body, but her physical presence was lessening. There was never going to be a time when it felt right to let her go, to say goodbye. But if there was ever a time, ever a moment, it was this last one. "I'm losing my connection with you, Dew."

This caught her off guard as she slumped down. "What? No! You can't!"

"Dew, it's going to be okay," Nathan said, bawling. He dreaded never seeing her, hearing her, holding her again. He held on to the space and closed his eyes. Her body no longer pushed against his arms. Her heartbeat faded from his skin. He imagined Dew as the small, kitten-sized lizard that would press her front paws against his cheeks to wake him up. Bright eyes.

Flickering tail. "I'm so very thankful to have had you in my life, for as long as I had."

"Nathan," Dew cried out, her voice wobbling and filled with pain. "Don't say that. Please, stop."

"I have to," Nathan said. He opened his eyes, and he let out a big sigh of relief as her color was dim but visible. He could still see her. Her tears soaked into the ground. She shrank to the point where Nathan could once again lift her up. He held her in his arms and squeezed, wishing for four more years. "Because I'm scared I won't be able to tell you that I love you, Dew. And I'll always love you."

To his horror, she was once again becoming invisible to him. Even though she wasn't expelling water, her weight was decreasing. He put her on the ground, not wanting to drop her. She leaned against his legs as she disappeared from his sight. He couldn't feel her. This was it. He felt it in his spirit. He could no longer see her nor hear her nor feel her. "Mom? Dad? Nali?" The three he called out for went to him and comforted him. "I can't see her. I can't hear her!"

Edward cried along with them. He wrapped Dew in a hug, hoping that would calm her down. She nuzzled her snout in the cradle of his jaw and neck and quietly lamented, "He can't hold me. He can't hold me. I want him to hold me."

Edward did the only thing he could think of. He reached out to Nathan's hand and interlaced their fingers together and pressed his own palm against the back of Dew's neck. With his own knuckles pressed against Nathan's cold hand, he guided Nathan in the motion of petting Dew's spine. He said to Nathan, "She's here." Dew's sniffles softened when the warmth of Edward's hand ran across the back of her neck to her tail. "He's here."

Edward then put his forehead against Nathan's and let Dew nuzzle in the space between their skulls. Through Edward, Dew said to Nathan, "Thank you for everything you have done for me."

Nathan said to Dew, "I wish I had more to give you."

Dew said, "You've given me more than you'll ever know. I love you, Nathan."

Then Edward reminded them, "This may not be how you both wanted it, but I'm still here. As long as I can see you, Dew, you'll have a way to connect to Nathan."

Nathan smiled and wiped some of the tears away. "I didn't want this. But I'm glad you're here, Edward."

Dew said, "Me too."

"You and I still have a lot of work, Dew," Edward said. "You have more songs to learn. And you have a river to return when you are strong enough. Plus, we have to give back the Obsidian Armor and Sacred Arrows."

"You're right," Dew said, some of her energy and life returning.

The three of them stood up, facing the sun. Nathan finally felt after all these years of raising Dew that she was in good hands. Edward was the best person to be her Hero. And to be honest, he was also Nathan's Hero. He felt a tinge of jealousy for not being able to join them as they returned Father Sun's property. But that part of his life was complete. And he was hopeful for the future he could make for himself and for his grandkids and for his grandkid's grandkids.

Edward placed Dew on the ground and let her run around. And after a while, she crawled up his back and rested on his neck, gazing longingly at Nathan. Edward petted her again, to reassure her that this wasn't the end, not yet. Dew pushed her tiny body against his hand. Now it was his turn to raise Dew. Even though there were dark clouds, powerful storms, in their paths, Edward felt confident that he and his family would be able to come up with solutions.

HWÉÉLDI

AFTER HIS DAD PARKED JANET'S SUV in the lot of
the Bosque Redondo Memorial a few miles south of Fort Sumner, New Mexico, Edward held his breath as he stepped out into
the bright, sunny, cloudless parking lot. Despite the clear air
enveloping them, there was a distinct heaviness in the atmosphere that weighed on Edward's chest. For his twelfth birthday,
Edward wanted to go to Hwééldi and see the place for himself.
Now that he was here, he wondered if it was okay to celebrate
his life in the midst of the location where so much suffering had
occurred.

Ted, Nathan, and Janet stepped out of the SUV, silent and
reverent, sadness on their faces. Janet rubbed Ted's shoulder and
gently smiled. Ted held her hand. Nathan folded his arms over
his stomach and the four of them walked toward the entrance

of the Bosque Redondo Memorial, a building in the shape of a large L. At the middle bend was a tall, triangular structure reaching toward the sun.

They walked on a spotless gray concrete trail. To their right was the trunk of a massive cottonwood tree and a sign that said it had been planted by Diné prisoners during their internment at Hwééldi. Closer to the gray and dry tree trunk was another sign asking children not to climb on it. Edward grew angry at the thought of adults letting children play on a testament to the survival of his Diné ancestors.

Edward took out his phone and snapped a picture to share with Grandma Lillian and Grandpa George. After Yitoo left, he had told her that he felt that she treated him like an "indian." She apologized and said she wasn't aware that she was treating him any differently. But his grandpa said that she did. And after some much needed discussion, the three of them were able to enter a new phase of their relationship. Since Grandma Lillian wasn't able to join them, she asked Edward to take many pictures so that she too could learn about the Long Walk and Hwééldi.

Nathan held the door open to let the three of them enter. To their left were a gift shop and restrooms. To their right was the shadowed entrance to an exhibit. They entered. Along the walls were quotes and faces of Diné prisoners. One that stuck out especially to Edward was from an Nde, Mescalero Apache, that read, "There was no water fit for drinking. We had been accustomed to the clear, cold water from the melting snow of the

White Mountain. We had to drink the muddy, ill-tasting water from the Pecos. It made us sick; it even made the horses sick." Edward read on another wall that in total, the estimated number of Diné prisoners was 9,500, with an additional 500 Mescalero Apache.

Farther into the exhibit was a long, concave wall, upon which were murals. Painted like Van Gogh's *Starry Night* by Diné artist Shonto Begay, three large murals depicted blue-clad US soldiers whipping a long line of Diné in the middle of winter. The Diné of the past huddled together in the falling snow. Among them, Edward saw a young boy who was about his age.

He couldn't help himself. Tears flooded down his cheeks. He imagined his ancestor: cold, hungry, and alone. Next to the boy was a tall man holding something wrapped in white linen on the back of his shoulders. Edward imagined that the man was the one who adopted his ancestor and took him as his own son. Even though they weren't related by blood, they were related through the clan system. The Diné people had found families and strength to endure Hwééldi.

Nathan walked up next to him and placed his hand on Edward's shoulder.

"You okay?" Nathan asked.

"They survived," Edward said.

"We survived," Nathan said. "They are us."

Edward leaned his head onto Nathan's shoulder. Nathan rubbed Edward's back as they pushed through the rest of the exhibit. Above, strings of white light gently glowed, and the sounds of feet walking came through speakers hiding in the dark ceilings. There were so many lights, some shining brighter than others, hanging lower than others. It was like staring into the Milky Way galaxy at night. At the end of the line of lights a plaque read, "10,000 lights for 10,000 lives."

"We survived," Edward repeated. Edward knew that Nathan didn't mean just the Long Walk. He also meant Yitoo, who was now in the Fifth World.

Since their fight in the Pacific Ocean three months ago, Edward had been experiencing flashes of memories that sometimes froze him stiff. Nathan helped him through these episodes and introduced him to mindfulness. Though not fully gone, and he didn't want them to be completely gone, his memories of Yitoo were losing their power to grip his throat and heart.

Their parents guided them to the next exhibit, which was outside.

They followed a well-worn path, with numbered signs indicating the audio tour segments of the memorial. In the cradle of tall cottonwood trees sat a boulder, topped with small smooth pebbles. The four of them stood in front of a pile of rocks, some smooth, some porous. Some gray, some white, some brown. On the rocks was a plaque in Diné. Edward didn't have the communication stone on his person. But he had been practicing reading the language out loud.

He read, "Ni'hokáá Diyin Dine'é bi'oodlą' biyi' bitsodizin dóó biyiin dóó bizaad dóó bi'ó'ool'įįł hólǫ́ éí bee nihidziil. Kodóó dził nihighan sinilígíí bii'jį' bee biih néidzá. Dííjįįdi

bee ał'ąą nídínéet'ą. T'áá éí díijįįdi bee hółdzilgo haz'ą. Si'ąh
Naagháí Bik'eh Hózhóón nidlįįgo yiildah.

Hózhǫ Náhasdlįį'

Hózhǫ Náhasdlįį'

Hózhǫ Náhasdlįį'

Hózhǫ Náhasdlįį'"

Edward took a picture of the plaque. He didn't want Nathan
to translate it. Because he himself wanted to be able to translate
it, even if that meant learning the Diné language.

A little farther down the dirt path was another cluster of
thoughtfully placed pebbles and a plaque: "These rocks were
carried from different parts of the Navajo reservation in Febru-
ary of 1971 in commemoration of the Navajo people who were
exiled and died here from 1863 to 1868." Diné were still bringing rocks from Diné Bikéyah to their ancestors who weren't
able to return home. A twig poked upward, and hanging off it
was a golden item in the shape of a heart with a purple interior.

On the other side was a vast expanse of open field. This was
where his ancestors suffered. This was where they missed Diné
Bikéyah, their homeland. This was where they were beaten.
This was where they starved. This was where they were murdered. This is where they survived. This is where childless
parents found orphans. This is where they grew food to eat.
This is where couples found love. This is where children were
born. This is where they endured so that future generations like
Edward and Nathan could live.

Ever since his dad told him of his ancestor's relocation story,

Edward had carried the story within his heart. The story wasn't just a collection of words. It had a life of its own. Sometimes, like now when the pain of the past was right in front of his eyes, the weight of the story grew and the horrors and injustice that had happened overwhelmed Edward.

Nathan seemed to sense Edward's turmoil and again rubbed his back.

But Edward had his family, which included Janet and Nathan. They helped him to carry the weight of the story. They helped him to navigate the anger that was now like red embers in his heart. At any moment, those embers could burst into raging flames.

Edward was glad to carry the story, and when it came time, he was going to tell his kids and grandkids about their ancestor who survived everything so that they could live here today. And he would be there to help them learn how to carry the weight of the story. Because even though the relocation occurred almost two centuries ago, its effects were still being felt. Its ramifications still reverberated throughout history. The Diné of today still endured the consequences of the relocation, of the stolen resources.

Later, Edward sat back down in the SUV. Edward had needed to go to Bosque Redondo to see for himself. He was glad he did. Because just like Yitoo and her anger, Hwééldi was now a part of his life going forward. Though, in his blood, in his being, in his soul, Hwééldi had always been there. Like the moon, Hwééldi would always be there. And like the moon dancing with the ocean tides, Hwééldi would invisibly push and pull at his emotions.

Like Nathan had taught him, Edward took a breath in and exhaled. He braved the thoughts and emotions and let them sift into his unconscious.

Edward gladly upheld the weight of the relocation story. It was his time to carry the weight so that past generations could rest. It was his story now. The story was him.

Edward looked forward outside of the windshield as Janet shifted into gear and drove back to Chandler. In his imagination, he saw lines of thousands of people taking the first step of 450 miles back to Diné Bikéyah—excitement, joy, happiness, in each and every single step. He imagined that his ancestor didn't look back and only looked forward. Their suffering had ended.

A NOTE FROM THE AUTHOR

YÁ'ÁT'ÉÉH SHIKEH DÓÓ SHI DINE'É. Hello, family and friends,

'Ahéhee' for reading *Heroes of the Water Monster*. Writing this book was a challenging yet valuable experience. Processing historical trauma, in particular, unearthed a lot of emotions. It is my hope that this book will start important conversations.

The initial idea for *Heroes of the Water Monster* came to me while I was revising my debut novel, *Healer of the Water Monster*. When Nathan ventured to the Third World, I wanted him to interact with another water monster there before meeting with Mother Water Monster. That water monster ultimately became Yitoo Bi'aanii. Since Pond was largely sickened by external forces, I wanted Yitoo to be afflicted by internal strife. I asked her the same questions that I asked Nathan to get to know him. I discovered that Yitoo was the first water monster to leave the Third World and eventually brought up the San Juan River all by herself. But I didn't know why she needed to return to the Third World to heal. It made sense that since the Holy Beings had been present for many eras, they would have experienced firsthand the horrors of the relocation of the Diné. I also knew that cities in the southwest were draining water from Lake Powell, which is fed by the San Juan River. These two topics—the relocation of the Diné and the theft of water—became intertwined with Yitoo. Her story needed to be told because Indigenous stories of the Era of Relocation have been silenced.

The relocation of my Diné ancestors began in 1862 when General Christopher Houston "Kit" Carson began his scorched-earth campaign by igniting cornfields and slaughtering livestock in what was then called the "Territory of Arizona," which had been claimed by the Confederate States of America during the US Civil War. Carson's brutal methods forced many Diné to surrender at Fort Defiance, where one hundred thirty years later, I would live and go to school. Carson forced Diné people to walk 450 miles to Bosque Redondo from late 1863 through 1864. My ancestors were separated into fifty groups and walked one of seven paths. Carson ordered his soldiers to kill any stragglers, be they sick, elderly, young, or pregnant. At Hwééldi, my ancestors struggled to farm the flat lands of Bosque Redondo for four years. Hastiin Ch'il Haajiní, and other naat'áanii-s (leaders), would negotiate with government representatives to produce Naaltsoos Sání, the Treaty of Bosque Redondo, the sixth and final treaty between the Diné Nation and the United States. On June 1, 1868, after the signing of Naaltsoos Sání, my ancestors were allowed to return to their original homelands, though significantly reduced and now called a reservation. I'm fortunate that my ancestors were able to return to a reduced portion of their original homelands—many Indigenous Nations do not have that consolation.

This is a highly condensed version of the Long Walk and

Hwééldi. Diné of the era weren't always peaceful and often fought with soldiers and neighboring Nations. While it is estimated that 10,000 individuals were held prisoner at Fort Sumner, there are no records of those murdered in prison camps like those at Fort Defiance or during the Long Walk.

The story of Edward's ancestor was based on my own maternal ancestor's story, especially the moment when, to save lives, the "mean-looking" nuns slapped food to the earth, making it inedible. However, I supplemented my story with research to ensure a more accurate and detailed account of the Long Walk. In doing so, I read *Navajo Stories of the Long Walk Period*, edited by Johnson Broderick, and traveled to Fort Sumner, New Mexico, to visit the place where my ancestors were imprisoned. Details such as the purple heart on a mound of rocks, an ancient oak tree stump, and the "10,000 lights for 10,000 lives" exhibit were informed by my July 2021 visit. There, I was exposed to many stories that revealed what had happened. Afterward, I cried in the parking lot before I returned to my mom's home in Fort Defiance, Arizona. Today the main street that runs through it is still called Kit Carson Drive.

The first time I heard about my maternal ancestors who survived the Era of Relocation, I was ten years old. As my mom told the story, she referred to places like Canyon de Chelly, Nazlini, Many Farms, and Dajiziih and recounted the violence that occurred there. These were places where I played with cousins, had family picnics, and herded cattle. I now saw them anew with tragedy and horror. My perception of the world around me had changed.

As my view of the land around me was reframed, my relationship to the United States became complicated and burdensome. This was a lot for a ten-year-old to process.

Both Nathan's and Edward's emotional journeys throughout *Heroes of the Water Monster* mirror my own processing of learning about the Long Walk and Hwééldi. I imagine many Indigenous children today also navigate these complex thoughts and emotions. Nathan has to come to terms with his participation in the dominant culture. Edward fights to find an identity that can encompass past injustice as well as future hopes. Edward sometimes refers to his ancestor's story as a weight.

For me, that weight is a collection of thirty pages, an estimated 4.8 ounces.

As an undergraduate at Yale University, I had access to world-class libraries, including the Beinecke Library. In its womb are massive tomes filled with firsthand historical documents, such as two Gutenberg Bibles and the Voynich Manuscript. While researching for a final paper, I learned that Beinecke had in its collection "Letters received by Kit Carson, 1856 Nov 9–1865 Aug 18." On the morning I read the letters, I prayed with corn pollen on the grass of Old Campus. At Beinecke, I checked in with the librarian and was guided into an underground, sterile, temperature- and humidity-controlled room. In front of me was a chest-high desk with a wooden book holder. I was asked to put on a paper mask and linen gloves, so I did. A few minutes later, another librarian wheeled a cart by and handed me a box. The mushroom smell of aged paper infiltrated the mask and wafted in my covered nostrils. I opened the box and saw a foam container that cradled a folder of papers.

The papers were pristine, if yellowed. Some edges had worn away. The dark gray letters on the papers had faded. I could barely decipher the fancy cursive. It was more ghost than words. But I could make out "Dear K. Carson." I could make out numbers scribbled on the sides. Were these numbers my ancestors being counted? I could make out "successful." What were the parameters of that success? The number of peaceful surrenders? The number of days they held my ancestors captive? The number of poisoned provisions given to my ancestors to cull their numbers so that relocating them would be an easier task? There were no books, no guides, no materials to help me process the ancestral trauma that I inherited. There still are none available for Indigenous children being introduced to this silenced history.

Indigenous children of all Nations eventually have to learn about the genocidal crimes inflicted on their ancestors. When they do, those children must find a way to navigate their complex relationship with a dominant society that was built upon their ancestors' bloodshed. All children, Indigenous or not, should learn about the Era of Relocation and the violence that begot their own hometowns.

I'm so grateful for the current rise in the study of intergenerational trauma. To add to that discussion, I want to talk about "inherited trauma." Whereas intergenerational trauma is about the negative habits, behaviors, and interactions between multiple generations, I believe inherited trauma is about the genes that are invisibly passed from one generation to the next.

For Edward, inherited trauma is described as a wound of his spirit that was passed down to him and that has always been there. I first came across this idea as a junior at Yale. I took a class called Animal Models of Clinical Disorders, which described the contributions animal lives had made toward the advancement of medicinal treatment for psychological disorders, including anxiety disorders like depression and PTSD. I learned about a breed of mice called C57BL/6, which are used in testing to examine the side effects of experimental medications. While not a one-to-one comparison, these animal experiments serve as the last stage of inquiry before human trials begin. Mice must exhibit symptoms of depression for a medicine to be tested on them. But these mice do not naturally come with depressive symptoms. These must be bred into them.

The researchers start with a generation that is exposed to environmental stresses, such as wet bedding, electrified cages, bright lights during the night, loud noises during eating. In that generation, a small percentage will show depression-like symptoms. Breeders then will isolate that small percentage and mate them. The second generation of C57BL/6 will be subjected to those same environmental stresses. There are increased rates of depression-like symptoms throughout Generation 2. Those individuals of Generation 2 who show depression-like symptoms will be isolated and bred. And that cycle continues until there is a significant percentage of individuals exhibiting symptoms of depression. That is Generation 5.

My generation is Generation 5. My maternal grandma's grandpa was the ancestor who inspired the prologue. He was Generation 1. His children, Generation 2, had to endure the whitewashing efforts of Bible-based institutions and adapting to the new Navajo Nation government. Generation 3, my grandma, had to endure the boarding school era, in which Indigenous children were forced to leave their homes and attend abusive boarding schools. My parents' generation revolted as part of the American Indian Movement of the 1970s. My generation grapples with the endangerment of Indigenous language, culture, and identity.

My book delves into the increasingly dire water crisis in the southwestern United States. As I finished writing the first draft in March 2020, reports on the low water level of Lake Powell were common. Now, as I write this author's note in May 2022, recent pictures of Lake Powell show it has fallen to terrifying low levels. Ancestral Puebloan ruins that had been submerged since the completion of Glen Dam in 1963 are now visible again.

The communities of the Phoenix valley receive water from two sources, the Salt River Project (SRP) and the Central Arizona Project (CAP). The SRP is the primarily source of water and hydroelectricity that supports the Phoenix valley through dams in both the Salt River and Verde River. SRP delivers water throughout the suburbs of Phoenix through miles of concrete canals. The CAP is a complex system of aqueducts, tunnels, pumping stations, underground siphons, and reservoirs that collectively move more than 1.4 million acre-feet of water each year, roughly 336 miles across the Sonoran Desert. The CAP transports water all the way to Tucson, Los Angeles, Las Vegas, and many other places. The Colorado River is a huge contributor of water to the CAP. And the San Juan River feeds into the Colorado River.

There are complex water laws in the southwestern United States, such as *Arizona v. California* (1963), which appropriates water rights for southwestern states and five Indigenous Nations, and the Groundwater Management Act of June 1980, which dictates groundwater reserves in Arizona.

I lived in the Phoenix valley after graduation from high school and worked two part-time jobs there during the summer of 2005. I would bike back and forth from my aunt's south Scottsdale apartment just north of Tempe in the 115-degree weather to save money for my upcoming fall tuition at Yale University. Along the four-mile bike ride, I passed several golf courses. More than two hundred golf courses are located in the Phoenix valley. If one eighteen-hole course needs about four acre-feet of water per year, that's roughly eight hundred acre-feet of water. An acre-foot of water is 325,851 gallons—enough to sustain three families for a year. Phoenix valley uses approximately 260,680,800 gallons of water annually for its golf courses.

It's wonderful that Phoenix has managed to grow. But consider the communities, not just Indigenous, that are suffering to facilitate water parks like Hurricane Harbor. I hope that, through my book, you are able to understand the ongoing damage caused by taking water out of its cycle and hoarding it in groundwater banks for the benefit of southwestern cities.

When I met Yitoo during the revising of *Healer of the Water Monster*, I knew her story needed to be told. I was entranced with her strength, her confidence, and her convictions. Whether it be the misuse of her waters or the wounds of the relocation, Yitoo had a lot to say and outdated attitudes to outgrow.

You may have noticed that I have used a lowercase "i" in "indian" during Edward and Grandma Lillian moments. I chose to use a lowercase "indian" to refer to the stereotype of Indigenous peoples. Several Nations prefer to call themselves "Indian." I personally do not. I wanted to respect those Nations and peoples that call themselves "Indian," as well as be able to talk about how non-Indigenous people often treat us as stereotypes.

Thank you again for reading *Heroes of the Water Monster*. For my non-Indigenous readers, if you feel guilt about the contents of this book, please put that aside; this book is not about guilt. It's the story of two resilient boys coping with their inherited trauma, negotiating conflicting identities, and believing that we all can change for the betterment of our descendants as well as for the health of this beautiful Earth we call home. For my Indigenous readers, yes, my generation is Generation 5. But consider this. If harming one generation is enough to raise rates of depression, then it stands to reason that it'll only take one generation loving the next to begin reversing those rates.

'Ahéhee'

Brian Young

GLOSSARY

I have decided not to include pronunciation in this glossary because some Diné accents and sounds just don't have a phonetic equivalent in English. But if you wish to hear the Diné language and perhaps some of these very words, please check out navajowotd.com, as they have a wonderful library of Diné words pronounced.

Family Terms

There are multiple variations of family terms, and certain contexts determine proper designation or colloquial usage. Let's take 'análí, for instance. In colloquial Diné, which often is mixed with English words, 'análí is used with a possessive prefix such as shi- (my), ni- (your), or bi- (his/her/its). Shinálí, ninálí, and binálí respectively. In English conversations mixed with Diné words, it's common to say my nálí, your nálí, or his/her/its nálí.

Cheii Correct spelling is 'acheii, which literally means maternal grandfather. Often when spoken with English, it's common to say and spell cheii without the 'a- at the beginning.

Másání Correct spelling is 'amásání, which literally means maternal grandmother. For context, Nali asked Edward to refer to her as maternal grandma. This is pretty common practice on the reservation for Diné Elders to refer to youths as their grandchildren and vice versa, even if they aren't related by blood. Another use is when Ted tells Edward to call his másání, Grandma Lillian. Even if the family member isn't Diné, Diné family members will still refer to them with Diné terminology.

Nálí Correct spelling is 'análí, which literally means paternal relationship. For context, Nathan occasionally uses nálí as opposed to Nali (without the accents) when talking to Edward; this is the correct terminology. Nali (without the accents) is an affectionate nickname for paternal grandparents, like "Nana."

nálí 'adzą́ą́ paternal grandmother

nálí hastiin paternal grandfather

Nálí Lady and Nálí Sir Some Diné children will refer to their paternal grandparents as Nálí Lady or Nálí Sir.

shínaaí my older brother

shinálí my paternal relation

shitsilí my younger brother

shiyáázh my son (mom to son)

shiye' my son (father to son)

Words and Short Phrases

'ahéhee'	thank you
'ałk'idą́ą́'	a long time ago
'ałtse'	wait
'aoo'	yes
Bilagáana	Anglo. Can also be used as a clan designation. In this context it is used as Edward's first clan, which he inherited from his Anglo mom.
chaha'oh	shade hut
Diné	Literally means person or people, but can mean Navajo people.
Diné Bikéyah	Literally means "the land of the Diné." But this refers to the actual traditional landscape of the Diné that is bordered by the Four Sacred Mountains in the cardinal directions and *not* the Diné Reservation, which has been reduced in size and exists only in Arizona, Utah, and New Mexico.
Diyin Diné'e	Holy Beings
Dook'o'oosłííd	Western sacred mountains. English name is San Francisco Peaks, near Flagstaff, Arizona.
'éí biniinaa	Literally: It is for that reason, because
'éí dooda	Literally: This is no. Understood to mean a firm no.

Gah Hahat'ee	Literally rabbit tracks, but refers to the star constellation of the tail end of Scorpius.
Ha'át'íísh̨ą'?	What?
Hajíínéí	Literally, Place of Emergence. Located just south of Farmington, New Mexico.
Hajíínéí Bahaane'	The Story of Emergence, the Diné creation story
Hastiin Ch'il Haajiní	Diné name for Chief Manuelito, who, along with other naat'áanii, signed Naaltsoos Sání and ended the Diné four-year internment at Hwééldi. Translates to "Man of the Black Plants Place." Some other names include Hashké Naabah and Naabah Jiłta.
Hwééldi	Literally means "Where They Suffered," but refers to Fort Sumner in Bosque Redondo, New Mexico, where approximately 9,500 Diné were held captive between 1863–68.
K'ad 'éí	Literally: Now it is, meaning these days, these times
Na'ashjé'ii 'Adzą́ą́	Spider Woman
Naaltsoos Sání	Literally "the old paper/book/text," but means "The Treaty of 1868"
naat'áanii	Leader. As used in the book, the Diné word naat'áanii is combined with the English plural -s.

Nahiłii	This is our respectful word for African American people and the multi-heritage identity of Afro-Diné. Can also be used as a clan.
N'dáá	Enemy Way Ceremony. Full term is Ana'í N'dáá. Very common to just use N'dáá in conversation.
shidóó	me too
Tábąąhá	Water's Edge Clan
tádídíín	Corn pollen
Todacheenie	Nathan's last name is an English spelling of the Diné clan Tódích'íínii, Bitter Water Clan. Before Hwééldi, Diné did not have last names. After the signing of Naaltsoos Sání and when Diné returned to the newly established Diné reservation, the United States government assigned Diné last names to help assimilate them. Several common Diné last names like Yazzie (yazhi), Nez (Neez), Begay (Biye') and many more were assigned to Diné. Some English last names, like Williams, were "given" to Diné by priests and nuns. The author's own last name, Young, was given to his distant paternal ancestor by a Mormon clergyman.
Tsidił	Stick Game
tsiiyééł	traditional Diné hair bun

Tsoodził	Southern Sacred Mountain, also known as Mount Taylor. Near Grants, New Mexico.
Txį'	Come on, let's go.
Yitoo Bi'aanii	These two words refer to the San Juan River, the largest river that runs through Diné Bikéyah, and also to the water monster Yitoo herself. It's important to note that this is not the actual name of the river and that the author didn't want to include the traditional name of the river, as it can have ceremonial context.

Sentences

'Ahéhee' Diyin shí 'éí Diné!	Thank God I'm Diné!
Dá'ák'ehshą'?	What about the cornfield?
Doo shił yá'át'ééhda.	I don't like it.
Ge'! 'Ashiiké dá'sinoołts'ą́ą́!	Be quiet! Listen to the boys!
Háadishą' Dew?	Where is Dew?
Haash wolyé 'ashkii yazhi?	What's your name, little boy?
Kwe'é doo nahałtin da.	There's no rain here.
Shí 'éí Edward yinishyé.	My name is Edward.
Wohsą́ ch'iyaan chaha'ohdi.	Eat. The food is at the shade hut.
Yá'át'ééh, shinálí 'ashkii!	Hello, my paternal grandson!
Yoostsah shaníaah	Give me the ring.

Numbers

t'ááłá'í	one
naaki	two
táá'	three
dį́į'	four
'ashdla'	five
hastą́ą́	six
tsosts'id	seven
tseebíí	eight
náhást'éí	nine
neeznáá	ten
ła' ts'áadah	eleven
naaki ts'áadah	twelve
táá' ts'áadah	thirteen
dį́į' ts'áadah	fourteen
'ashdla' ts'áadah	fifteen
hastą́ą́' ts'áadah	sixteen
tsosts'id ts'áadah	seventeen
tseebíí ts'áadah	eighteen
náhást'éí ts'áadah	nineteen
naadiin	twenty
naadiin doó bi'ąą t'ááłá'í	twenty-one
naadiin dóó bi'ąą naaki	twenty-two
naadiin dóó bi'ąą táá'	twenty-three
naadiin dóó bi'ąą dį́į'	twenty-four
naadiin dóó bi'ąą 'ashdla'	twenty-five

naadiin dóó bi'ąą hastą́ą́	twenty-six
naadiin dóó bi'ąą tsosts'id	twenty-seven
naadiin dóó bi'ąą tseebíí	twenty-eight
naadiin dóó bi'ąą náhást'éí	twenty-nine

ACKNOWLEDGMENTS

I want to first and foremost thank my readers. I had been so nervous when publishing my previous novel, *Healer of the Water Monster*. I could not have asked for a better reception. You have all been so welcoming to Nathan's journey and generous with compliments and critiques. Thank you for supporting my early career in publishing. Truly, 'ayóó 'ahéhee'!

Thank you to my critique partners, who provided valuable feedback on earlier versions of *Heroes of the Water Monster*. Shelby Wardlaw, your amazing insight really did help bring this book to its final form. I can't thank you or praise your intellect enough! Alex Uloa, my friend, thank you for being so eager to read *Heroes of the Water Monster* and informing me about one of the appealing aspects of my first book. Natalie Little Simpson, thanks for stepping up and providing me with your insight! Of course, Darci Schummer as well as Rain Newcomb, thank you so much for quickly reading my manuscript and providing crucial last-minute observations before I submitted the final revision! And last but most certainly not least, my gratitude to the entire Native children's literature critique group led by Andrea Rogers.

Shimá Pauletta White, shizhé'é Tom White, Jr., shádí Naomi Young, shínaaí Brandon Young, shimásání Jessie Williams, shicheii John Williams, Sr. 'Ahéhee' 'aadoo' 'ayóó 'áníínish'ni. Thank you for constantly supporting me through the highs and lows of a creative career. And to all my cousins who supported me as well as teased me. And to all my cousins whom I teased.

'Ahéhee', Tiffany Tracy! Thank you for pointing out all the small details and providing the name for Hastiin Ch'il Haajiní. I'm so proud of everything that you are doing for the Ganado community!

Rosemary Brosnan and Auntie Cynthia Leitich Smith! My superhero team of editors! I am completely overwhelmed by both your trust in not only me, but also all the wonderful Indigenous authors for whom Heartdrum provides a home. The work that you both have done, are doing, and continue to do is so very important for all children, Indigenous and non-Indigenous. With you two, we authors are able to reach children who may feel forgotten and tell them they are seen and they are loved.

Thank you to all the individuals at HarperCollins and Heartdrum, including Courtney Stevenson and Aubrey Churchward! I can't forget Shaun Taylor-Corbett, the voice actor for both my audiobooks. Thank you so much, Shaun, for putting so much effort, hard work, and all that talent into bringing my books to life. And a grand thank-you to senior production editor Jessica Berg and copy editor Jacqueline Hornberger for combing through my grammar and spelling mistakes, of which there were a lot!

Dan Mandel, thank you for representing me and advocating on my behalf! I can't wait to see what we will accomplish together with both these books and future books! But also, your guidance, patience, and knowledge have been extremely valuable for me and my growth as a storyteller! Thank you.

Thank you to all the librarians and teachers who are doing the hard work of putting my books and others into the hands of young people. You are on the front lines fighting against censorship and have the incredibly valuable job of ensuring diverse stories reach all children.

I have to thank my cats, too, Cali and Fez. Without the two of you napping on me during my writing sessions, *Heroes of the Water Monster* may have taken longer to finish. Thank you both for providing me with a sense of routine as well as responsibility all throughout the quarantine.

'Aadoo' 'ahéhee' to my ancestors who survived everything so I could be alive today telling stories. Lastly, 'ahéhee' Diyin Diné'e.

A Note from

CYNTHIA LEITICH SMITH,

Author and Co-Curator of Heartdrum

Dear Reader,

In a way, we are all always living in the past, present, and future. Let's talk about all three. In this story, our heroes of today—Edward and Nathan—learn about generations of painful history between the Diné and the US government. Do you know what that's like? I do. I am Muscogee, not Diné, but my tribal Nation was also relocated by force. The US government moved us from our ancestral lands in the southeastern United States to Indian Territory, now called Oklahoma, in the 1830s. That journey is sometimes referred to as "The Trail of Tears."

Maybe you're thinking, the 1830s Trail of Tears? The 1860s Navajo Long Walk? How could what happened so long ago still matter today? Maybe it matters most because those stories are still unfolding. We can affect what happens next for the better.

Today almost 600 resilient Native Nations survive and at times prosper within the borders of the United States, even though all but 1 percent of Indigenous ancestral land has been taken from them. The Muscogee are still struggling against the state and US government for our land, and we're not alone in that. Plus, as a result of relocations and land loss, Native peoples are especially vulnerable to climate change and have lost natural resources.

What do you know about your ancestors? Like Edward, my ancestors include both Native people and white settlers who displaced them. Edward sometimes refers to himself as "half Anglo" and "half Diné." But Edward is one whole person with a supportive family and a purpose in this world, with one whole body, heart, and mind. He is a blessing, just like you.

The novel is published by Heartdrum, a Native-focused imprint of HarperCollins Children's Books, which offers stories about young Native heroes by Native and First Nations authors and illustrators. I'm deeply honored to include this book on our list because it's a page-turner that respectfully considers our relationship with water, with the Earth, with each other, and with our communities. It is honest about traumatic history in a way that helps us heal, that helps us hope, and it does all that through the lens of Diné identity and the vision of young Diné heroes.

Mvto,

Cynthia Leitich Smth

Author and filmmaker BRIAN YOUNG is a graduate of both Yale University, with a bachelor's degree in film studies, and Columbia University, with a master's degree in creative writing fiction. An enrolled member of the Navajo Nation, he grew up on the Diné Homelands but now currently lives in Brooklyn, New York. As an undergraduate, Brian won a prestigious Sundance Ford Foundation Fellowship with one of his feature-length scripts. He has worked on several short films, including *Tsídii Nááts'íílid—Rainbow Bird* and *A Conversation on Race with Native Americans* for the short documentary series produced by the *New York Times*. Brian is currently working on another book for young readers. In addition to film and writing, Brian also works as a personal trainer, both online and in person.

CYNTHIA LEITICH SMITH is the bestselling, acclaimed author of books for all ages, including *Rain Is Not My Indian Name*, *Indian Shoes*, *Jingle Dancer*, and *Hearts Unbroken*, which won the American Indian Library Association's Youth Literature Award; she is also the anthologist of *Ancestor Approved: Intertribal Stories for Kids*. She was named a NSK Neustadt Laureate, which honors outstanding achievement in the world of children's and young adult literature. Cynthia is the author-curator of Heartdrum, a Native-focused imprint at HarperCollins Children's Books, and serves as the Katherine Paterson Inaugural Endowed Chair on the faculty of the MFA program in Writing for Children and Young Adults at Vermont College of Fine Arts. She is a citizen of the Muscogee (Creek)

Nation and lives in Austin, Texas. You can visit Cynthia online at www.cynthialeitichsmith.com.

In 2014, We Need Diverse Books (WNDB) began as a simple hashtag on Twitter. The social media campaign soon grew into a 501(c)(3) nonprofit with a team that spans the globe. WNDB is supported by a network of writers, illustrators, agents, editors, teachers, librarians, and book lovers, all united under the same goal—to create a world where every child can see themselves in the pages of a book. You can learn more about WNDB programs at www.diversebooks.org.